The Experts Praise
Deranged
by Jacob Stone

"*Deranged* is a dark and different serial killer novel that will haunt the reader long after the book is closed and back on the shelf. Author Jacob Stone transfixes us with dread, and something more. He has the rare capacity to startle. Read if you dare."
—John Lutz

"*Deranged* is a fascinating and exciting blend of misdirection, topsy-turvy, and violence."
—Reed Farrel Coleman

"Gutsy and written with such casual grace, as if the author were sitting across the bar from me, telling me the story, *Deranged* just might be one of the most compelling, thrilling and truth be told, at times look-away-from-page-frightening serial killer novels I've read in a long, long time."
—Vincent Zandri

"Los Angeles has seldom seen such grisly fun. It's James Ellroy meets Alfred Hitchcock in a bloody, yet bizarrely humorous romp on the psychotic side of the street."
—Paul Levine

"This series comes out of the gate swinging with the first offering, *Deranged*. Morris Brick's determination and grit make him a great hero for a thriller series. The surprise twists really kept me engaged. I hope to see Brick have a long shelf life."
—Outofthegutteronline.com

Also by Jacob Stone

DERANGED
CRAZED
MALICIOUS
CRUEL
UNLEASHED

Cruel

A Morris Brick Thriller

Jacob Stone

LYRICAL UNDERGROUND
Kensington Publishing Corp.
www.kensingtonbooks.com

First Electronic Edition: September 2018
eISBN-13: 978-1-5161-0638-7
eISBN-10: 1-5161-0638-5

First Print Edition: September 2018
ISBN-13: 978-1-5161-0639-4
ISBN-10: 1-5161-0639-3

Printed in the United States of America

To my good friend Vinod Bhardwaj,
who likes plenty of twists in his mysteries

Prologue

The rat grew frantic in its efforts to escape the trap, its front claws a blur as they scratched against the wire mesh. This one was older than the juveniles already collected, and showed the scars of a lifetime spent skulking through Los Angeles alleyways and sewers. Half of one ear had been torn off, its grayish-black fur matted, and a dozen wounds scabbed over. While the rat was larger than the others, it was still emaciated enough to be able to squeeze through a hole the size of a quarter. Rats like this one were crucial for what was coming.

The newspaper stories from 2001 didn't mention rats, and neither did the ones from 1984. That had to be because the reporters hadn't been told about them, or really about any of the specifics. In 1984, the newspaper and TV reporters described the murders only as depraved and sickening. A police officer must've given them that description, and someone with a touch of poetry in his soul named the killer the Nightmare Man. That name stuck—both in 1984 and in 2001—but it didn't fully do the killer justice. While horrific, monstrous things were done to the victims, they were things that could only have come from the nightmares of a lunatic.

Just as some species of cicadas awaken only every seventeen years, the same was true of the Nightmare Man. October second would mark the seventeen-year anniversary of the start of the last killing spree, and new victims had already been chosen. They were both the least and most fortunate people alive. They would be dying the worst deaths imaginable, but they would have a kind of immortality, their fates forever entwined with the Nightmare Man. Because of that, they would never be forgotten.

The cage was picked up, and the rat inside backed up and got on its hind legs, its small black eyes shining with malevolence as it bared its teeth. It was an ugly thing and would do nicely for what was needed.

A homeless woman lay curled in a fetal position as she slept beside a dumpster. She stirred as the cage holding the rat was carried past her. Her red-rimmed eyes cracked open, her round, craggy face turning toward the soft padding of footsteps. In a raspy croak that sounded as if her throat had been scraped raw with sandpaper, she asked for money. Even from several feet away, the sour smell of cheap gin on her breath assaulted the senses. A decision now had to be made: whether to kill the old woman or ignore her. A moment of reflection revealed a third option—simply hand the homeless woman a twenty-dollar bill, and that was what was done. The woman mumbled something unintelligible as she accepted the money. She turned away as she hid the bill within her layers of clothing, and then she presumably fell back to sleep.

That was how it needed to be. It wasn't time yet for the Nightmare Man to awaken from his slumber. October second was still a full ten days away. That was when the killings would start again. Besides, snuffing out the life of this old woman wasn't necessary. Her alcohol-addled mind wouldn't later connect this late-night intrusion of her makeshift home with the Nightmare Man's return.

But the Nightmare Man was coming.

And Los Angeles would soon be weeping tears of blood.

Chapter 1

The toy poodle–pit bull mix was lying on her stomach, her paws covering a short, stubby snout. Lori Fletcher's heart melted when she saw her.

"Her name is Sally," Brian said. Rail-thin and gangly, the teenager wore a stained T-shirt, torn jeans, and what Lori hoped was only mud-encrusted tennis sneakers. He was a volunteer at the animal shelter and was showing her the dogs available for adoption. *Just a kid*, she thought, *barely seventeen, if that.* A few times she caught him sneaking peeks at her. She found him adorable, almost as much as the poodle–pit bull mix in the cage. He carried a loose-leaf binder that provided information about each dog, and he cleared his throat so his voice wouldn't crack as he read the sparse notes that had been provided about Sally, telling Lori the dog displayed a gentle temperament, would be good with children, and appeared to be only six months old. "Do you want me to open the cage so you can say hello to her?"

Lori wasn't there to adopt a soft, cuddly sweetheart like this mix, but against her better judgment she nodded. Brian unlatched the cage and opened the metal door, and the dog stood up and began slowly wagging her tail. Ever so cautiously the pooch edged toward the opening so she could stick her stubby nose out of the cage. The next thing Lori knew, she had the dog squirming in her arms as she hugged the poodle–pit bull mix to her chest, and the dog likewise struggled to lick her face. Lori broke out laughing. It had been an unusually stressful few weeks, and she needed something like this more than she could've imagined. She was smitten.

"Love at first sight," Brian said, a note of jealousy in his voice. He showed a smart-alecky grin. "Or maybe it's love at first lick."

The dog was far more toy poodle than pit bull. While she had a pit bull's square-shaped snout and blocky body, she was a small thing weighing less than twenty pounds with a poodle's soft downy fur. But she wasn't what Lori had in mind. The reason she needed a dog was to protect her from *him*. Except she didn't know who *he* was.

A fear she couldn't quite understand had been worming its way into her consciousness for weeks, and then four days ago she awoke with a profound thought screaming in her brain: *he* is going to do terrible things to you. She tried to dismiss this as simply a manifestation of her growing anxiety, except the certainty that *he* existed seemed so real that it left her shaken. It made no sense. She knew that, and for several days she tried to convince herself she'd only had a bad dream, and that was the only reason for the unease gnawing at her. Logically, that was what it had to be, except she couldn't remember anything about the dream, and the fear that a killer was waiting for her in the shadows became overwhelming. Maybe she was suffering from a nervous breakdown. Maybe the explanation was as simple as that, but when she woke up this morning sobbing in terror that *he* was soon going to do depraved and horrible things to her, she believed it as much as she ever believed anything. She decided she had two choices: check herself in for psychiatric evaluation or get a dog to protect her. As much as Sally tugged at her heartstrings, the little fluff ball wouldn't be able to protect her from a gust of wind. So she steeled herself and handed the dog back to Brian.

"I should look at other dogs before making a decision," she said.

The teenager's eyes widened with surprise, as he must've been sure Lori had found her match, but he placed the dog back in the cage, and as the door latched shut, the poodle–pit bull mix let out a heartbroken whine. This struck Lori like a dagger. She almost relented, but that ever-pervasive thought echoed in her head. *He's out there, and he'll be coming for you soon.*

Brian continued the tour. Most of the dogs up for adoption were pit bulls. There was one Chihuahua and a beagle and pug mix, but just about every other dog seemed to be pit bulls or pit bull mixes. Lori knew they had a reputation for ferocity, but that was probably only if they had been badly mistreated or trained that way, and the ones she saw all looked like loveable sweethearts, just like Sally. None of them would be able to protect her from her boogeyman...if he in fact existed.

When Brian brought her to a cage holding a large, angry-looking beast, Lori knew she'd found her protector. The animal had a thick, squat body, a large head, and a coal-black coat mottled with reddish-brown streaks. The dog gave her a sinister, dead-eyed stare. As she moved closer to the cage, a threatening noise between a snarl and a growl rumbled out of the beast's throat. If it was meant to scare Lori off, it didn't work. In fact, it had the opposite effect. The ferocity made her feel safe. She asked Brian if she could meet the dog.

"Really?" he asked, his voice rising an octave.

"He looks to me like he could use a good home."

Brian consulted the loose-leaf binder, flipping through the pages until he found the one matching the cage number. His eyes scrunched up as he looked from the page to the dog and back to the page. "It says here his name's Lucy," he said.

Lori could see that the dog was male, and one that hadn't been neutered. "That's an odd name for him."

"Very odd," Brian agreed. He read more of the notes associated with the animal. "The veterinarian who examined him thinks he's part Rottweiler and part Doberman. A hundred and twenty pounds. He's had all his shots." The teenager smirked. "If you adopt him, you should change his name to Lucky."

"Why's that?"

"He's only got three days left to be adopted before being put down. Are you sure you want me to take him out of his cage?"

The teenager seemed nervous to put his fingers anywhere near Lucy. Lori smiled sweetly at him and told him she'd do it. She had grown up with two Rhodesian ridgebacks, and large dogs didn't intimidate her. She also knew the secret to a dog's heart. Lucy made more snarling, growling noises and bared his fangs as she unlatched the cage and opened it. But the dog stayed where he was and didn't move until Lori reached into her pocket and took out a bacon-flavored treat. The dog moved quickly then, snatching the treat away, somehow leaving her fingers intact. When Lori offered another treat, this one held in the palm of her hand, the dog was more careful about taking it. He even consented to let her scratch him behind the ear and thump him on the side.

As Lori stood beside the animal, she felt safe for the first time in days. She smiled at him. *I'll save your life and you'll save mine.* The dog cocked his head and gave her a quizzical look in return.

"I found my dog," she told Brian. "Can I take him home with me?"

Chapter 2

Morris Brick had not been to Luzana's before, and for good reason. The restaurant on North Cahuenga Boulevard had a reputation for putting a serious dent in its customers' wallets, but even if that wasn't the case, there was little chance he would've been able to get a table there. Luzana's had become Los Angeles's most exclusive hotspot. A place for Hollywood royalty, sports celebrities, and the ultra-rich to be seen and noticed. Morris might've become a minor celebrity after years of catching depraved serial killers, but that still wouldn't have bought him a table reservation at Luzana's, and so it only mildly surprised him when the maître d'hôtel gave him the snootiest look he had ever seen. He was genuinely surprised, however, after the man peered over his stand to see that the pig-like grunt just heard had come from Parker, Morris's all-white bull terrier, that he made a shooing gesture with both hands. That was just plain rude!

Morris arched an eyebrow and, keeping his voice amiable, asked, "Am I supposed to guess that means you have no tables available? At twenty past two on a Tuesday?"

If it were possible, the maître d' would've climbed onto a stepladder so he could look even further down his nose at Morris. "Apparently," he mumbled under his breath.

Morris stood his ground and lazily rubbed his jaw. If he were the vindictive type, he could've called in a favor at the mayor's office and had the place shut down for a kitchen violation—imagined or real, it didn't matter. After all, six months ago he and his team at Morris Brick Investigations, commonly known as MBI, very likely saved the lives of hundreds of thousands of fellow Angelenos, and at a heavy cost. Charlie Bogle had almost died after being shot in the chest and hadn't been the same since, even quitting MBI two months ago, and Morris himself had taken shrapnel to the leg from a booby trap, and it was only since last month that he was able to put away his cane. But as tempted as he was to drag the maître d' out from behind the stand and teach him some manners, he maintained a calm demeanor and told him he was meeting a friend. "Philip Stonehedge. He's already here," he said.

The maître d' opened his eyes wide with incredulity. Stonehedge was high up on Hollywood's A-list, and not only that, he was dating the gorgeous Brie Evans, who sat near the top of the list. But since there was a remote chance Morris might be telling the truth, he asked for Morris's name and made a phone call, keeping his voice low so Morris couldn't eavesdrop. Shortly afterward, a waiter came bustling out of the main dining room and whispered something to the maître d', whose attitude quickly changed.

It was almost as if a magic wand had been waved—in less time than it took to snap one's fingers, his contempt transformed to full-blown obsequiousness. He bowed and asked Morris to follow him, and as he led them through the crowded dining room filled with Hollywood royalty and other studio muckety-mucks and onward to the equally bustling outdoor patio, Morris resisted the urge to plant a kick onto the man's well-padded derriere.

Parker had been behaving himself, but he suddenly grunted excitedly and lurched forward as he strained against his leash. The bull terrier must've spotted Stonehedge, who was grinning at them from his table, the thick, jagged scar running down his cheek giving his grin a sardonic quality. The actor had gotten the scar from being slashed with a gun barrel. This happened after he had arranged with the mayor's office to tag along with Morris on the Skull Cracker Killer investigation, although it wasn't SCK who did the slashing but a vicious criminal by the name of Alex Malfi who didn't appreciate the actor trying to interfere with a Beverly Hills jewelry store robbery. Malfi further showed his displeasure toward Stonehedge by shooting him in the thigh, and the actor would've died if it hadn't been for Morris's later heroics.

Stonehedge left the table to playfully tussle with Parker, then shook Morris's hand and reached over to bring him in for a hug. The maître d' stood deferentially off to the side until Stonehedge slipped him a fifty. Morris and Parker joined Stonehedge at the table, which already had several platters of food waiting for them. When the bull terrier grunted impatiently, the actor fed him a piece of meat from one of the platters.

"Wood-grilled lamb tenderloin wrapped in jamón ibérico," the actor said, beaming. "Absolutely delicious."

Morris knew enough Spanish to guess that jamón ibérico was a kind of expensive imported ham. Given the way Parker wolfed it down and grunted for more, the dog must've concurred with Stonehedge's assessment.

"Don't give him too much," Morris said. "He needs to lose a few pounds." Stonehedge laughed at that. "Don't we all?"

That was true for Morris. He needed to drop ten pounds from his waistline, but for someone who enjoyed gourmet food as much as Stonehedge, his friend somehow stayed as lean as a marathon runner. Before he could object, Stonehedge fed Parker another piece of lamb. Morris snared a piece for himself and had to agree it was exceptional. A waitress came over to take his drink order. Stonehedge had a bottle of champagne already at the table. When Morris tried ordering a beer, his friend stopped him.

"You're not seeing me off with a beer," he insisted. Then to the waitress, "My buddy will have a *le daiquiri*."

Before Morris could say anything, the waitress was rushing away from the table. "*Le daiquiri* as opposed to a daiquiri?" he asked.

"It's the *le* that makes it so special," the actor said with a straight face. "When you taste it, you'll be glad I changed your order. If not, you can always have her bring you a beer. Besides, this is the last chance I'll have in four months to be so obnoxious with you."

"At least you admit it."

Stonehedge lifted his champagne glass, his eyes narrowing as he gazed at the slightly rose-colored bubbly. "I'm nothing if not painfully self-aware of my indulgences and faults." He took a sip of his drink and turned again to Morris, his lips showing a pensive smile. "I'm glad you were able to make it. And I'm glad you were able to bring the little guy along."

"He never would've forgiven me if he knew I'd cost him a mooching opportunity at Luzana's."

As if on command, Parker let out a grunt. Stonehedge fed the dog what looked like a blackened piece of meat from another platter. "Truffle-encrusted Wagyu beef," he said. "It's even better than the lamb."

Morris whistled Parker over and ordered the bull terrier to lie down. The dog did as he was commanded, but not without letting out a few unhappy grumbles.

"I'm not sure I'll be able to get him to eat his dog food after this," Morris complained.

"Eh, if you put it in front of him, he'll eat it."

That was mostly true. Parker rarely ever walked away from his dish when there was still food in it. He was also a champion moocher, and Morris himself had proven over the years to be a soft touch, but he was trying to change his ways since Parker's last visit to the veterinarian. That was three weeks ago, and the veterinarian confirmed what Natalie had been telling him: that Parker needed to lose weight or it could cause health problems later on.

Morris asked, "When are you leaving?"

Stonehedge took another sip of his champagne. "Flying out of LAX eight this evening, and with losing eight hours I won't be arriving in Dublin until two tomorrow. Then a two-hour drive to Galway." His expression grew wistful. "My last decent food until then."

"This time you're making a romantic comedy?"

Stonehedge had taken what looked like a fancy slider from one of the platters and was munching on that. He waited until he swallowed his food before nodding. "You've got to try one of these, Morris. They're amazing. But yeah, that's right. *Stumbling in the Rain*. Not the best title for a rom-com, but the script's good, and my co-star is the lovely Claire Rose. The film will be a nice change of pace from the thrillers I've been making of late."

Morris took Stonehedge's advice and tried one of the sliders, and it was every bit as good as his friend had claimed. The filling was a thick slab of bacon coated with a sweet bean garlic glaze. He didn't have the heart to deprive Parker of bacon that delicious, and he scraped off the garlic glaze and fed the rest of the slider to his dog. Tomorrow would be another day to get back onto Parker's diet—and his own, for that matter.

Stonehedge watched with an amused grin but held back any comment as their waitress had returned with *le daiquiri*. Morris took a sip and had to admit it was better than any beer he could've ordered.

"A shame Brie isn't co-starring with you," Morris said.

Stonehedge made a face at that idea. "They wanted her, but Brie's tied up for the next two months. Probably better that we're not acting together. Competition's not the best thing for actors in a relationship. But we'll be seeing each other. Next week she's flying to Munich for a promotional event, and I'll hop over for a visit and take advantage of the beginning of Oktoberfest. But enough about that. How about yourself? Any interesting cases?"

"Mostly run-of-the-mill insurance fraud work." Morris had grabbed another piece of wood-grilled lamb and fed it to a grateful Parker. "The most interesting of which was a stolen coin collection I closed last week. The collection was appraised six months ago at one point two million and was supposedly stolen three months later in a home burglary. It turned out that the owner had sold off the collection to several private buyers and then staged the burglary. What he really bought for himself was a grand larceny charge."

"You're right. Sounds pretty run-of-the-mill."

"You can say what you're really thinking. Boring."

"Well, yeah, compared to hunting serial killers."

"After that psycho Jason Dorsage, I'm fine with boring."

"You say that now, but just wait until you're chasing after your next serial killer. Knowing my luck, it will be while I'm in Ireland, and I'll miss all the fun. And—" The actor abruptly stopped talking and snapped his fingers to get Morris's attention. "Hello? Are you still there? Morris, buddy, you faded on me, like you went away somewhere deep in your head."

"What?" A hard grimace tightened Morris's lips into a thin line. "Just a random thought. Nothing worth mentioning."

Stonehedge had been right, and Morris was lying now. It was more than just a random thought that had distracted him. In fact, he was so distracted that he had fed Parker another piece of lamb without realizing he had done so, and the bull terrier didn't mind this absentminded lapse.

He hadn't thought about the Nightmare Man murders in years, but something caused a disturbing fact about those killings to resurface in his mind. Maybe it was because of what Stonehedge had been talking about, or maybe something else had triggered it, but whatever it was, it occurred to him that October second would be the seventeen-year anniversary of when the last killings started.

The Nightmare Man had never been caught. When the first set of killings happened thirty-four years ago, a witness had described the killer as a man in his late forties. Even if the Nightmare Man was still alive, he'd be close to eighty now, if not older.

Still, Morris couldn't help feeling a sense of dread knowing what might be coming in only a week.

Chapter 3

Culver City, 1984

The killer known as the Nightmare Man entered the bedroom and saw that Mary Beth Williamson was sleeping on her stomach. He got a pair of socks from a dresser drawer and forced them into her mouth so she wouldn't be able to scream. Before she could sputter awake and realize what was happening, he flipped her on her back and tied her wrists and ankles with nylon rope. He then used a razor-sharp hunting knife to cut off her cotton pajamas.

As she lay naked in the semidarkness of the room, her eyes met his, and he could see first fear and then defiance flooding her eyes. That would change soon enough. Once he started pulling off her fingernails there would only be a desperate pleading for him to stop. Later, she'd be lost completely in her pain. He sorted out the contents of his gym bag, picked up the needle-nose pliers, and went to work.

The other night he had watched *Live and Let Die* on video with his wife and sons. For his money, Sean Connery was the only true Bond, but the movie's title song had stuck in his head, and as he used the hunting knife to carve away thick pieces of Mary Beth's flesh, he found himself absently singing the line "When you got a job to do you got to do it well." *So true.*

Later, when he was using a cigarette lighter to heat up the end of the thin metal rod that he used to brand his victims' wounds, he caught the look in her eyes. She was no longer pleading for him to stop but instead was desperately trying to ask him a question. Why her?

It was a good question, because he could've picked thousands of other women in LA. So why her? Opportunity was one of the reasons. Her husband was an intern at Cedars-Sinai, and when the killer had gotten into their house three weeks ago using the spare key that they kept hidden in a fake rock, he found the husband's work schedule and knew the husband wouldn't be getting off work until eight in the morning. The killer had also used the opportunity to break the latch on one of the windows in the spare bedroom, so even if the wife started using the chain door locks while her husband was gone because of the Nightmare Man, the killer would be able to enter the house without making any noise. But the truth was, he'd have little trouble getting into any house or apartment, and it wouldn't much matter if he found a husband or boyfriend in bed with his victim.

So why her? Mary Beth Williamson was twenty-eight. On the plump side, but pleasingly so, as the killer's mother might've said. Medium-length brown hair, pleasant enough face, a curvy and attractive body even with the added thirty pounds she carried. The killer had spent time watching her. He knew she worked as a nurse and that she appeared to be a pleasant and friendly woman. The killer had to admit there was really no particular reason why he chose her. It was just bad luck on her part, plain and simple. But what would've been the point of telling her that?

Chapter 4

Los Angeles, the present

Lori couldn't help smiling when she realized why her new dog—a male—had been named Lucy. It had to be short for Lucifer.

"That wasn't a nice thing to do to you," she told the dog. "How can anyone expect you not to live up to a name like that? But we're changing things. Brian at the shelter had a most excellent idea, and so I'm changing your name from this point on to Lucky. How do you like them apples?"

The dog cocked his head and looked at her as if she were crazy. He was a scary-looking animal. Ugly, too, with his thick, blocky head and the whites of his eyes a yellowish-red color as if they were oozing blood and pus. None of that mattered to her. Quite the opposite, she was beginning to find a certain beauty in his scary ugliness, and after a somewhat standoffish first hour together, they'd been getting along just fine. The bacon-flavored treats she gave him helped, as did the two hot dogs she bought him at the Santa Monica pier. But what really sealed the deal was that the dog sensed she felt safe with him. Even more so, that she needed him. If the unknown boogeyman that she believed existed broke into her apartment while she slept, Lucky would protect her. She knew in her heart that was true, and because of that she already felt a deep affection toward the dog, even though he'd been in her life less than three hours. She stopped to hug him tightly around his thick neck. Lucky groaned as she did this, but otherwise tolerated it, and she broke out laughing when she saw what could only be described as a look of embarrassment contorting his face.

They'd been walking along a pathway on the cliff that overlooked Santa Monica State Beach. She had wanted to tire the dog out before she brought him to her apartment, and the mission seemed to have been accomplished.

Lucky had been moving more sluggishly the last few minutes and began using a stalling tactic of sniffing each bush and tree they came across for what seemed like an excessive amount of time. She took him to a bench shaded by a palm tree, poured water into a paper cup, and held it for dog. After Lucky had his drink, he lay on the ground, his thick body heavy against her legs. Lori felt mostly content as she looked out onto the ocean, although one thought nagged at her: How was she going to sneak Lucky into her apartment? And how could she possibly keep his presence a secret? She sat worrying about that for several minutes until finally making a decision, resolve hardening her features.

She got off the bench and tugged on Lucky's leash, coaxing him to his feet.

"Come on, big guy," she said. "Time to take you home."

* * * *

Nathan caught her before she was able to sneak Lucky into the elevator. He was the live-in superintendent for Lori's building. A short, squat man in his fifties who always seemed to wear the same dirty undershirt badly yellowed with age and perspiration and even dirtier khakis, and whose body odor was pungent enough that Lori needed to breathe through her mouth when he was around. Nathan also had a habit of barely moving his lips when he talked, as if he were always practicing a ventriloquism act.

"Dogs aren't allowed," he said.

Once again his lips showed less movement than someone shivering from the cold. It was disorienting to Lori watching him talk, like trying to watch a foreign movie that had been poorly dubbed so that the mouths and sound were out of sync. Nathan also seemed to have a way of sneaking up on her when she least wanted to see him, and because of that she was ready for him and had her game plan figured out.

She argued, "Mrs. Weinstein has a Pomeranian!"

He made a face as if he had tasted something unpleasant. "That's what you call that thing? It's always yapping. Gives me a headache."

"I've been with Lucky for hours now and he hasn't barked once."

"It don't matter. Weinstein got permission to have that yappy thing. You don't have permission. You need to write a letter to the landlord and get permission."

Lori didn't quite bat her eyes at him, but she came close. "Nathan, I'm a twenty-five-year-old woman living alone in the city. I don't feel safe. I need Lucky here to feel safe."

"The building's safe," he argued.

"That might be true, but I don't feel safe walking alone outside."

"Neighborhood's safe also."

"I don't only walk in this neighborhood."

He shifted his eyes so that he was looking past her right shoulder, and a blush reddened his cheeks. "You're very pretty," he said. "You could get married if you want."

"Thank you, but even if that were true, I'm not dating anyone right now, so that solution won't help me today. You don't want to be responsible for me being hurt or worse, do you?"

His face reddened more. "Nothing I can do," he insisted. "Rules are rules."

Lori had half a pound of roast beef in her oversized handbag, which was the main reason Lucky had been behaving himself—his attention focused solely on her bag. While she was talking with the super, she had unzipped her bag and pulled out a slice, which she held to Nathan. He gave it and then her a baffled look, as if he thought she was trying to bribe him with cold cuts.

"Why don't you feed this to Lucky?"

It took him a moment to make sense of what she was suggesting. His eyes instantly dulled, as if he were going to flatly refuse, but he just as quickly weakened and accepted the meat, which he held out to Lucky. The dog snatched it out of his hand without taking off any fingers, but he also wagged his tail slightly as if he was still trying to decide whether the squat super was friend or foe. Lori gave the super another slice of roast beef to feed Lucky, and this time the dog made up his mind and let out an appreciative grunt. He even pushed his thick head closer to the super so the man could pet him.

Nathan looked perturbed by all this as he struggled to make a decision, but Lori saw something melt in his eyes. She knew the man liked her and found her attractive. She also knew he was harmless, and his feelings for her might very well have been along the lines of a brother toward a much younger sister (even though there was a good twenty-five years separating them) rather than any romantic longings. She also had no doubt that he was a loner and had guessed he would warm up to Lucky if given a chance. It looked like she was right.

"If he bothers other tenants or makes a nuisance of himself—"

"He won't! I promise. And I won't be leaving him alone in my apartment. I'll be taking him to work with me each day."

The super's mouth pinched as if he were suffering indigestion. But this was just for show. A decision had already been made. He cautiously began rubbing Lucky behind his ear, and a contented noise rumbled out of the dog's throat. Kindred spirits.

"I'll let you in on a secret," he confided. "When a letter goes to the landlord, he calls me to make the decision. You can keep him as long as he don't cause any trouble."

Lori could've kissed him, except it would've confused the situation. "Thank you so much, Nathan. And he won't cause any trouble. I'll make sure of it."

The super shifted his gaze from the dog to Lori. He smiled, revealing cracked and chipped teeth stained worse than his undershirt. It might've been the first time she had ever seen his teeth.

He said, "If you want to let him eat Weinstein's yappy little dog, that will be okay with me. The thing gives me a headache. But make sure he don't cause no other trouble."

Chapter 5

Three years ago, Morris Brick was a star within the LAPD after solving three high-profile serial killer cases in a span of seven years. His last investigation as a homicide detective had him chasing down the Hillside Cannibal Killer, which not only made him a national celebrity but also almost made him the Cannibal's last victim. When he decided to quit the department and start MBI, Police Commissioner Martin Hadley made only a perfunctory effort at best to talk him out of it. While that might've surprised others, Morris pretty much expected it from Hadley—after all, the two of them strongly disliked each other and had been butting heads since he made detective. Hadley, however, went ballistic when he found out Morris had arranged for three other LAPD homicide detectives—Charlie Bogle, Fred Lemmon, and Dennis Polk—to join him in his new venture. The police commissioner would've blown a gasket entirely if he'd known Morris also took copies of his cold cases with him on his way out the door.

Morris had no intention of actively working any of these unsolved crimes, but he wanted the files in case inspiration struck. Of all of them, the ones he prayed most to be solved were the Nightmare Man murders. He also dreaded the thought of ever opening the thick manila folder that held the sickening details and secrets of those killings.

It was a little after four when he returned with Parker in tow to MBI's office suite on Wilshire Boulevard. He'd been coaxed by Stonehedge to have three *le daiquiris* (his actor friend was right—they were delicious), but he could've had half a dozen more and it wouldn't have mattered. Thinking about the Nightmare Man sobered him up more than guzzling a thermos of black coffee or dumping a bucket of ice water on his head.

He was fourteen when the Nightmare Man first struck, but even though he had been almost a decade away from becoming a police officer, he was still connected with those murders since his dad, who was then an LAPD homicide detective, was the lead investigator. He didn't see his dad much during the seventeen days that the killings took place, nor the four months that followed as his dad continued to chase dead ends. The times that he did see him, Sam Brick had tried to hide the horror of the killings from his family. He never talked about them. Not a word. But there were cracks in the façade he put up, moments when Morris caught a glimpse of the weariness his dad tried so hard to conceal.

It wasn't as much a coincidence as it might've seemed when in 2001 he made detective at thirty-one and only a month later was assigned to the case when the murders started up again. All he ever wanted to do as a kid was follow in his dad's footsteps and become a police detective, and somehow it seemed fitting that he'd finish the job his dad started and be the one to catch the Nightmare Man. But it didn't happen. Just as in 1984, the Nightmare Man slipped away after seventeen days of bloody carnage, his crimes remaining unsolved.

Morris dug the Nightmare Man folder from its hiding place under a pile of boxes and other papers stored away in the back of his coat closet. He hadn't been aware of it until then, but at a subconscious level he must've been trying to hide the file's existence—that had to be why he'd buried it where he had. The other cold case files were kept in his bottom desk drawer.

Parker had accompanied Morris to the closet, making sure to stick his nose into things. The bull terrier followed Morris back to his desk and with a grunt lowered himself onto the carpeted floor. Within minutes he was lying on his side and snoring heavily. It was tiring work mooching as much as Parker had done that afternoon!

For several minutes Morris sat Buddha-like, staring at the folder. He hadn't touched it since dropping it onto his desk, and the thought of doing so gave him an uneasy, hollow feeling deep in his stomach as if he had swallowed a peach pit. More a delaying tactic than actually wanting coffee, he left his office and walked to the kitchen area. He found the coffeepot holding an inch of cold, congealed, grayish sludge that must've been left over from yesterday. Before meeting with Stonehedge, he'd been out of the office tracking down several crates of stolen machinery parts for a client. Likewise, Lemmon and Polk were out on assignment. Adam Felger, MBI's millennial computer and hacking specialist, whom Morris talked to briefly when he returned from his late lunch, drank only Red Bull and had an impressive collection of empty cans stacked up in his office, and

Greta Lindstrom, MBI's office manager and receptionist, eschewed coffee for bottled water.

Morris scrubbed the glass carafe clean and started a fresh pot brewing. Several times during the year he had considered replacing the antiquated coffeemaker with a single cup brewer that worked with individual-sized flavored pods, but he was old-fashioned when it came to coffee and liked the idea of always having a pot available.

The coffee finished brewing, and he stared at it, reluctant to pour himself a cup. Once he did, he'd be done with excuses for not opening the Nightmare Man folder. As he stood silently he thought about the approaching seventeen-year anniversary and how that number held a special significance for the killer. As with the killings in 1984, those in 2001 also took place over a seventeen-day period. The victims were all women. All of them were found naked in bed, and with each murder the killer pulled off seventeen finger- and toenails and used a hunting knife to slice off seventeen pieces of flesh, and then arranged all this at the foot of the bed into a grisly "17." But that wasn't all he did to the victims. There were the seventeen burn marks found on each of them. As painful and disfiguring as these wounds and burns were, none of that was what killed these women. It was the way he used a rat to end their lives that still made Morris queasy whenever he'd let himself think about it, and there wasn't much else he had ever encountered as a homicide detective that made him queasy.

Morris decided he wasn't in the mood for coffee after all. Without any further procrastination, he walked back to his office, sat down behind his desk, and opened the Nightmare Man folder. The first page was a police drawing from 1984. The witness lived in the same apartment building as the victim and saw the suspected killer when the man was leaving through the building's back door at three a.m. carrying a large gym bag over his shoulder—a bag large enough to hold a rat cage. The parking lot behind the building was poorly lit, and the witness, a twenty-three-year-old man by the name of Levi Bergdahl, was standing in the shadows and wouldn't have been seen by someone leaving the apartment building. The suspect's face, however, would've been lit up enough by an exterior doorway light for Bergdahl to have gotten a clear view of him and be able to provide the details he'd given to the police sketch artist. Bergdahl had been drinking that night for several hours before coming home, but he insisted he wasn't drunk, and Morris's dad decided he was credible. The sketch was shown to the other residents in the building, and nobody knew the man, so he had either broken into the building late at night to kill Denise Lowenstein—the

Nightmare Man's fourth victim—or to burglarize another apartment, except none of the apartments other than Lowenstein's were broken into that night.

It had been over fifteen years since Morris had last looked at the police sketch, but the image was still vivid in his mind. A long, narrow face lined by deep grooves. No beard or mustache. In the darkness of the night, the witness couldn't tell whether the suspect's hair was black or a shade of brown, or even whether it had any gray, but insisted it was cut short and that some kind of hair gel had been used to slick it back against the skull and keep it from touching the suspect's ears, which were long and had thick lobes. The nose, like the man's face, was long and narrow, and possibly bent as if it had once been broken and never set properly. The drawing looked to Morris like the face of an ex-convict who'd done hard time. Bergdahl further claimed the suspect wore a dark gray jacket, dark pants, and gloves. He had watched quietly from the shadows as the suspect left the building and fled down an alleyway to an adjoining street. While Bergdahl thought the man was suspicious, and was in fact frightened by him, he didn't contact the police until after he found out Denise Lowenstein had been murdered by the Nightmare Man.

Morris's dad had had the same thought about the police sketch looking like an ex-convict and had gone through stacks of prisoner mugshot books without any luck. The convicts he found who resembled the sketch were either still in prison when the murders took place or had airtight alibis.

The next sheet of paper in the folder was a drawing Morris had made that aged the 1984 suspect by seventeen years, and like his dad he had spent dozens of hours looking at mugshot books and prisoner photos without any luck. Morris gave this drawing only a cursory look before moving on to the police and medical examiner notes and the profiler reports. He read all of these carefully—both the notes and reports from 1984 and 2001. When he was done, he picked up the crime scene photos, his jaw muscles tightening as he steeled himself to look at them. Carefully, methodically, he studied each of the photos, even the ones that showed how the rats were used, as he hoped to glean a nugget of useful information that might've escaped him and the other police and FBI investigators over the years. It was as painful this time as it had been every other time he had seen them, and as in the past, no hidden secret was revealed.

Once he was done, he arranged the thick stack of pages into a neat pile and placed them back into the manila folder and, instead of hiding it in the back of his closet, he left it on top of his desk. If Levi Bergdahl's witness account was worth a damn and the person he had described was the Nightmare Man and not a random burglar, the killer would be in his eighties today. And that would only be if he were still alive. But what if Bergdahl was wrong? Or even if he was right? Couldn't an eighty-year-old psychopath still kill, especially one as depraved as this killer and who'd been waiting seventeen years to take more lives? The odds were the Nightmare Man was gone forever. Logically Morris knew that, but he still couldn't shake the uneasy feeling deep in his stomach that they weren't done with this maniac yet.

He absently drummed his fingers against the surface of his desk, then made a phone call. After four rings, Hadley answered, his voice gruff and exasperated as he demanded to know why Morris was calling.

"Do you know what day it will be a week from today?"

"I'm busy," Hadley grumbled. "If you got something to say, spit it out."

"October second."

"You don't think I've got a calendar and can see that?"

"It will be the seventeen-year anniversary of when the Nightmare Man started killing again."

There was a fat second of silence, then Hadley's frog-like voice croaking, "So?"

"You don't think you should be doing something about it?"

"Like what?"

"How about warning the public? Or maybe sending out extra patrols and checking alleys for anyone collecting rats?" Morris could hear his voice growing harsher as he added, "Or following up on the idea my dad was working thirty-four years ago, and what I wanted to try seventeen years ago."

"You won't give up on that, will you? Forget it, Brick, I'm not wasting departmental resources chasing a ghost. If this maniac is still alive, he's a feeble old man rotting away in either a prison cell or a nursing home. And if you think you can use this to drum up business for your pissant little firm, forget that also. I swear, Brick, if you start showing up on TV worrying the public about this, I'll find a way to pull your license and shut you down. And don't even think about calling your slick Boy Scout friend at the mayor's office."

"Martin, women could be dying soon. In the worst possible way."

"Yeah, well, that's my headache if it happens, not yours."

Hadley disconnected the call from his end.

A soft groan came from the floor. Morris looked down to see Parker stretching all four legs, the bull terrier's eyes open as he waited to see what Morris would do next.

What he wanted to do was forget all about the Nightmare Man, but he didn't think that was possible, at least not entirely. Maybe if October second came and went without the murders starting up again.

Morris checked his watch. A little before five. He got Greta on the phone. Two more insurance fraud cases had come in that day. They still had their share of corporate investigations, divorces, and occasional missing persons, but the insurance fraud cases were becoming their bread and butter. Not the worst thing in the world, and much better than thinking about serial killers. But the work could wait until tomorrow. He used the point of his shoe to lightly rub Parker's chest. The bull terrier lifted his head to give Morris a questioning look.

"What do you say we cut out early and I take you to the dog park?" Morris asked. "See if we can work off some of that rich food you mooched off me?"

Parker answered by flipping himself onto his feet, his thick, ropy tail wagging steadily.

Chapter 6

Morris called his wife from the dog park. A minute ago Parker had been playing tag with a newly made friend, each dog taking turns grabbing the baseball from the other, then chasing the opponent until they could grab the ball back. The other dog was faster than Parker, but the bull terrier was significantly stronger and could tackle the larger dog if he got close enough. The other dog also couldn't take the ball away from Parker if he didn't let him. After twenty minutes of this, Parker either got bored or winded. Whichever it was, he let the baseball drop from his mouth and wandered off to sniff some bushes. Likewise, the other dog trotted off to join her owner.

Natalie asked about lunch with Stonehedge. "You didn't let Parker mooch up all the food, did you?"

"Not all, but I was weak," Morris admitted. "And Parker's ridiculously talented in his wheedling ways. It didn't help matters that I got distracted."

"About what?"

"An old case. Not worth mentioning."

"You don't sound so sure of that."

Natalie was a trained therapist and good at what she did. She was especially good at picking up on all sorts of clues, including changes of inflections in Morris's voice and reading his mood.

"I'm being an alarmist, that's all. It's really not worth talking about since the case is as cold as they come and nothing new has happened. It's just a feeling I have. Anyway, I am at the dog park now with Parker, the one on De Longpre Avenue."

"Our little guy behaving himself?"

"Like a champ. I threw him a baseball until my arm nearly fell off, then in the nick of time he made friends with one of those tall, thin gray dogs—a Weimer-something. The two of them played tag for a while. Now Parker's watering some bushes."

"A Weimaraner. I believe that's the name of the breed of dog he played with."

"Yep. Sounds right. I'm thinking of picking up either Chinese, Indian, or pizza for dinner. Your preference?"

"Chinese would be wonderful. Seven Star?"

"Where else? Should I order the usual?"

"Hmm. I'll try something new tonight. Order me the crispy fish with spicy chili sauce. I've been thinking of that dish since seeing it on the menu last time we were there."

Morris was a creature of habit. It was near sacrilege for him not to order his favorite food at a restaurant. After all, why take the chance? But he didn't argue with his wife. She was going to be at the office a little while longer typing up client notes, and he told her he should have dinner waiting for them by the time she got home.

He wandered over to where Parker had dropped the baseball. The leather covering was half chewed off, and what was left had gotten fairly well slimed with saliva from both dogs. Still, the ball would be useable at least one more time. Morris did a deep bend on his creaky knees and rubbed the ball against the dry grass until it was merely damp instead of sodden. Then he whistled for Parker, who came charging out of the bushes toward him with a clownish grin only a bull terrier could give.

* * * *

Morris didn't beat Natalie home as he expected. His wife pulled into the driveway just ahead of him and stood with hands on hips waiting for him and Parker. She was a slender, petite brunette with mesmerizing brown eyes, and after twenty-five years of marriage her smile could bring a lump to Morris's throat. He still had a hard time believing how lucky he was when she fell in love with him all those years ago.

Parker had spotted Natalie also and was squirming in his seat and grunting excitedly. Morris reached over and opened the passenger door so the bull terrier could rush out, his tail beating at a faster rate than a metronome set to its quickest tempo. This distraction gave Morris time to go around to the trunk and get the bags of takeout food without Parker starting up with his mooching ways. Whenever he picked up takeout food with Parker in the car, he had to store it away in the trunk to keep it safe and keep the dog's mooching from going into overdrive.

Natalie was on her knees, partly wrestling with the bull terrier and partly trying to keep him from licking her face wet. Her bright smile dimmed with concern as she looked into Morris's eyes. She disentangled herself from Parker so she could give him a kiss.

"Hon, you're still worrying about that cold case," she said. "I can see it weighing on you."

Morris took hold of her hand. Parker, grinning happily, pushed his nose against the paper bag holding cartons of crispy fish, kung pao chicken, Peking ravioli, and pork fried rice.

"You're right, of course," Morris acknowledged. "But I've got no reason to be worrying about it. Nothing new has happened."

"Are you sure you don't want to talk about it?"

Morris made a pained face. "I'd rather not."

They went inside, heading straight to the kitchen. He hid the takeout bag in the oven—a trick so Parker wouldn't think the delicious-smelling food was imminent, otherwise there wasn't a chance the bull terrier would've eaten his dog food. As it was, he sniffed the ridiculously expensive low-fat, high-protein, and grain-free dry food that Morris had poured into his bowl before consenting to eat it. The veterinarian had recommended a different and cheaper brand, but Rachel had gotten into the act and researched the healthiest food they should be feeding Parker, and Morris wasn't going to argue about it. If he tried, he'd lose. His daughter was now a third-year law student at UCLA with plans of being a prosecutor, and she was damned persistent when it came to something she was passionate about.

With this subterfuge done, Natalie set the table while Morris got out an already opened bottle of Riesling for Natalie and a bottle of a heavily spiced lager for himself that Stonehedge had recommended. They waited until Parker licked his bowl clean before Morris brought out the Chinese food from the oven and dished it out onto two plates.

Parker's mooching was halfhearted at best after emptying out a bowl of his food and all of his earlier mooching, and after a while he gave up completely to lie down by Natalie's feet. As much as they tried to make small talk, a pall hung over the room. After several minutes, Natalie asked whether it was the Nightmare Man case that had Morris so distracted.

Morris put his chopsticks down as he appraised his wife.

She was just so instinctive.

He asked, "Has there been anything on TV about the approaching anniversary of those killings?"

"No, nothing. But no other murders ever tore you up like those did."

"That's true," he agreed.

There shouldn't have been anyone in the media sniffing around about the Nightmare Man killings. They were never told the significance of the number seventeen to the killer, nor did they know that the killings restarted on the anniversary of the Nightmare Man's first murder. In 2001 they didn't find the body until five days after the murder had taken place, and they didn't bother to correct the media's misunderstanding about the date of when the killing had happened.

"Nat, I've got no reason to believe this killer is still alive, or that he's coming back. It's just a feeling I can't shake. I tried calling Hadley to remind him of what might be coming, and he blew me off. Worse, actually. He threatened to shut down MBI if I made any noise to the media or anyone else about it."

Her expression became pensive. "But you're not giving up that easily," she said.

"No, I'm not," he admitted.

Chapter 7

Vincent Scalise and Frank Colgan were sitting in Vincent's new Lincoln sedan with its lights off and the engine running. Scalise's nickname among his colleagues was "Dapper Vince," which made sense since he always dressed stylishly in a suit, although the wide ties and Italian oxfords he wore bordered on a mafia *chic* look. Colgan usually dressed for work in a suit and tie also, but on his lumpy body, his suits never looked stylish, only rumpled. He was given the nickname "Irish," which made sense in a way because of his red hair and beefy red face that always looked as if he'd been drinking whiskey, but he seldom drank alcohol and didn't have any Irish blood in him. His old man's family were Italian, and they shortened their surname from Colganatti to Colgan when they arrived on Ellis Island a hundred years earlier, and his mom was a large German woman.

Colgan took two sandwiches out of a paper bag and handed one to Scalise. "Roast beef," he said. Scalise unwrapped the sandwich and couldn't help sneering at it. Supermarket-bought white bread. Irish couldn't even have the imagination to stop at a bakery and buy a loaf of sourdough or ciabatta! He took a bite, and no surprise the bread had been smeared with a thick layer of mayonnaise. They'd known each other over ten years, and Scalise must've told Colgan dozens of times that he preferred mustard on his roast beef sandwiches, but the guy refused to listen. Scalise made a disgusted face but didn't bother this time to complain about the mayonnaise and instead continued to eat. It was well past midnight, and they could have a long night ahead of them. The tip they had was that Alvin Rothman would be rousted sometime over the next few hours by a phone call, which would send the deadbeat fleeing from one of the apartment buildings lining the street. If they knew which building Rothman was holed up in, they'd already be kicking down doors.

It turned out they didn't have to wait hours. They were still working on their sandwiches when a pear-shaped man emerged from a vestibule door three buildings away. The man stood frozen, looking in both directions as if he were unsure whether it was safe. He then scurried down the steps and onto the sidewalk.

"I think that's our scumbag," Colgan said.

Scalise tossed what was left of his sandwich out the window. He left the lights off as he pulled away from the curb and followed the man. A Prius might have been quieter, but the Lincoln barely made a purr, and that was why Scalise was able to get close enough to make sure it was Rothman without Rothman realizing he had company. Only after Scalise gunned the engine and jumped the curb did Rothman look behind his shoulder, and by then it was too late. The Lincoln clipped him and sent him tumbling onto the sidewalk. By the time he picked himself up, Colgan had exited the vehicle and was standing behind him. A punch to the kidneys dropped Rothman to his knees. Scalise popped the trunk and left the engine running, first checking the front right bumper for any damage, then rubbing a small area above the bumper on his pride and joy with a handkerchief to make sure there wasn't a dent before joining Rothman and Colgan.

Scalise bent low so he could whisper into Rothman's ear. "You're lucky your fat scumbag ass didn't put a dent in my car."

Rothman's face was a frozen rictus, his body seized up by pain. He gasped out, "You broke my leg."

"You think I broke his leg?" Scalise asked his partner.

Colgan said, "Not the way he got up after being knocked down."

"There you go again," Scalise said to Rothman. "Lying to me, just like you've been lying to me for weeks. But don't worry. After tonight I'll be doing more than just breaking your legs."

Scalise winked at Colgan, and they lifted Rothman by his elbows to his feet and rushed him toward the back of the car.

"Wait," Rothman pleaded. "I got something big I can trade you."

Colgan snorted out an angry laugh. "This guy never stops, does he?"

"I swear this is huge!"

Scalise signaled his partner to slow down. "What do you got?"

"We have a deal then? If I tell you, you'll let me go tonight?"

Scalise pulled a switchblade from his pocket and flicked the five-inch blade open.

"You tell me what you got right now or I'll cut out your heart and leave it right where you're standing. I swear to God."

Rothman's skin paled to the color of milk, and his eyes ping-ponged first to the blade and then to Scalise's face. "It's about Melanie Penza," he forced out, his voice a squeak.

"What about Mrs. Penza?"

"She's cheating on the old man." Rothman tried smiling, but it came out as something sickly. "It's what you should expect if you marry a young thing who looks like she does."

Scalise gave Colgan a questioning look.

"I think he's a lying scumbag."

"My thoughts exactly," Scalise said. "You can't trust a word out of his mouth."

They started moving Rothman toward the back of the Lincoln again.

"I'm not lying, I swear," Rothman insisted, his voice rapid-fire and in a high pitch. "The guy she's seeing is big. If you knew who he was, you'd know how much money this is worth. Three times what I owe. Easy."

Scalise closed up his knife with his thumb and put it away. This wasn't worth getting blood on his clothing. Instead, he cuffed Rothman on the ear.

"Then how about you tell me while you're still breathing," he growled.

Rothman gave them a name. Scalise shot Colgan another questioning look, because if Rothman was telling the truth it was every bit as big as he claimed. Colgan shrugged, indicating he was undecided about the veracity of Rothman's revelation.

Scalise asked, "Why should I believe a word out of your mouth?"

"Because I took photos on my phone."

Scalise snapped his fingers and held his hand out, palm up. Rothman, his large fleshy face folding into a dejected frown, pulled a cell phone from his pants pocket. After unlocking it with the password, he handed it over. As Scalise scrolled through the photos, Rothman's expression only grew more miserable. It was the look of someone whose winning lottery ticket had been set on fire and all he could do was watch it burn.

Scalise whistled softly as he found the first photo showing Melanie Penza walking into a bungalow with the guy Rothman had told them about. This was every bit as big as Rothman had said it was. Bigger, actually.

"Where was this taken?" he asked.

As morose as any human being could look, Rothman said, "Santa Monica."

Scalise cuffed him again on the ear. "Quit being wise. Give me an address."

Rothman gave him an address.

Scalise exchanged a look with Colgan, and each man took hold of one of Rothman's elbows, rushed him over to the open car trunk, and threw him in headfirst. Rothman was actually surprised by this, squeaking out several times that they had a deal. He tried to turn himself around and scramble out of the trunk, but Colgan had gotten the jumper cables. He wrapped them around Rothman's neck and pulled them tight. Rothman clawed at his throat, but it didn't do him any good. Soon his eyes were bugging out and his face turning a deep purple, and then his body fell limp back into the trunk.

The plan that night had been only to rough Rothman up and scare him into paying some of the forty grand he owed, but Rothman gambled trying to escape a beating, and like all the other bets he'd been making lately, he lost badly. What he told them was too big to let him live. He should've expected what happened.

An hour and a half later, Scalise and Colgan were digging a grave in the Santa Monica Mountains. The temperature had dropped to fifty degrees, but even so both men were soon drenched in sweat. They took turns digging. This wasn't going to be a shallow grave. They couldn't afford to have an animal dig up the body or have the body rise out of the grave because of flooding. Joe Penza was eating a forty-grand loss because of this, and once Rothman was buried he needed to stay buried. At that moment it was Colgan's turn to dig.

"This is dynamite," Colgan murmured to himself, shaking his head as if he were in awe.

He'd already said this at least a dozen times since they had left downtown Los Angeles. Scalise took a drag on a cigarette and blew the smoke out of his nose. He noticed that the cigarette had burnt down to the filter, and he flicked the stub into the hole. Colgan continued to dig for several more minutes while Scalise stood silently watching.

Colgan tossed the shovel out of the grave. "Four feet should be enough," he grunted. He held out his hand to Scalise to pull him out. Instead of taking the hand, Scalise reached inside his jacket and pulled a .40-caliber pistol from a shoulder holster. Colgan looked on in disbelief before asking Scalise what he was doing.

"Only what I have to."

"After all the years we've known each other, you're going to do something like this?" Colgan asked, aggrieved.

Scalise swallowed back a crack about how anyone who insisted on putting mayonnaise on roast beef deserved to be shot in the chest and decided to be magnanimous about it. The fact was he liked Colgan, and so he showed regret in his eyes and a rare moment of honesty. "I feel terrible about it. But you've been saying it yourself. This is dynamite."

Colgan froze as if he were deciding whether to try escaping or go after Scalise. Before he made a decision, Scalise shot him in the chest, the hollow-point bullet punching a fist-sized hole out of his back. Colgan fell dead.

The photo Rothman had taken had to be worth at least a hundred grand if handled right. It could also get whoever had the photo killed. Even if Scalise could've trusted Colgan not to screw things up, he wasn't about to share a hundred grand with him, which meant Colgan had to die that night no matter what Scalise might've thought about him.

Scalise didn't mind the rough stuff he did for Big Joe Penza, which included robbing banks, extortion, collections, and hijacking the occasional truck. The truth was, he enjoyed it, but what had it gotten him? After fifteen years of working for Penza, he had a closet full of tailored suits, a new Lincoln, and twenty grand stashed away. That was it. He was never going to get rich doing this shit. Three weeks ago he had met a Russian who told him how he could make millions by embracing new technologies, namely something called ransomware. The way he explained it to Scalise, this was a computer virus that would screw up someone's computer unless they paid money to make the virus go away. They'd only charge each victim two hundred dollars, but if the virus spread to hundreds of thousands of computers, it would add up. This Russian had a team of computer experts in one of those former Soviet republics with a name that was impossible to pronounce, and he promised Scalise he could get a ransomware concern off the ground with a seventy-five grand investment, and they'd be fifty-fifty partners. Scalise believed him, which meant the moment Rothman showed them his photo, Colgan was a dead man.

Scalise said a silent prayer for the soul of his ex-partner, then rolled Rothman's corpse into the grave.

He first filled up the hole, then layered stones, leaves, and other debris on top to hide the freshly dug grave. While he did this, he thought about the story he was going to give Big Joe Penza about Rothman's disappearance, and Colgan's also. By the time he was done, he was satisfied with what he had come up with.

During his drive back to Los Angeles, Scalise thought only about how he was going to use the dynamite Rothman had given him.

Chapter 8

Over the last three days Lucky had gotten used to people knocking on Lori's office door, and when her boss, Alice Green, stuck her head in, the oversized Rottweiler-Doberman mix barely budged.

Alice, who was a slender and attractive woman in her early fifties, grinned and asked how the big galoot was doing. That had been her nickname for Lucky from the start, and even though Lori didn't know at the time what it meant, the nickname sounded so right that she started calling Lucky it also. When she later looked the term up online, she couldn't help smiling thinking how perfectly it fit the big guy.

Lucky lifted his enormous head from the floor, fixed his yellowish-reddish eyes on Alice, and let out a deep-throated moan before dropping his head with a thud back to the floor. Since his skull was probably harder than concrete, it was doubtful he felt the impact.

Alice shifted her gaze to Lori and asked how the Cheswick assignment was coming. "Do you think you'll have it done by five?"

"Faster than that. I should have it finished up within the hour. Do you want a sneak preview?"

"Sure."

Alice came around Lori's desk and positioned herself so she could get a look at the computer monitor and the graphics Lori had been designing. "Excellent," she said, beaming. "You made a good decision adopting that big galoot." Somewhat maternally, she added, "You've been so much more relaxed and at peace since doing that, and it's showing in your work." Before turning to leave the office, she gave Lori's shoulder a friendly squeeze.

Lori wiped away some moisture from her eyes. "Thanks again, Alice, for letting me bring him to work."

"I'm happy I did." Alice was still beaming. "He adds a nice presence here. I have to admit, I didn't think that would be the case when I first saw him."

That was an understatement. When Lori brought Lucky to the office that first morning, he certainly raised some eyebrows. She had discussed with Alice about her wanting to get a dog and bringing him to work, and she even confided in her boss her reason why, although she lied when she told Alice she knew her fear was unreasonable. Her fear was the opposite of that, even though the idea of it was insane. But she knew in her heart *he* was out there and she knew *he* was waiting to do terrible things to her, even though she didn't have any idea who *he* was. At the time Alice gave her blessing, but that first morning Lori could see concern flooding Alice's eyes when she saw what she was getting with Lucky, and that she was on the verge of changing her mind and banning the dog from the office. But Jerry Harrison in accounting, bless him, fearlessly approached the dog, and Lucky proved to be a gentle soul, even with his big galoot appearance. After that others in the office approached him, including Alice, and he ended up winning over the office.

Looks could be deceiving. Lucky turned out to be a big softy even though he looked like he could scare the bejesus out of the demon dog from *The Omen*. Still, Lori had no doubt that when the time came, the dog would save her from *him*. She knew that this man existed in the real world and not just in her nightmares. She also knew he would be coming for her soon. He'd wait until late at night when she would be alone in bed and helpless. She couldn't say how she knew this, but she did and with the same certainty as the knowledge that she needed to breathe to live. And she knew that when *he* came for her, Lucky would become every bit as ferocious as he appeared. And because of that, she felt safe.

She focused her attention back on her work so she could finish the assignment within the hour as promised.

Chapter 9

Morris was running late, and it didn't help that he had to park three blocks away from where he was meeting Charlie Bogle. He half jogged to his destination, and by the time he reached the front door of the Bottom Shelf his neck was damp and sweat dotted his forehead. He glanced at his watch and saw that it was twenty past eight. Yeah, he was going to get grief for this.

The basement-level watering hole was a block from the Wilcox Avenue precinct, and for the past three decades it had served principally as a hangout for cops. It didn't surprise him that at that hour on a Friday night the place was packed. Almost any night after eight the Bottom Shelf was full with brothers and sisters in blue. He squeezed his way through the crowd, trading handshakes and small talk with officers he knew. He spotted Bogle sitting alone at a table in the back nursing a beer. When Bogle saw him approaching, he showed nothing in his expression. Morris took the seat across from him.

Morris said, "Yeah, I'm late. Sorry."

"Never mind that. Where's your twin?" Bogle deadpanned.

Morris smiled thinly. His hair, which was cropped close to the scalp, was still mostly dark brown with only some gray at the temples, while Parker's fur was white, but with his short, compact body, spindly legs, thick long nose, and big ears, he and Parker proved the old adage of an owner resembling his dog. Given his somewhat comical looks, it made it all the more remarkable that he had ended up with a dark-haired beauty like Natalie.

"Nat doesn't work Fridays, so the little guy's keeping her company. You're looking good. Babysitting the Hollywood elite seems to suit you."

He hadn't seen Bogle since his investigator had left MBI two months ago, and the change seemed to have done him a world of good. The heaviness that had been weighing Bogle down since he was shot in the chest was gone. But there were other changes, too. He looked more fit, more tan. When a smile cracked Bogle's face, Morris caught a familiar glint in his eyes, one that he hadn't seen since that fateful day.

"I do more than just fix problems for spoiled brat actors," Bogle said. "That's part of it, of course. Some of it's pretty heavy lifting. For example, I had to deal with a nasty piece of blackmail just last week. But the studio has standard investigation work also, like intellectual property theft and employee background checks. Anyway, going to Starlight Pictures has been a good change. Thanks again for helping me get the job."

"I was happy to do so, even though I hated to see you leave MBI. But who am I to stand in the way of progress? Charlie, I'm glad you could make it tonight, especially on such short notice. I hope I didn't make you cancel a date with a hot actress."

Morris said that half-jokingly. Bogle was good-looking in a tough guy sort of way and had a reputation for dating around, which finally caught up to him a year ago when his wife divorced him. Now that he was head of security at Starlight Pictures, Morris had no doubt his former investigator was juggling a bevy of gorgeous starlets.

Bogle half closed his eyelids. "I didn't have to cancel anything," he said. "Those days are long gone. Jenny and I are talking, and things are getting better between us. She might even give me another chance. We'll see." The glint that had shone in his eyes dimmed. "I never told you or anyone else this, but when I almost died six months ago I didn't see a bright light or a tunnel or anything else. It was like a light switch being turned off, and there was only nothing until the doctors brought me back." He lifted his beer and took just enough of a sip to wet his lips. "It made me think long and hard about what's important in life, and for me it's being back with Jenny and having a family again. But enough of such maudlin talk. I'm surprised I haven't read anything in the papers yet about you putting a bullet in Polk's ass. I was sure without me there as a buffer you would've done that by now."

Morris chuckled. "It's been tempting," he admitted.

A waitress came over to take his order. He gave Bogle a questioning look and asked if he wanted wings. Bogle gave him a what-do-you-think look back, and Morris told the waitress to bring him a Guinness draft, another beer for Bogle, and a large order of wings with hot sauce. Once the waitress left, Bogle asked how things were at MBI.

"Busy," Morris said. "One of the big insurance companies has been giving us their tougher fraud cases, and that's now making up over half our business."

"No more serial killer cases, huh?"

"Not yet. But that's sort of what I wanted to talk to you about. Back in 2001 you were working on the organized crime task force, right?"

Bogle picked up his beer, peered at what was left in the glass, and drained it. "Morris, you've got a good memory. But yeah, after I was promoted to detective in 2000, I was assigned to Vice and worked on the OC task force until I joined you at Homicide and Robbery in 2005. Why?"

Morris dug into the briefcase he had brought with him and pulled out the two police sketches he had of the Nightmare Man. He showed Bogle the first drawing and explained that it was how a witness had described the suspect back in 1984.

"I was fifteen back then," Bogle said.

"I know. I was fourteen. But here's a drawing of the same perp showing how he might've looked in 2001. Any thoughts?"

Morris handed him the second drawing. Bogle studied it for a solid minute before handing it back.

"In 2001 I was trying to crack a smuggling ring at the docks, and this joker could be any one of a dozen low-level mob guys I encountered. The first drawing you showed me—the one where your perp's in his forties—that one looked more familiar, but I can't think of why."

"They're both of the Nightmare Man."

Bogle made a face, as if he couldn't believe he didn't recognize the drawings. "I remember them now. Both when I was a teenager and later when I was on the force. You think that psycho was working for the mob?"

"It was a theory my dad had. He worked the 1984 killings."

Bogle lazily scratched his neck. "I never knew that. Small world, huh, what with you working the 2001 murders. Did you find a mob connection then?"

The waitress returned with the beers and wings. Morris waited patiently as she deposited them on the table. After she left, he took a long drink of his Guinness.

"I was blocked," he said. "I was new to Homicide, and the senior detective they partnered me with was none other than Martin Hadley. He didn't see any merit in that line of investigation."

"Good old Hadley was always a political animal. Since the idea was yours, he wouldn't want to give it a chance of paying off and seeing you outshine him."

"That might've been part of it, but I think it was more vindictiveness on his part. Martin knew it was my dad's idea, and he was still harboring a grudge against my dad for back in the day royally reaming him out in front of the precinct over one of his stupider blunders."

Bogle snorted out an angry laugh. "I'd pay a month's rent to be able to go back in time and have a front row seat for that." He picked up a wing and chewed it slowly, an eyebrow raised as he studied Morris. "Why worry about this Nightmare Man business now?"

Morris took another long drink. He lowered the half-filled glass back to the table, fixed his eyes on it, and began rolling it between his hands, somehow keeping the stout from sloshing out. Keeping his voice low, he explained why the number seventeen meant something significant to the killer. He further explained that Tuesday would be the seventeen-year anniversary of the start of the Nightmare Man's 2001 killing spree, just as the first spree back in 1984 had also started on October second.

"And you think this guy is waiting to start killing again? Even if this psycho is still alive, he's got to be in his eighties by now."

"People are running marathons in their eighties these days."

"Yeah, but this is different. Has there ever been an active serial killer that old?"

"I don't know. But this guy is a special kind of sickness, and he well earned the name he was given. I wouldn't put it past him to keep killing as long as he can draw breath into his body."

"This is all based on a gut feeling and nothing else?"

"That's all," he admitted.

Bogle sat back in the booth and tugged on his lower lip as he mulled this over. He had known Morris long enough to know that a person could go broke betting against his friend's gut feelings.

"So what are you going to do?" he asked.

"I tried calling Hadley, and it went as well as you could probably guess. Namely, he threatened to pull MBI's license if I went public with my concerns, or even if he found out I was doing anything private with them. But the hell with him. I'm going to do what I should've done seventeen years ago, which is dig into the mob angle." He placed both police sketches flat on the table so they faced Bogle. "Can you think of someone connected back in 2001 who'd know if this guy was a mob hitman?"

"That's an easy one. It would be the same guy you'd search out today."

"Big Joe Penza?"

"He'd be the guy. He took over for his old man around the time I joined the OC task force, and he would've been intimate with all the players. He would've known them all back in 1984 also."

Morris's lips twisted into a grim smile. "I guess I'll be looking to have a chat with Big Joe Penza."

Chapter 10

"Dapper Vince" Scalise sucked on his Cohiba Esplendidos, blew a smoke ring from his mouth, and watched absently as the bluish-gray smoke dissipated into the air-conditioned room. The actor Ben Chandler was also smoking a Cohiba, both men lighting up after their steak dinners. Chandler was holding his cigar between the index and middle fingers on his left hand so he could use his right to pick up the twenty-five-year-old single malt scotch that went for eighty dollars a glass.

The city of Los Angeles prohibited smoking inside a restaurant, so even though Scalise and Chandler were in a private room at Palace 21 they were still violating the no-smoking ordinance. But that didn't matter. No employee wanting to keep his teeth was going to tell Scalise to put out a cigar, and even if the waitstaff serving them hadn't recognized the danger Scalise represented, they were too starstruck by Chandler to complain about what the two men were doing.

"Cigar's not bad," Scalise noted, hamming it up as if he were actually a connoisseur of expensive cigars. Every blue moon Joe Penza would hand some out from his private stash, and occasionally Scalise would take one off a mark, but usually he smoked more moderately priced cigars. "Nice flavor. Good burn. Not the best I ever had, though. That would be an Opus X. Ever try one of those?"

"I haven't, but next time we get together I'll make sure I have a box of them." Chandler's face was lit up brighter than any kid who ever raced down the stairs to open Christmas presents. "Vincent, I can't thank you enough for seeing me. It's going to be a huge help."

Scalise raised an eyebrow. "Just because you buy me dinner, a few drinks, and a cigar you think we're on a first-name basis?"

Chandler stiffened. "My mistake. I meant *Mr. Scalise.*"

A smile cracked the gangster's face. "You should see the way you look right now, like you're about to keel over. Benny, you need to learn how to take a joke. Damn right we're on a first-name basis. But I gotta tell you, it's getting tiring hearing you thank me all night."

Some pink peppered Chandler's cheeks as he recovered from his scare. "Still, it means a lot to me," he said.

Scalise leaned back in his chair. He was the picture of nonchalance as he blew out another smoke ring and sipped his scotch. Expensive scotch was something he knew well. A handful of downtown restaurant owners were on his collection list. These guys were degenerate gamblers and in deep to Penza, and whenever they came up short, Scalise, in exchange for giving them an extra week and not breaking their arms, would confiscate a bottle or two of their best single malts from the bar, while his former partner "Irish" Colgan would get a steak dinner packed up to go, his price for letting the owner keep his teeth.

"What else was I going to do?" he asked. "I've known Billy Dunn since forever. If he's going to ask me to do this favor for you, then that's what I'm going to do." His eyes dulled as he puffed out more cigar smoke. "I should've called you three weeks ago when Billy first asked, but I got busy. My apologies."

"No need to apologize. I know you're getting sick of me thanking you, so I'll just say it one last time. I can't possibly tell you how thrilled I was when I got your call today."

The thin smile Scalise showed wasn't much different than a cold-blooded reptile's. He winked to show what he was about to say was bull. "I don't know why you think hanging out with me is going to help you with that movie role. You got the wrong idea about what I do, 'cause I'm nothing more than an average schmo working a job. Whoever told you I'm connected with the mob is nuts."

Chandler didn't need the wink to know that Vincent Scalise was an important player in Big Joe Penza's organization. From what he'd been told, Scalise did everything from breaking legs to robbing banks.

"Sure, but I heard you know people," Chandler said, being as diplomatic as he could about it.

Another wink from Scalise. "I know some big talkers. Nothing more than knockaround guys who think they're bigshots. These clowns tell a good story, but that's all it is—a story. You'll meet some of them at the poker game later tonight."

A wind chime noise sounded. Scalise wrestled his cell phone from his jacket pocket and squinted at a new text message. "We got to wrap up this party. There's an errand I need to do. Afterward I'll take you to that poker game I've been telling you about."

Scalise drained what was left in his glass, and Chandler did the same. The two men walked out of the private room with cigars in hand. They collected dirty looks as they walked through the main dining room, but even if people didn't know who Scalise was, they were still smart enough not to say anything to him.

Chapter 11

Van Nuys, October 8, 2001

Cynthia Leary lay naked on her back, trussed up like a Thanksgiving turkey, with a pair of socks stuffed in her mouth to keep her from yelling for help. He sat down next to her and touched her cheek and felt the coolness of the skin. His hand moved down her body, and she shuddered when he let his fingers linger on her left nipple. It was rock hard. Could she possibly be aroused right now? He had to find out the answer to that! He reached down and felt that she was as dry as sandpaper. No, it wasn't sexual arousal that made her nipples so hard, but fear. That was good. He so much preferred fear.

He didn't want to get any blood on his clothing so he stood up and removed his shirt and pants. Being a gentleman, he asked her if she'd mind if he took off his underwear, and since she didn't tell him not to, he stripped off his briefs. It was no surprise that his penis stood erect and was far harder than her nipples. More than that, it was throbbing. You couldn't blame him for being excited. It had been excruciating waiting all these years to begin the Nightmare Man's new killing spree. When he took the first victim five days ago he was like a teenage boy having sex for the first time, rushing through it so fast that he barely had time to enjoy the experience. The same wasn't going to be true tonight. He would use a slow hand with Cynthia and make sure to squeeze every drop of pain out of her. Just thinking of that brought him close to climaxing. He excused himself and used her bathroom to take care of the matter at hand, flushing away any potential DNA evidence.

When he returned to her cramped bedroom, he apologized for his absence and then emptied the contents of the gym bag he had brought, lining up each item on the bed alongside her. He made sure to put the metal cage holding the rat right next to her head. The rat inside was oh-so-hungry. Angry, also. He felt his heart flutter as he saw how liquid with fear her eyes had become.

Cynthia Leary. Twenty-seven. A hopeful actress working as a waitress. Her small one-bedroom Van Nuys apartment was what a Realtor might generously call cozy, at least if the Realtor was a big enough liar. The bedroom was smaller than most jail cells and could barely fit her single bed. Well, that would just make tonight all that more intimate.

There was enough ambient light in the room to see her long, skinny body. He doubted she'd had a good meal in years, and not just so she could pay rent for this dump, but more because she hoped to be famous someday. All that scrimping and saving and starving herself to chase after her dream, and this was what it came down to. How terribly sad.

He bent over so he could whisper in her ear.

"You'll be famous," he promised her. "Everybody will soon be talking about you. They'll be showing your picture on TV and in the newspapers. After they find you, of course."

He had to add that last caveat. It had been five days since he took this spree's first victim, and still no mention about it on the news. Eventually that would change, but it had annoyed him to no end. He was so looking forward to seeing the fear that these murders would be causing. That was half the fun, after all.

He picked up the needle-nose pliers he'd brought, climbed on top of her so that he straddled her, and took his time pulling off her fingernails. He made sure to work even slower later, and he made a conscious effort to liberally use the smelling salts he'd brought.

This was the way it was meant to be. After all these years, he finally discovered his true self.

Finally. Finally.

Chapter 12

Los Angeles, the present

Lori Fletcher lay curled on the couch watching one of the recent *Furious* movies and fighting to keep her eyelids open. She shouldn't have been struggling so hard to stay awake. It wasn't that late, and all the noise and action and Vin Diesel's biceps should've been enough to keep her from drifting off. But it had been an emotionally wrought few weeks—really a rollercoaster swinging her from the depths of despair as she was convinced that an unknown boogeyman was going to get her, to feeling safe after she adopted Lucky. While she might've been sleeping soundly once that big galoot came into her life, she also had to make up for many troubled nights before that. Exhaustion overtook her. The last snippet of the movie she remembered were cars being airdropped into the Caucasus Mountains, and then the world faded on her.

The next thing she was aware of was a hellacious racket, something much louder than the *Furious* movie still playing on the TV. In her semi-conscious state, all she could think was that a wild beast had gotten into her apartment. As she became more awake she realized the noise was coming from Lucky. She nearly fell off the couch as she stumbled to the source of the noise, her heart jackrabbiting in her chest.

Sure enough, Lucky barked with such violence that he was nearly frothing at the mouth, hackles raised along his spine. For all the good it would do, since the dog outweighed her and was powerful enough to drag her wherever he wanted to go, Lori clicked the leash onto his collar and swung the door open. *He is out there and Lucky will tear his throat out!* But there was no one in the hallway other than Mrs. Granauche from two doors down, who had stepped out of her apartment and was giving her a sour, accusatory look. Lori had convinced herself that when her boogeyman came *he* would bring a stench of death with him, but there was nothing other than a jasmine scent that must've come from Janice Howell, who lived in the neighboring apartment.

Mrs. Granauche, a seventy-two-year-old widow, complained that the dog's late-night barking had woken her. Lori apologized profusely and promised it wouldn't happen again. Mrs. Granauche grudgingly accepted this and disappeared back into her apartment. Lucky, for his part, stood in the hallway sniffing, his barking having turned into a low, rumbling growl.

"What was it?" Lori demanded.

The dog fixed his yellowish-red eyes on her and whimpered.

She wanted to take Lucky outside to see if he could sniff out whoever it was that had set him off, but she didn't have her keys, so she had to first run back inside to get them. Once she had her apartment locked up and secure, she brought Lucky to the elevator. The dog was still sniffing in the air as if he were trying to pick up the scent of what had spooked him so badly. He continued making his aggrieved rumbling noises as they rode the elevator down to the lobby.

Once she got him outside, the dog stood sniffing in the air, searching for a scent he couldn't find. She lived in a residential area, and at that hour there were no pedestrians walking about and no cars driving away. If it was her boogeyman who had upset the dog, he had since disappeared. It occurred to her then that Lucky might've only had a nightmare. After all, he had his own baggage, and God only knew what abuse the poor thing had suffered before ending up at the rescue shelter. Lori stood silently as she scratched the dog behind his ear and studied him.

"Is that what happened," she asked, "you had a bad dream?"

Lucky sneezed, the action loud and violent.

"Or maybe something in the movie spooked you? What was I thinking playing anything called *Furious* after what we've been through?" She watched as Lucky looked at her with utter befuddlement, as if he had no idea why he had gone Defcon One minutes earlier. "What do you say we go for a long walk? See if we can rid ourselves of these bad dreams?"

Lucky sneezed again, this one seemingly an agreement to her suggestion.

Chapter 13

Scalise was doing the chauffeuring. He explained earlier that night that he loved driving. "It don't matter to me whether I'm stuck in traffic or cruising the freeway at eighty," he had told Chandler, "where else am I going to be that's as comfortable as the front seat of my Lincoln?"

Chandler didn't share Scalise's appreciation for driving around Los Angeles, but he tactfully agreed with him. What the hell, it meant he didn't have to drive.

Soon after leaving Palace 21, Scalise's mood darkened. It came quickly, like a thunderstorm blowing in, and as the gangster sat brooding behind the wheel, the tension seemed to roll off him in waves. It became suffocating, and Chandler almost asked to get out of the car, but he was curious about what was behind this change. What held him back even more was that filming for his new gangster movie started Monday, and he knew he wouldn't be able to channel the necessary bravado on set if he chickened out now. He tried to ignore his growing unease, but after several minutes he couldn't help himself from nervously asking Scalise if something was wrong.

Scalise gave the actor a quick sideways glance, a glint showing in his dark eyes. "Why should something be wrong?" he asked in a soft, menacing voice.

The implied violence in Scalice's tone was unmistakable. "I don't know," Chandler stammered, his voice dropping to a whisper. It wasn't just a single butterfly fluttering around in his stomach but a whole swarm of them now. "I just thought you looked worried, that's all."

"What was it you said? I couldn't hear you with the way you're mumbling under your breath."

Reluctantly the actor repeated himself.

"So you're telling me you can just look at me and know that, huh? Or are you saying you're a mind reader?"

"Neither," Chandler said.

"You're sure you can't tell what I'm thinking right now?"

"That I should keep my mouth shut."

"What do you know, you can read minds after all."

Scalise's brooding continued until he stopped the Lincoln in front of a shuttered warehouse advertising that it was available for rent. As quickly as someone snapping his fingers, his moodiness lifted and he returned to his earlier buoyant self. He gave Chandler what appeared to be a playful punch in the shoulder, but the pain from the blow radiated all the way down to the actor's wrist.

A grin cracked Scalise's face. "Benny boy, you look like you're about to get sick. What's wrong, you can't take a joke?"

Confused, Chandler asked, "What was the joke?"

"The way you've been acting like I'm some sort of mob guy, I thought I'd play the part and give you my best Joe Pesci from *Goodfellas*. Look, I'm no gangster, I just know a few people from the old neighborhood, that's all. This errand shouldn't take no more than five minutes, and afterward we'll go to the poker game I've been telling you about. While I'm busy, I need you to stay in the car." Scalise's eyes dimmed as a thought came to him. He added, "If you see some clown sneaking up on me, hit the horn. You got it?"

If you see some clown sneaking up on me... The actor didn't trust himself to speak. He knew his voice would crack if he said anything, so instead he bit his bottom lip to keep his emotions in check. This had long ago stopped being fun and games, but now this? What had he gotten himself into?

Scalise slapped him playfully twice on the jaw, both slaps making Chandler wince. A deadly smile froze the gangster's lips as he pulled the car away from the curb and drove onto the shuttered warehouse's driveway and continued to a parking lot in back. A man was leaning against a car parked along the far end of the lot. The headlights hit his face, and Chandler recognized him. Bobby Gallo, Big Joe Penza's right-hand man. He had the reputation of being a full-blown psycho. His friend Billy Dunn had promised him that while Vincent Scalise was colorful and an evening with him would be memorable, Chandler would walk away with at worst a few scrapes as long as he behaved himself. That promise was the only thing that had kept Chandler from jumping out of the car earlier. He knew the same wasn't true of Bobby Gallo. But both men worked for the same boss. This was just a quick errand. There was no reason for Chandler to be feeling cold sweat dripping down his back.

Scalise stopped the car fifty feet from Gallo. The keys were left in the ignition with the engine running and the car in neutral. A growing sense of terror took hold as Chandler realized this meant Scalise thought there might be a need for a quick getaway. His nerves weren't helped any when he saw Gallo looking past Scalise so he could stare right at him. He thought about opening the door and running, but his leg muscles had turned to jelly and he knew he wouldn't get far if he tried. Instead he watched Scalise approach Gallo and then the two men engaging in what looked like an amicable conversation. When a third man emerged from the shadows behind Scalise, the actor froze. Before he remembered the horn, the man grabbed Scalise in a bear hug. Gallo stepped forward and pulled a switchblade from Scalise's pocket. The Lincoln's headlights glimmered off the steel blade as it sprung open. Chandler watched as the blade was plunged into Scalise's stomach and then as it sliced upward. He stared dumbfounded as Gallo pulled a big-ass gun from a shoulder holster and started moving in his direction.

Chandler woke up from whatever stupor he had drifted into and dropped so he was out of sight. In one of his movies, the character he played found himself in a similar situation. What his character did when the bad guy came running at him spitting bullets from an Uzi was reach across the driver's seat and push down on the gas pedal with one hand while using the other to shift the car into reverse so he could drive away. In the movie, this was done by a stuntman. This time Chandler did it, and the car shot backward like a rocket until it slammed into a retaining wall.

The crash jolted him, but he was otherwise unhurt. He looked up enough to see Gallo was still chasing him, but he had put more distance between them. Whatever damage he had done to the car, it wasn't enough to keep it from driving. While still lying across the driver's seat, he spun the steering wheel enough so he could maneuver the car out of the parking lot and onto the street. Only then did he risk putting the car in park and climbing onto the driver's seat. He floored the gas pedal and ran red lights after that.

He had spent weeks researching his upcoming role, reading everything he could about Big Joe Penza and his organization. The one recurring theme he kept coming across was that anyone who came forward to testify against Big Joe or his top guns ended up dead well before trial.

He had no idea where it would be safe for him to go. All he knew for certain was that he was in big trouble.

Chapter 14

Lori woke up the next morning with Lucky treating her face like a tasty lollipop. She pulled away from the wet, sandpapery tongue and struggled to open her eyes against the sunlight flooding the room. As she realized why her face was wet and what Lucky was doing to her, she bolted upright, fully awake. A double espresso wouldn't have worked as well.

"Ugh, I've been kissed by a dog," she said, giggling softly to herself as she repeated Lucy van Pelt's line from the old Peanuts TV special that she had watched every year as a kid. Lucky cocked his head to one side and stared at her as if she were crazy.

"Yeah, I know, you big galoot, kind of silly of me, huh?"

She squinted at the alarm clock on the shelf next to her. It was past ten o'clock. She hadn't slept this late in ages. Of course, it helped that she and Lucky had gone on a two-hour hike around West Hollywood last night and didn't get back to her apartment until after one. Not only did the walking tire them both out, but it was liberating, especially watching one particular predatory-looking dude cross the street after seeing Lucky.

"Let me guess, your bladder's bursting?"

The dog made a noise that was part growl, part whimper. Lori rolled out of bed, put on a pair of running shorts and a T-shirt, made a pit stop herself, and then took an increasingly impatient Lucky out into the hallway. She spotted Mrs. Weinstein by the elevator with her Pomeranian. The little fur ball started yapping up a storm as if he wanted to take on the bigger dog. If Lucky wanted to he could swallow the Pomeranian whole, but for his part he watched silently, his head cocked to one side. Mrs. Weinstein shot Lori an accusatory look, as if this was her doing. Well, discretion was the better part of valor. She abruptly turned away and led Lucky toward the stairs, and the big galoot didn't put up a fight.

They made a quick trip around the block while Lucky watered shrubs and killed swaths of grass, and other dog owners they passed hastily crossed the street and stared at Lori as if they were blaming her for bringing this unsightly beast into their neighborhood. She smiled back as if everything was fine in the world. Heck, their dogs were the ones straining at the leash to get at Lucky, not the other way around. After looping the block, Lori stopped off at a nearby bakery to get herself a croissant and coffee and a blueberry muffin for the big galoot. Her plans that day were to go to the office and get a head start on her assignments. She figured she owed Alice that for being so good about letting her bring Lucky into work. First, though, she needed to take a shower.

As she watched Lucky gobble up the muffin, she wondered again about the way he had acted the other night. Bad memories. That had to be it.

* * * *

The plan was to tire the big galoot out at the dog park so he'd snooze later when Lori brought him to work. Earlier in the week she had bought a ball thrower—a plastic thingamajig with a long handle and a cup to hold a tennis ball. She counted seven other dogs of varying sizes at the park. While Lucky appeared indifferent to them, she had no idea what he'd do once he was off the leash, since she hadn't taken that step yet. It would be terrible if he attacked one of them.

"What do you think, big guy, are you going to be good?" she asked.

Lucky gave her an inscrutable look.

She kept him on the leash and introduced him to each dog and was relieved that he behaved himself, although two of the owners came running over to drag their dogs away.

"So I can trust you, huh?" Lori asked.

She felt certain that if a dog was capable of shrugging, Lucky would've done so right then. She unhooked his leash, loaded the ball thrower with a tennis ball, and let it fly. The salesclerk had told her she'd be able to throw a ball a hundred feet with it. The ball sailed farther than that, maybe as much as half the length of a football field. Lucky took off after it, his long legs making deer-like strides. Lori watched with amazement at how fast he ran, but he didn't stop when he reached the ball. Instead he kept running straight at the three-foot-high fence bordering the park. Instead of turning back, Lucky effortlessly leapt over it. Soon after that he disappeared from sight. Lori knew he wasn't coming back.

Chapter 15

Monday afternoon, Parker kept Morris company while he sat in his car and staked out a downtown warehouse on Seventh Street. He lowered a pair of binoculars, almost strained a jaw muscle yawning, and made a face after sipping coffee that had gotten cold an hour ago. His cell phone rang. Detective Marty Wright.

"I got what you asked for earlier," Wright said. "Big Joe Penza is shopping for clothes right now."

"Marty, thanks for coming through. Drinks on me wherever and whenever, you name the place and time."

"Don't think I won't be collecting," Wright threatened. "I plan to put a heavy dent in your wallet. Or your expense account. Whatever it is you hotshot private cops use these days."

"Whichever it is, it will be a tax write-off. Where's Big Joe shopping?"

"Some fancy-ass shop on Rodeo Drive. I'm not even going to try to pronounce the name." Wright spelled out the name of the store and gave the street address.

Lemmon was on assignment in San Diego, and last Morris had checked, Polk had tracked a suspect in a fraud case to Long Beach. He didn't want to give up on his stakeout, but he also didn't want to miss his opportunity to talk with Penza. He called Felger, and MBI's computer and hacking specialist sounded excited to do fieldwork.

"Bring a thermos of coffee, otherwise you'll be dozing off in an hour. Also bring an empty jug so you can return the coffee. I need you to watch for a van with the following license plate." Morris read him the plate number he had scribbled on a scrap of paper. "If it shows up, mark the time and take photos of it. Greta will get you a camera. How quickly can you get here?"

"Fifteen minutes?"

"Make it ten. Call me when you're in your car and I'll give you more instructions."

He started the engine and pulled away from the curb. Parker lifted his head and gave him a questioning look. There was a chance the van would show up before Felger arrived, but if it did, he would still catch the van on its way out. It couldn't be helped. Morris needed to talk to Penza, and he wasn't going to miss his opportunity.

* * * *

The name of the fancy-ass store that Wright didn't want to try pronouncing was *Hjälte*, which Morris figured meant something in either German or one of the Scandinavian languages. He brought Parker with him. The place looked more like a modern art museum than a clothing store. Abstract paintings decorated the walls, and light-colored woods and chrome filled the store's interior. The merchandise was discreetly hidden away in sleek cabinets with not a single mannequin in sight—which Morris guessed would've been too gauche. He spotted two thick-necked types standing in the back by the dressing rooms, but before he could get very far, a salesclerk intercepted him. The man was a featherweight and impeccably dressed in one of the store's chic suits. He also must've correctly appraised the value of the seventeen-year-old suit Morris wore and came to the conclusion that Morris wasn't the caliber of customer that Hjälte wanted. He looked genuinely apologetic as he informed him that dogs weren't allowed in the store, which was as good an excuse as any. Morris flashed him the badge the mayor's office had provided the MBI investigators so they could do work for the city.

"That's okay. The dog's been deputized," he said with a straight face.

He walked around the flustered salesclerk. Parker, who was wagging his tail, let out one of his happy pig grunts. The two thick-necked types guarding the dressing room area weren't as impressed by the badge. They stood blocking Morris's way, and they weren't about to budge. Given their sizes and apparent low centers of gravity, it would've taken a hydraulic jack to move either of those human boulders.

"I just want to talk to your boss for five minutes," Morris said.

"Mr. Penza's busy. Beat it."

Parker let out an impatient grunt. The hired muscle glared at the bull terrier to show that he wasn't impressed by him either.

"How about you give him my name and see if he's willing to talk to me?"

The hired muscle refused to take Morris's business card and demanded a photo ID. Reluctantly Morris handed over his driver's license, and the muscle disappeared into the dressing room area. The other thick-necked goon took his place. It didn't take long for his partner to return and signal with a tilt of his head that it was okay for Morris to pass. The goon stepped aside, and Morris passed him and collected his license from the other hired muscle. This one warned Morris that he might want to leave Parker with him.

"Mr. Penza doesn't like dogs," he said.

"I'll keep him with me. Besides, how could anyone not like this little guy?"

The man's eyes glazed over. "Suit yourself," he said.

Morris smiled thinly at what was most likely an unintentional choice of words to use in a men's clothing store. As Parker trotted past them, he let out a grunt to show he didn't much care for the pun, intentional or not.

Big Joe Penza earned his nickname. Standing six feet four and weighing close to three hundred pounds, he appeared big rather than fat. A mountain of a man. Morris found him at the end of the hallway standing in front of a three-panel dressing mirror and scowling harshly at all of his reflections. The reason for his scowl might've been because the suit he had on was meant for someone thirty years younger than himself. He was trying to shed years off his age, and not just by buying hip new clothing. While no tattoos or piercings yet, he had the type of tan a man only got from religiously using a tanning booth. Hair plugs filled in the large bald spot Morris had noticed from a photograph taken of Penza years earlier, and what was now a full head of hair had been dyed yellow. The hair, dye job, and tan didn't change the fact that he had the heavily lined face of a sixty-year-old man showing all of its scars.

"Stylish," Morris said.

Penza turned his scowl toward Morris. "Is that supposed to be funny?" he demanded.

"Not at all."

Penza eyed him carefully, then glanced downward at Parker before giving Morris another critical look. "Because if I thought you were cracking wise I'd have my boys toss you out of here on your ass. And your mutt also. What do you want?"

Morris didn't bother to correct him about Parker being a purebred bull terrier. He dug the two police sketches out of his briefcase and handed the 1984 drawing over to Penza. Penza gave it a cursory look before handing it back.

"Why should that mean anything to me?"

"That was how a witness described the Nightmare Man back in 1984."

Penza's eyes dimmed as if he were remembering back to that year. "Again, so what?" he asked.

"My old man was the lead detective on that case. He believed the killer was a professional. If anyone back then knew all of the hired guns working in Los Angeles, it would be you."

"Yeah? That's news to me."

Morris made a waving away gesture with his hand. "This is off the record," he said. "I don't care about what you did back then or what you're doing now. All I care about is finding out who this guy was."

"That doesn't make any sense. 1984 was a long time ago. Why bother with this now?"

Morris handed him the other drawing. "This is what he could've looked like seventeen years later in 2001."

Penza gave the police sketch a quick look. "Again, so?"

"Tomorrow will be seventeen years from when he last started killing again."

"You think there's a pattern?"

"I know there is."

Penza's expression weakened. He used one of his sausage-sized thumbs to absently rub his jaw. "I heard awful things were done to those young women," he said.

"Worse than awful."

While Penza continued to rub his jaw, his gaze shifted past Morris as if he were staring at something far off in the distance. Morris could almost see the calculations running through the mob boss's head as he tried to make up his mind about something. He stopped rubbing his jaw, and when he looked back at Morris, his eyes were half-lidded and held as much warmth as ice.

"It's too bad I can't tell you who he is," Penza said. "Those two drawing could be dozens of different guys I've seen over the years. Hell, I used to have a barber who looked like those drawings. And to think, three times a week I let him put a razor to my throat."

Morris gave the crime boss a hard look. "This cute act doesn't suit you. The guy I'm looking for was in the game, and you should damn well know who he was."

"I got no idea what game you're talking about."

"Why'd you bother seeing me if you were only going to stonewall me?"

A smirk cracked Penza's lips. "Because I know your reputation. I know you're supposed to be like your dog over there. A bulldog when you take on work—"

"He's a bull terrier."

Penza glared at Morris. "Don't be smart with me. I'm not a dog person. Okay? You're making another assumption that just because I don't know anything about hitmen don't mean I can't help you. Back in 1984 I heard something through the grapevine that might help you figure out who that guy is."

"What do you want in return?"

"For you to bring someone to me. You ever hear of an actor named Benjamin Chandler? I want to talk to him, but the problem is I'm having a tough time finding him."

Even if Morris hadn't caught the glimmer of anger that flared in Penza's eyes when he mentioned Chandler's name, the way the muscles bunched around the mob boss's mouth would've been a dead giveaway by itself.

"I'm not going to find a guy for you so you can rough him up or worse."

"That's not what this is. I only want to talk to him. Face-to-face."

"What about?"

Another flare of anger, but it died out quickly. "It's personal," he said.

After drinks with Bogle, Morris had researched Penza on the internet and knew the mob boss had married a girl last year young enough to be his granddaughter. He'd found pictures of her. A gorgeous blonde who showed this funny Cheshire cat smile in each of the photos. Morris understood why Penza had gotten the hair plugs and dye job, and why he was now trying on a young man's suit.

"It's about your wife," he said.

Penza seemed surprised by what Morris had said. Scared also in a way. "Did you hear something?" he asked.

"Not a word. But I've been a detective almost as long as you've been a criminal. I may not have been a math major in college, but I can figure things out, especially what one and one adds up to. I can't be a party to you hurting Chandler."

Penza deflated right then. Not a lot, but enough to make his face craggier, so that he looked every bit his sixty years. If anything, his full head of yellow hair only made him look older.

"I'll level with you," he said. "When I first heard about that scumbag and Melanie, I wanted to disfigure him so no woman would ever again look at him as pretty." Penza's eyes wavered, and something close to fear showed in them. "But now I just want to talk to him. I swear that's all. It can even be someplace public. I don't care."

Morris understood him. A frightened, aging man who desperately wanted to hold on to his much younger wife, even if it meant debasing himself. He said, "If I find him, you'll have to agree to safeguards so that no one gets hurt."

"Yeah, sure." Penza jutted out his chin as he regained some of his bluster. He pointed a thick, heavy index finger at Morris. "But Brick, if I find him before you do, the deal's off and the information I got stays bottled up for good. So you better do your bulldog trick and be fast about it."

Parker let out an annoyed grunt as if he'd just been insulted.

Morris asked, "How do I get in touch with you?"

"Hand over your phone."

Morris did as asked, and Penza keyed a phone number into Morris's contacts.

"That's for a burner, so don't be cute and give the number to organized crime. It won't do them any good."

Morris took the phone back. "How come you're so hard to find?" he asked. "I had my computer guy try to get a home address or phone number for you, and he came up empty. He never came up empty before."

Penza smiled. "A secret," he said. "Maybe I'll tell you if you bring me that actor."

For a reason he couldn't explain, that annoyed Morris. "Want my advice about the suit?" he asked.

Penza gave him a quick look up and down. "Fashion advice from someone dressed like you? I don't think so."

He turned back to the three-panel mirror. As far as he was concerned, they were done. That was just fine for Morris also. Given the way Parker grunted, it was just fine with him too.

Chapter 16

In Bobby Gallo's opinion, the redheaded chick who answered the door could've used a few pounds on her. That was the problem with Los Angeles: all these skinny-assed broads who preferred to look like sticks instead of real women. She had a pretty face, though. He had to give her credit for that, especially with how scared she was looking. He couldn't blame her for that even though he hadn't done anything yet to frighten her. A minnow should be scared when a shark approaches. Before she could say a word, Gallo had a hand covering her mouth and was walking her back into the Venice townhouse. Tommy Stanton closed the door as he followed them inside.

Gallo whispered into the woman's ear, "Unless you want me to break your neck, you don't make a sound, understand?"

She understood. Tears welled up in her eyes. It was quite a trick the way she seemed nearly weightless, putting up no resistance as he walked her into the living room and sat her down on an expensive-looking mauve-colored satin sofa. She was proving herself smarter than some of them, at least so far. This was the seventh place he had gone looking for Chandler, and while he hadn't killed any of the others he had to get violent with three of them to shut them up.

He kept her company on the sofa while Stanton searched the townhouse. She refused to look at him and sat stiffly tugging at her fingers like she was trying to pull them off. Her face had crumpled badly, and her lips were quivering up a storm. She didn't make a sound, though. *Smart girl*. She had a nice set of pearly-white teeth, and it would be a shame if he had to slap them out of her mouth. He looked her over more carefully and appreciated better why she was one of Chandler's fuck buddies. She might've been skinny, but she also had nice, long legs that looked like they could wrap tightly around a man. Pert breasts also. He thought briefly about taking off her clothes and giving her a try to see if she deserved the comments Chandler had written about her in his little black book, but he quickly shot down that idea. He didn't have time for fun and games. He needed to find the pretty boy actor before Big Joe did. What a mess this was becoming. But to be fair, it could've been so much worse.

He was lucky Vinnie Scalise made such a bonehead play. After he used Scalise's own knife on him, he and Stanton took Scalise to a private location where he had all the necessary tools to make Scalise talk. It took some work, but in the end he was able to make Scalise spill his guts, both figuratively and literally. He found out about that sneaky prick Rothman taking pictures of him and Melanie outside the Santa Monica bungalow. He had no idea anyone had followed them there. The thought of Rothman selling those photos to Big Joe still made him shiver, but fortunately that lowlife scumbag had other plans for them—plans he never got to put into motion. He also found out about Scalise killing Rothman and Frank Colgan and burying their bodies, and he gave a version of that story to Big Joe so he could justify killing Scalise to him. The version he gave Big Joe was that Scalise killed Rothman and Colgan so he could steal twenty grand he got off of Rothman. Big Joe was skeptical since the story made little sense—in order to believe it you'd have to believe Scalise was a complete idiot, but Gallo was able to tell him where the bodies were buried and hand over to Big Joe the twenty grand he had gotten from a hidden cache Scalise had told him about while his guts were spilling out and he was begging to be put out of his misery.

It helped that he didn't just tell Big Joe his story about Scalise but also showed him a photo with Chandler expertly photoshopped into it so that it looked as if Melanie was heading into the bungalow with the actor. Melanie was furious when he warned her about his plans, but she quieted down once he got her to listen to reason. They'd been sneaking around together for six months, and she'd been anxious for the last few weeks about Big Joe suspecting something. So why not give him Chandler? Penza had become a lovesick fool willing to humiliate himself to keep from losing a dish like Melanie. He wasn't going to hurt her. All he really wanted was to be convinced that the cheating was over. If Gallo was wrong and Big Joe hurt Melanie, or worse, well that would be a shame. She might not have had as much meat on her as he usually liked, but she was a hot piece of ass and a lot of fun in the sack. He might have even developed feelings for her. But he wanted more than just her. He wanted everything Big Joe had, and piece by piece he was putting his plans in place so he could take it all.

Stanton came into the room shaking his head. The actor wasn't hiding out there. Gallo took hold of the redhead's delicate chin and turned it so she had to look at him.

"I'm going to ask you questions, and don't lie to me, because if you do I'll know it and it won't be good for you. Do you understand me?"

"Yes."

Gallo smiled thinly, seeing a spark of defiance in her eyes. She was tougher than she looked.

"When did you last see Ben Chandler?"

The question surprised her. "Over a week ago," she said, her voice halting.

"How about texts or phone calls from him?"

Her eyes went distant as if she were giving the question intense thought. "The same," she said.

Gallo snapped his fingers. "Your phone."

"It's on the countertop in the kitchen."

Without Gallo having to ask, Stanton retrieved it while the woman stayed under Gallo's watchful eye. After she unlocked the phone, Gallo scanned through the text messages and phone log. She had told him the truth. The last texts from the actor came nine days ago—a flurry of naked selfies that were sent between them. Once again, there was that glint of defiance in her eyes as he studied the text messages and photos. When he was done, he handed her back her phone.

"You don't want to go to the cops or tell anyone about this visit," he said. "If you do, I'll find out about it and it won't go well for you. You understand that, right?"

She bit her lip to keep from crying. Gallo wasn't sure whether it was out of anger, fear, or relief. He touched her cheek and let his hand linger, enjoying the coolness of her skin and watching her struggle to keep from bolting away from him. A real shame. If he had time, he could have fun with her.

He signaled Stanton with a tilt of his head. Without another word the two men left the townhouse. Once they were back in Gallo's Audi, he picked up Chandler's little black book from where he'd left it on the center console, and after marking an *X* next to the redhead's name he chose the next entry in the book for them to visit. This was a guy in West Hollywood who sold the actor coke. Maybe they'd find Chandler this way, or maybe he'd hear about the actor surfacing somewhere, and he'd get him then—even if he had to fly halfway around the world. He couldn't afford for Chandler to live long enough to find his way to Big Joe.

Gallo gritted his teeth remembering how Big Joe had acted when he told him about Melanie and the pretty boy actor. He'd been sure that Big Joe would want the actor chopped up into fish bait and dumped into the Pacific. Instead, Big Joe wanted the actor found so he could talk with him. Gallo was embarrassed for the mob boss. If nothing else, it showed just how soft Penza had become, and how badly he needed to be replaced by someone with some balls on him.

But that was for later. For now Gallo had to make sure Penza never talked with that actor. Benjamin Chandler had to disappear from the planet. Gallo's own life depended on it.

Chapter 17

Morris left a message when he tried calling Charlie Bogle. He did the same right afterward with Dennis Polk. When his phone jangled it turned out to be Bogle calling him back first.

Morris said, "I had a talk with Big Joe Penza today."

"Is that so?"

"Yep. He even intimated that he'll give me the name of the Nightmare Man if I give him something in return."

"Yeah?"

"That's what he intimated."

"Do you believe him?"

"I don't know," Morris admitted.

"What does he want?"

"A face-to-face with an actor named Benjamin Chandler."

Bogle's voice tightened as he asked why.

"Big Joe thinks his wife had an affair with Chandler. He wants closure, at least that's what he's intimating."

"A lot of intimating going on over there. Again, do you believe him?"

"Hell if I know. But if I bring him Chandler, I'll make sure it's safe. Charlie, you must know why I'm calling. Adam did his thing and discovered this actor Chandler is starring in a Starlight Pictures production that was supposed to start filming today."

"Yeah, I know. I got a call earlier that he didn't show up for the shoot and he's not answering his cell phone. I was about to head over to his Beverly Hills home. You want to join me? It will be like old times."

"Two heads are better than one," Morris said.

"Three if you count Parker. Assuming you bring him."

"Yep, I've got the little guy today. Give me Chandler's address and I'll meet you there."

"Better yet, I'll swing over to MBI and pick you up. Parker also." Without missing a beat, he added, "While you're waiting, why don't you call Annie Walsh or one of your other contacts in the LAPD and get a trace going on Chandler's credit cards."

Morris chuckled. "So the truth comes out. You just want me tagging along so you can get that trace."

There was a sniffing sound from Bogle's end, as if his feelings had been hurt. "Morris, don't be so paranoid. It will be fun, you and me hunting down a wayward actor together. Besides, you want him found as badly as the studio does, and a credit card trace might be the fastest way."

Bogle didn't mention the obvious. That finding Benjamin Chandler through a credit card would only work if he were still alive to be using one. It had occurred to Morris when he was talking with Penza that the mob boss was only playing him, and that the actor could already be dead and buried in a landfill. Penza could be using him to set up an alibi in the event that Chandler's body later surfaced and word got out about his wife's affair with the actor.

"I'll do my best to sweet-talk Detective Walsh," Morris promised.

After he got off the phone, he did just that and ended up trading a trace on Benjamin Chandler's credit cards for buying Annie drinks and food at her favorite watering hole at a date and time to be determined. Maybe he'd bring Marty Wright along and they could make it a party. Annie was curious about the interest in Chandler and somewhat dubiously accepted Morris's version of the truth: that the actor didn't show up on set that day and he was doing Charlie Bogle a favor. Just as he was getting off the phone with Annie, Polk called.

"I'm driving back from Long Beach now," Polk said.

"Were you able to wrap up the fraud case?"

"With a bow. A big polka dot one. The mink coats that were supposed to be stolen? Nope. I've got video of them being sold out of the back of a van by the store's owner. So what do you got that's so important?"

"I need you to put a tail on someone. Melanie Penza."

"Penza, as in Big Joe Penza?"

"Yeah, Melanie's his fourth and current wife."

Polk sounded apprehensive as he asked, "We've got Big Joe as a client now?"

"No, but we're looking for a friend of hers. An actor by the name of Benjamin Chandler. I'll text you photos of both of them."

"I know who he is. I've seen him in movies. Not very smart of the guy, playing footsies with Penza's wife. Where do I pick up the tail on the wife?"

"This is where it gets tricky. I've been speaking with Marty Wright out of Organized Crime, and they don't know where Penza lives. Adam, though, has been looking into it, and he's found places where the tabloids have taken photos of the wife. Spas, restaurants, shops. Give Adam a call and he'll send you the list he came up with."

"The client has a limit regarding how much money I can spread around at these places so I get a call when she shows?"

Morris didn't bother to tell him there was no client, although there was a chance Bogle would be able to get Starlight Pictures to reimburse them for whatever expenses MBI laid out.

He said, "Spend what you need to, just keep a record of it."

"Will do. I'll be stopping by MBI. I've got a few ideas of my own, and need to pick up some equipment."

* * * *

Benjamin Chandler lived in what would be considered a second-tier neighborhood for Beverly Hills. There were no ridiculously sized mansions, and none of the properties had tennis courts or private gates. While the homes were not modest by any stretch, they were squeezed onto lot sizes that were roughly a third of an acre. Still, even in Beverly Hills, there were neighborhoods several tiers below this one.

Benjamin Chandler owned a two-story traditional house that Morris guessed was built in the forties, but still worth close to ten million dollars. The front was exposed to the street with twenty-five-foot-high hedges providing privacy on both sides and in the back.

Bogle pulled his late-model Lexus that he'd bought used with eighty thousand miles on it into the circular drive, and he and Morris, with Parker plodding along, tried the front door. If the bell rang inside, they couldn't tell—either it was broken or the construction was too solid to leak out any noise. Whichever it was, no one answered. The same after Bogle rapped his knuckles against the oak door. It didn't surprise either of them when they investigated the back of the house and found the power line had been cut. Nor when they saw that a panel had been punched out from one of the patio doors. Neither bothered to mention the obvious—that the power line was cut to disable the alarm system.

The door with the missing glass panel had been left unlocked. They entered the house. Morris and Bogle had worked together long enough as homicide detectives that they could communicate with simple gestures, and Morris indicated with his index finger that he'd take the second floor. Bogle began a search of the first floor. As Morris headed up the stairs, he could tell from Parker's demeanor that the house was empty. If there'd been anyone lurking inside, Parker's ears would've perked right up and he would've grown tense, but instead the bull terrier remained his usual happy self. A quick search of the five bedrooms and three bathrooms on the second level showed nothing unusual. No blood, no signs of violence, nothing to indicate the house had been robbed, and no Benjamin Chandler. When he was done, he and Parker met Bogle by the front door.

"What do you think?" Bogle asked.

Morris made a *who-knows* gesture with his hands.

"Yeah, I know. But one or more persons other than Chandler forced their way into the house. Could be some of Big Joe Penza's boys."

"There are no signs of a struggle," Morris offered.

"They could've cleaned up after themselves. Or gotten him out cleanly."

"If it was the first, they would've cleaned up the broken glass and fixed the door. The power line also. I don't think it's the second. I just can't see Penza volunteering to me that he had a beef with Chandler if he'd already grabbed him."

"What is it then?"

"I'm sure it's what it looks like. Penza's boys broke in looking for Chandler. Odds are good Chandler got spooked before that and is on the run."

"Or he's already buried in the desert."

"It's possible. I just don't think it's likely."

Bogle made a face as if he had bitten into a habanero pepper. "We need to get the police involved," he said.

"If we do, we'll have to tell them about your actor and Penza's wife," Morris said. "Odds are that juicy bit of gossip will leak out, especially if Hadley finds out about it."

Bogle said, "Which he will. By the end of the day that bastard will be trading it for a future favor."

"Easy to guess who his trading partner would be. Margot Denoir. She lives for stories like this, and no doubt we'd be watching a giddy-as-all-hell Margot repeating this gossip tomorrow morning on *The Hollywood Peeper.* I'm sure your studio wouldn't mind the publicity."

Bogle groaned as he realized what else would happen if word of Chandler and Penza's wife's affair were made public. "Big Joe would be out for blood if this got out," he said.

"I'm not entirely convinced Penza only wants to talk to your actor," Morris said. "But if this story gets out and he's made into a public laughingstock, he'll have to save face by hurting Chandler. At the very least, disfiguring him, but more likely than not, torturing him for days before making him disappear for good. Probably better if we don't make this a police matter, at least until we know more."

Bogle showed a grim smile. "My employer would fire me on the spot if they knew I was keeping this from them."

"No doubt," Morris agreed.

Chapter 18

Annie Walsh called to tell Morris that Chandler last used a credit card at a downtown Los Angeles restaurant. "Palace 21 on South Flower, Friday night. The charge was put in at eleven eighteen. One thousand six hundred dollars even."

Morris thanked her and told Bogle about the call. Bogle let out a low whistle. "That's my monthly rent payment," he said in amazement. "The way these actors burn through money. Must've been some party."

"One can only imagine."

"Friday night, huh? Three days missing and counting."

"Yeah."

On the way to the restaurant, Morris had Bogle stop at a food truck so he could buy Parker a pork taco. The bull terrier had been on his best behavior so far that day, and Morris wanted to make sure it stayed that way when they got to Palace 21. The taco mostly did the trick. It was only a little after five when they walked into the restaurant, but half the tables were already occupied, and the smell of delicious grilled food was drifting in from the kitchen. Parker, though, kept his mooching attempts to a minimum and only let out a single unhappy pig grunt about not getting any handouts.

They found the waiter who had served Chandler. A good-looking man in his late twenties who had the look of someone who was waiting tables only until he got his big break in Hollywood. He told them the actor had used one of their private rooms but that it wasn't for a party—that Chandler only entertained a single guest.

"Describe the person," Morris said.

"Scary."

"Scary how?" Bogle asked.

"Like Al Pacino from *Scarface*." The waiter cleared his throat and lowered his voice so that no one passing by could hear him. "We get all types of moneyed customers, and it doesn't take long to recognize the ones you need to be careful around. He was one of those."

The waiter gave them a physical description. Late thirties, dark hair, lean, but with a wiry toughness that you don't want to mess with. He added, "The man was dressed sharply in a pinstripe suit, I think Giorgio Armani. The wide tie was a giveaway. So were the dark gray Italian oxfords."

"That's a pretty good memory for someone who was here three days ago," Bogle noted.

"True," the waiter agreed. "Partly it was because I'm a fan of Mr. Chandler, partly because some customers make an impression. This guy made a serious impression."

"I'd like to get you with a police artist," Morris said.

"You want a sketch of this guy?"

"For starters," Morris said.

"We might have a video of him. There's a surveillance camera by the front door, and I think the recordings are kept for a week."

"That would be even better," Morris acknowledged. "How were Mr. Chandler and his guest getting along?"

"I'd say they were chummy." The waiter lowered his voice more and said, "I wasn't trying to eavesdrop, but you hear things. From what I could tell, Mr. Chandler is going to be playing a gangster in his next movie and his um, guest, was helping him prepare for the part."

"That's true," Bogle told Morris. He muttered under his breath, "These damn method actors."

The waiter wetted his lips and said, "When Mr. Chandler was settling the bill, I overheard his guest saying that he needed to take care of some business before they could go to an all-night poker game."

"Were any names mentioned?"

"None." An alarmed look showed in his eyes. "Is Mr. Chandler in trouble?"

"I don't know."

"I hope not." The waiter showed an apologetic smile. "I'm a big fan of his work. I'm an even bigger fan of people who tip twenty-five percent."

Morris gave him his card in case he thought of anything else that could help them identify the mystery guest. The manager of Palace 21 was able to locate video of Chandler and another man walking into the restaurant together last Friday evening, and he emailed Morris several photos that were cropped so that they only showed the mystery man. The waiter had been right. Al Pacino from *Scarface* was a near-perfect way to describe the guy.

Once they were back in the car, Morris emailed the photos to Marty Wright and asked for help identifying the man. At that time it was past six, and they went back to the food truck and ordered more tacos—two each for Morris and Bogle, and another one for Parker. They were finishing up their meal when Morris got a call back from Wright. He put his phone on speaker so Bogle could listen in.

"The guy in the photo is Vincent Scalise," Wright said. "He works for Big Joe Penza. We've got a long list of felonies we like him for, including several murders, but no luck so far in building a case that could get past a grand jury, let alone convict the scumbag."

"A scary dude then."

"Yeah, I'd say so. Here's something interesting. Saturday morning his pride and joy, a new Lincoln Continental, was found ditched in a downtown alleyway. The car was dented up pretty good, but no blood inside or out. Since then we've been looking for Scalise but can't find him. We can't find the guy he likes to run with either. A knuckle dragger by the name of Frank Colgan."

"Where was the car found?"

Wright gave him the address. "What's your interest in this?" he asked.

"I'm not entirely sure right now," Morris said. "I'll tell you more when the picture gets a little clearer."

"This is going to cost you," Wright grumbled. "Forget beer. When I collect payment I'll be drinking only top-shelf booze."

"I'll start the paperwork now for a second mortgage."

Morris disconnected the call. Bogle's eyes were glazed with a thousand-yard stare. "This doesn't make any sense," he said. "Why would one of Penza's boys be palling around Friday night with Chandler if the guy was banging Penza's wife? And why would the two of them both disappear?"

Morris had a few thoughts on the matter, as he was sure Bogle did. "We need more clarity," he said. He checked the time. It was almost seven. They'd check out the alley where Scalise's Lincoln was found and see if that helped spark any additional ideas. More likely than not the clarity he sought would be coming in the days that followed.

He pulled away from the curb, his mind buzzing with possibilities. The question that most distracted him was whether Penza wanted Chandler found because he believed the actor had had an affair with his wife or because Chandler had witnessed what happened to Vincent Scalise after the two of them left Palace 21. And if it was the latter, why would Penza make up a story about Chandler and his wife? And how was he able to seem so convincing?

Morris had an idea. It was fuzzy and needed more focus, and his gut told him the additional clarity would come once Polk started tailing Melanie Penza.

Or maybe after another talk with Big Joe.

Chapter 19

The owner of the dwelling stood in the shadows and watched as the seconds ticked to midnight. Finally! October second! So many years waiting for this. The owner's heart pounded with the realization of what would soon be happening.

There were so many misconceptions about the Nightmare Man, including the dates for when the killings started in 1984 and again in 2001. According to the news reports, October second was when his reign of terror began in 1984, which wasn't entirely true. The media had it completely wrong in 2001. After he awoke from a seventeen-year hibernation to once again continue his glorious depravity, they reported that the first killing happened five days later than it did. *Fake news.*

Reasonable people could argue that the anniversary date should be October third. In 1984 and 2001, the torture began late at night when it was still October second, but in both cases the victims continued breathing until the wee hours of October third, and only then were their lives snuffed out in the cruelest possible way.

Furniture was moved aside, revealing a door that led to the special room. There was no doorknob, but a key was used and the door swung inward. The owner's hand felt along the wall for a switch. A single sixty-watt bulb turned on.

This was where the rats were kept, each in individual cages. If they were housed within a single cage, they'd tear each other apart in a cannibalistic fury. All five of them were hungry and angry. It was important that they be kept on the verge of starvation and fed only enough to remain alive. One of them soon enough would be gorging itself. In the days that followed the others would be doing the same.

This special room was a holy place. A temple of sorts. Stories of the Nightmare Man's murders were archived. Photos hung on the walls. Souvenirs taken from the 2001 victims were kept in a place of reverence on a small hand-built altar. The newspapers and TV stations never reported about the souvenirs. Perhaps they never knew about them. Perhaps the police never knew about them either. These were only small tokens. A lipstick canister. Glass earrings. Sunglasses. Panties. Stockings. Items that could easily be overlooked. Soon more souvenirs would join them.

The room held more than just the rats and artifacts from the past killings. Also stored away were photographs of the future victims, all of them taken as they lay sleeping and unaware. Each of them had been visited at least a half dozen times over the last two months. These visits occurred in the wee hours, and as the women slept, they were whispered to and told what would soon be happening to them. How the Nightmare Man would be coming for them. Sometimes they'd wake up, but they'd be too groggy to realize that a stranger was hiding just out of sight. Sometimes they'd fall back into a fitful sleep. Occasionally they'd get up for a while, but eventually they'd come back to bed, never realizing that they had company. When it was safe, the visitor would slip out of the apartment and disappear into the night, giddy from the excitement, and not just from these nocturnal visits, but from knowing what was coming.

Such a long wait. The last few years were especially torturous, each day seemingly an eternity. But in only a little more than twenty-four hours it would be starting up again….

The needle-nose pliers were picked up. Such a delicate tool, but they played an important role for what was coming. So did the hunting knife. It had been sharpened so that it could slice through an avocado pit. What it was soon going to be cutting would be significantly softer.

All the tools and devices that were needed were kept in this special room. All of them maintained. All of them ready. None, though, was more important than the rats. They were what was truly nightmarish about the killings.

The blood would soon be flowing. The thought of that made it so one could almost smell its coppery-metallic odor. Even more, could almost taste it. What would be done to the five women who were chosen would be far worse than any nightmare. Just like it had been in 1984 and in 2001. Just like it would be in another seventeen years.

The Nightmare Man would always be waking after his long slumber.

Chapter 20

"Do you mind if I join you?"

Lori was too groggy after a fitful night of sleeping to realize that the slight woman standing by her table holding a coffee and pumpkin-spice muffin was talking to her, at least at first. A quick look around showed that all of the other tables in the bakery were taken, and once she finally understood what the woman was asking her, she nodded, embarrassed that she had sat like a doofus for a good thirty seconds before responding. The woman took the seat across from her and held out her hand.

"Rosalyn," the woman said.

It was a small, delicate hand, which made sense because it was attached to a small, delicate-looking woman. She was somewhat older than Lori. Early thirties, thin, light brown mousy hair that framed a moon-shaped face, slightly upturned nose. Not a very memorable face. Plain, bordering on pretty. The kind that you see a dozen times a day. Maybe that was why she seemed vaguely familiar.

Lori took the hand and introduced herself.

"Thank you for letting me sit here," Rosalyn said. "I got here ten minutes too late this morning. Maybe sometime in the future if you come in and the place is crowded, I'll be able to return the favor."

"I wouldn't mind that at all," Lori said. Something about this woman put her at ease, and she found herself smiling despite her fatigue and anxiety. "It would be nice having company when I come here."

"Nobody should eat breakfast alone."

Rosalyn said this so earnestly that Lori broke out laughing. "True, that," she said.

Rosalyn winked at her. "We can be pioneers starting a new tradition in West Hollywood," she said. "Strangers sitting together at breakfast, whether it be at diners, bakeries, or wherever. Wouldn't that be nice? Although you're not exactly a stranger. I've seen you in the neighborhood walking a huge black dog. That's the kind of dog that gets your attention."

For several minutes Lori had been feeling like her old self. Carefree and unworried. Thinking of Lucky brought back feelings of impending doom. For a brief heartbeat she imagined a voice whispering in her ear: *he's coming for you and he'll be doing terrible things to you.*

"Are you okay?" Rosalyn asked, her eyes opening wide with alarm. "You just turned white as a sheet."

Lori had no doubt that was true. She felt so cold all at once. Lightheaded, too. She picked up her coffee in both hands and took a long drink, trying to draw some warmth into her body. She heard a catch in her voice as she told Rosalyn how Lucky had run away. Her voice sounded so distant to her own ears that it seemed nearly impossible to think that it came from her.

"I'm so sorry," Rosalyn said, compassion flooding her face. "I saw the lost dog posters you put up around the neighborhood, but I guess I was being a ditz, or maybe hoping you'd found him already. I do chatter on sometimes. But a dog that looks like yours can't hide for long. Someone will find him and contact you. I'm sure of it."

Lori lowered her gaze to the coffee mug she was holding. Her lips pressed together so tightly that the muscles around her mouth began to ache. She knew this other woman was only trying to be helpful, but right then she only wanted to be left alone in her misery. After a long, uncomfortable silence, Rosalyn seemed to sense that also. She murmured an apology and left the table.

Chapter 21

Morris and Bogle tracked Benjamin Chandler's agent to a private room at Cedars-Sinai Medical Center. The agent, Matt Brownstein, had a thick bandage wrapped around his skull and one of his eyes. The other eye had been blackened, his jaw swollen, and his left arm bent in a ninety-degree angle with a fiberglass cast that started at the shoulder and ended at the wrist. His blackened eye shifted toward Parker when the bull terrier made a pig grunt.

"Mr. Brownstein?" Morris asked.

Brownstein didn't answer him and shifted his gaze back to the TV, his bruised face settling into a sullen expression. A soap opera was on, and a fiery brunette was staring angrily at a smug-looking blonde with big hair. Bogle used the remote to turn off the TV. Before Brownstein could object, Morris showed him his badge.

"I know about you," Brownstein said, his voice slurring because of his injured jaw. "You're that ex-homicide cop who caught all those serial killers. You consulted on *The Carver*. Another movie also. If you ever want film representation, give me a call. I'll get you better gigs."

"Thanks. I'll think about it. I also want to make sure you're Matthew Brownstein because the hospital has you registered as Ira Gold."

Brownstein winced as if from a piercing pain. When the pain passed, he acknowledged that he had checked in under an alias. "I don't want clients seeing me like this," he said. "In this town they'd flee me like rats from a sinking ship. Or fleas from a drowning rat." He shifted his blackened eye toward Morris to give him an appraising look. "I'm surprised you were able to find me."

"It wasn't easy," Morris said. "In fact, it took all morning."

A knowing smile twisted Brownstein's lips. "But you got connections."

"I do," Morris admitted. "You want to tell me what happened?"

"Why? You're investigating what happened to me?"

From out of the corner of his eye, Morris caught Bogle smiling thinly and knew what his friend was thinking. *Another Hollywood smart-ass.*

"I'm looking for one of your clients. Benjamin Chandler. I'm guessing his disappearance and your injuries are related."

"I doubt that." Brownstein was a scrawny man with not quite enough flesh on his face. He reminded Morris of Niles from the old TV show *Frasier*, and the churlish look Brownstein showed made him appear even more like the sitcom character. "I slipped in the shower," he insisted stubbornly. "I don't know how that could have any connection with Ben going missing."

"So you know your client's missing?"

"Of course I do. The film company called yesterday to bellyache about Ben not showing up on set."

Bogle caught Morris's eye as he slipped his cell phone from his jacket pocket and stepped out of the room. He was going to call his bosses at Starlight Pictures and check whether they had called like Brownstein was saying.

"Your partner checking up on me, huh?" the film agent said, a glint of amusement briefly displaying in his eye before pain wiped it away. "He must be an ex-cop also."

"Your client is in trouble," Morris said. "The odds are good that the same bent-nosed thug who worked you over is going to do far worse to Chandler if he finds him before I do. You could help him by filing a police complaint against your assailant."

"It wouldn't help me any," Brownstein complained bitterly under his breath. He caught himself and focused his good eye on Morris. "Look," he said, "Ben's a fun guy to hang with, and he's been a good earner for me. But he's only one client, and while I genuinely like him, I like breathing more. So all I'm saying on the matter is that I slipped."

"Can you give me a name? Off the record?"

"Sure. Dove."

Brownstein said this with a straight face, and it took Morris a second to realize he was referring to Dove soap and he wasn't going to budge from his slipping in the shower story. Charlie Bogle walked back into the room and offered a curt nod to let Morris know the agent was telling the truth about the studio calling him yesterday.

"If Chandler was going to hide out for a few days, where would he go?"

The obstinacy in Brownstein's good eye weakened. "He'd probably fly to Maui. He loves that island."

"He didn't fly anywhere. He's too afraid to use a credit card. And he didn't drive to Mexico either."

Brownstein's lips pursed as he gave the matter more thought. Half a minute ticked off before he turned back to Morris.

"Ben's a bit of a hound dog. A guy with a girl in every port, or in his case, in every LA neighborhood. He's also old-fashioned in that he keeps a little black book in his night table drawer. I think it's something he read Sinatra did, or one of his other idols, I'm kind of fuzzy right now from the pain medication. Get that black book and check the addresses. You'll find Ben hiding in one of the beds."

Morris's cell phone rang. Polk. He stepped away to take the call.

"I picked up Melanie Penza's trail," Polk said, sounding pleased with himself. "Some of the money I spread around paid off, and I got a call that she's at a bistro on Rodeo Drive. The lady's sitting alone at an outdoor table, and I'm parked half a block away looking at her right now with field glasses. A nice dish. Her, not the salad she ordered."

"Good. Let me know how this progresses."

"Will do."

Morris turned back to Brownstein, kept his voice from dripping with sarcasm as he thanked him for his help, then signaled Bogle that they had a little black book to find. Brownstein seemed surprised by their imminent departure.

"Do you have a lead on where to find Ben?" he asked.

"Not exactly."

Despite himself, Brownstein asked, "What did Ben do to get himself in this trouble?"

Morris said, "Either something incredibly stupid, or this is all nothing more than bad luck."

Parker had been lying quietly on the floor. A short whistle from Morris had the bull terrier flipping himself onto his feet, and Parker happily led the way out of the hospital room.

Chapter 22

While Melanie Penza sat alone eating salad and sipping on what Polk guessed was an herbal ice tea given the hibiscus flower floating in it, he sat in his car and munched on one of the salami and American cheese with mustard on rye sandwiches he had packed away earlier that morning. He had brought a copy of the *Los Angeles Times* and had spread open the sports section. This was partly so he could hide that he was surreptitiously using his field glasses to spy on Joe Penza's twenty-seven-year-old blond dish of a wife and partly so he could read how the LA Rams were planning to fix their stagnant offense. He'd been doing this kind of work long enough that he could put away the field glasses and know by instinct when she left the table, but it was still better to keep an occasional eye on her in case someone stopped by to talk to her.

Polk continued to do serious damage to his sandwich as he held up the sports section to use as camouflage while sneaking another quick peek at Melanie Penza. A knock on the driver's side window caught him by surprise. He turned his neck and saw a scruffy-looking teenager holding a skateboard grinning at him. Polk lowered the window.

"You're spying on someone in that café," the kid said, his grin spreading so that it was an ear-to-ear job.

"Is that so?"

"Yep. Definitely. You must be a cop."

"You figured me out."

The kid looked so ridiculously pleased with himself that he could burst. "I knew it! What can I do to help?"

Polk gave the kid a hard look and decided it would be better to keep him busy than to chase him away.

"What's your name?" he asked.

"Finn."

Polk made a face as he dug his wallet out of his back pocket and pulled a business card from one of the compartments. He handed the card to the kid, who gave it a careful read.

"It says here you're a private cop," the kid said.

Polk showed him his badge. "Deputized by the city," he said. "I'm a little bit of both public and private. You see that blond babe sitting at that table? The looker? I want you to take your skateboard and hang around by the front door, and when she leaves text me the plate number and model of her car. You think you can do that?"

An intensity burned on Finn's face. "Sure," he said, his voice cracking.

"If you make contact with her, I swear to God I'll break your neck. Your skateboard also."

"I won't. You got my word."

Polk took a twenty from his wallet and handed it to Finn. "I'm counting on you," he said.

Finn's expression became one of deadly seriousness. He dropped his skateboard onto the sidewalk, got on it, jumped the curb, and headed toward the restaurant's front entrance, zipping across four lanes of traffic and ignoring the cars blasting their horns at him as he maneuvered around them. Polk smiled watching him. The enthusiasm of youth.

He wasn't counting on anything from Finn, but twenty dollars was a small price to pay to keep the kid from causing him trouble. Once Finn was out of sight, he continued munching on his sandwich, reading about the Rams' offensive woes, and using his field glasses to make sure Penza's pretty behind was still seated at the table. When his gut instinct told him it was about time for her to be finishing her lunch, he looked through the field glasses and saw that she was settling up with a waitress. He waited until traffic was clear and then swung a U-turn so he could pick her up by the valet station. Immediately he heard a burst of a police siren. It had to be from an unmarked car.

Polk wanted to ignore it, but he had a couple of minutes before he'd be losing his prey. He pulled over to double-park and watched in his rear-view mirror as the unmarked Dodge Charger with blue and red flashing lights pulled up behind him. He knew the detective who stepped out of the car. Darryl White. The two of them had never liked each other when Polk was on the force, to put it kindly. As far as he was concerned, White was a pencil-necked geek who more often than not mucked up his investigations, and White made it known he considered Polk a lout who needed a good ass-kicking. He wasn't the only one on the force who believed that, but White's holier-than-thou attitude particularly bugged him.

Polk attempted to appear unconcerned as he watched White casually stroll up to his driver's side window. He showed White the badge deputizing him. The detective didn't seem impressed.

"I'm on a job," Polk said.

"You made an illegal U-turn across four lanes of traffic."

"Mail MBI the ticket. Otherwise you're going to screw up my investigation."

"Uh uh," White said. "We're playing this by the book. License and registration."

Polk maintained an inscrutable expression as he handed these over. He didn't want to give White any satisfaction. He also got out his cell phone.

"You know what this is for?" he said. "I'll be calling my boss, Morris Brick. Morris will be calling his buddy in the mayor's office, and this time tomorrow you'll be busted down to patrolman and walking a beat in Skid Row. Hope you got yourself a comfortable pair of shoes. For your wife's sake, I also hope you got a good supplemental life insurance policy."

"How about you shut your trap?"

White walked back to his unmarked Charger, and Polk called Morris and gave him a quick rundown on what was happening. "I'm about to lose my target because of this jerkoff," he complained. "If I take off, White will make it into a police chase, and I'll be starring on the six o'clock news."

"I'll see what I can do," Morris promised.

Morris must've done something, because a minute later White left his car and was walking back to Polk. The detective had a hard sneer frozen on his face, but he also had a look in his eyes of someone who'd been seriously chastised.

White handed him back his license and registration and told him to get lost. Polk peeled away from the curb, not giving him a chance to change his mind.

Melanie Penza was already gone. Finn, though, had texted him make, model, and license plate number. He had also texted that she had taken a right onto Santa Monica Boulevard. Not bad for twenty dollars. If the kid's information turned out to be good, he'd find a way to slip him more money, maybe even use him for future jobs, but that was something he'd think about later. Melanie Penza had a two-minute head start on him, and for now he had to worry about finding her.

Two blocks ahead he spotted a yellow BMW convertible taking a right onto North Canon Drive. He sped up and watched as she pulled up to a day spa and handed the car over to the valet. There was public parking on the same block, and he guessed that was where the valet would be taking the car. He had to circle the block to get back to the public garage, but sure enough he spotted the yellow BMW convertible, its plate matching Finn's text. He pulled into a nearby spot, and as he walked past Melanie Penza's car, he dropped to one knee so he could better tie his shoes. He also used the opportunity to attach a GPS tracking device to the BMW's undercarriage.

Swift move, he thought with a smirk.

A minute later he was loitering near the entrance of the spa. Not long after that he spotted a man heading into the spa who looked familiar enough that Polk snapped a photo of him with his cell phone. The man was in his late thirties and looked like someone who could've played linebacker in high school and kept himself in football shape. Broad shoulders, square jaw, narrow waist, impeccably dressed in a light gray suit and matching Italian loafers. A good-looking Hollywood type, except there was a hardness about him that these actors and movie executives didn't have; there was also something reptilian about his eyes. Polk knew he had seen him before, but he couldn't figure out where. He texted the photo to Morris.

* * * *

They didn't find a little black book in Benjamin Chandler's bedroom or any of the other rooms they searched. They were discussing what their next step should be when Morris received a text from Polk filling him in on what had happened so far and asking if he knew who the man in the photo was. The man looked familiar to Morris, but he couldn't place him. He showed the photo to Charlie Bogle.

"That's Bobby Gallo," Bogle said. "Big Joe Penza's right-hand man."

"Interesting," Morris said. Parker was lying on his side, and Morris absently began rubbing the dog's chest with the toe of his shoe. Parker stretched his legs and let out a satisfied grunt. "I guess it could be a coincidence that Big Joe's wife and top guy are getting massages at the same spa at the same time."

Bogle kept his poker face firmly intact as he offered, "Or body wraps. I'm not sure exactly what they are, but I hear they're hot now. At least Jenny mentioned something to me about scheduling one for Friday."

Morris smiled thinly. "I don't see Bobby Gallo as a body wrap type of guy, or him getting a facial either. A spa, though, would be a good place for lovers to meet clandestinely. So what happened last Friday? Benjamin

Chandler is palling around with Vincent Scalise, and they spot Gallo and Melanie Penza together? Something violent goes down making Scalise disappear and Chandler go on the run? Gallo then convinces Big Joe that Melanie's having an affair with Chandler?"

"It adds up," Bogle said. "Although Chandler could've been iced along with Scalise."

"I don't think so. Odds are Gallo has the actor's little black book and is going through it looking for him and sending others—like Brownstein— to the hospital. I think Big Joe was being sincere with me. He honestly believes Chandler was having an affair with his wife and only wants to talk to him. Gallo cannot allow that to happen."

Bogle tugged on his lower lip. "If we're right about him," he said.

As far as Morris was concerned, it added up, or at least it appeared to. He could go to Big Joe with what they had, but it would be better if he could show the mob boss a photo of Melanie and Gallo together.

"What do you think?" he asked Bogle. "Should we give it a day or two to see if we can get a more incriminating photo?"

Bogle grimaced, and Morris knew why. Waiting would give Gallo more time to hunt for Benjamin Chandler, but while they could build a good story around what they had, it was still at this point only a story. If Big Joe didn't buy it, Gallo and Melanie Penza could discover that they'd been found out, which would make things tougher for everyone.

Bogle said, "I don't like it, but that's probably the best way to go."

Morris called Polk to tell him the guy in the photo was Bobby Gallo, and when Polk suggested he join him on the stakeout so he could take Gallo when he left the spa, Morris agreed that made sense.

Chapter 23

Before going to bed, Lori Fletcher had washed down a sedative with three glasses of wine. The sedative had been given to her by a coworker, Heather Mackey, who was a year older and also worked as a graphic designer. Heather had insisted Lori tell her why she looked so exhausted, and after she broke down and confided in her about being terrified that a nameless boogeyman was out to get her even though she knew her fear was irrational, Heather invited her to spend the night at her apartment. She almost accepted her coworker's offer, but she wanted to be home in case Lucky was found. In her heart she believed that was going to happen. Lucky would be returned that night, and she'd be safe and protected. By ten she gave up hope that Lucky would be brought back to her. She also knew that her only chance of sleeping was if she took the sedative, so she swallowed it down with a glass of Riesling. One glass didn't seem enough, so she drank another, and then another after that. The third glass did the trick, as it soon became a struggle to keep her eyelids open. Somehow she made it to her bedroom, and the last thing she remembered was crawling under the covers. Then blackness until waking up.

She didn't fully wake up—at least not right away. The sedative and wine had left her too groggy to make sense of what was happening to her. Even with the fuzzy feeling in her brain, she knew something was very wrong. All of her fingers ached, and most of her toes did also. It was a dull, throbbing pain. A pain that made her want to curl up in a ball and cry. Except she couldn't do that. It dawned on her that she couldn't move her hands or feet. She was on her back and she couldn't move much at all. She couldn't see anything either. It was darker in her room than it should've been. There was no ambient light. There should've been something from her radio alarm clock on the built-in next to her bed, and also from the smoke alarm detector. Her fear grew as she realized why it was so dark, and why she couldn't move her hands and feet. A blindfold had been wrapped around her face, and her hands and feet had been bound.

Oh my God! He was with her now and he was doing horrible things to her! In her panic, she understood why her fingers and toes ached as much as they did. *He* had pulled her fingernails off and was now doing the same with her toenails. In fact, she felt something hard and metallic biting down on the nail of her big toe, the one on her left foot, and she tried to scream when she felt the nail being ripped from the flesh.

Only a dull, muffled sound came out of her. The fuzziness filling up her mouth wasn't because of the wine and sedative but because she'd been gagged.

She was fully awake then. Her heart pounded wildly in her chest. This was real and not a hallucination. *He* was with her and there was no one to protect her.

She realized she was naked. *He* had taken her pajamas off. She was completely exposed. But she knew that was the least of her problems.

Two more toenails were ripped off. Both times she tried to scream, both times the gag muffled her.

She wanted to beg for her life. To promise anything if he'd only let her live. But the gag kept her from being able to do anything but make sickening noises. Soon she felt the knife blade cutting into her, and that was when the real pain started.

She passed out several times from the pain, but each time he'd bring her back to consciousness by making her inhale a noxious chemical. Before he started burning her, she just wanted to die. Over and over again, she prayed for it to end.

She was woken up one last time by the noxious fumes. The gag had been taken out of her mouth. She filled up her lungs with air and opened her mouth to scream. Before she could, something cold and metallic was pushed into her throat. She began gagging, but the object was hollow and wasn't going to suffocate her. Still, it kept her from being able to scream.

It was funny what might pop into a person's head during a time like this. Cutting through her sheer terror and agony was a thought about the voice that had been whispering to her for weeks, the one warning her that *he* was going to do terrible things to her. It was a voice she imagined hearing only in her dreams, but would linger throughout the day, echoing dimly in her consciousness. It occurred to her why the voice sounded vaguely familiar. She silently mouthed *wow* as she realized where she had heard it before. Even though she was in shock, and even with everything that was happening to her, the thought left her stunned.

Was it possible?

The blindfold was taken off. She wanted to see her tormenter and at least have the satisfaction to know if she was right about the voice, but her eyes first sought out the source of her gagging, and she saw that a hollow pipe had been shoved into her mouth. Something a plumber would use. Then a squealing noise froze her. It was the sound that a small, angry animal might make. She couldn't look away as a gloved hand holding a squirming rat appeared in front of her eyes. The rat was clawing and biting furiously at the glove, but the glove looked heavy and thick, and would protect her boogeyman from the sharp fangs and claws.

A cold, unbearable horror filled Lori as she realized why the hollow pipe had been pushed into her throat and what was going to be done with the rat.

This was beyond her worst nightmare. Beyond anyone's.

The only solace she had was knowing death would be coming quickly once the rat was used.

Chapter 24

Nathan wasn't having a particularly good morning. It was bad enough that his allergies were acting up, but the tenants in 4C were having plumbing problems. Sludge from the pipes had backed up into their bathtub, and of course the tenants thought the thick blackish-colored sludge was something other than what it was. He had to first calm them down, and they were rip-snorting mad, and then he had to spend an hour snaking out the pipe. Dirty, unpleasant work. When he was done, he knocked on Lori Fletcher's door. She lived in 3C, the apartment directly below 4C, and there was a good chance she was having the same issue. She didn't answer the door. A shame. He wouldn't have minded seeing her. A cute girl, and to be honest about it, he had a little thing for her, even if she was way too young for him. And way too pretty. He thought about letting himself into her apartment and snaking out the pipe so she wouldn't have any problems, but if he did that she wouldn't call him later when she did have a problem, and he'd miss out on being able to spend time with her, even if it was just him in her bathroom while she was elsewhere in the apartment.

Sighing heavily, he took the elevator down to the basement. He had more work he needed to do. A broken disposal in 5M, a dripping faucet in 4K, 1G complaining about ants, but he first wanted to wash the sludge off his arms.

Nathan stepped into his studio apartment and the intercom began buzzing. He almost ignored it. He had enough work stacked up as it was, and he was feeling cranky after being elbow deep in sludge and his throat felt coated from allergies. But whoever it was would just keep buzzing. When the people here had problems they acted as if it were the world's worst catastrophe, and they expected him to jump right on it. God forbid he take time to wash off some sludge or make coffee. He answered the intercom, growling out something that sounded like "yeah."

"Hi, is this the building's super? I found a dog that I think belongs to one of your tenants."

It had to be Lori Fletcher's dog. Weinstein's little yappy thing had been yapping his head off earlier this morning, and he hadn't seen Lucky for a few days. He hadn't realized the dog was missing, but it explained why Lori had been moping when he saw her Sunday.

"I'll be right up," he grumbled over the intercom.

He took the stairs to the first floor and saw a good-looking millennial-type in the vestibule area with Lucky. There was no mistaking that dog. Nathan felt an affinity to him. An ugly as heck animal with a heart of gold, at least he believed that to be the case. He couldn't help feeling annoyed seeing the guy who had found him. Thin, well groomed with a hipster goatee, and neatly dressed in chinos, a pullover cotton long-sleeve shirt, and boat shoes with no socks. Just the type Lori would go for, especially since she'd be grateful to him for finding her dog. Nathan felt a hot flush of jealousy thinking Lori would agree to go on a date with this millennial-dude if he were to ask her.

Nathan opened the vestibule door, and the guy introduced himself as Dillon Hardwick and explained that he had found Lucky three days earlier. "I didn't see the lost dog poster until late last night. The owner is named Lori Fletcher? I tried calling her this morning, but she didn't answer her phone, so I thought I'd stop by and see if I could catch her at home."

"She's not in her apartment," Nathan uttered with the same enthusiasm he would've shown if he were about to have a tooth drilled. "Ms. Fletcher's probably at work."

"Do you know where that is?"

He was a super, not a personal secretary for the people living here! Why would he keep a record of where these people worked? The oblivious smile on Hardwick's face annoyed him, and he wanted to tell him to hand over the dog and get lost. If he did that, he'd be able to play the hero later when he reunited Lori with Lucky. But he knew it would make Lori happy if the dog were brought to her now.

"I have to do work in Ms. Fletcher's apartment. If you don't cause any trouble, you can come up with me. There might be something in her apartment that says where she works."

Nathan stepped aside to let Hardwick bring Lucky into the building, then led the way into the elevator. He got a small degree of satisfaction seeing how careful Hardwick was not to brush against him and get any grime on his white cotton shirt, also seeing the way he wrinkled his nose once they were in the elevator together. Some people might've taken offense at that, but Nathan was glad he could make him uncomfortable.

Instead of taking the elevator back to the third floor, he first took it to the basement so he could get the drum machine and other tools he needed to snake out Lori's bathtub line. On the way back to the elevator he handed Hardwick his tool chest. Hardwick was too polite to decline carrying it, and Nathan smiled inwardly seeing his reaction to having to get his hands a little dirty. It was a tight fit back in the elevator with the drum machine and Lucky taking up space, and once again Nathan got a small bit of satisfaction seeing Hardwick trying so hard not to get any grime on his pristine clothing.

Nathan was rolling the eighty-five-pound drum machine down the hallway, and Lucky's reaction when they got close to Lori's door spooked him. The dog became agitated, howling as if he were in agony and straining on his leash, dragging Hardwick right to the door. Nathan fumbled with his oversized keychain, searching for the key that matched Lori's door.

"Something smells really bad in there," Hardwick said.

He was right. The odor was unmistakable. An outhouse-type smell. Nathan had noticed it earlier but dismissed it, thinking it was from the sludge coating his arms. His hand shook as he used the matching key to unlock the door. He began blinking wildly, pinpricks on his legs and arms, a coldness pushing deep into his skull. The sound of the dog's agonized howling became muffled as if the animal were a hundred yards away. It shocked him when he realized he was moving toward the source of the stench. Lori's bedroom.

"Oh my God."

This came from Hardwick. Nathan had forgotten all about him. He took another step into the bedroom, trying to make sense of the crude "17" assembled on the floor. Horror overtook him as he realized it was made up of grisly pieces of severed flesh and human fingernails, maybe toenails also. In a daze he stumbled closer to the bed and saw what was left of Lori. Her lips had been sewn shut, but something was causing her lips and cheeks to push out. He couldn't look away from it. It was both horrifying and fascinating. What could possibly be causing that?

Something forced its way through her lips. He moved closer, and when he realized what it was, he fainted dead away.

Chapter 25

Natalie had taken Parker to her office that morning, so today it was just Morris and Bogle. They had followed Bobby Gallo to a Bel-Air address and watched from a distance as Gallo knocked on a door and then as he and a muscle-bound associate forced their way in after a man wearing a silk bathrobe answered the door. This was the third home they had followed Gallo to, and the third one they had witnessed him breaking into. He was still hunting for Benjamin Chandler.

Yesterday Gallo had left the spa before they arrived, so Polk picked up his tail, and Morris and Bogle took over following Melanie Penza. They had an uneventful rest of the day watching her. After she had left the spa, she spent several hours shopping before calling it quits. They did, however, discover that she and Big Joe lived in an exclusive downtown Los Angeles condo building. He called Marty Wright with the information, and Wright thanked him for it and told him he'd look into it. "Penza must own it under a different name, probably using a shell company," Wright had said. "We suspect he owns several condos downtown and moves to different ones every few months."

Polk had called Morris later that night to tell him he had followed Gallo to five tony addresses around Los Angeles until Gallo gave up his search to spend several hours at a strip club and then bring two of the dancers back with him to his high-rise apartment. Polk had brought along an extra GPS tracking device and attached it to the undercarriage of Gallo's car so Morris would have an easy time picking up his tail the next day.

After twenty minutes outside the Bel-Air address, Bogle became fidgety. He drained what was left of the coffee he'd bought earlier, crumpled the cardboard cup, and tossed it to the floor, his expression one of disgust.

"We should get the police involved," he said. "Home invasion. Assault and battery. Aggravated mayhem."

Morris sighed. They'd had this argument already. "No chance any of these people will press charges against him. And it won't help us with Penza. The opposite, actually. We need that incriminating photo, and we don't need Gallo knowing we're onto him."

"If he finds Chandler in one of these houses, he'll kill him."

"Not in front of witnesses. And not where the body can be found. He'll want to take Chandler someplace private, and we'll intercept him before he can do that."

Bogle said, "You're making an assumption. You don't know that for a fact."

Morris made a shrugging motion with his shoulders and hands. What Bogle said was of course true, but he'd say it was more an educated guess than an assumption. It made too much sense for it to be any other way, at least as long as Big Joe had told him the truth, and he was fairly certain the man had leveled with him. If Penza had tasked Gallo with finding Chandler and bringing the actor back to him, then Gallo couldn't afford to kill Chandler in a way that his body would be discovered. Even if Penza had sent Gallo out to find and kill the actor, Gallo would still want to bring him to a secluded location before doing the deed, and he'd also want to make sure that the body disappeared forever. The murder of a Hollywood celebrity would bring down a lot of heat, and it would be far better for the celebrity's disappearance to be added to the list of Los Angeles's unsolved mysteries.

"There's got to be a better way for us to find Chandler than following these animals," Bogle complained.

Morris shrugged again. He had called Philip Stonehedge in Ireland earlier that morning and was able to catch him during a break. Stonehedge didn't know Benjamin Chandler, but he told Morris he'd make some calls and see what he could find out. Gallo was the one with Chandler's little black book, so until Annie Walsh saw more credit card activity from Chandler or Stonehedge was able to give them some leads, following Gallo was all they had.

Morris's cell phone rang. He gave the caller ID a quick glance. He had to clear his throat before asking Hadley whether this was about the Nightmare Man. A purely rhetorical question on his part, because what else could it be?

Hadley's normal blustery voice had been reduced to something chastened and hollow. "I don't know how it's possible, but that psycho is back," he said, as if he couldn't believe it. "Goddamn it, why couldn't he have stayed gone?"

* * * *

Morris found Doug Gilman waiting outside the West Hollywood apartment building. Gilman was the mayor's deputy assistant and, for the last six months, also Rachel's boyfriend. Eighteen months ago he arranged for MBI to take the lead on the SCK investigation once the murders moved cross-country from New York to Los Angeles. It turned out to be a good career move for him and led to his promotion after Morris and MBI solved the case that had baffled both FBI and New York officials for five years. It also put political pressure on the mayor's office to keep bringing MBI into other serial killer cases so they could assure the good people of Los Angeles they were doing everything possible to catch the fiend terrorizing them.

Gilman gave Morris a curt nod and held up paperwork that he needed signed. Morris had taken a taxi from Bel-Air so Bogle could continue tailing Bobby Gallo, and he and Gilman had talked over the phone, working out the details for MBI to be hired and take the lead in the investigation. While Gilman looked impatient and harried, his skin appeared its usual tanned color, and that was all Morris needed to see to be sure that the mayor's deputy assistant hadn't yet ventured inside the dead woman's apartment. Gilman tended to get green around the gills when in the proximity of a dead body, and Morris had seen it happen after Gilman simply heard the grisly details of a murder. What the Nightmare Man did to his victims went far beyond what Gilman might've previously glimpsed. Or what any sane person could ever imagine.

Morris took the eleven-page contract from Gilman. Most of it was boilerplate, and the payment rate had already been set by the city when MBI was hired for the SCK investigation, but he read over the two clauses that mattered to him: the one that gave MBI autonomy to handle the investigation as they saw fit and ignore any directives from Police Commissioner Hadley, and the other that allowed MBI to control the message given to the media. After verifying that the clauses were as they had discussed, he asked Gilman for a pen and signed the contract with a gold-plated Cross pen that had likely been given to Gilman as a college graduation present, or maybe something he had given himself after his promotion.

"I remember the Nightmare Man murders when they happened in 2001," Gilman confided once he had the signed contract stored away in a briefcase and the pen handed back to him and secured within his inside suit jacket pocket. "I was thirteen at the time. They scared the heck out of me even though nobody ever said what was done to the women." He shivered noticeably. "Just hearing the name of the killer gave me the willies. I'm sure what I imagined had to be far worse than what happened."

Gilman had said the last part more as a hopeful question. Morris knew he didn't want to know any details, but he couldn't help himself from shaking his head. Gilman winced, his mouth weakening. He was likely picturing even worse things happening to the victims than he had imagined as a thirteen-year-old.

"Try not to think about it," Morris suggested.

"Easier said than done." Gilman gritted his teeth and shook his head violently as if he were shaking and clearing an Etch A Sketch. "I gave myself a crash course on the Nightmare Man after finding out about this murder. Not any of the details about what was done to his victims, but other aspects. When I was thirteen I must've heard about how these murders also happened in 1984, but that seventeen-year gap didn't make an impression on me then. It did today." Gilman gave Morris a hard, flinty look. Stone cold enough to be impressive, and Morris realized that this was Rachel's influence, that her toughness was beginning to rub off on him. "Tell me straight," Gilman asked in a voice every bit as hard and flinty as his stare, "should Commissioner Hadley have been prepared for this?"

"I don't know," Morris admitted. "We knew the number seventeen held some sort of importance with this psycho, so if he was going to start killing again, this is when you'd expect it. Hadley, though, had good reason to believe he would either be in his eighties or dead, which makes it a tough call to frighten a population for something you don't think has much chance of happening."

"They're going to be frightened when they hear about this."

"They will," Morris agreed.

"I saw the police drawings of the suspect. The one done in 1984 and the one made in 2001 where he was aged seventeen years. How come that didn't lead to his arrest?"

"I couldn't tell you. My dad led the investigation back in 1984, and he believed the witness was legit. But sometimes a police sketch just isn't enough, even if it's a good one."

Gilman asked, "Was everything done back then that could've been done?"

"No. There was an avenue of investigation that I thought should've been taken that wasn't."

"Why wasn't it?"

Morris showed a pained smile. "Chalk it up to office politics. It happens. But I'll be looking into it now. In fact, I have been for the last few days."

"Really? You've been expecting this?"

"I thought it was a possibility."

"Did you call Hadley? Never mind that." From the way Gilman began fidgeting, he didn't want to hear the answer, probably already knowing what it would be. He peered at his watch and frowned. "I have to give a press briefing in a half hour. I'll make sure to get those two police sketches to the media, and I'll get a third drawing made with the suspect aged another seventeen years. We've got a hotline number already set up, and I'll give that plenty of attention. Anything I should mention in particular? Leave out?"

"The public needs to be vigilant. Hadley is going to love this since it's going to generate hundreds of false calls, but it can't be helped. Ask for people to call the hotline number if they see anyone suspicious in their building or neighborhood late at night. You need to stress that. This psycho is far from done."

"I'll get the message out. Don't worry."

"People need to be careful about who they open their doors to. If you don't know the person, you don't open the door. Period. I also would like to see everyone get better door locks."

He expected his last comment to elicit a groan from Gilman, and it did. "Morris, as thrilled as our local locksmith association would be for me to announce something like that, it would cause a panic, and the mayor would have my head."

"Figure out a way to imply it then. As far as things not to mention, don't give any details about the murder. Think of this as a virus we're trying to contain. The last thing we want is to spawn any copycats."

"Don't worry about that. I couldn't give out any details even if I wanted to. I don't have them."

They shook hands. Gilman turned to leave, but he looked back at Morris, worry weakening his eyes and mouth, the hard flinty look from earlier completely erased.

"The victim, Lori Fletcher, is close to the same age as Rachel. I have a recent photo of her that I'll be giving to the media. She was very pretty. Petite, dark-haired. Looked a lot like Rachel. Should I be concerned?"

The ten previous victims were all Caucasians. Their ages ranged between twenty-two and forty-seven. Four of them were either married or living with someone. Three of the victims were killed when their partners were either working a graveyard shift or traveling on business; in the fourth case, the husband had been rendered unconscious with chloroform and was found bound and gagged in the same bedroom where his wife was butchered. The victims were brunettes, blondes, and redheads. Some were pretty, others not. Socioeconomically, they ranged from white-collar middle class to wealthy. As far as Morris could tell, the killer showed no discernable pattern in choosing his victims.

Morris said, "We should all be concerned."

Chapter 26

On his way to the apartment, Morris walked past at least a dozen patrolmen and plainclothes officers. Hadley wasn't one of them. It didn't surprise him that the police commissioner was keeping his distance. When he saw Detective Greg Malevich standing outside the apartment taking a smoke break, he asked if Detective Walsh was inside.

"Annie's back at the Wilcox Avenue station interviewing the two unlucky citizens who found the victim." Malevich took a drag on his electronic cigarette and blew the vapor out from the side of his mouth. "One of the neighbors is home, and I got nothing from her other than she's not happy that I'm out here smoking. A few minutes ago she stepped into the hallway to give me the evil eye. I'd go outside, but I'm waiting for other neighbors. Besides, there's no secondhand smoke from these things." He scowled at the pen-shaped device, and under his breath added, "I need to get that smell of death out of my throat. I've been tasting it ever since going in there."

Morris clapped Malevich on the shoulder. He well understood the sentiment.

The victim's door had security plates on the doorjamb and the edge of the door that interlocked and would keep someone from breaking in with a crowbar. The weak point, though, was the lock. Any standard door lock can be picked given enough time. Morris opened the unlocked door, waved over one of the crime scene specialists, and asked her to turn the deadbolt once he closed the door. He took out his lockpicks, and after he heard the click of the deadbolt being turned he went to work. Malevich saw what he was doing and timed him. While Morris worked on the lock, he asked Malevich about the electronic cigarette. "Aside from the occasional cigar, I didn't know you smoked," he said.

Malevich took the device from his mouth and frowned at it. "Back when I was in the Army, I was two packs a day," he said. "I quit cold turkey once I was discharged and met Keira. I can't explain the impulse that made me do it, but two weeks ago I picked this up at a vape shop in Venice. Keira would not be happy if she knew. This is only my third time using it, but I got to tell you, Morris, I'm glad I got it right now. Not exactly a PSA moment, huh?"

Morris was noncommittal about his answer. He knew the stresses in working Homicide, and he knew what was waiting for him inside this apartment. Whatever you have to do to make it through the day.

It took him four minutes and eighteen seconds to unlock the door. Not the worst lock he'd ever encountered, but certainly not the best either. The killer could've had a key or been skilled with a lockpick.

"Not bad," Malevich noted with a thin smile. "When you get sick of running MBI, you can start your next career as a cat burglar."

With his best poker face, Morris said, "Parker would not approve."

He headed inside the apartment. Joining the young woman who had locked the door for him were several other crime scene specialists, all of them busy in the small living room either vacuuming up fibers, hair, and other tiny debris from the floor or searching surfaces for prints. The bathroom door was open, and Morris spotted a specialist inside examining the bathtub drain.

He nodded to the specialists he knew from his time on the force and continued on to the bedroom. From force of habit he wrinkled his nose at the smell of disinfectant. As nauseating as he found the odor, the stench it covered up would be worse. When the victim died she would've evacuated her bowels, and there would've been other unpleasant odors mingled in with it. Burnt flesh. The coppery, metallic smell given off by spilt blood. And an odor that was hard to define, but was nonetheless unmistakable and potent: Fear.

Morris closed the door behind him after stepping into the room. He first glanced toward the foot of the bed where the grisly "17" should've been. It had been removed, but a bloodstain left behind outlined the message. The medical examiner, Roger Smichen, was examining the body. He looked up to offer a bleak smile.

A weariness showed in the ME's eyes, and his smile reflected something tragic. Smichen was long and bony, and his scalp completely bald and his face hairless aside from sparse, light brown eyebrows. It might've been the way the light struck his sunken cheeks, or it could've been because of the overall gloominess of the situation, but he appeared paler than usual, more cadaverous.

"As much as I enjoy your company, Morris, it's a shame to see you dragged into yet another of these depraved murders," he said. "Especially given that this one stands far apart from any I've ever seen."

He knew Morris had resigned from the force and started MBI because he'd had his fill of serial killers, yet this was the fourth time he and MBI had been brought into one of these cases.

"This is unfinished business for me," Morris said.

"You worked the murders back in 2001?"

"Yeah." The sight of the victim flashed Morris back to the others. The same cruel damage had been done to her. She'd been left naked on the bed, and large lumps of flesh had been cut away, nails torn off, small circular burn marks showing on her raw wounds. If he looked closely enough, he knew he'd see ligature marks on her wrists and ankles from the killer binding them. In the other murders, the killer had used nylon rope.

The ME had inserted a clamp in her mouth to keep it open so he could more thoroughly examine her throat. Morris dreaded moving any closer. He didn't want to see a rat's tail protruding from her throat. Something, though, was different. There were puncture marks on her lips that he hadn't seen with the other victims.

"2001 was before my time," Smichen said somewhat whimsically. "I was still in Indiana then learning the craft of my trade, or I guess you could say, preparing for the big leagues here in LA. I haven't had a chance yet to look at the autopsy reports for the earlier victims. Any obvious differences you can see?"

Morris could see that all of her fingernails had been pulled off, and all but three toenails. "How many wounds?" he asked, his voice coming out as a growl.

"Seventeen. The same number of burns, all of which are circular, one-eighth-inch diameter. He must've heated a metal rod and used that to burn her."

"The same as with the other victims."

Smichen pulled off one of his latex gloves and pushed his hand over his scalp. This was a mannerism Morris had seen once before from the ME when he was dealing with a particularly cruel murder. Something to briefly get his mind off what had been done to the victim.

"This was all done while she was still alive," Smichen said. "I'm sure you've seen the outline of the message he left for us. Any idea why the number seventeen is so important to him?"

"We never figured it out." Despite himself, Morris's voice still came out as a heavy growl. He also realized his hands had clenched into fists. He concentrated to unclench his fingers so they would hang loosely at his side. A trick he learned years ago was if you forced your body to relax, your mind often would relax too. "There's a rat lodged in her throat, right?"

"No. There was a rat that had been either coaxed or forced into the victim's throat and blocked her air passage long enough for her to die from asphyxiation. You can see this from these swollen veins and signs of cyanosis." Smichen pointed out the several veins that had swollen on her face and neck and a bluish discoloration on the inside of her lower lip. "When she was found, the rat had crawled out of the throat and was trying to force its way from her mouth."

"That's different," Morris said. "With the other victims, the rats had been pushed through a hollow pipe and into the victim's trachea. They were dead when they were removed, and from their broken limbs and other damage, the ME thought a narrow metal rod was used to push them deep into the throat."

"I found a circular abrasion along the back of the throat indicating that a hollow pipe with a quarter-inch diameter was used, which, as I've since found out, is just big enough for a juvenile rat to squeeze through. I also found singed fur and a bruise on the rat's hindquarters that showed it was pushed with ostensibly the same rod that was used to burn the victim, just not hard enough to cause the same damage you claim was done to those other rats, or for it to remain lodged in the throat. This rat, though, was very much alive, or at least it was when it was removed from her. It has since been sent to the lab to be examined."

Morris moved closer to the body. "What happened to her lips?"

"They were sewn together. If they hadn't been, the rat would've escaped."

"That wasn't done with the other victims. Time of death?"

"Between midnight and three in the morning. I'll have her taken back soon for a full autopsy, and I'll see if I can narrow it down more."

Smichen stood. He made a face as he stretched and worked out a kink in his back. "I've been at this an hour already," he explained. "I'm not as young as I used to be. Anything I should be looking for?"

"Ammonium carbonate was used with the other victims to keep them conscious."

"Good enough. I'll check for elevated liver enzymes." Smichen showed a pained expression as he continued to knead his long, bony fingers into his lower back. "I'm getting too old for this," he said. "I'd been thinking I could hold on for another five years, but after today I'm not so sure. Did I ever tell you that my wife and I are thinking of retiring to Lisbon?"

"Portugal?"

"That's right. Donna and I have been there four times on vacation. Stunning city. On our last trip we did some house hunting. I could buy a nice villa for half of what I could sell my house for here. The idea of a quiet life is very appealing right now."

"You'd get bored. Do you even speak Portuguese?"

"We'll learn it."

"A nice fantasy," Morris said. "Crime scene photos already taken?"

The wistfulness softening Smichen's eyes faded as he snapped back to the reality of the situation. "Of course. The killer's twisted little message wouldn't have been removed otherwise. How many more of these victims should I be expecting?"

"If he follows the same pattern he did in 1984 and 2001, four more over the next seventeen days unless I catch him first."

"For God's sake, catch him then. I don't want to see another victim who suffered the way this poor girl did."

"I'll be doing whatever I can," Morris promised.

Chapter 27

Morris called Natalie to tell her that the Nightmare Man was back. "He butchered a young woman in West Hollywood last night. There were a few twisted alterations from his past methods, but otherwise it's him."

"The city wants you leading the investigation, and you accepted."

Natalie said this in a purely matter-of-fact tone, without a hint of hurt or accusation. Still, he felt a pang of guilt. When he left the force, he had promised her he was done dealing with murderers, especially serial killers, but he had still ended up being dragged into those other serial killer investigations, all of which had taken a toll on him, and on her also. He knew full well the worry and stress he was going to put her through while he chased the Nightmare Man.

"They do, and I did," he admitted. "I'm sorry, Nat. I know I made you that promise."

"Hon, I relieved you from it after you stopped that last madman from wreaking havoc and killing thousands. You're too good at what you do for me to keep you from hunting these monsters. That would be the height of selfishness."

"Nat, that's not true at all. You've got every right to want to lead a normal life."

"I'm quite happy with my life. I've got a wonderful daughter, a husband I love, and a bull terrier I adore, even if he is getting a little tubby. And speaking of Parker, how about picking up the little guy?"

Morris heard over the phone a familiar grunt, and he could see in his mind's eye Parker lying on his side by Natalie's feet, stretching his legs, and grunting on hearing his name.

"I'd rather he stay with you."

"Uh uh. Morris, darling, I don't need the protection. This madman never strikes until late at night, right? So I'll be just fine. But I'll feel better knowing Parker's keeping you company, especially since you'll be out late like you always are when you're hunting these killers."

"Charlie Bogle will be keep me company."

"Charlie's a good guy, but it's not the same. Parker helps keep you even-keeled and calm. Anyway, this is something I'm insisting on. It's not open for discussion."

"Your foot's down," he said.

"Exactly."

They'd been married long enough for him to know when he had a chance of changing her mind, and this wasn't one of those times. "I'll swing by within the hour," he promised. "Could you give Rachel a call? You can use the pretense of letting her know that I'll be installing a new lock on her apartment door, but see if you can talk her into moving back home for a few weeks, or at least while the Nightmare Man is still at large. I'd try, but I know our daughter well enough to know that I wouldn't get anywhere."

"But I might if I act as if I'm scared to be home alone and want her company?"

"That's what I was thinking."

"It won't work, hon. She'll see through my subterfuge. But I'll give it a shot. Maybe she'll take pity on us. Is there anything I should tell Rachel to look out for?"

"We don't know how he gets into his victims' homes," he said. "What's that term new age types use for paying attention to what's going on around you?"

"Mindfulness."

"That's what Rachel needs to be."

"You can be mindful, but you practice mindfulness."

Morris smiled at his wife's precision. "However you explain it to our daughter, she can't let her guard down. She has to be aware if there's someone lurking in the hallway waiting to force his way in when she opens her door, and she can't let anyone inside her apartment that she doesn't know. At least the lock I ordered for her can't be picked, so that's one less thing we have to worry about. Hopefully, you'll be able to work your magic and she'll come home tonight so that will be something else off our minds. I'll see you soon."

"The little guy and I will be waiting."

Morris had other calls to make. The first was a quick one to Marty Wright. After that he called Polk to let him know the Nightmare Man was back and that they were going to be working the case.

Polk let out a low whistle as if he were sorting out in his mind the ramifications. "I was a patrolman when he surfaced the last time. When was that again?"

"2001."

"Seventeen years later, and the bastard's back, huh? You were part of that 2001 investigation, weren't you?"

"Low man on the totem pole."

"I was a kid when this lunatic first struck. What year was that?"

"1984."

Polk let out another low whistle. "This guy's like cicadas, has to come out every seventeen years to annoy the shit out of everyone. So what do you want me to do? Drop my tail on the lady Penza and head back to the office?"

"Keep following her for now."

"Are you sure? We've got a lunatic on the loose. As much as I enjoy following this blond babe from her condo to a Pilates studio to a nail salon, then an intimate apparel shop, and now a bikini wax salon, I'd rather be putting my detective prowess to better use, namely, helping you catch this Nightmare Man joker."

"This might be related. It's complicated."

"Boss, if you say so. But this is a story I'm going to want to hear when you have time."

"Later. You have my word. I'm guessing from her routine today she's got a hot date planned for tonight. If it's not with Big Joe, you'll be able to wrap up your tail on her today."

"One can hope. I've got my camera ready if the opportunity arises."

After Polk, Morris next called Bogle to fill him in on what had happened and to get an update on Bobby Gallo. Bogle was still tailing him, and the gangster was still causing mayhem. After that, Morris had quick calls with Fred Lemmon and Annie Walsh. He then headed to the Wilcox Avenue precinct. He needed the crime scene photos for what he had in mind, but he also needed to fill Walsh in on why it was so important that they find Benjamin Chandler.

Chapter 28

Detective Annie Walsh told Morris that the two people who had discovered Lori Fletcher's body were still in the precinct in case he wanted to talk to them. "They both exhibited signs that they were suffering from shock, so I've got them talking to counselors."

"One of them was the building's super?"

"That's right." Walsh consulted her notepad. "Nathan Slotnick, age fifty-two, no criminal record. He's been working as a live-in maintenance man at the apartment building for twenty-three years." Walsh gave her notepad another look, then explained how Slotnick and Dillon Hardwick ended up in Lori Fletcher's apartment that morning. "Hardwick confided that he found a photo of Lori Fletcher online, thought she was pretty, and wanted to meet her. Here's the kicker. He'd been keeping her dog since he found it, if you could call that beast a dog—it looks more like Cujo's worst nightmare. He saw one of Fletcher's lost dog posters last night when he was walking the animal but thought it was too late to call her. If he had, she'd probably be alive now."

"Ah, hell."

"Yeah, I know." A hard, angry glint showed in Walsh's emerald-green eyes. "I already checked that Hardwick tried calling Fletcher at 8:02 this morning like he said. I'll be following up with both Slotnick and Hardwick, but I don't see either of them being involved, or that they have anything more they can tell us."

Morris pulled his shoulders back, stretching them. It had been a long day so far, and he knew it was going to get a lot longer. He noted that when he was in the apartment building he hadn't spotted any surveillance cameras. "Please tell me they have hidden ones."

"I asked Slotnick that, and no such luck."

"Of course not. That would be too easy. When did Hardwick find Fletcher's dog?"

Walsh flipped through several pages of her notepad before finding the answer. "Saturday afternoon. Around three. The dog had knocked over a garbage can and was scrounging for food."

"How come he didn't use the dog's tags to track down the owner?"

"The dog had slipped out of his collar," Walsh said. "From what I could get out of Slotnick, Fletcher got the dog because she was afraid."

"Psychic."

"If you believe in that." Her face scrunched up to show she was highly dubious about something. "What you told me earlier about Penza, do you really believe that? He can tell you who this Nightmare Man maniac is?"

"I don't know. I think he has something. I just don't know how good it is."

"He'll only tell you if you bring him that actor, Benjamin Chandler?"

"That's what he's saying."

Walsh's eyes slitted and her mouth pinched as anger peppered her cheeks. "We should pick up that fat load and lose him in the system for a few days. I'm sure we could sweat out of him whatever he has."

"I'd say he's more hefty than fat. Anyway, squeezing him wouldn't do any good, so that's why I need you to keep looking for any credit card use by Benjamin Chandler."

Walsh's eyes narrowed more. "You must've been expecting the Nightmare Man to start killing again. Did you warn Hadley?"

Morris's involuntary grimace answered that.

"Bastard," Walsh spat out.

"It would've been a tough call for Hadley to do anything," Morris offered.

"Not for me."

Morris forced a smile. "That's why I keep saying you should be promoted to commissioner."

"Don't say it too loudly. Hadley would can my ass if he hears that."

"I've always got a job for you at MBI."

"Thanks, but no thanks. I'd end up shooting Polk within a week."

"No court would convict you. While I'm chasing Chandler, I'd like you to look into the victim's background. I don't think there's much chance she knew the Nightmare Man—the profiler who worked the other murders was convinced he chose his victims randomly—but there might've been some incidental contact between the two of them."

"Sure. Makes sense."

"I asked Fred to assist you. He's driving back from San Diego. Expect his call."

"As long as it's not Polk," she deadpanned.

Morris checked the time. "I better get going," he said. "I promised Nat I'd pick up Parker within the hour, and she'll give me holy hell if I don't follow through."

"Tell Nat to be careful."

He told Walsh he planned to do exactly that. He didn't explain that he'd be asking Natalie to get his spare .32-caliber pistol out of the lockbox in the bedroom and to keep the gun at her side tonight until he returned home. In fact, he was going to make it a condition for him taking Parker.

Chapter 29

Morris wanted to surprise Big Joe Penza, but Marty Wright wasn't able to give him Penza's location, so he had to call the mob boss's burner phone.

"You got that actor?" Penza asked, sounding surprised.

"You think I'd be calling you otherwise?"

They went back and forth over potential meeting places until Penza suggested a downtown restaurant. "They got a private room that I use. You got my word I'll be there alone. If you're the suspicious type, you can check it out first and make sure none of my boys are around before you bring that scumbag actor inside with you."

Morris mostly believed what he had told Annie Walsh about Penza being stubborn about giving up any information unless Chandler was brought to him, but he had to try. If the mob boss had a heart bigger than an ice cube, there was a chance Morris would be able to convince him to do the right thing. Regardless, he wouldn't be able to concentrate on a damn thing if he didn't give it a try.

When he and Parker walked into the private room Penza had arranged, the mob boss was sitting alone with a steak dinner, a basket of garlic bread, and bottle of red. He finished chewing a mouthful of beef tenderloin before winking at Morris.

"I thought you'd be the suspicious type," Penza said. "All you cops and ex-cops are paranoid as all hell. So are you satisfied I don't got any of my boys around?" He squinted, confusion muddling his expression as he tried to figure out what Morris was taking out of his briefcase. "What are those? Photos?"

Morris answered him by walking up to his table and spreading out in front of him the crime scene photos taken of Lori Fletcher's corpse as if they were a deck of cards. Penza gave them a curious look. Once he realized what they were, he sat back heavily in his chair, his thick arms crossing his chest.

"Why'd you show me that?" he demanded.

"This young woman was named Lori Fletcher. She was only twenty-five. She didn't deserve what happened to her. If you had told me what you know about the Nightmare Man instead of sending me on a wild-goose chase, she might be alive right now."

Penza stared with hurt at Morris, his jaw muscles tightly clenching. He said, "I gave you my word earlier. You're the one with no honor."

Morris laughed. "I've got no honor? Because I'm trying to stop more women from being butchered?"

Penza pointed a thick finger at Morris. "Don't you put that on me. You knew my price. If the information I have could help you stop this guy, then you should've worked harder to bring me that actor. This is on you, not me."

Penza's thick lips curled downward into a look of peevishness. As far as he was concerned, his argument made perfect sense, and Morris could see he had little chance of changing his mind. But he had to try.

"This Nightmare Man psycho will be killing more women if he's not stopped. It could be your wife next. Or one of your daughters. Doesn't that matter to you?"

Penza's peevishness turned to irritation. "Bad enough you lie to me. Bad enough that you show me those *ferkakte* pictures to ruin my meal. But now you're going to put your shortcomings on me? Go to hell."

He pushed his plate away. Parker, who'd been fixated on the steak, let out an impatient whimper. Penza's gaze shifted to the bull terrier. He looked surprised, as if he hadn't noticed the dog before. Muscles quickly bunched along his jaw, his eyes bulging with spitefulness. A grown man about to throw a temper tantrum. He shook his finger at the dog.

"You're not getting a single scrap of this, you mangy mutt," he spat out. "I'll have the kitchen throw it away before you get any of it." His upper lip curled into a churlish sneer. "Ugly bullet-headed thing. I wouldn't be surprised if you were part alley cat."

Parker let out an insulted bark.

Morris kept a tight hold on the bull terrier's leash as he collected the photos and put them back in his briefcase. They weren't doing him any good with Penza. It was doubtful Penza noticed, as he remained locked in a staring match with Parker.

"Why are you so convinced your wife was having an affair with Benjamin Chandler?" Morris asked.

Penza looked up to meet Morris's eyes, his face reddening as if he were incensed by the question.

"None of your damn business," he forced out, his voice a raspy growl. He wrestled a burner phone from his pants pocket, dropped it on the table, and slammed it with the meaty part of his fist, breaking the phone into pieces. "You can take this with you on your way out. I'm done with you."

Morris had pushed Penza too hard. He coaxed a reluctant Parker to turn around. The bull terrier was being stubborn, still thinking he had a chance of getting some of the uneaten steak, but no amount of mooching would help this time. Parker let out an angry pig-grunt as he trotted alongside Morris toward the door. Penza must have gotten out his cell phone, because before Morris left the room, he heard Penza ordering an underling to pick him up at the restaurant and to bring along a couple of boys in case an ex-cop wiseass and his mongrel ugly-as-sin dog were still bothering him.

Chapter 30

Morris was parked a block away from Dominick's, the steakhouse where he had met Big Joe Penza. Parker lay on the passenger seat moping, the look on his face a dictionary perfect definition for the word *hangdog*. It had been a personal affront to the bull terrier to see most of a steak go uneaten and not be able to mooch as much as a single bite. Morris scratched Parker behind the ear as he waited for Penza to leave the restaurant, and given the way the dog's thick, ropy tail began slowly thumping the seat, that seemed to help mollify his hurt feelings.

Morris had little doubt that if he found Chandler and brought him to Penza that the mob boss would tell him what he knew. If he reneged on their agreement, Morris would empty a full clip into Penza's knees if needed to get him to talk. The problem now was since the burner phone had been destroyed, he would have to keep a tail on Penza so he knew where to find him. He'd already called Fred Lemmon to let him know there was a change in plans—that instead of teaming with Annie Walsh he would have to take over the tail for Morris once he got back to LA. Fred was still an hour outside the city but would call him once he was back at MBI. Morris could've sworn he heard a note of disappointment in the investigator's voice, and he wondered about that. As far as he knew, Fred and Corrine were happily married. Maybe he'd only imagined what he thought he heard.

A black Cadillac sedan pulled up to the front of the restaurant. It would be a cliché if this were Penza's car, but life was chock full of clichés, and it didn't surprise Morris when a minute later Penza lumbered out of the restaurant and worked his large body into the backseat of the sedan. When the car pulled away from the curb, Morris followed it, making sure to keep half a block's distance from the Cadillac.

He followed Penza to a Russian bathhouse in West Hollywood. So the mob boss needed a spritz after his disappointing meal. Morris drove past the bathhouse, swung an illegal U-turn, and parked half a block away on the other side of the street. He watched as Penza walked into the bathhouse accompanied by a thick-necked bodyguard.

Morris called Charlie Bogle, got an update regarding the mayhem Bobby Gallo was wreaking, then filled Bogle in on what had happened.

"You had to poke the bear," Bogle said.

"Yeah, I know. It was a mistake. But I thought I had a chance of appealing to his better nature."

"Bull. You were pissed and you wanted to vent."

"Probably some truth to that."

Bogle snorted on his end. "You think?"

"Okay, a lot of truth."

"Morris, you know I trust your judgment and I don't want to look a gift horse in the mouth with you helping me track down Chandler, but how about you tell me slowly and in small, understandable words why your dad was so convinced the Nightmare Man murders were connected to the mob?"

Morris explained his dad's reason.

"How does that explain what happened in 2001? Or yesterday?"

"I don't know," Morris admitted.

A call came in from Fred. Morris put Bogle on hold so he could take it. Fred had just pulled into the MBI parking lot and would soon be ready to take over Penza's tail.

* * * *

The woman wouldn't stop sobbing. Annie Walsh fully understood the reason: Her coworker had just been murdered by a serial killer. Still, Walsh had a tough time sitting still and generating empathy as she waited for the woman to get a grip. Before the waterworks started, she had told Walsh that Lori Fletcher had been in fear for her life.

The coworker, Heather Mackey, had gone through a third of a box of tissues before her crying subsided to a gasping sniffles. It might've only been a temporary break before the waterworks started up again in earnest, so Walsh jumped in and asked her who had been threatening Fletcher.

That confused Mackey enough to put a halt to her crying. "I didn't say anyone was threatening her."

"You said she'd been afraid."

"But not because anyone was threatening her. It was because of her dreams." Her mouth crumbled a bit as she thought more about that and added, "Or I guess I should say her nightmares."

"You're saying she had dreams someone was going to hurt her?"

"That's right." She gasped, and her voice took on an astonished tone as she added, "I guess you could say Lori had a premonition this was going to happen."

Yeah right. Another witness claiming the victim had been psychic. Walsh didn't buy it for a second. "How long ago did you two talk about this?"

Mackey gave Walsh a stunned look. "Yesterday," she said. "My God, was it only yesterday? It seems so much longer ago."

"Tell me everything she told you."

"Lori was looking exhausted, like she hadn't slept in days. I took her aside and asked what was wrong, and she confided to me that she'd been having this irrational fear that someone was going to do terrible things to her. I thought maybe an ex was threatening her, but when I pressed her on it she swore that wasn't the case. She insisted that it was something from her dreams. That she'd wake up feeling like someone had been whispering to her, telling her that *he* was going to do terrible things to her, but she had no idea who this person was. Somehow she knew what was going to happen."

"Was this the first time she'd mentioned this to you?"

Mackey stared at the remains of a tissue she'd been shredding, as if she were noticing it for the first time. "Yes. I knew several weeks ago something was bothering her. She just looked so worried. But when I tried asking her about it, she insisted it was nothing. Then she adopted Lucky and she seemed like her old self again. I guess over the weekend Lucky ran off, and on Monday Lori was back to looking miserable again. Yesterday I forced her to talk to me. I wouldn't take no for an answer."

"Were the two of you friends?"

Mackey showed a bleak smile. "We're the only graphic designers working here." Her eyes became wet with tears as she realized that wasn't true anymore. She blinked back the tears. "We ate lunch together most days. We'd go out for drinks after work. When she told me how anxious she'd been feeling, I invited her to spend the night at my apartment, but she insisted she wanted to be home in case someone found Lucky. Maybe she believed this killer would get her no matter where she was. I thought if she had a good night's sleep she'd be able to get past this craziness, so I gave her some Valiums."

Her head jerked to one side as if she'd been slapped, and she brought the knuckle of her index finger to her mouth.

"What if it was because of the Valium that Lori's dead?" she asked. "Taking it could've left her helpless. She could be alive now if I hadn't given it to her."

"It wouldn't have mattered," Walsh said. Morris had filled her in enough about the Nightmare Man's past killings for her to know this was true. Several of his long-ago victims had been overpowered and knocked unconscious with chloroform. Lori Fletcher was as good as dead the moment the Nightmare Man had picked her out to be one of his victims. Maybe if her monstrous dog hadn't run off things would've been different, but he had. "I can't go into details, but whether or not she took a Valium last night wouldn't have mattered. If anything, it might've helped to keep her calmer and lessen the suffering."

Mackey's mouth dropped open as she stared at Walsh, and then her face crumbled completely and she started bawling. Walsh still had more questions for her, particularly about Lori Fletcher's past boyfriends or strangers Fletcher might've mentioned. It was going to be a while before she'd get a chance to ask them. No doubt Mackey would be going through many more tissues.

Walsh was going to have to work on her bedside manner.

Chapter 31

The lock Morris had ordered for Rachel had been delivered earlier that day to MBI, but he needed to go home to pick up his tool bag. This gave him a chance to make himself a cold meatloaf sandwich and feed Parker his food. Of course he had to wait until the bull terrier licked his bowl clean before he went near the refrigerator. He took pity on the dog, who was still sulking over his failed mooching experience, and added a thick slice of meatloaf to the bowl. By the time they left the house, Parker was in better spirits.

Natalie was planning to be at her office until nine that night. They had talked on the phone, and he knew she hadn't been able to convince their daughter to spend time at home while this madman was terrorizing Los Angeles. That was pretty much what he had expected. Rachel had inherited his stubbornness, and when her mind was made up, she could take it to a whole different level. Even more so than Parker at his most mulish.

His early detection system went off when they were still five doors away from Rachel's apartment, and Parker started grunting excitedly, his tail-wagging going into overdrive. So Rachel was home. He checked his watch. Twenty past six. Why wouldn't she be?

He knocked on her door, and when Rachel answered she had her hands on her hips and was giving Morris an exceptionally stern look. That didn't last as she immediately had to deal with Parker's onslaught. Within seconds she was on the floor laughing as she wrestled with the bull terrier and tried to keep him from licking her face. By the time she disengaged herself from Parker, Morris was halfway done installing the new lock.

"You think you can come in here and put whatever lock you want on my door?" she demanded coldly.

"Pretty much."

There was cold silence, then, "I thought the last lock you installed couldn't be picked."

Morris had two more screws to put in before he'd be done. "The key could be copied. This one can't."

He gave each screw one more try with the screwdriver to make sure they were in solid, tested the lock, then got off his knees and onto his feet, slowly straightening his back. Rachel was still on the floor hugging Parker, who was in seventh heaven. The bull terrier might've ostensibly been Morris's dog, but Rachel was his true love. Morris showed her the key for the new lock.

"See those four magnets? The way they're positioned makes this key impossible to duplicate, and the lock impossible to pick. No one is getting in here unless you let them in. And you be careful who you let in."

Rachel's tough act softened. She accepted the three factory-made keys for the lock. She then got to her feet and moved in for a hug. Morris held her tightly.

"I wish you'd come home until this mess is over," he said.

"Come on, Dad, with the new lock my place is safer than Fort Knox. The semester just started. I have to be in class, and I can't be hiding out at home every time you hunt a serial killer."

"This one's different. I have a history with him. So did your granddad."

Morris's cell phone rang. He kissed Rachel's forehead before breaking off the hug so he could check the caller ID. The White Swan Hotel in Galway. He answered the phone, and an excited Philip Stonehedge told him he'd been calling around Hollywood like Morris had asked.

"I have a good idea where Benjamin Chandler is hiding out," Stonehedge said. "From what I'm hearing, Chandler is one of these method actors who takes things way too far when he prepares for a role. Three years ago he was going to star in *Sons of the Apocalypse*, a biker gang crime film that ended up getting canned, and he started hanging out with a badass biker gang, got involved in a melee at a North Hollywood strip club, and broke some serious biker dude's jaw. According to a reliable source, he hid out at his agent's cabin in Wrightwood until things could be worked out and he could show his face around town without having it shot off."

Wrightwood was a small mountain town an hour and forty-five minutes outside of Los Angeles. So Brownstein had lied to him. Maybe he'd heard something through the grapevine, knew Morris had been in touch with Big Joe Penza, and thought he was protecting his client. Morris was impressed that Brownstein had taken the beating he had from Gallo without giving up Chandler. The fact that Brownstein pointed them to Chandler's little black book meant that the book wouldn't lead them to his mountain cabin.

Morris asked, "How reliable is your source?"

"Very reliable. She was with Chandler at the cabin. She's also married, and her husband believed she was on location for a shoot. She asked that I not give out her name."

"Did she give you an address for this cabin?"

Stonehedge laughed. "Come on, man, you have to know I'd get that address before calling you. This isn't my first rodeo, you know. I'll text it to you."

"Thanks, Phil. You really came through for me."

"That's what I do, and that's why I keep telling you to make me a part-time PI at your firm."

They'd talked about this before, and Morris knew Stonehedge was partly serious—that he wanted to work as a PI between movie gigs. As with those other times, Morris told him they'd discuss this more after Stonehedge retired from acting.

As Stonehedge had promised, he texted Morris the cabin's address. Morris looked away from his phone to see Rachel and Parker staring at him intently.

"A lead?" Rachel asked.

"A lead that might get me to a legitimate lead."

"In other words, you're still groping in the dark."

"Hopefully, it's better than that, but I'll know more later tonight."

"Don't be out too late. Mom needs you at home."

Concern showed in Rachel's eyes. Morris promised her he'd be heading home as soon as he checked out this new lead.

Rachel came in for another hug, and Morris gave her another kiss on the forehead. She was twenty-four and in another year would be starting her career as a tough-as-nails prosecutor, but there were times when he had a hard time seeing her as anything other than the skinny little six-year-old girl he had comforted after she fell off her bicycle and badly skinned her knees. This was one of those times.

"Be careful, sweetheart," he said. "Don't let anyone in here you don't know. I'm serious. If someone comes knocking on your door dressed as a cop, call me. I'll come over and make sure he really is one."

He wanted to ask whether Doug Gilman would be sleeping over. Although Gilman and his daughter had been a couple for over six months, this was still a subject he hadn't broached with her, or with Gilman, as tempted as he might've been. He'd feel better knowing Rachel wasn't alone while the Nightmare Man was out there.

"I'll be fine. Just be careful yourself, okay?"

"How about I leave Parker with you?"

Rachel didn't exactly roll her eyes, but she came close. "Come on, Dad, that wouldn't work. I've got law school plus twenty hours each week at my job. Parker would be miserable left alone all day."

"I could drop him off at night and pick him up in the morning."

No hint of an eye roll this time, only a patronizing smile. "Dad, I love you, but it's time for you and the little guy to get going."

Morris took the hint. She was just too stubborn. Once her mind was made up, that was it. It had always been that way with her. He almost asked if he could search her apartment before he left to make sure the Nightmare Man hadn't gotten in and was hiding somewhere inside, but he knew if he did that he'd get the full eye roll, and for good reason. Forget one in a million, there wasn't even a possibility of that happening. If there was someone else inside the apartment, Parker would've let him know already.

He needed to get a grip. Badly. He had demonstrated that earlier with the way he handled Big Joe Penza. Of course, what he really needed was to put the Nightmare Man out of commission, and he needed to do it before anyone else got hurt.

He told Rachel one more time to be careful, and she somehow restrained herself from showing her exasperation. He led Parker out of the apartment, and after the door closed behind him, he stood quietly and listened for the lock to turn. Only after he heard it did he head for the elevator.

Chapter 32

Charlie Bogle wouldn't let the argument drop. He insisted, "Brownstein didn't do his client any favors."

Morris shrugged halfheartedly. This had been going on for a while now. After he left Rachel's apartment, he'd called Bogle to fill him in on Stonehedge's discovery. Bogle had earlier watched Gallo drop off his thug associate and followed him to his high-rise apartment building. Since it appeared as if the gangster was done for the night, they decided to meet at MBI and drive to the mountain town of Wrightwood together.

"These agents are a pain in the ass," Bogle muttered half under his breath.

"Brownstein thought he was protecting him," Morris said.

"How exactly was he doing that? He knows I work for Starlight Pictures. He also knows who you are."

"I'm sure the painkillers they're giving him clouded his judgment."

Morris's cell phone rang. Dennis Polk. He put the phone on speaker.

"I got the goods," Polk said, sounding pleased with himself. "Not just one photo, but a couple of dozen."

"Is that so?"

"Damn straight. Melanie Penza was prettying herself up for a big date, like we thought. Thirty minutes ago she met up in Malibu with her boyfriend."

"Bobby Gallo?"

"That's right."

Bogle checked the time and frowned. "Gallo must've gone back to his place for a quick shower and change. I'm betting he left right after I gave up his tail."

"Is that Charlie Bogle?" Polk asked.

"The one and only," Bogle said. "How are tricks?"

"Not too shabby. When I see you next we'll catch up over some beers."

"Not if I see you first."

"Ha ha. Always the joker."

Morris interrupted them, saying, "Where are they meeting?"

"Yeah, the lovestruck couple," Polk said. "They're using a beachfront home. Nice place, very secluded. But that didn't stop me from snapping shots of them entering the home together. They didn't waste any time either, and let me tell you, those two are noisy in bed. A lot of passion, also a lot of screaming, grunting, and dirty talk. A couple of alley cats going at it would make less noise. I could hear them loud and clear from outside the front door, and with the racket those two made, they never heard me pick the door lock or realize I was right outside the bedroom taking pictures of them *in flagrante delicto*."

"When did you learn Latin?" Bogle asked.

"You pick things up," Polk said. "I also know *e pluribus unum*. I can't tell you what it means, though."

Morris asked, "Do the photos clearly show their faces?"

Polk chuckled. "Among other things."

"Okay. Good. Fred is keeping a tail on Big Joe. Give him a call and meet up with him. Charlie and I will join the two of you when we can. We'll tackle Big Joe then."

"Sounds like a plan," Polk said.

The call ended, and they drove in silence for several minutes before Bogle muttered thanks. The reason for this was Morris no longer needed to bring Benjamin Chandler to Big Joe in order to get what the mob boss knew about the Nightmare Man. Polk's photos were all that were needed. He could've turned the car around and headed back to Los Angeles, and not too many people would've blamed him if he had done exactly that. He didn't need to explain to his friend of over twenty years why he was continuing on to Wrightwood. They had a deal. Bogle needed to bring Chandler back to Los Angeles, and Morris wasn't about to leave him hanging out to dry.

* * * *

The cabin was set forty yards back from the road and further hidden behind a copse of pines. Even if it wasn't dusk, it would've been easy to miss, and Morris had to circle back before he found the narrow dirt driveway. The lights were off inside the cabin, and it didn't appear as if anyone was home, but as they drove up, Bogle pointed out that the blinds covering the window on the left had moved.

"Someone's peeking out," Morris said.

"Benjamin Chandler."

"Let's hope so."

"Ten to one he rabbits," Bogle said.

"A sucker's bet," Morris said.

"Front or back?"

"Back."

Morris pulled the car to a stop, and he took Parker with him, got a flashlight from the trunk, and continued to the back of the cabin while Bogle went straight to the front door. A BMW convertible had been tucked away behind the cabin so it couldn't be seen from the front, and a porch door was swinging back and forth. Parker's ears perked up, and he stood as still as a marble statue. Morris heard noises from the direction where Parker was staring, and in the dusk he saw a person scrambling up a mountain path. It had to be Chandler, and he already had a hundred-yard lead on them. Morris groaned. His creaky knees couldn't handle chasing someone up a mountain.

He yelled out that they had been sent from Starlight Pictures to bring him back. That only seemed to make the man run faster, at least until he slipped and fell on his face. Bogle soon joined Morris, and they watched as the man fought to get back on his feet.

"I tried telling him who we are," Morris said.

"He's in full-blown panic," Bogle observed.

The man was fading from view as he scrambled up the path.

"It's possible he didn't hear me," Morris said. "The guy's got to be part mountain goat. I'm not up to chasing after him."

Bogle said, "Neither am I."

They both turned to Parker, who looked more than up to the task.

Morris took him off his leash, then gave the dog an encouraging shove and ordered him to go get him. The bull terrier shot up the path.

"We better go up after him," Morris said.

Bogle asked, "Your dog's not going to hurt him, is he?"

"Depends how much of a fight he puts up. He'd get hurt worse if we didn't do anything. There's got to be rattlesnakes up there."

The flashlight proved useful as they made their way up the trail, allowing them to make sure they didn't step on loose stones. They moved at a more leisurely pace than either Parker or the man who they presumed was Benjamin Chandler. Still, even in the cool mountain air, they were both sweating badly five minutes later when they found the bull terrier and the man he had chased up the path.

Morris was relieved to see that the man was in fact Benjamin Chandler. If it hadn't been him, he was going to have some explaining to do, especially seeing that the actor had been knocked onto his back, and Parker now stood on his chest, growling, with the actor's right forearm gripped in his mouth. Even without the flashlight, Morris could see Chandler's eyes were liquid with fear.

The actor screamed out, "I won't say anything to the police, I swear to God!"

"Relax," Morris grunted as he pulled Parker off the actor and had him release the forearm. No denying that Nat was right, the little guy needed to lose a few. "We're here to save your ass. Scout's honor."

Bogle offered Chandler his hand and helped him to his feet. He introduced himself and Morris. The actor slowly rubbed the forearm Parker had used for a game of tug-of-war. From what Morris could tell, the skin hadn't been broken, and if the actor had a broken bone, they'd know it already. His arm was probably bruised, but no worse than that.

Chandler looked incapable of saying a word. He blinked wildly as he looked first at Bogle, then at Morris, and finally at Parker. The bull terrier was back on his leash and grinning happily as if nothing had happened.

"I thought you were sent by Penza," the actor said finally, as if he were in a daze.

"How about we get off this mountain and back into your cabin?" Morris said. "You look like you could use a stiff drink. You got anything down there?"

"An eighteen-year-old Glenmorangie."

Bogle asked, "Is that a girl or a scotch?"

Chandler was too shaken up to get the joke. "Scotch whisky."

"Okay," Morris said. "Let's pour a few and explain the situation to you. Are you able to walk? Do you need help?"

When Morris had first flashed the light on Chandler, the actor's face had been a ghastly white, but now some color was seeping back into his cheeks and his eyes looked less fearful.

"You have no idea how scared I was," he said. "When I saw your car driving up, I was sure I was a dead man. But to answer your question, I'm okay. At least I think so."

He held out his hand in front of him, and there was only a slight tremor.

Morris handed him the flashlight, and Chandler led the way down the path. Bogle sidled up to Morris and asked in a low voice, "When were you ever a Boy Scout?"

"I never said I was. But Rachel was a Girl Scout for years, and with all the Thin Mints and Samoas I ate, I earned my honorary title." He pointed his chin at his dog and added, "So did Parker."

Chapter 33

"I'm looking for Big Joe Penza."

The tuxedoed maître d'hôtel at the Russian restaurant Vanya's was a fleshy man with heavy-lidded, sleepy eyes and a small amount of wispy hair framing his scalp. He gave Morris a bored look and in a thick accent mumbled something that could've been: "Don't know who that is."

It was almost midnight, and while a scattering of customers still sat at tables, the restaurant felt about as lively as a tomb. Parker, for his part, nearly unhinged his jaw yawning.

Lemmon and Polk had accompanied Morris into the restaurant, while Bogle and Chandler sat two blocks away in Morris's car waiting for his call. Morris held out Benjamin Chandler's driver's license.

"Penza will want to see this."

The maître d' gave the license an indifferent look.

Morris dug into his wallet and folded a twenty-dollar bill around the license. The maître d'hôtel conceded then to take the money and license. In that same thick accent that sounded as if his mouth was full of marbles, he mumbled something that Morris took as: "You wait here."

The man walked off toward the back of the restaurant before disappearing down a hallway. It didn't take long for him to come back and wave Morris and the others to follow him. He led them to a room in the back where Big Joe Penza and six others sat at a table playing poker, drinking vodka, and eating caviar, smoked fish, and other appetizers. Morris noted that Big Joe liked his private dining rooms.

Penza raised an eyebrow and jokingly remarked, "You brought a small mob with you, huh? Too bad, it looks like I got you outnumbered."

"True," Morris agreed. "But your poker buddies need to get lost. We need to talk privately."

"That so? How'd you know where I was?"

"I had a tail on you since I left you earlier."

Penza's thick lips froze into a mirthless smile. "You'll tell me later how you managed that," he said. "How come I don't see that actor with you? This another trick of yours? A manufactured license?"

He said this mostly as a joke, but Morris picked up the threat in his voice. That if he wasn't bringing him Chandler, there would be problems.

"The license is legit. We found him and you'll be seeing him soon, but there are matters we need to discuss first."

Penza's eyes glazed. He didn't like being told what to do, but he accepted that he needed to send his poker friends away. "A half hour break, boys, no more than that," he promised them. "Order whatever you want, put it on my tab."

There was an undercurrent of grumbling, but the men filed out of the room. Once the door closed behind the last one, Morris told Penza that he'd also put a tail on Melanie.

Polk had his camera with him. A top-of-the-line Nikon with a telephoto zoom lens. He showed Penza on the camera's viewfinder the photos he had taken. At first Penza smirked as if this was an elaborate joke, but once the pictures moved from the outside of the Malibu home to the bedroom, his smirk disappeared.

"These are real?" he asked, incredulously.

"I wouldn't know how to fake something like that," Polk said.

Morris said, "Chandler never had an affair with your wife. He doesn't know her. Never met her. He did, however, witness Bobby Gallo stabbing another of your associates. A knuckle-buster named Vincent Scalise. That's why he's been hiding."

"Why'd Bobby tell me what he did?"

This was said innocently enough. Morris didn't need to tell Penza what was obvious. That Gallo was covering up his own affair, and at the same time he needed cover to make sure Chandler disappeared and never had a chance to tell Penza what he had witnessed. It took a few seconds, but from the way the mob boss's eyes dimmed, he saw that also.

"I want to hear this from that actor's mouth," Penza demanded stubbornly.

"Sure."

Morris got Bogle on the phone and told him to bring Chandler to the restaurant. While they waited for Bogle and Chandler, Penza demanded to know where the photos had been taken. Morris gave him the Malibu address.

"They're still there?"

"As far as I know."

This was a lie. Morris had earlier called Marty Wright and given him the story of Chandler witnessing Gallo stabbing Scalise, and Wright arranged for the organized crime unit to pick Gallo up. An hour ago, Morris got a call that Gallo had been arrested. They would try to flip him. Melanie Penza was also picked up, but in her case it was more for her own protection. They were going to offer her a witness protection deal to turn on her husband. With some luck Penza would be behind bars by tomorrow, but Morris didn't need to tell him that.

Penza signaled with his sausage-sized thumb for Morris and his crew to leave the room. "When that actor shows up, you knock on the door, and I'll let you know when you can come in. For now, scram."

Morris didn't argue. Penza wanted to make phone calls in private. It didn't matter. It would take at least forty minutes for the leg breakers he'd be sending after Gallo to discover that the Malibu home was empty, and by that time Morris would've gotten from Penza what he needed. Before turning for the door, he grabbed two pieces of lamb from a platter of shish kebab and fed them to Parker. The mob boss glowered at him but swallowed back whatever it was he wanted to say.

"He earned it," Morris explained. "It's partly because of him we're able to bring Benjamin Chandler to you tonight."

"Ugly bloodhound," Penza muttered, impatient for Morris and the others to leave so he could sic his thugs after Gallo, and possibly also after his wife. Morris didn't bother to correct him regarding Parker's pedigree.

Instead of waiting by the door, they moved back to the main dining hall so they could be on the lookout for Bogle and Chandler. Penza's poker buddies were laughing it up at one of the tables. Polk stared longingly at their half-open bottle of vodka.

"I could use a drink right now," Polk said.

"Only one?" Lemmon asked.

"Hell, I'd take a bottle of that fermented potato juice."

Morris said, "Let's see how the night goes."

Parker let out a satisfied pig-grunt, his tail still wagging from the lamb.

Lemmon laughed as he watched the dog. "I swear, Big Joe looked like he wanted to stab you in the hand for feeding Parker."

"No doubt," Morris agreed.

He spotted Bogle and Chandler walking into the restaurant and waved them over, then led the way back to Penza's private dining room. He didn't bother knocking. The hell with Penza. When he walked into the room, Penza glared at him and then turned his glare toward Chandler.

"If you don't know my wife, then explain this," Penza demanded coldly.

He held up a cell phone that showed a photo of Chandler and Melanie Penza together outside a Santa Monica bungalow. The actor approached Penza and gave the photo a curious look before smiling to himself.

"That was from *People* magazine," Chandler explained. "Not that exact photo, of course. The real photo was a publicity shot with me and Jane Wickford, an up-and-coming actress. If you look online, I'm sure you could find the original. Someone photoshopped your wife into this one."

From the look in Penza's eyes, he already knew that would be the answer, but he had to play the tough guy.

Morris said, "You're square then with Mr. Chandler? No remaining issues?"

"Tell him to beat it," Penza said.

Bogle spoke up, saying, "I'll make sure Mr. Chandler gets home safely." He clapped Morris on the shoulder and winked at both Polk and Lemmon before escorting Chandler out of the room.

Morris sat down next to Penza. Polk and Lemmon also took seats at the table. Morris told them to pour themselves shots, that they had earned it. He fed Parker another piece of lamb kebab and spread caviar on a piece of small toast for himself. He'd had caviar a few times in the past and had so far never really cared for it but thought someday he might develop a taste. As he took a bite, he realized today was not that day.

"You're making yourself right at home, I see," Penza complained.

"Damn straight," Morris said. He poured himself a shot of vodka and mouthed *l'chaim* to Polk and Lemmon, who had done the same. After downing the drink, he slammed the glass on the table. A brightness burned in his eyes when he turned back to Penza.

"I went far above and beyond my end of the deal, and me and my associates are hungry and thirsty after running around all day solving your marital and organizational problems. Now you're going to tell me what you know about the Nightmare Man."

He was sick of Penza and disgusted that this man had made him spend costly days jumping through hoops before being willing to help him stop a depraved serial killer. Maybe he wouldn't empty a clip into Penza, but he could feel a meanness building inside, and he was going to do whatever it took to get Penza to tell him what he knew.

Penza's thick lips were pushed into a belligerent frown, but something broke in his eyes. He pushed a thick hand through his yellow-dyed hair, a sudden weariness aging him well past his sixty years.

"It's about time I told someone this," he said.

Chapter 34

Los Angeles, 1984

Torture will be necessary.

That was the message written neatly on the letter a prospective client sent to Ed Blount's post office box. They weren't supposed to do that. They were only supposed to send the address of their own post office box so Blount could arrange a time and place for them to meet. Blount shrugged off this indiscretion, figuring the prospective client wanted to make sure he knew up front what the job entailed in case he had qualms about torture. He didn't. He was a professional. Half of his jobs were for the Penza family, half were freelance, and he had no problem doing whatever was necessary. More than a few times he needed to beat information out of a target, and there had been jobs with the Penza family that required the target to be left a bloody mess to send the right message. He got no enjoyment when he had to make a target suffer, nor when he killed them, but it didn't bother him either. It was a job. It paid the bills.

Almost three a.m. Aside from those working graveyard, the city's inhabitants were mostly tucked away for the night. It had been ten minutes since Blount had seen another car on the road, and the same wouldn't have been true an hour ago. North Hollywood would've been buzzing then with activity, and cops would've been cruising for drunks. In another hour, Los Angeles would be waking up and early morning delivery trucks would start snaking through the city streets. Now was the time of night when Blount liked to work.

His headlights cut through the murky grayness as he drove along North La Brea Avenue. There was too much ambient light from businesses and streetlamps for the night to ever get pitch-black in Los Angeles. That was a shame. Blount would've preferred to travel in complete darkness.

The man he was meeting didn't know Blount's name and never would. The same wasn't true for Blount. He had sent instructions detailing the time and location for a meeting to a post office box and hired someone to watch for when the letter was picked up so that the prospective client could be followed. In this way, he discovered that the man's name was Donald Trilling. Blount now knew enough about him to feel comfortable taking the job. Trilling was by all accounts an upstanding citizen. Someone wealthy enough to own a home in Brentwood and investment properties in Venice, and equally important to Blount, no police record or arrests. There was no reason to suspect that the police or other law enforcement officials would be squeezing Trilling to contact Blount. Still, that scenario wasn't impossible.

The meeting place was in the back of a supermarket parking lot. The only car there when Blount arrived was Trilling's silver Mercedes. He pulled up to the left of it and signaled with a wave of his hand for Trilling to get out of his car, and then to come around to his door. Trilling looked confused. Blount waited for him, then rolled down his window, and told him to lift up his shirt. Trilling stared at him with an awkward smile before realizing Blount wanted to make sure he wasn't wearing a wire. He smirked as he lifted up his cotton-knit long-sleeve shirt to show he didn't have a recording device taped to his torso. When Blount told him to lower his pants, Trilling made a you-got-to-be-kidding-me face, but he did as he was told, just as he did when Blount told him to drop his briefs.

"Satisfied?" Trilling asked.

"Get dressed and get in the car."

"How about I check you out for a wire," Trilling suggested with the same smirk he had shown earlier.

"How about you quit being a wise guy before I break both your arms and leave you here."

The smirk froze on Trilling's face, becoming something brittle and plastic. Blount could see Trilling considered challenging him, but he made the smart decision not to do so. He walked around to the passenger side of the car, got in, and then looked surprised when Blount backed up and drove out of the parking lot.

"What are you doing?" he asked.

Blount held up an index finger, leaving a clear message: Not another word.

He had to make sure no one was following Trilling, but he also wanted to take Trilling to a remote spot in the Hollywood Hills. He had a shovel and a bag of lime in the trunk, and if things went south it would be a better place to leave his body.

Trilling held his tongue for several minutes before asking where they were going.

Blount was satisfied no one was following them. "Someplace we can talk privately," he said.

"We couldn't have done that in the parking lot?"

"Not private enough."

Trilling smiled at that. "One can never be too safe in your line of work, huh?"

Blount didn't answer him and Trilling didn't waste his breath asking any further questions. Blount got onto Mulholland Drive, followed that for several miles, then pulled onto a dirt road. After driving deeper into the hills, he stopped the car and turned off the lights. No one would be able to see them where they were parked. He turned to Trilling and asked him to tell him about the job.

"I want my wife killed," Trilling said. "And I have specific instructions for how I want it done."

Trilling handed Blount a carefully folded sheet of paper. The hitman used a penlight to read what amounted to a short laundry list of tortures. He had assumed that the torture would be to extract information, but that wasn't going to be the case. Trilling simply wanted to inflict terrible pain on his wife before she died. There were only four items on the list. The first three would be cruel, but simple enough to do. The last—the one involving a live rat—was just plain demented.

"If your wife were to die like this, the police would be zeroing in on you. Even if I made her body disappear afterward, you'd be their chief suspect. The smart thing would be for her death to look like a suicide or accident."

"Her death can't be that easy, not after what that bitch has put me through." Trilling's voice took on a petulant note as he added, "Marjorie's death has to be exactly the way I wrote it down. I put a lot of thought into it. I know what she's terrified most of, and doing what I'm asking will make her final minutes a living nightmare. You're the professional, you'll just have to figure out a way to do it so I'm not suspected."

Blount saw a way to do it. It was an awful idea, awful enough that it gave him a moment of pause. He even saw a way to carry out the last item—which was making Trilling's wife choke to death on a live rat. At first it didn't seem possible. His fist would be way too big to fit inside someone's mouth, so how could he shove a rat down a woman's throat? If he broke apart her jaw like a pistachio shell, she'd either die on the spot or go into shock. But he knew rats could squeeze through small holes. He'd have to do some research, but he had an idea of how it could be done.

Blount didn't believe in heaven or hell, which was just as well, because if there was such a thing as hell he was already damned. If he carried out his idea and hell existed, he'd be taking an express trip to its deepest, darkest, most demonic level.

"There is a way to do it," he said. "But it will cost you. Four hundred grand."

This was far more than his standard twenty grand charge for a hit. Even in the darkness of the car, he could see Trilling opening his eyes wide with surprise.

"Why so much?" Trilling asked.

"I have to hide her death among others."

"I don't get what you're saying."

"I'll make it look like a serial killer is on the loose. Others will have to die in the same way."

Trilling let out an insipid giggle that he had the good sense to cut off. "That's absolutely brilliant," he said. "I was wondering how this could be done so I could escape police scrutiny, but that would work nicely. Yes, indeed. How many other women will you be killing?"

"Four in total, including your wife."

"Make it five. That seems like a better number for a serial killer. Yes, that would keep the police too busy to look at husbands or other family members."

"Half a million then. A hundred grand a victim."

"Deal. Can I choose the four other victims?"

"Absolutely not."

"A pity," Trilling said, and he sounded truly disappointed. "It would've been exciting picking out the other four, but c'est la vie."

The hundred grand a victim price was beyond exorbitant, even with what was required. Blount threw out that number so Trilling would turn him down. That was what he was expecting, and that would've given him an excuse to drag Trilling out of the car and leave his corpse in the hills for the coyotes to gnaw on. Trilling deserved to die for what he was asking from him. But half a million dollars would be a game changer. With that kind of money he'd be able to take Lauren and the boys someplace where Penza wouldn't be able to reach him—maybe upper Michigan, or a small town in Iowa. He'd then buy a quick oil change franchise. Or a doughnut shop. Or any legit business so he'd be out of the game. He hadn't realized until right then how much he wanted out.

Five more hits and he'd be done. That's how he had to look at it. These women were only going to be targets like any of his other past targets, and it didn't matter how repulsive he found his client.

He made necessary arrangements with Trilling, then turned the car around and headed back to North Hollywood.

Chapter 35

The cutoff age for the youth fall baseball league was sixteen, but Sam Brick guessed the kid at the plate had to be almost twenty. Tall, rangy, big shouldered, already growing a mustache. He obviously wasn't twice as big as Morris, but it sure felt that way. It didn't surprise Brick when the kid smoked a shot down the third-base line. What did surprise him was when his son dove to his right and stretched out fully so he could catch the ball, then scrambled back to his feet and doubled off the runner who'd been on first. The poor baserunner probably thought he could score on the play and had reached second before he realized the ball was caught. What fourteen-year-old makes a play like that? That was a major-league play. No doubt about it! Brick was on his feet cheering wildly. So were all the other parents in the stands, even the ones whose kids were playing for the other team. He was also proud of the way Morris handled it. Didn't even crack a smile. He got back into his crouch and kept his focus only on getting the final out of the game.

Esther, Morris's six-year-old sister, had been squirming in her seat the last two innings. She tugged on Brick's coat jacket.

"This is so boring I might die," she announced in a breathless voice, a hand raised to her forehead, the tiny palm facing outward as if she might faint any second now. "Can't we leave yet? Please?"

Brick couldn't help grinning. What was really eating at Esther was all the attention her big brother was getting. While Morris was quiet and reserved, Esther was a natural-born actress, and it bugged her when she wasn't the center of attention. Like Morris, she was small for her age, with thin pipe cleaner legs and arms. Morris, though, physically took after him.

He might've been short, but he had a fireplug body. Esther was a redhead like her mom and was going to be a beauty when she grew up.

"Thanks to your brother's heroics the game won't be lasting too much longer. We'll pick up Mom afterward and go out for pizza and ice cream. How does that sound?"

"I just don't know if I can stand it another minute," she said, hamming it up.

Brick tousled her hair. "Give it your best shot, okay, sweetie?"

Esther let out an overly dramatic sigh. "If I must."

The next batter grounded out to second. Game over.

Brick and his daughter made their way to the field. While Morris celebrated with his team, Esther held on to Brick's arm and swung around as if she were playing on a jungle gym. The celebration ended, and Morris joined them.

Brick extended his hand. "Quite a game, son," he said. "You were easily the star."

Morris grinned sheepishly as he took his dad's hand. "I did okay," he said.

"I'd say more than okay. A home run, two other hits, outstanding plays at third."

Esther let go of her dad's arm and rolled her eyes with exasperation. "Big deal," she exclaimed. "All Morris does is fall like this."

She flopped onto the grass field with all the grace of a duck doing ballet, her thin arms and legs flailing awkwardly.

Morris broke out laughing. "Esther the pest," he said.

Esther was quickly on her feet, her face animated with passion, her tiny fists clenched. "Morris the booger head!" she shouted.

Morris's grin became something wicked. "Dad," he said, "is it too late to trade the little pest for a dog? Even one of those annoying toy poodles? Any dog would be better behaved."

"Booger head!" Esther yelled.

Brick was struggling not to laugh. Before he could scold either of them, the large cumbersome cellular telephone that he carried for work rang. Morris and Esther stopped their feud to watch him. They knew that calls that came over this phone were serious business. He answered the phone and listened quietly as he was told about the dead woman who had been found and the things that were done to her. The good humor he'd been feeling only seconds earlier was gone. Even though Morris and Esther hadn't heard the call, they could tell something bad had happened, and their expressions became subdued as well. Little Esther started crying. Brick corralled his daughter and smoothed her hair, trying to comfort her.

"You have to go to work?" Morris asked.

Brick tousled his hair. He lifted Esther with one arm and kissed her softly on the top of her head. "Let's get the two of you home," he said. "Mom will take you for pizza and ice cream."

Chapter 36

Los Angeles, after midnight, October 10, 1984

The client was supposed to be away on a business trip. That was what they had agreed, anyway. Blount cut the phone lines, disabling the security system, and broke in through a patio door. It didn't surprise him when he found Trilling sitting in the dark on the steps leading to the bedrooms on the second floor.

"Are you having second thoughts?" Blount asked in a whisper.

Trilling's face was mostly hidden in shadows, but there was enough moonlight filtering in to see that his face was tense with anticipation.

"Certainly not," he said. "I want to watch, perhaps even help, so I wanted to tell you not to use chloroform on me."

Blount smiled thinly. When they made their arrangements, Trilling demanded that at least one other victim have a husband, since otherwise it could look suspicious if his wife was the only married victim. It made sense, so Blount agreed, and at the time Trilling asked what he would do when he found a husband or boyfriend in bed with a victim. Blount explained that he'd be bringing chloroform and extra rope along so he could knock them out, then tie and gag them, and Trilling seemed satisfied with the answer. So this was why he was anxiously waiting for him—he was afraid Blount would sneak into the bedroom and knock him out before he could stop him, and then he'd miss all the fun.

"I won't use chloroform on you," Blount promised. He held out his hand, and Trilling handed over the crystal glass he'd been holding. Blount gave it a sniff. Bourbon, top quality stuff. "I'll wash this out. You go back to bed and act as if nothing is going to happen. And for God's sake, don't wake your wife."

Trilling got to his feet and did as ordered. Blount watched his client until he disappeared up the stairs and into his bedroom; then he left his oversized gym bag by the stairs and brought the glass back to the kitchen. He kept his leather gloves on while he washed out the glass. He probably could've just left it in the sink, but for all he knew forensics could've had the technology to figure out that the bourbon had been poured near the time the Nightmare Man began torturing Trilling's wife. That was the name the media had given him. The Nightmare Man. Why not? It made as much sense as anything, and at least they were buying into the serial killer angle.

Marjorie Trilling would be the third woman killed by the Nightmare Man. The first two killings had gone off without a hitch, at least in a way. Blount had taken out more targets during his twenty-plus-year career than he could remember, and none of them were anything other than a job. Once they were done, they were forgotten. Just as a butcher would feel cutting a slab of beef into steaks. This was different. Blount found himself haunted by those two women. He tried telling himself that death was death, and what he put the women through didn't matter, just like it didn't matter when he had once skinned a target for Penza. That hit was on a guy in Penza's organization who had started talking with the cops, and as far as Blount was concerned, the guy deserved the hell he went through before he finally cut the man's throat. But the two women he had chosen were innocents who didn't deserve what had happened to them. The same was true of Marjorie Trilling. If Trilling had only paid him to turn the light off on his wife, Blount wouldn't have a problem, but these killings weighed on him in a way he never would've imagined possible. If it wasn't for the half million dollars at the finish line, Blount would've gladly changed his target for the night.

The arrangement he made was for Trilling to transfer a hundred grand to a Cayman Island account as a down payment, a hundred and fifty grand once Marjorie Trilling was murdered, and the rest after the fifth murder. Blount discovered that Trilling was very wealthy and had over thirty million dollars in assets. Trilling had been planning his wife's demise for several years, making sure he had enough money in a tangled web of shell companies so the payments couldn't be traced by law enforcement.

When Blount saw Trilling waiting for him, he considered forcing Trilling to transfer the remaining four hundred grand that was owed and then doing all the things to Trilling that the smug prick wanted done to his wife. But that was only a nice fantasy. The problem was Trilling might not be able to transfer money from his home. More likely, he needed to go to an office or bank to enact a transfer, and because of that the sonofabitch would be alive when morning came, and it would be his wife who would soon be dying a nightmarish death.

Whenever Blount went out on a job, he brought along a leather sap, a beaver-tail-shaped weapon weighted at one end with half a pound of lead. Doctors have their stethoscopes, surgeons their scalpels, but Blount's tool was his sap, and he was just as skilled at using it. A flick of the wrist, and he could hit a mark in the kidneys and leave him unable to breathe and helpless. Swinging the sap a little harder and striking right above the ear, he'd knock the person unconscious. Harder still, and he'd cave in a skull. He took the sap from where he had it tucked away under his belt and lightly slapped the rounded end against his palm. He'd keep his promise to Trilling. He wouldn't use chloroform on him, but he'd be damned if that sick bastard would have a front-row seat to his wife's murder.

Blount got the nylon rope out of the gym bag, measured and cut the lengths he'd be needing, and shoved those into his jacket pocket. He kept the sap in his right hand and used his left to carry the bulky gym bag he had brought along. The bag held not only the tools he'd be using, but a box-like metal trap for catching rats. As he made his way up the stairs, he heard the rat that had been caught two weeks earlier frantically scurrying about.

Trilling had two teenage daughters who were attending boarding school. He also used to have a live-in housekeeper, but he had let her go six months ago in anticipation of this night. So now it was only Trilling and his wife at home. Blount walked silently into the bedroom. He left the gym bag at the foot of the king-sized bed and moved quickly to where Trilling lay in a fetal position, trying to pretend he was asleep. At the last second he heard Blount approaching, and when he lifted his head, the sap struck him above the right temple. The blow made a soft thud and sent Trilling deep into dreamland.

The wife was sleeping soundly on her stomach. Blount lowered the quilt covering her and had her wrists bound before she woke up. He next bound her ankles, then rolled her onto her back. She stared up at him groggily for several seconds before realizing what was happening.

"Please, don't hurt us," she begged. "My husband will pay you whatever you want."

He wanted to apologize to her, but instead he laughed. He couldn't help himself.

She screamed as she understood who he was. The Nightmare Man. He didn't need to gag her since nobody would hear her, but he also didn't need a headache either. He found a pair of men's socks in a dresser drawer and used that to shut her up. He then used the remaining rope to hogtie Trilling and leave him on his stomach.

He got the hunting knife from the bag and used it to cut off the wife's pajamas. After that he went to work. As he did the terrible things to the woman that Trilling had paid him to do, he kept telling himself that this was only a job, but he knew he was lying to himself. This had become something else. This was something he'd have to live with, just like the other two women, and the two that he still had to butcher in the cruelest possible way. But it was also his way out. Given enough time and distance, these killings would become faint memories, possibly even memories he wouldn't be sure actually ever happened. At least he had to hope so.

He methodically set about doing every single torture that Trilling had specified. Trilling wanted seventeen cuts and burns and the same number of nails pulled out to signify each year he had spent with his wife, and it was Blount's idea to arrange the severed flesh and torn nails into a gruesome "17" at the foot of the bed. That was what serial killers did, right? Left twisted messages behind? It would leave the cops chasing their tails trying to figure out what it meant, and if any of them got the smart idea to see how many years Trilling and his wife had been married, they'd discover that they had only just had their fifteenth anniversary. While they'd been together seventeen years, they'd been married only fifteen.

Blount took almost two hours to complete the torture and killing. He didn't rush it. If he was going to take on a job, he would damn well do it right. If the client wanted the victim woken up with smelling salts every time she passed out, then that's what he did, even though it took longer to bring her back each time she lost consciousness. He also had to keep reheating the metal rod with a cigarette lighter after each burn. The only time he hurried things up and didn't quite live up to the spirit of the deal he made was with the rat, but he felt he could be forgiven for that.

He was packing up when his client started moaning. It was a soft moan that showed he hadn't fully woken up. Blount didn't bother checking on him. Instead, he finished his packing and left the room.

Chapter 37

Los Angeles, November 14, 1984

Sam Brick's commanding officer, Captain Jim Marshall, smiled as if he were waiting for a punch line that he was beginning to realize wasn't coming.

"You can't be serious," he said.

"It adds up," Brick argued stubbornly.

"Good God, man! You're saying a contract killer invented the Nightmare Man so he could hide a paid-for-hire murder among the victims of a serial killing spree? Don't you realize how insane that sounds?"

"Serial killers learn and adapt," Brick said. "Their methods change as they grow bolder and need bigger thrills. This guy"—he pointed a thumb toward the sketch a witness had provided after the fourth victim—"had an elaborate methodology from the beginning that never changed."

"We don't know what he did before the Nightmare Man murders. He could be responsible for other deaths."

"It's possible," Brick admitted. "But for him to then go from killing people in more mundane ways to becoming the Nightmare Man would be like a sports car going from zero to a hundred in seven seconds. Theoretically, who knows? I've just never heard of it."

Marshall looked confused. "Are you talking about a sports car or a serial killer?"

"Either."

"For all we know, this lunatic could have bodies planted throughout Death Valley. He could've been refining his technique for years."

"Again, it's possible," Brick conceded. "But I don't believe that's the case. It's more likely the client gave a hitman instructions for how he wanted his wife tortured and murdered."

Marshall cleared his throat, which Brick knew meant his commanding officer was losing patience. "The client being Donald Trilling," he said.

"He's the one with enough money to hire someone to do this."

"Sam, he's also a victim. He was violently assaulted and nearly put into a coma. He's lucky he didn't suffer permanent damage. He's also lucky he was found when he was. A couple of days tied up like that and he could've died from dehydration."

"He was tapped with a leather sap," Brick said, touching above his right temple to show where Trilling had been hit. "Just hard enough to knock him out, but not seriously hurt him. That sounds like something a mob connected guy would be good at. I also don't think it was all that surprising how quickly he was found. Just a coincidence he had an early morning meeting scheduled the next day so his secretary would get worried and send the police to his house?"

"What evidence do you have that Mr. Trilling would want his wife murdered? A girlfriend? Life insurance policy?"

Brick shrugged. Trilling was wealthy—he didn't need to kill his wife for additional money. Besides, you don't have your wife butchered the way Marjorie Trilling was if money was the only motive. Trilling's secretary was young and extremely attractive, but she seemed sincere about why she sent the police to Trilling's home that early morning on October tenth. Or maybe she was just a convincing actress. If Donald Trilling was having an affair, Brick hadn't found evidence of it yet, but he knew there had to be another woman, and he'd find her eventually.

"Sam, you don't have any solid evidence—not of marital discord or anything, and you're going to accuse Mr. Trilling of something this horrendous?"

"My gut's telling me he's our guy," Brick said. "And Jim, I do have something. Marjorie Trilling's psychiatrist told me about her rat phobia."

Marshall cleared his throat again, making more noise than before. From the look he gave Brick, his impatience had given way to irritation. "A lot of women are afraid of rats," he insisted.

"This went far beyond normal fear. According to Dr. Berman, the way she died would've been beyond excruciating. Jim, if you authorize a financial investigation into Trilling, I'll bet my pension we find a money transfer he can't explain."

Marshall's eyes glazed. "Sam, I'm not taking your pension," he said. "Find me something. Not just idle speculation, but something real. If this killer is a hired gun like you think, then find me evidence. Until then, keep away from Mr. Trilling. That's an order. The poor guy has suffered enough."

Marshall wasn't going to give Brick a chance to argue any further. As far as he was concerned, they were done, and to prove the point, he picked up a report from his desk and pretended to read it. Brick accepted that he was fighting a lost cause. He took the police sketch of the Nightmare Man and left Marshall's office, managing as much dignity as he could muster.

He knew it would be a tough sell given all the sympathy Trilling had been generating in the press. As far as the media was concerned, he was the poster boy for victim of the year given that the Nightmare Man not only murdered his wife but left him beaten and hogtied on the same blood-soaked bed as his wife's mutilated corpse. When Brick interviewed him, Trilling gave him all the right answers, even managed to squeeze out a few tears as he struggled to bravely hold it together, but Brick picked up an underlying smugness. There was something off about the guy, something very wrong. He was sure of it. But suspecting something and proving it were two different things, and so far he had gotten nowhere. The mob informants who saw the police sketch claimed they didn't know the killer, which didn't mean much. They could've been lying, or if the hired gun had ties to the mob, the man might've been known only to Salvatore Penza and a handful of other higher-ups. Joe Penza, Sal's big ox of a kid, would probably know him also.

Brick's gaze wandered to a framed photo on his desk of Ruthie, Morris, and Esther that had been taken earlier in the year. He'd seen so little of his family since getting the call about the first victim, missing Morris's baseball games and Esther's big dance recital and barely spending any waking minutes with his wife. He decided he deserved some time with them now, even if it was only with their photo. He pushed the chair back and swung his feet onto the desk. He soon found himself chuckling thinking of little Esther. Such a firecracker. She'd been furious with him for missing her recital, and she made sure he knew it. Most days she'd already be asleep when he got home, but those few times when he got home early enough to see her, she made sure to give him the silent treatment. He chuckled again. His daughter could hold a grudge. He had no doubt that she was going to be a handful as a teenager. Not like Morris at all. That kid was as even-keeled as they came. He had gotten a call from his son's coach just last week about a scout from the Dodgers being at the game. When the scout talked with the coach, he singled Morris out, telling the coach Morris had all the tools to play pro ball someday, that all he needed was a growth spurt. That night Brick made sure to get home early enough to see his kids, and when he took Morris aside to tell him what the coach had said, his son shrugged it off as if it were no big deal.

His gaze focused on Ruthie. He'd hit the jackpot with her, no question about it. A beautiful woman and a gentle soul. But she wasn't a pushover, that was for sure. As sweet as she was, she was also a rock who held the family together and did everything that needed to be done whenever Brick found himself submerged in one of his investigations. He also knew he frustrated her. He had walled off this part of his life from his family, and she wanted to be let inside. She was convinced that if he opened up to her about the job, she'd be able to comfort him, but he wasn't about to let any of the sickness that he routinely waded in stain her or his kids.

"Hey, Sam, don't you have a lunatic you need to be catching?"

Brick turned to see Lenny Girsten, a big smart-alecky grin stretched across his face. A moan eased out of Brick as he swung his feet from the desk.

"I'm trying," he said.

"That's not what it looked like to me."

Brick tapped his skull. "Just deep in thought, that's all. You should try it once in a while."

"Nah, I could hurt myself doing that." Girsten was still grinning, but it turned sickly. "It's been almost a month since that lunatic killed anyone. What do you think, is he done?"

Brick was sure the killing was over for now. The last victim had been found October twentieth, making it seventeen days from when the first victim was discovered. This was yet another reason to think it was a hitman. That "seventeen" stuff was too obvious, too neat, almost as if someone were trying to convince the police this was a serial killer. But that didn't mean the hitman had retired the Nightmare Man for good. Brick could see the sonofabitch using it again if a contract required it, say if a woman's death would bring too much heat on the client, even if the death were made to look like a suicide or accident.

"Hard to say," Brick admitted.

"Then how about you catch the bastard so the good people of this city can sleep easy again?"

Girsten gave a quick salute and walked off. Brick's gaze shifted to the thick file sitting on his desk for the Nightmare Man murders, for all the good it would do him. He was going to solve this when he found the hitman Donald Trilling hired.

He had to just keep digging. In his gut he knew Trilling was guilty as sin.

Chapter 38

Donald Trilling had his shirt and pants off before he realized Blount was sitting in his bedroom.

"You don't have to put your clothes back on for my sake," Blount said. "I've already seen you with your pants down. You might as well be comfortable."

"Thanks."

Blount said, "I hope I didn't startle you."

Trilling's skin color had turned a ghastly white as he stood by the dresser wearing only briefs and a pair of black ankle dress socks. Blount guessed he was trying to decide whether to run, fight, or pretend the visit was normal. The man had enough wits about him to see the futility of running or fighting, so all that was left was to act as if there was nothing unusual about the hitman he had hired showing up late at night in his bedroom. He walked over to one of the two walk-in closets in the room and retrieved a silk robe, which he slipped on and tied the belt to keep closed. Blount didn't bother moving. He had already searched the house, and he knew Trilling's only gun was kept downstairs in his private study.

With the robe now on, Trilling walked over to the bed and sat on the edge so that he faced Blount. He crossed a bony knee over the other.

"I hope you didn't take offense at my not answering your asinine question," he said, his voice and manner dripping with ice. A wealthy man trying to assert his dominance and take control of the situation. "I paid you what I owed you, even though I'm not at all happy that you cold-cocked me and refused to follow my instructions. Why are you here?"

"I followed your instructions to a *t*," Blount said. "You asked me not to use chloroform on you, and I didn't."

"I also told you I wanted to watch you kill my dear Marjorie."

"It had to look right. The crime scene boys would know the whole picture from the angle of the blow, so it had to be done the way I did it. I didn't count on you having such a soft skull and being out as long as you were."

Trilling looked mad enough to chew glass. It was an act. Blount knew he had to be terrified. And for good reason.

"What are you doing here?" he demanded in the same ice-dripping voice from earlier.

"We need to talk."

"Should we go downstairs? Perhaps talk over a glass of fine bourbon? I keep a bottle of Old Fitzgerald in my study."

"Here is just fine." Blount smiled inwardly at seeing Trilling hide his disappointment over not luring him to where he kept a .38-caliber pistol in a bottom desk drawer. He added, "I'm hearing rumblings that the cops are looking at you more closely for your wife's death."

"That's preposterous!"

"Maybe, maybe not. What matters is that things could get messy if they find out about your girlfriend. You've been careful, I'll give you credit for that. You've at least been smart enough not to bring her here or take her any place public. But it didn't take me long to find out you've been screwing the twenty-something blonde you've got shacked up in your Venice townhouse. Cops will figure it out eventually."

This had an impact on Trilling. Blount could almost see the calculations churning in the man's mind as he tried to figure out how much his girlfriend's discovery could hurt.

"It wouldn't matter if the police found out about Jasmine," Trilling said. "It's impossible for them to unravel the money transfers I made. They wouldn't be able to prove anything."

"Unless your girlfriend knows something."

"She doesn't."

"She'll need to convince me of that."

Blount got off the chair, collected the shirt and pants Trilling had left carefully folded on his dresser bureau, and brought them over to him. Trilling stood dumbfounded.

"Get dressed," Blount said. "We're going to visit Ms. Jasmine Hennery."

"At this hour?"

"She'll make time for you. I'm sure of it."

"How would talking with Jasmine help?" Dread showed in Trilling's face as a thought occurred to him. "My God, you're not going to come right out and ask her if she knew about my plans for Marjorie?"

"Don't be an idiot," Blount said. "The three of us will have a friendly chat, maybe over some bourbon. I won't be mentioning your wife, but I'll have a good idea after a half hour whether your girlfriend knows anything or even suspects that you're involved in your wife's death."

"What happens then?"

"If your girlfriend passes my test, she lives; otherwise, she disappears tonight. Free of charge. You won't owe me a dime."

Trilling's eyes opened wide, a stunned look on his face. "What if you think Jasmine knows something and you're wrong?"

"You get yourself another girlfriend. It's not that big a deal. But I'm a pro. I know what I'm doing. I don't make mistakes. Now take your clothes and get dressed."

Trilling did as he was told. He looked scared as he buttoned his shirt. Blount decided it wasn't because his girlfriend knew something, but that he was afraid Blount would err on the side of caution. Maybe the coldhearted bastard had feelings for her after all and wasn't just screwing her because she was a hot piece of ass.

Blount asked, "Did your wife cheat on you?"

Donald Trilling was stepping a leg through his pants, and he gave Blount a distracted look, no doubt deep in thought over what would soon be happening to his girlfriend.

"I've been wondering why your wife had to die the way she did," Blount said.

"How's that your concern?"

"It's not. It's just something I've been thinking about."

"Are you married?"

"I am."

"Then I'm sure you have a good idea already. These bitches know how to make you feel this small." Trilling demonstrated by showing his thumb and index finger held one inch apart. "Nothing's ever good enough, and they make sure to let you know in all these little ways how disappointed they are in you. I hated that bitch." Trilling's expression grew reflective, and he added, "Jasmine is all sweet and niceness now, but I'm sure over time that will change. It could be that you'll be keeping me from ever seeing that side of her."

Trilling finished putting on his pants. Then the idiot turned his back on Blount. The hitman stepped behind him and used the crook of his arm to put him in a choke hold and bent him backward so Trilling would be in too awkward a position to put up any fight. Ten seconds later he was unconscious. For some reason suicides by hanging seemed more authentic when the victim was disrobed, so Blount removed Trilling's pants and shirt, then wrapped the silk sash from the bathrobe twice around Trilling's neck and carried the unconscious man to the closet. He secured the two ends of the sash between the top of the door and the frame so he could leave Trilling hanging. Trilling sputtered awake at the end and clawed vainly at the sash around his neck. Blount could've held his arms and stopped him, but he didn't bother. Suicides did the same. It was a natural reaction. Soon Trilling stopped struggling and his head drooped toward his chest.

Blount had earlier found a footstool in what had been the wife's closet. He got it, placed it under Trilling's limp body, and knocked it over so it would look like the dead man had kicked it out from under him. After that he went downstairs to the study and used letterhead and a fountain pen from the desk to write a suicide note. He had brought along what Trilling had sent to his post office box, and he carefully mimicked Trilling's small, neat print. The gist of the note was that Trilling was tortured by the knowledge that he could've saved his wife from the Nightmare Man if only he had woken up a minute earlier that fateful night, and that he didn't see the point in living any longer without the only woman he'd ever loved. He didn't sign the note. Suicide notes were seldom signed.

There was some truth in what he had told Trilling. He had heard whispers that a homicide detective was showing a sketch of the Nightmare Man to mobbed-up guys. This detective would only be doing that if he suspected Trilling of hiring a contract killer to orchestrate the Nightmare Man murders. Even so, the sketch didn't look like Blount, and even if this detective had been able to get Trilling to talk, the client never knew his name, and Blount had one of those faces that blended into the crowd. In three weeks Blount would be moving to Grand Rapids, Michigan, to start a new life, and if Trilling had lived, it was doubtful he'd be able to cause Blount any trouble.

A contract killer assumes certain risks, and under normal circumstances Blount accepted that, but not with these Nightmare Man murders. These were different. He would do whatever was necessary to make sure his wife and boys never learned of his involvement. But that wasn't why he killed Trilling. He did that because the man deserved to die. Blount might've carried out the assignment, but Trilling was the one who gave birth to the Nightmare Man and unleashed that evil into the world. What kind of man wants his wife murdered like that? Or agrees to have four innocent women butchered in the same manner? Because his wife might've sighed or rolled her eyes one too many times? Blount's only regret was that he had to make Trilling's death look like a suicide; otherwise, he would've gladly brought the Nightmare Man back one more time.

He'd been wearing leather gloves since entering Trilling's home, so prints weren't a concern. He read over the suicide note and was satisfied with it. A minute later he left the house from the same patio door he had entered after picking the lock, and disappeared into the night.

Chapter 39

Los Angeles, the present

"You were right about the guy being a hired gun," Joe Penza said. "A hard case by the name of Ed Blount. He was a freelancer whose home base was in LA, but he did jobs throughout the country."

Morris vaguely remembered the name. Back in 2001 he had looked at photos and mugshots of every suspected hitman, but he didn't remember Blount resembling the 1984 sketch.

"He was arrested for capital murder," Morris said as he pulled that fact from a deeply stored memory. "A contract killing."

"That's right. He was convicted, too."

"You recognized Ed Blount from the sketch?"

"Forget that drawing," Penza said. "The only thing that paper's good for is picking up after your mutt. Ever hear of Vittorio Capotondi?"

"No."

"That figures. He was well before your time." Penza's eyelids lowered and his facial muscles relaxed as he reminisced. "The man was a genius, a true craftsman. He made masks you couldn't tell were masks unless you were right next to the guy wearing it. Blount would've had several made for himself, and he'd be wearing one if he was out doing a hit where he could be seen. So like I said, forget that drawing."

"So let's say the sketch is worthless—"

"Which I'm saying it is."

"Okay, so how'd you know it's Blount?"

Penza sat back heavily in his chair and began rubbing his thick lower lip with his thumb. "This is all off the record."

"Yeah, we agreed to that already."

"I still want you imagining me saying the word hypothetical over and over again so I don't have to keep saying it."

"Agreed."

Penza breathed in deeply, inflating his barrel chest, then letting the air out slowly like a tire that had been punctured. He nodded to himself, as if making up his mind.

"After those *ferkakte* murders happened, my old man heard from a freelancer who was offered a job to kill a rich guy's wife."

Morris said, "The rich guy being Donald Trilling."

"Yeah. This Trilling character had special requirements for how his wife had to be done. Some real sicko stuff that ended with her having a live rat stuffed down her throat. The freelancer turned it down. It was too sick for him to want anything to do with, but when Trilling's wife turned out to be one of the women killed by this so-called Nightmare Man, he put two and two together and figured that someone else took on the job."

"Name of the freelancer?"

"Uh uh. You don't need it and you're not getting it."

"Okay. Forget that. How about you explain why this would matter to your old man or this anonymous freelancer?"

Penza's jaw dropped as if he were incredulous. "You think we're savages?" he asked. Anger flashed in his eyes, and his voice sounded strained as he explained, "There's what's right and what's wrong. You want someone iced, okay, that's your business, but you're going to torture and kill four other women in a sicko way to hide the hit? That's just wrong and can't be tolerated. My old man thought so, and so did I." He crossed his arms over his chest. "It had to be dealt with."

"How'd you figure it was Blount?"

"My old man did some digging. I won't say exactly what he found out, but it pointed to Blount, and it made sense he'd be the guy. I wasn't kidding before what I said about him being a hard case. A guy with ice water instead of blood. When the client, Trilling, was found hung from his closet to make it look like a suicide, we knew for sure it was Blount."

"Why was that?"

Penza smiled. "His signature move."

"So it wasn't just bad luck Blount got picked up for another hit?"

Penza's smile stretched another inch. "Like I said, Blount had to be taken care of, but he wasn't the type of guy you send a couple of boys after. You do that with a guy like him, and there's a better chance your boys get sent back in pieces. Something else had to be done."

"So you framed him."

"Me, personally? Nah. But let's just say Blount must've been surprised when the cops found a gun where they did. Or a shirt buried in the hamper with the target's dried blood on it."

Morris remembered something about Ed Blount from his research in 2001. "He died in prison," he said.

"Yeah, he did," Penza said. "When those murders started up again that second time, I wanted to see if any freelancers got the bright idea to hide a contract in those killings, because my old man was right. Someone willing to do that needs to be permanently shut down. I can guarantee you none of the women killed in 2001 had contracts on them. I hate to be the bearer of bad news, but whoever took over for Blount did so for strictly personal reasons, not business."

Chapter 40

Morris stopped off at an all-night supermarket on the way home. This detour cost him ten minutes, and it was a few minutes after two a.m. when he pulled into his driveway. Parker consented to let out a soft moan but otherwise didn't move. Even when Morris got out of the car and walked around to the passenger side so he could open the door, the bull terrier remained curled up on the seat. Morris studied Parker lying like a lump, as if the bull terrier lacked the energy to move as much as a muscle. Morris sat on his heels to put him closer to eye level with the dog and rubbed Parker's snout. "You look beat," he said.

Parker opened his eyes, but showed no intention of budging.

"Too beat to move, huh?" Morris asked. "I can't blame you. It's been a long day, and tiring, with you racing halfway up a mountain. If you want to sleep here, that's okay with me. It's a shame, though, you'll be missing out on scrambled eggs and bacon."

The word *bacon* did the trick. Parker grunted several times as he pushed himself to his feet and jumped out of the car. Morris got the groceries out of the trunk, and Parker plodded alongside him as they made their way to the front door.

A light was on in the living room. Natalie was waiting up for them, her feet curled under her as she sat on the couch reading a book she had started the other day, an allegorical fable about a man who believed he had to weed a field every day or the world would come to an end. Morris saw that she had his spare .32-caliber pistol on the couch next to her and was glad to see she had taken his warning seriously.

Parker might've been worn out, but he worked up enough energy to scamper over to Natalie, his body squirming and tail wagging as she hugged him around his thick neck. Morris bent over her for a kiss, and to retrieve the gun and drop it in his jacket pocket.

"So is the guy crazy or is he really saving the world each day?" he asked, referring to the book.

"I don't know yet. The author's being awfully cagey about it. I think he's going to make me wait until the last page to find out."

She waved Morris over for a more satisfying kiss than the peck he had given her while she was occupied with Parker, and he complied.

"That's better," she said, her eyes half-closed. "Almost worth staying up for. What's in the grocery bag?"

"It was supposed to be tomorrow's breakfast, but I promised the little guy I'd cook up some bacon and eggs now." The word *bacon* elicited another grunt from Parker, and Morris good-naturedly thumped the dog on the side. "The only way I was getting him out of the car was by bribing him or carrying him, and I didn't feel up to carrying him. You want me to cook you up some?"

"Sounds good."

Natalie joined Morris and Parker in the kitchen. She started a pot of chamomile tea for them while he layered strips of bacon into a frying pan. He would've preferred coffee, but he wasn't going to suggest that at this hour and have Natalie throw a potholder at his head. As it was he planned to be up by six so he'd be at MBI by seven, and if he was lucky he'd catch three hours of sleep. While he kept a watch on the bacon, he told Natalie about what Big Joe Penza had told him.

"Do you believe him?" she asked.

"He wasn't intentionally lying."

"But was he telling the truth?"

Morris said, "Some of it, certainly. My dad was convinced Donald Trilling hired a contract killer for his wife, and what Penza said adds up. Whether he's right about Ed Blount, I don't know. We'll have to look into it and see what we can find."

"Then what?"

A weariness had crept into Morris's eyes. "If Blount invented the Nightmare Man, we'll have to figure out who he told his secret to."

The first batch of bacon had fried to the crispness Morris and Natalie liked, which was fine with Parker since he wasn't picky about how the bacon was cooked so long as he got some. Morris used a spatula to get the bacon out of the pan and onto folded paper towels so the paper would soak up the grease. He poured the grease from the pan into an empty coffee can and started up another batch of bacon. Parker was lying on the floor, too tired to bother mooching, and Natalie looked like she was too absorbed in thinking about what Morris had told her to ask any more questions. For several minutes the only sounds in the kitchen were the refrigerator humming and bacon sizzling. Once the second batch was done, Morris poured out half the remaining bacon grease from the frying pan and used what was left, mixed with a pat of butter, for the scrambled eggs.

"The secret of Chef Morris," Natalie observed.

"It's what makes them so good."

"And so fattening."

Morris said, "You only live once."

The eggs cooked quickly, and Morris spooned portions for himself and Natalie onto plates and put Parker's into his bowl. The bull terrier groaned like an old man as he pushed himself to his feet and plodded over to the late-night snack.

"The little guy's really dragging," Natalie said, smiling wistfully as she watched Parker. "He's chewing his food instead of inhaling it."

"I never thought I'd see that." Morris fought off a yawn and the urge to close his eyes. The day was catching up to him as well. He probably could've had high-octane coffee instead of the herbal tea without it costing him any sleep.

Natalie was looking at him with concern. "You're going to have another busy day tomorrow," she noted.

"I expect so," Morris agreed.

Chapter 41

The moonfaced woman with the mousy brown hair never suspected she was being followed. The freak had waited for her across the street from her apartment building, then shadowed her after she stepped outside. He kept his distance, watching as she hummed to herself, oblivious to the world around her, even to the strangers she passed. Head in the clouds. That's what his dear departed mother would've said. He was being far more careful than he needed to be, and he snickered thinking of how he'd have to poke her in the back before she'd notice him. But he didn't poke her. Instead, he watched as she entered the bakery four blocks from where she lived.

He had brought along field glasses, and he used them to spy inside the bakery and see that she was sitting at a table facing away from the door. She wouldn't see him if he were to go in there, and there wasn't any reason for him not to, especially since a chocolate croissant and cappuccino would really hit the spot right then. He might've been a freak, but he liked the niceties of life. He crossed the street, walked into the bakery, and took a table so he could surreptitiously watch her.

A waitress came over. He could see worry lines creeping around her eyes and mouth, and he knew what must've been on her mind. He wanted to tell her not to worry about the Nightmare Man, that she wasn't going to be one of his victims, but it would've sounded crazy if he had said that. So he smiled sweetly at her, but it was insulting the way she reacted. It was almost as if he had jumped at her and yelled *boo*. Outwardly, he didn't look like a freak. Clean-cut, dressed nicely, some would even say good-looking. But the waitress had somehow seen him for what he really was. Well, that was just too bad. He had tried being nice. No one could say otherwise. He looked away from her and turned his attention to the moonfaced woman he had followed. Rosalyn Krate. The woman who was ordained to be the Nightmare Man's fifth victim.

Rosalyn was sitting alone. That wasn't true two days ago. He had followed her that day to the bakery, but it was later in the morning when she got there and the bakery was already crowded. He didn't think she'd be able to get a table, so he didn't risk venturing inside, thinking there'd be too great a chance she'd see him. Instead he was content with watching her through field glasses. But she had been bold, joining another woman at a table. When he recognized who the woman was, he laughed so hard that it brought tears to his eyes. The audacity of it was really quite remarkable.

The waitress returned with a croissant and cappuccino. She seemed especially anxious when she dropped the food off at his table, as if she were still spooked by his smile, or possibly what she believed she saw inside him. *Women. What are you going to do?*

He took a bite of the croissant. Tasty, yes indeed. It looked like Rosalyn had ordered a bran muffin and coffee. Doubtful she'd be finding her muffin as tasty as the croissant. Really a shame. She should be living it up. It wasn't as if she had that many breakfasts left. By his count, fifteen, assuming she didn't skip any.

The thought struck him that he knew exactly how and when she was going to die. It was mind-blowing in a way. Sure, there were inmates on death row you could say the same about, but some of them would get reprieves, or at least there was a chance the governor of their state would step in and delay the inevitable. And of course, there were those with illnesses or severe injuries whose days, even minutes, were numbered. But this was different. Rosalyn was a healthy, relatively young woman, yet her fate was cast in stone. Late at night on October nineteenth her torture would begin, and sometime in the early hours of October twentieth she would be expiring. After her glorious death, the Nightmare Man would be disappearing once again. Of course, you can't keep a good man down, and in 2035 the Nightmare Man would be returning. New victims would be chosen and the bloody cycle would start all over again.

The thought of it gave him goose bumps.

He glanced at his watch and was disappointed to see it was already time for him to leave. After all, he was a busy freak with things to do and people to see.

Chapter 42

Extra chairs had to be brought into MBI's lone conference room, leaving barely any elbow room around the long, oval-shaped table as the occupants finished up their bagels and cream cheese and drank coffee. While it might've been a tight squeeze, they at least didn't have to worry about a persistent bull terrier mooching from them, since Morris had left Parker with Natalie that morning. He didn't have the heart to drag Parker out of the house, and he figured the dog could benefit from taking it easy and spending a day snoozing by Natalie's feet. Along with MBI's full crew and the four LAPD detectives who'd been assigned to the investigation were Doug Gilman, LA Police Commissioner Martin Hadley, FBI profiler Gloria Finston, and chief medical examiner Roger Smichen.

Hadley glared at his watch and then at Morris. "Why the blazes haven't you started yet?" he demanded.

"Charlie Bogle should be here any minute."

Hadley didn't look happy about being kept waiting. He grumbled, "I thought he quit this Mickey Mouse company."

"I told you we should've named ourselves MMC," Polk said.

That got a laugh out of Lemmon and caused Hadley to stare bullets both his and Polk's way. Morris had to bite his tongue to keep from joining in. He winked at Annie Walsh when he caught her doing the same.

"Charlie's been helping with the investigation," Morris explained as he drew Hadley's glare back to himself. "We spoke this morning, and he wants to see this through to its conclusion. We're lucky to have him joining us."

"I wholeheartedly agree," Gloria Finston said, her thin lips pressing into a tiny v smile. "Even if we're kept waiting another minute or two."

Finston had worked with MBI on their last two serial killer investigations. A small, dark-haired woman in her forties. Morris liked her and respected her abilities and insight.

There was a rap on the door. Without waiting for an invitation, Bogle walked in and closed the door behind him. He scanned the room, exchanged quick nods with Morris, Polk, and Lemmon, then took the empty chair left near the door.

"Sorry, no room at the big boys' table," Polk remarked.

"I'll survive," Bogle said.

Hadley was rapidly losing patience. "Are you clowns done yet? For Chrissakes, we've got a madman out there!"

Morris was going on three hours of sleep. That morning he woke up at five thirty, skipped showering and shaving, and headed straight to MBI where he'd been since ten past six so he could learn what he could about Ed Blount and prepare for the meeting. Lemmon, Polk, and Felger had all been in the office since seven doing the same. He swallowed back the crack he wanted to make about how nice it was that Hadley finally understood the urgency of the situation, and instead asked Felger to get things started. As good as it might've felt to tell Hadley off, it wouldn't have done him any good.

Felger did whatever magic he needed to project the screen from his laptop onto a blank wall. On the same wall was a map of Los Angeles County in which the locations of the Nightmare Man murders had been marked off with colored thumbtacks—blue for 1984, red for 2001, and a lone yellow tack for Lori Fletcher's West Hollywood address. Morris waited for several of the participants to move their chairs so they could see Ed Blount's mugshot photo from 1984 before telling them what Big Joe Penza had told him last night. He had expected resistance from Hadley and was surprised that the police commissioner sat quietly rubbing his jaw, his thick lips pulled into a scowl.

Morris told them Blount had died in prison in 1992.

Walsh asked, "Of what?"

"Liver cancer."

"You really think he was the Nightmare Man back in 1984?" Gilman asked.

"I don't know," Morris admitted. "What Joe Penza said only makes sense if Donald Trilling hired a contract killer to murder his wife, and the only way that makes sense is if this same killer invented the Nightmare Man to hide Marjorie Trilling's murder among the other victims. I trust that Penza believes it was Ed Blount, and I'd like to attack this in two ways: see if we can tie Blount to the 1984 murders, and at the same time find out who he trained to be the next Nightmare Man."

Gilman looked confused, his brow deeply furrowed. He asked, "Why would he do that?"

"He could've been bragging," Bogle offered.

"Or he could've been a fucked-in-the-head psycho who wanted to see his work continue," Walsh said angrily.

"Both are of course possibilities," Finston acknowledged, her small dark eyes contemplative as she rubbed her nearly nonexistent chin with a bone-thin thumb. "He could've also been unburdening himself. Liver cancer is an especially painful way to die, and even a coldblooded contract killer could've grown remorseful over taking on such a cruel job. Assuming he turns out to be the first Nightmare Man."

"I hope this bastard died a rotten, miserable death," Walsh said. "Assuming he was the Nightmare Man."

Morris asked Felger to move to the next screen, which showed the relevant information they'd been able to find about Blount: where he had lived in Irvine, the name of the auto repair garage he supposedly had worked at as a mechanic, and details about his capital murder arrest and conviction. Morris waited until everyone had a chance to absorb what was on the screen, then signaled Felger to move to the next one, which showed names and addresses for three men named Blount. Two of them were within an hour of Los Angeles; the third lived in Ohio.

"Blount had three sons," Morris explained. "Fred, Polk, Annie, each of you take one and see what you can get out of them."

Fred piped in, "Dibs on the one in Irvine."

"I'll take Anaheim," Walsh said.

"Which leaves me Toledo," Polk said. "That's fine with me. I hear it's beautiful this time of year."

"That's only because you need your hearing checked," Fred said with a straight face. Then to Morris, "Do we let them know this is about the Nightmare Man?"

"You won't have a choice. You'll need to show them the 1984 sketch. If Blount was using a mask like Penza thinks, one of them could've seen it. Maybe one of them also saw their dad collecting rats. Since you're going to Irvine, talk to the owner of the garage where he worked and drop by his old home. The current owner bought it from his wife, since deceased. Maybe they found something in it."

"What about the rest of us?" Greg Malevich asked, referring also to the other two LAPD detectives at the meeting, Ray Vestra and Franklin Strong.

"The warden at the state prison in Ashfield will be sending over prisoner records for anyone who could've had contact with Blount and was released before October 2001. I need you to get Gloria their police files, and she'll be doing triage on them. I'd like you, Ray, and Franklin to investigate them, tackling first the ones Gloria thinks are most likely to be our new Nightmare Man. The rest of us will join you as we free up."

Hadley asked bluntly in a tone implying Morris planned to be loafing, "Handing out all the heavy lifting, eh, Brick? What about yourself?"

Morris understood Hadley, which didn't necessarily make his petulance any easier to take. He had a guilty conscience about stopping Morris from more aggressively pursuing the hitman angle back in 2001, and he was trying to hide it under bluster. Showing far more patience than Hadley deserved, he explained that the warden who was on the job back in '92 had since retired but was still living in Ashfield. "Charlie and I will be driving up to the prison to pick up Blount's records, and while we're up there we'll be talking with the former warden. If you want, you can join us."

Hadley's round, jowly face reddened with indignation. He cleared his throat, then announced that he had more important things to do.

Morris was done giving Hadley any benefit of the doubt. He ignored him to turn to the ME. "Roger, your findings?"

Smichen had been sitting quietly until then, looking almost as if he were meditating. A tall and bony version of Buddha. He consulted his notes.

"From the victim's blood loss and the amount of clotting that had occurred, I was able to determine that her injuries were sustained over a one- to two-hour period and, as with past victims, elevated liver enzymes were found. In other words, she was tortured for up to two hours, and the killer used smelling salts to keep her conscious. The only differences I was able to find between this murder and the others were what I'd already mentioned to you, namely the rat was more gently prodded into her throat and her mouth was sewn shut afterward with a common household thread sold at dozens of stores in the Los Angeles area. Death was from asphyxiation caused by a foreign object blocking her air passage. The same as with the other victims."

Polk said, "The foreign object being a rat."

Smichen gave him a sideways glance. "I thought that would be obvious."

"It was," Morris agreed. "Roger, could you examine the 1984 and 2001 medical examiner reports, see if you can find any indications that different perpetrators committed the murders?"

"To support your theory that a new Nightmare Man took over in 2001?"

"Exactly."

"Will do," the ME said.

Morris was planning to give a speech about how they were up against a ticking clock. That unless they stopped this maniac, he would be brutally killing four more women over the next sixteen days. As he looked at how tightly wound everyone appeared to be—even Polk—he realized a pep talk wasn't necessary. Far from it. Everyone in the room, even Hadley, was chomping at the bit to see this psycho caught.

"All right, then," he said.

Chapter 43

Joplin Cole found the guy on the elliptical machine next to her creepy. She was thirty-five minutes into her program when she spotted him walking into the gym. At first glance he appeared normal enough, and there were likely women who'd find him attractive. Short blond hair, bronze tan, blue eyes, a gymnast body. But something about him gave her the shivers. She at first tried to be kind about it, blaming it on how anxious she'd been feeling over the last few weeks, but then he made a beeline toward the neighboring elliptical machine, and since then her internal creep meter had been buzzing off the charts. She only had another six minutes to go or she would've moved to another machine.

He asked her, "Do you come here often?"

She kept her stare focused straight ahead and forced out between breaths, "Not...interested."

The machine had her working hard, the speed ratcheting up so that she was pumping her legs at a four-minute-mile pace and a steep incline level. The last thing she wanted was to deal with this creep, and she wished he'd take the hint and find a different machine, or at the very least, leave her alone. But it didn't seem like that would be the case, and before too long she could feel his presence once again intruding on her.

"I wasn't hitting on you," he said, as if he were insulted. "I was only trying to be friendly."

Joplin was nearing the home stretch and only had four minutes and twenty seconds to go. *Just ignore the creep,* she thought. Except it was easier said than done. She could see enough out of her peripheral vision to know he was still watching her, and there was something darkly oppressive about it, almost as if she could feel the weight of it pressing against her chest.

A minute went by in which she tried to focus only on her breathing and the burning in her leg and chest muscles. *You can do it. The rest of the world doesn't exist right now. Mr. Creepy doesn't exist. It's just you and the machine. Three minutes to go. You can do it—*

"My name's Dale."

Joplin looked over to see him smiling as he held out his hand to her, actually expecting her to take it. There was something about the look in his eyes and the unnaturalness of his smile that made her feel like she was an insect he was studying under a piece of glass. She abruptly stopped her machine and jumped off, moving fast to get away from him.

"Wow, the rudeness of some people."

She turned back to see the condescending look he gave her as if she were the one who had something wrong with her. She almost headed back to him so she could tell him off, but a cruelty shining in his eyes stopped her. The guy was more than just a creep. There was something dangerous about him. She was sure of it.

She continued on to the front desk and told the woman working there that she wanted to complain about one of the other gym members. "Mr. Creepy on elliptical number eighteen wouldn't stop harassing me."

"What exactly did he do?"

Joplin stood tongue-tied as she thought about what the guy had actually done. He introduced himself and told her his name. He held out his hand to her. He complained that she had been rude. Such unpardonable crimes. But she wasn't crazy. She knew what she had recognized in his expression, and she trusted the vibe she picked up. Still, she'd sound unhinged if she made those complaints out loud.

Blushing with embarrassment, she said, "He wouldn't take no for an answer."

The woman laughed, and her voice was soft and oddly sensual as she said, "I don't think there are many guys here who'd willingly take no from you. Not too many gals either. You're gorgeous."

Joplin's blush deepened. The woman was in her early thirties, maybe six or seven years older than herself. She vaguely remembered seeing her on other occasions at the front desk but had never really paid attention to her before. Now that she was, what she thought had been a plain, unremarkable face with a slightly upturned nose was actually quite pretty, especially with the sly smile she was showing.

She held out her hand. "Joplin," she said.

"Rosalyn."

The woman's smile grew bold as they shook hands, and calling it a handshake wouldn't do it justice. There was some heavy duty flirting going on, no question about it. Joplin had never been interested in a sexual relationship with a woman before, but it wasn't as if she'd been having such great luck with guys. She'd broken up with her last boyfriend a month ago when she caught the jerk in bed with a coworker he used to insist was a platonic friend and nothing more. God, she'd been so blind. She'd wasted two years with the jerk, and almost three years with the guy before him, and that one turned out to be an even bigger jerk. Maybe it wouldn't be the worst thing in the world to try something different. There was something appealing about Rosalyn. A delicateness. And it would be nice to have company while this crazy Nightmare Man stuff was going on. Maybe she'd sleep better.

She'd give it a night to think about. If she was feeling this way tomorrow morning, she'd come back to the gym, and she and Rosalyn could continue their flirting.

"It was wonderful meeting you, Rosalyn."

"Joplin is such an interesting name," Rosalyn said with a curious smile. "Were your parents from Missouri?"

Joplin rolled her eyes, because she had told this story too many times during her twenty-six years. "No, they were fans of Janis Joplin, and I guess they figured it would be hipper to name me Joplin than Janis."

"It suits you. I so much enjoyed meeting you also and hope to see you again, the sooner the better."

"Me too."

Chapter 44

Charlie Bogle told Morris to put away his car keys, that he'd drive them to Ashfield. Morris fished inside his pants pocket for a quarter so they could flip for it, but when he found himself too bleary-eyed to make out whether it was heads or tails, he asked Bogle how much sleep he'd gotten the night before.

"A good six hours. I feel as fresh as a daisy."

"That's double what I got. Must be nice working for a big movie studio and living the soft life."

Bogle got a chuckle from that. "So I'm driving."

"Looks that way."

They piled into Bogle's car, and once they were underway Morris asked how his boss at Starlight Pictures took it when he asked for a leave of absence to work on this investigation.

"Not thrilled, but he understood."

"Did Benjamin Chandler show up on set?"

"He did. I dropped by at eight to check on him. A little bruised, but he seemed to be doing okay."

"No complaints about Parker knocking him down?"

"You're worried about being sued?"

"A little," Morris admitted.

"Don't be. If anything, I think he's embarrassed by the incident. It wouldn't help his macho image if word of that got out." Bogle scratched lazily at his jaw, his eyes taking on a faraway look as if he were deep in thought. "I didn't know you'd trained Parker to do something like that."

"I didn't. To be honest I wasn't sure what he would do. The little guy probably thought he was playing a game."

"He sure rocketed up that mountain path," Bogle said, chuckling under his breath. "I'm not saying Parker's a lightweight, but the only reason he knocked Chandler down was because he was in a panic. Chandler, not Parker."

"Probably true."

Morris lowered the back of his seat, closed his eyes, and soon drifted off. His ringing phone woke him. He worked the phone out of his pocket and saw it was Gloria Finston.

"Ashfield State Prison sent over a list of inmates who were released by October 2001 and whose incarcerations overlapped with Blount's," she said. "Three hundred and seventeen names. We'll start collecting their police records and see where their residences were when the 2001 murders took place, but I'd like to focus on the ones who had contact with Blount after he was diagnosed with cancer."

"Sounds like a smart plan."

"Morris, did I wake you? Your voice sounds froggy."

"I was dozing."

"I apologize. You looked tired at the meeting. I should've waited to call you, but when you get Blount's prison records, please call me back with the date of his cancer diagnosis."

Morris checked his watch. They'd only been on the road twenty minutes and still had almost two more hours of driving before they'd be in Ashfield.

"I'll call the warden now and see if he can get you that date."

"Also check whether he was housed in a different section of the prison once he became ill. It would be helpful to get a list of prisoners who had exposure to him at that time. It's possible he confided in another prisoner who repeated the story to someone else."

He had already thought of that scenario and quickly dismissed it from his mind. If that was what had happened—Blount telling his secrets to another prisoner only to have that person tell it to someone else in a demented version of the telephone game, the odds were that the Nightmare Man's grisly formula would've been altered during the retelling. More importantly, the number of people they'd have to investigate would explode exponentially, and they wouldn't have a prayer of catching the Nightmare Man in this way. It made sense to focus the investigation in a way that gave them a chance of catching the killer. Still, it would help getting that second list, and he promised Finston he'd work on it.

Finston's voice lowered as she said, "You realize, Morris, you're betting the farm that what Mr. Penza told you is true. Even if he's right that Donald

Trilling hired a contract killer, he could be wrong about Ed Blount being the one hired."

"It's a gamble," Morris acknowledged, "but it's all we got until we find a witness. Anyway, a bet with fifty percent odds is at least even money."

"Those are the odds you're giving on Mr. Penza's information panning out?"

"Pretty much."

"It's a good thing I'm not a betting person," Finston said. "I'm not sure I'd be willing to take those odds."

Morris had put the phone on speaker so Bogle could listen in, and after he got off the call, Bogle commented that the FBI profiler was being a Debbie Downer.

"More like the voice of reason," Morris said.

He closed his eyes, hoping to doze off again.

Chapter 45

Lemmon found George Blount working at a plumbing supply store in Irvine. Blount had been twelve years old when his dad was arrested, and at forty-six he looked like a scrawnier version of the senior Blount's mugshot photo.

Lemmon had talked to Blount earlier on the phone, so his arrival wasn't a surprise. "We should talk someplace private," he suggested. "My car is probably as good a place as any."

Blount looked like he had questions he was eager to ask, but he held back, and after talking with his supervisor, followed Lemmon to the parking lot where Lemmon had left his car. Before arriving at the plumbing supply store, Lemmon had stopped at a doughnut shop, and he offered Blount coffee and a doughnut. Blount accepted the coffee but turned down the doughnut.

"I'm confused," Blount said. "On the phone you said this is about a murder investigation?"

Lemmon had a mouthful of chocolate glazed, so all he could do was nod as a couple of crumbs tumbled out of his mouth. *Unbelievable, I'm becoming Polk!*

"How would that be possible? My dad died in prison in 1992. Is this about his conviction? Is the case being reopened?"

Lemmon held a finger up while he took a sip of coffee to wash down the doughnut. He wiped a hand across his mouth to brush away any further crumbs. *If Polk only knew!*

"No, these are for different murders."

"Murders, as in plural?"

"Yeah."

Blount looked crushed at that news. "Oh dear lord," he moaned.

"This shouldn't be much of a surprise," Lemmon said. "You knew your dad was a hitman."

Blount had put down his coffee so he could hold his head in his hands. "I knew he was convicted of murdering a lowlife pimp. That's all I knew."

The lowlife pimp Blount referred to had been the owner of a mobbed-up Hollywood massage parlor, and if Penza was right then Ed Blount had been framed for the murder, but it would've only confused the issue to mention that to the younger Blount.

"You never suspected your dad before his arrest?"

Blount lifted his head, his face showing a washed-out look. "I don't know what I suspected," he said. "Before my dad was arrested, we were planning to move to Michigan. Did you know that?"

"No, I didn't."

"Grand Rapids. My dad was buying his own business, and then that arrest had to happen."

"He'd recently come into a lot of money?"

That thought apparently stunned Blount. "I don't know," he said.

"How was your family financially after your dad went to prison?"

"We did okay." Blount's eyes took on a distant look as he must've been going back decades in his mind. "My mom worked, and my dad had saved some money. When he died there must've been life insurance, because there was money for us to go to college."

Blount didn't look too sure about this, perhaps wondering for the first time where the money had come from. The senior Blount would've charged a large sum to create the Nightmare Man, and that would explain a family-saving windfall, probably from an offshore account that Blount had told his wife about. None of this was definitive proof, but it added up.

Lemmon asked, "Is there anything that you can look back on now that makes you think your dad worked as a contract killer?"

Blount shook his head, but a shadow fell over his eyes, and that told Lemmon there was something.

"What was it?" he demanded.

"Nothing really." Blount tried smiling at Lemmon, but it didn't stick. "I was thinking of my dad's workshop," he said. "This was a room he had set up in the basement. It had a separate entrance, and he always kept it padlocked. Nobody but him was allowed inside. Not me, my brothers, or my mom. It was off-limits, and there would've been hell to pay if any of us ever went in there. I hadn't thought about that room in years."

"You ever sneak in there?"

"I didn't have the guts," Blount admitted.

"How about later when your dad was in custody?"

"The police had a warrant to search our home. I remember them cutting off the padlock. The next day I looked inside and saw the workshop was empty." He managed a dismal smile. "I told you we were planning to move to Michigan. My dad had already cleaned it out."

Suspicious behavior for being a hitman, but again, not definitive proof that the senior Blount had been the Nightmare Man.

"Ever see your dad bringing rats into the workshop?"

"What?"

"Live rats. In cages."

"No, of course not."

There was that shadow again.

"What aren't you telling me?"

"Nothing, really," Blount said. "My younger brother Jack was the baby of the family. A hell-raiser, and a defiant little bugger. The type who if you warn him not to do something, he'll break his neck trying to do it. He bragged once about breaking into our dad's workshop. I thought he was making it up."

"He saw caged rats?"

"I don't know. I have this vague memory about him saying something about rats, but I can't tell you what it was. Or even if I only dreamt it." He gave Lemmon an imploring look. "What's this all about?"

Lemmon said, "It's better that I don't tell you in case we're wrong."

Blount's expression became something brittle, almost as if he had guessed it was about the Nightmare Man.

"Could you be wrong?" he asked.

"I don't think so."

Chapter 46

Jamie Siegel smiled wickedly. She leaned forward and said, "There's a guy eyeballing you like you wouldn't believe."

Jamie was Joplin's best friend at work. The J&J twins, as their supervisor liked to call them, on that day had decided to walk to a bistro four blocks from the office. The place had a golden beet salad to die for, and Joplin had been jonesing for it all morning.

"Is he worth a look?" Joplin asked.

She was still thinking about Rosalyn. The idea of having a fling with the pretty and petite woman from the gym was both exciting and off-putting. There was definitely an attraction, and she hadn't closed the door on the possibility, but she hadn't decided yet to open that door all the way either so she could step through it. If there was a hot guy showing heavy interest, why not consider it?

"He might be," Jamie said. "Thirties, blond, preppy. Looks like he's in shape." She giggled. "He could give you a good cardio workout."

A sickening feeling overwhelmed Joplin. Was it possible the creep had followed her to work and now to the bistro?

Jamie gave her a concerned look. She reached across the table and touched her hand. "It's just some dude licking his chops. Come on, Joplin, what's there to get so upset about?"

She sat paralyzed, as if any movement, especially looking behind her, would be impossible. Then a hot white anger flashed within her, directed equally at herself and at the man who might be the creep. It pissed her off that she'd give anyone that kind of power over her.

She was barely aware of looking over her shoulder and seeing that it was in fact the creep from this morning. The next thing she knew, she was on her feet and storming over to where the creep named *Dale* was sitting.

"Oh, hi," he said, a grin breaking over his face as if they were actually friends. "So it is you."

"You're stalking me," she accused.

He made a face, as if he couldn't understand why she'd say that. "What? No, of course not." The bastard winked at her. "I was minding my own business when I quite innocently spotted you, or at least someone who I thought might be the same infuriatingly rude but foxy-as-hell babe from the gym. Sweetheart, that's all that happened."

"I know what you did," she said, her voice sounding strange to her own ears, as if it were coming from someone else. "I know you followed me here so you could spy on me. I know you're nothing more than a creep who gets his jollies trying to frighten women like me."

"You're so wrong," he said. "I was looking your way only because I was trying to figure out if you were really the same person from before. I thought if you were it would be kismet, like maybe we were meant to be." He frowned at that. "It turns out I couldn't have been more wrong."

Her eyes narrowed as she stared at him. The bastard was actually trying to act as if he were the aggrieved party. Without realizing it, her hands had clenched into tight fists, her knuckles bone white.

"You leave here now or I'll scream," she said.

"Sweetheart, you need help."

"Don't test me."

He looked away from her, trying to act as if she wasn't there.

"Leave me alone, you creep!" she screamed as loudly as she could.

That surprised the creep named Dale, and he appeared startled, as if that was the last thing he expected her to do. She felt immense satisfaction from his reaction. Then his expression changed, becoming something savage. His true self showing through. It only lasted a heartbeat, if even that long, but it caused Joplin to stumble several steps back from the table.

He was quickly on his feet, his wallet out. He flung a couple of twenties onto the table, then he was moving fast toward Joplin. She would've screamed again, except she was too frightened. He didn't come at her to strike her, but so he could lean in and whisper something into her ear. After that he was rushing past her and out of the restaurant.

Oh my God. Did that really just happen?

The waitress and Jamie hurried over to Joplin. Her friend took hold of her hand.

"Sweetie, you're as cold as ice. Are you okay?"

She struggled to fight back tears. What the creep had whispered left her shaking.

Chapter 47

Bill Schofield invited Morris and Bogle to join him for lunch. "I can make you boys ham and cheese sandwiches and coffee. How's that sound?"

"Sounds awfully good," Morris said.

"Much appreciated," Bogle added.

Schofield, who had been the warden at Ashfield State Prison during the time Ed Blount was incarcerated, was in his early seventies. A tall, lean man, he had gray hair, a matching bushy mustache that mostly hid his mouth, and even bushier eyebrows. He looked pretty much the way Morris would envision the sheriff of this dusty town a hundred years ago.

They followed Schofield through his modest ranch-style home. The rooms were clean and neat and filled with pictures of Schofield's family throughout the years, including a growing brood of grandkids.

He brought them into a 1970s kitchen with a faded yellow Formica countertop and what looked like its original appliances and cabinets. The former warden ordered Morris and Bogle to sit at the kitchen table while he prepared lunch.

"The missus is babysitting my youngest girl's little ones, so we got the house to ourselves." He peered out the kitchen window toward the backyard. "I figured it's a nice day, so we'll take lunch on the patio. Assuming you boys don't mind some fresh air."

"If you didn't offer, I would've asked," Bogle said.

Morris voiced a similar sentiment. He nodded toward a photo of a brindle-colored bull terrier attached by a magnet to the refrigerator. He'd already noticed the dog bed in the den and the water and food bowls in the kitchen so he knew the answer, but he asked anyway, "The bull terrier in the photo—is she yours?"

"Yep," Schofield said. "That's Queenie. She can be a handful with company, so I asked Mary to take her, which she would've done anyway. The grandkids adore the dog." He gave Morris an appraising look. "Most people confuse her with a pit bull."

"I'm a member of the club," Morris said. He worked his phone out of his pocket, fiddled with it, and brought up a picture of Parker. Schofield came over to get a look. Morris handed him the phone.

"A fine looking fella," he said.

"That he is," Morris agreed.

Schofield handed the phone back and left to make the sandwiches. Somehow it seemed right when the former warden dug a loaf of white bread, American cheese, and a package of Oscar Mayer ham from his refrigerator. When he took out a jar of mayonnaise, Morris cleared his throat and asked if he could have mustard on his sandwich instead. Schofield gave him a disapproving look and muttered something under his breath, but most likely because Morris was a fellow bull terrier owner, he was willing to comply with the request.

"I got plain yellow," he grumbled. "No Dijon or nothing fancy like that."

"I wouldn't want anything else," Morris said.

That put Morris back in Schofield's good graces. He raised an eyebrow at Bogle, who told him mayonnaise would be just fine. Once the food was ready and they were sitting on the patio, Schofield asked what their visit was all about.

Morris said, "As I told you on the phone, we're investigating an active murder case that we believe is connected to one of your past inmates."

"You see, that's what got me curious." Schofield might've been smiling from the way the skin crinkled around his eyes, but it was hard to know for sure without being able to see the corners of his mouth. "I retired as warden in 2006, and that's had me wondering all morning how there's anything I could tell you that's worth a whit. Or are you here just grasping at straws?"

"We're doing a bit of that too," Morris admitted. He liked Schofield, and not just because of his choice in dogs. He recognized him as a straight shooter and saw no reason not to level with him. "We think one of your former prisoners might've committed the Nightmare Man murders back in 1984."

Schofield was slowly and methodically chewing a bite of his sandwich when Morris said that, and if it had any effect on him he didn't show it.

"There was another one just the other day," the retired warden said once he was done with the bite of food. "First one in a whole lot of years if I remember right. A young gal. Very pretty from the photo they showed on the news. You think this former inmate is involved in this poor gal's death?"

"Indirectly. He died in your facility in '92. The theory we're working on is he passed along his secrets to another prisoner, and this is the one who's continuing the killings."

"The inmate's name?"

"Ed Blount."

"I remember him," Schofield said. "Vaguely, but still remarkable given how many thousands of inmates have passed through Ashfield during my time as warden. A wolf in human skin. That was my impression. I don't think I could say anything more about him." He took another bite of his sandwich and chewed it thoroughly before asking, "How sure are you about this?"

"Everything we've got is circumstantial," Morris said. "But there's a lot of it, and more keeps dripping in."

He wasn't kidding about the last part. He'd already spoken to Lemmon and Walsh, and they both told him the same stories about Blount's padlocked workshop. Lemmon had found that Blount's former home had been torn down and a new house stood in its place, and the garage the hitman worked at had long since been sold, so there was nothing more to get there, but Polk was on a flight to Cleveland and would be driving into Toledo by five o'clock Los Angeles time so he could talk to the youngest of Blount's sons. Morris was hoping that the *hell-raiser*, Jack Blount, had once snuck into his dad's workshop like his two brothers believed, and that he'd be able to give them something to definitively prove Ed Blount was the first Nightmare Man. If not this still seemed like their best course of investigation, at least until a witness came forward or something else broke.

Schofield lay his half-eaten sandwich back onto his plate. "How about we get down to business then?"

Morris said, "On the way here we stopped at the prison to get a copy of Blount's records." He picked up the briefcase he'd brought along and pulled out a manila folder filled with freshly photocopied pages. "I was surprised to see that there's no mention of him being diagnosed with cancer."

Morris handed the folder over to Schofield. The former warden frowned as he flipped through the pages. His frown deepened as he found the page he was looking for.

"That's because his cancer was discovered during the autopsy," he said. "It happens sometimes. These inmates all have different pain tolerances, and if they don't complain about there being a problem, whatever's making them sick is not going to be found." He read further through the autopsy report. "Says here his weight at the time of his death was a hundred and thirty-two pounds. My memory was of a much bigger, stockier man. A guard should've noticed the weight loss and reported it, but again, these things slip through."

"There was no toxicology report," Bogle pointed out.

"There wouldn't have been," Schofield said. "Not once the coroner found his body ravaged by cancer."

Morris asked, "How prevalent was heroin in Ashfield back in '92?"

"It was there, just like all other prisons," Schofield said. "Some things you just can't keep out, no matter how hard you try." He was holding the report nearly an arm's length away, squinting at it. "There's nothing mentioned about drug paraphernalia being found by the body. You thinking he might've checked out intentionally?"

"The guy's serving life without parole and has to know he's dying of cancer. It seems like a reasonable possibility."

"How would it help you to know that?"

"I'm just trying to get a complete picture. But if he was using, I'd like to know who sold him the stuff."

Schofield let out a low whistle. "We're talking about what might've happened more than twenty-five years ago," he said. "That's an awfully tall order."

"It might be, but if you can give me names of prison guards who would've known who was dealing back then, it would be a help. You never know what memories might shake loose. I'd also like names of guards who would've paid attention to whom Blount spent time with, especially during his last year."

The skin once again crinkled near Schofield's eyes, suggesting that there was a smile being hidden by his mustache.

"I was right before about you coming here grasping for straws," he said. "But I'll give it some thought, maybe make some phone calls, and see what names I can get for you."

Morris had finished his sandwich and coffee. Bogle also. Morris stood and offered Schofield his hand.

"That's all I can ask for," he said. "And at this point, any straw you can hand me, no matter how flimsy, is better than what I've got."

* * * *

Morris talked with Gloria Finston during the drive back to Los Angeles. Thanks to deaths, hospitalizations, recidivism, and relocations to other countries, both voluntary and forced, they'd been able to narrow the list of ex-inmates to eighty-seven, of which only twenty-four were still in circulation.

"You've been busy," Morris said.

"We have been," Gloria agreed. "As it turns out, all twenty-four of these ex-convicts were released after Blount's death, so knowing the date of his cancer diagnosis wouldn't have helped."

"Any of these twenty-four stand out as more likely than the others?"

"Not at this time," she said. "They were all sentenced for violent crimes. I've done a cursory look at their police records, and they all have some level of sociopathic tendencies. Seven of them were at one time charged with sexual assault, and those are the ones I'm directing Greg, Ray, and Franklin to focus on first."

"Sounds like a good plan." Morris grew silent as he stared out the window. They were twenty minutes outside of Ashfield, and his mind drifted as he looked out over the terrain. For miles all he could see were small trees planted in rows. They must've been fruit trees of some kind, but they seemed too small for orange trees, and it must've been the wrong season for fruit to be growing. He shook himself out of his daydreaming. "Let's assume I'm right about Blount. Is there anything special about the pathology of whoever took over for him?"

"The new killer would be a sadist," the FBI profiler said. "Also an opportunist. Other than that, it's hard to say."

After he got off the phone with Finston, he called Margot Denoir, host of the hugely popular Los Angeles morning show *The Hollywood Peeper*. She'd earlier left eight messages with him, and she picked up his call before the first ring finished.

Morris said, "You're supposed to let it ring a few times so you don't appear too desperate."

She laughed at that. "What's the point of that, darling? You'd see right through me. Besides, it's a waste to play hard to get when the other party knows that it will take all of two seconds to get your panties off."

"When you're right, you're right," he agreed. "How'd you like to get me on the air tonight at eight for a special edition of *The Hollywood Peeper*?"

"Is this in regard to the Nightmare Man?"

"What else?"

"A scoop?"

"Of course."

"I'll see what I can do," she said. "Give me fifteen minutes before you call anyone else. Promise?"

"You got it."

Margot didn't need fifteen minutes. She called back six minutes later sounding breathless.

"Darling, you wouldn't believe the hoops the bean counters here made me jump through," she said. "But it's all arranged. Be at the studio by seven thirty. And please do bring your delightful dog. Our switchboard lit up like you wouldn't believe when you had him with you last time."

"As long as you don't call him delightful to his face. I don't want Parker getting a swelled head."

"Deal."

Morris got off the phone with Margot, and Bogle, showing a smart-alecky smile, asked, "What's this about your dog being delightful?"

"Never mind," Morris said.

"Must be some Hollywood thing," Bogle said. "I can't imagine Bill Schofield calling his bull terrier, or any dog, delightful."

"Neither can I."

"Your good buddy Stonehedge, on the other hand…?"

Morris gave Bogle a sideways glance to see his deadpan expression. "Hard to say."

Later, when they were a half hour from Los Angeles, Morris got a call from Roger Smichen.

"I did find a difference between the 1984 and 2001 murders," Smichen said. "The 2001 victims had higher elevated levels of liver enzymes."

"He used more smelling salts on them."

"Yes, exactly. Neither the 1984 or 2001 coroner reports provide the level of clotting, so it's very possible that the 2001 murders took longer to carry out. It's also possible that the killer was more intent on keeping his victims awake, and because of that used more ammonium carbonate. It's also possible that the 1984 killer was more skilled in administering it, so was able to use less for the same effect. Whichever it turns out to be, it's a strong indication that different individuals performed the 1984 and 2001 murders."

"Okay, thanks, Roger."

"You might want to hold off thanking me just yet. Ms. Fletcher's murder shows a similar level of elevated liver enzymes as the 1984 victims."

Morris groaned at what that implied. Yet a third Nightmare Man.

"The killer could simply be refining his technique from 2001," Morris offered. "There were other changes that were obviously deliberate. The sewn lips. The way the rat was left."

"It's possible," Smichen admitted.

He had put the call on speaker so Bogle could listen in. After he ended the call, Bogle asked, "We got someone new taking over this year?"

Morris hoped that wasn't the case. It was going to be hard enough tracking down a second Nightmare Man without having to worry about a third. He felt exhausted right then as if the weariness hit him like his namesake, a ton of bricks. It soon became a struggle to keep his eyes open, but napping now wouldn't do any good, and would only leave him groggier when he had to wake up in twenty minutes. What he needed was coffee, maybe a full pot, or better yet, have Bogle find a Starbucks so they could hook him up to an IV, the higher the octane the better. Especially since he knew tonight was going to be another long one. If he was lucky, he'd be home by one.

"Hell if I know," Morris admitted.

Chapter 48

"You send me to Toledo and what do I do?"

Morris was distracted from his phone conversation with Polk by the cameraman signaling that they would be live in three minutes. Margot Denoir had swapped out the easy chair on the set for a loveseat so that he and Parker could sit on it together instead of Parker lying on the floor like last time. The bull terrier was blissfully gnawing on a rawhide bone while Morris listened to Polk and Margot looked on with heightened expectation. Nobody was better at smelling sensational ratings than Margot.

"I've got less than three minutes," Morris told Polk. "Whatever you got, tell me it quickly."

"I delivered, that's what I did," Polk said, sounding disappointed that he couldn't play out his news more dramatically. "If Jack Blount was once a hell-raiser, he isn't anymore. Now he's an accountant. Kind of a milquetoast at present if you ask me."

"Speed it up," Morris said. "I'm going live with Margot Denoir in two and a half minutes."

"Okay, okay. Take all the fun out of it for me, why don't you? A long story short, he never broke into his old man's workshop like his brothers thought. What he did was hide in the bushes when his old man cleaned out the workshop, and after his old man left some boxes in the car and headed back for more, the younger Blount rummaged through them, saw what he thought were metal cage traps for catching rats, and also found a certain mask that he salvaged and kept all these years. And I got it now."

"The mask looks like the '84 police sketch?"

"Exactly like it."

"Jesus," Morris said.

"Yeah, I know."

"Text me a photo."

"You got it, boss."

"Sounds like something big," Margot said after Morris got off the phone.

Morris told her that was an understatement. When the text came in, he saw Polk had been right. It had to be the mask Ed Blount wore when a witness saw him leaving Denise Lowenstein's apartment building.

"I'm forwarding you a photo," Morris said. "We'll need to get this on the air."

The cameraman was counting down from ten. Margot must've arranged with her assistant to wait until the count reached three before rushing onto the set, distracting Parker with a treat, and grabbing the rawhide bone. God only knew why. Maybe Margot thought Parker would look more photogenic lying on the loveseat without the bone, but if Morris knew she'd been planning that, he would've explained why it was a bad idea. Since he didn't, it surprised him as much as it did Parker, and he didn't have a chance to grab his dog in time.

A split second later the cameraman signaled they were live, Margot went into her wide-eyed breathless act, and Parker bounded off the loveseat and landed in Margot's lap. The bull terrier proceeded to lick her mouth and cheeks, streaking her expertly applied makeup. The look of stunned amazement on Margot's face as she was left sputtering in midsentence was priceless. No one was better on the local TV scene at faking shock and outrage on the air than Margot, but right then her audience was seeing the real thing. Morris took his time grabbing Parker and carrying him back to the loveseat. He wasn't happy with the dumb stunt Margot had pulled.

"Parker's clearly a big fan of yours," he said, tongue in cheek.

Margot was too flustered to speak, which might've been a first for her. The moment passed.

"He must be," she said with an exaggerated sense of mortification. "I guess I should be thankful I'm still wearing my bra."

While her makeup was ruined, Margot's poofy blond hair remained undisturbed. Given all the styling mousse she used, it was doubtful a hurricane could have budged it. She wagged a finger at Parker. "Now you behave yourself! It usually takes at least three dates to get as far with me as you just did, buster!"

Parker thought she was playing a game with him, and he let out a couple of pig grunts as he tried to squirm free from Morris's grasp, but Morris held tight. He mouthed to Margot to bring Parker back his bone. The director must've picked up on it because seconds later the assistant was hurrying over with the partially chewed rawhide bone. Soon after that the bull terrier was gnawing on it and once again ignoring all the activity around him.

"Well, that was exciting," Margot declared. As fast as someone could snap their fingers, her expression became deathly somber. "We all need moments of levity during such difficult times. When we come back from commercial break, famed serial killer hunter Morris Brick will be revealing to us shocking new developments in the Nightmare Man case."

There wasn't supposed to be a commercial break at that time, but there also wasn't a TV director alive who would've risked Margot's ire right then. The cameraman signaled they were off the air, and Margot bellowed for her makeup artist. A skinny woman in her sixties rushed onto the set and began feverishly fixing the damage Parker had done.

"I should have your dog stuffed and mounted for what he did," Margot said.

"When we go live again, I should put you on my knee and spank you for what you did," Morris growled back at her. "With all the stimuli on the set and his toy being grabbed from him, he got overly excited and thought you were playing with him. He reacted exactly the way you should've expected."

Margot sat sullenly after that. As her makeup artist was finishing up, she complained, "I must've looked absolutely hideous."

"The most stunningly gorgeous woman on morning TV?" Morris said. "Not possible."

"Your flattery won't change the fact that I'll be a laughingstock!"

"If that's so, you'll be laughing all the way to the bank. Your ratings will be off the charts with the news I'll be breaking."

Talk of high ratings appeased her. The cameraman began to count down from five, and when he reached one, Margot's expression instantly transformed into one reflecting the utmost urgency.

"Exclusive to *The Hollywood Peeper*, we will be revealing the identity of the first Nightmare Man. I say *first*, because there have actually been two of these demented killers."

"That's right," Morris said. He gave the director a prearranged nod, and Ed Blount's mugshot, the 1984 police sketch, and the photo of the mask Polk had sent were shown on a split screen, and Morris told the whole sordid story of why he believed Ed Blount created the Nightmare Man.

"That's simply incredible," Margot said in her patented breathless voice as she raised a hand to her throat so that her fingers grazed the base of it.

Saying it aloud, it sounded impossible, but Morris knew it was true.

"This hired killer, Ed Blount—he died in prison in 1992?"

"That's right."

"So who is the second Nightmare Man?"

"We don't know yet, but we believe it's someone he met while in Ashfield State Prison. We're now looking at the inmates he had contact with, and we can use any help the public can provide."

Morris then made an appeal to viewers asking them to call the hotline number if they saw anything unusual near Lori Fletcher's apartment building during the weeks leading up to the murder. He also asked the same of anyone who might know someone catching and keeping live rats. This of course got Margot's curiosity, and she tried her damnedest to pry out of him whatever salacious details she could about what the Nightmare Man did with rats. She didn't get anywhere, and she must've known she wouldn't, but that didn't stop her from giving it her all. If nothing else, it made for riveting television and would send her audience's imaginations into overdrive, although nothing they came up with would match the sickening truth of what was done with them.

Revealing crucial information was always a dilemma for a number of reasons: First and most obvious in this case was the potential of being overwhelmed with false leads involving rats. Another factor that weighed heavily on Morris was that he might inspire copycat killers to come up with their own creative ways to use rats in a murder. But when he discussed this with Gloria Finston, she suggested he mention the rats. Even if nobody saw the killer collecting them, the killer could be worried that someone did, and the added stress could lead to him slipping up. She was convinced they had more to gain than to lose, and he agreed with her.

Margot finally gave up on pressing him about the rats, and he caught a glimmer in her eyes and a flash of a cunning smile. She didn't quite wink at him, but she just as well could've.

She said, "It seems that Police Commissioner Martin Hadley made the right call in bringing you and your firm, MBI, into this investigation."

He always suspected Hadley and Margot traded favors—that he slipped her confidential information in exchange for favorable treatment on her show, at least more favorable than he deserved. This proved it beyond any doubt.

Morris said with a straight face, "The man's a visionary."

Chapter 49

Joplin was alone in her apartment watching *The Hollywood Peeper*, and when that former cop Brick talked about what they had discovered about the Nightmare Man it left her too numb to move. She was affected at such a deep primeval level, and even if her life depended on it she wouldn't have been able to explain why. The same was true yesterday when she had seen the story on the news about the Nightmare Man resurfacing after seventeen years to take a new victim. Those stories had left her feeling far more vulnerable than she would've imagined possible, but she took solace knowing that the police had a sketch of the suspected killer and that they believed this man was now in his eighties. At least she had an idea of who to look out for. Now that had been taken away. Still, why would this news leave her nearly stricken with terror? Then she remembered the creep from earlier and understood her subconscious reaction. Almost as if he were in the living room with her, she heard clearly in her mind the words that the creep had whispered to her just before he fled the restaurant.

I'll be getting my jollies when I see stories about you on TV.

Was it possible he was the Nightmare Man? Joplin thought the creep had been in his early thirties. She remembered the ex-cop saying this new killer would've been in prison at the same time as the man they were now convinced was the first Nightmare Man, and he died in 1992. She was too numb with fear to do simple math in her head, but wouldn't that make the creep way too young to be the killer? But what if the ex-cop was wrong? That police sketch they showed was done in 1984, and it took them all these years to realize they'd been wrong about that!

The Nightmare Man could be anyone.

That thought crystalized in her mind. *He could be anyone.* She made a decision. She'd call the police and tell them about the creep. What was his name? Dale, at least that's what he'd told her. She wished she had played along and gotten his phone number. Too late now for that, but they should be able to figure out who he was from the gym's membership records.

Her cell phone was in her purse, which she had left in the kitchen. She got to her feet, but her legs felt so rubbery she almost fell back onto the couch.

This is insane. Get a grip! There's no reason to be so freaked out by this!

Thinking of the word *freaked* made her giggle, and it took her a few seconds to realize why. Dale wasn't a creep but an outright freak. She also had the thought that a shot of vodka would help steady her, and she could use that! She waited for her legs to feel less rubbery, then headed to the small galley kitchen off the living room.

She kept the vodka in the refrigerator. It tasted so much better chilled. This last bottle she'd bought only a week ago, and she was surprised to see it was already half gone. She normally wasn't a big drinker, and in the past would go a month or longer without any alcohol, but the last few weeks she'd been anxious and had been having a shot or two almost nightly. At first she attributed it to her breakup with Richard, but lately she realized there was something else working on her and fraying at her nerves. When she saw the stories yesterday about the Nightmare Man killing a woman her age in her very same neighborhood, she had a bizarre realization that her recent anxiety and the Nightmare Man were connected, even though she only had a vague memory of him from when she was nine and stories about him were all over the TV. She wondered if she had had a premonition about him coming back and murdering more women. It was almost as if someone had whispered in her ear that this would be happening. She even had a crazy thought that she had heard those whispers. God, was she going crazy?

She poured herself a generous double shot of vodka and drank it straight, not even mixing in any orange juice. It helped. She felt steadier, and when she held her hand out in front of her face, she detected only a slight tremor. She decided another drink would help even more, and she poured herself another couple of ounces, and this time sipped it. Once her glass was empty, she brought the vodka bottle, glass, and her purse back to the living room. She plopped down on the couch, being extra careful not to spill any of the vodka, especially since she was already feeling its effect. She poured herself one more drink, and she giggled as she dug her phone out of her pocketbook. Instead of calling the police, she called Richard.

When she reached voicemail, she hung up and called him again. This time he answered on the fourth ring.

"What do you want?" he demanded coldly.

"Wow," she said. "You can't even be nice and say *hi, Joplin, how are you*?"

"You got it, babe."

"Really? We were together for two years! After all the times we fucked, you can't even be a little nice to me?"

"What a charming mouth on you."

"I'm sorry. I didn't call to fight. But you could be a little nice to me."

"Do I really need to remind you of all the *nice* things you said to me?"

Joplin's hand shook as she poured herself yet more vodka. Richard could be so infuriatingly smug when he wanted to be. She took a deep breath and concentrated to keep her voice under control.

"Do I really need to remind you that I found you in my bed screwing whatsherface?"

"Her name is Debra. And I thought it was *our* bed?"

Joplin's mouth gaped open. Did he really just say that?

"You're joking, right?" she asked.

"Why don't you ask me where I'm living now?"

"What?"

"Aren't you at least curious after you kicked me out of *our* apartment without any notice?"

"You were screwing her right in front of me!"

"Mistakes happen, Joplin. It wasn't as if we were married, or I didn't catch you flirting openly with your good buddy Connor."

She had no idea what he was talking about. She did have a friend at work named Connor, but he was gay. There was never any flirting, only outrageous joking, and Richard knew that, but then again, he was a lawyer, and he was good at talking circles around her.

"You know Connor is gay," she said.

"That doesn't matter. Flirting is flirting, regardless."

He said this in such a mean-spirited way that she understood all he wanted to do was hurt her, and that he must've been looking forward to this for weeks. She also knew he had to be shacked up with his so-called platonic friend Debra, and he was just dying to rub that in her face.

"You know Richard, you really are a Dick!"

"Lovely," he said. "Exactly what I should've expected from you."

She disconnected the call. She couldn't believe she had actually called to reconcile and invite him over for the night. For almost two years he had completely bamboozled her, making her think he was charming and witty, but eventually he showed her what he really was: a cruel, selfish bastard! He couldn't even apologize for cheating on her, instead he had to try to turn things around so that she was the one who had wronged him!

At first she was furious, but then she started giggling, and she realized she was inebriated. More than that, she was flat-out blotto.

She stared bleary-eyed at the vodka bottle and saw it was almost empty. She had poured nearly half a bottle down her throat. A full bottle was seven hundred fifty milliliters, and she struggled to work out in her head how many ounces half of that would be. Her thinking was too fuzzy to figure it out, but she knew it had to be more than she'd ever drunk when she was in college.

I'll be paying for this tomorrow, she thought. She also made a promise that this was it; she wouldn't be buying another bottle tomorrow. She was done letting any guy make her anxious—whether it was Dick the Prick or the Nightmare Man. She thought suddenly of Rosalyn and smiled. Yeah, she was ready to try something different. Even if she was badly hungover, she'd be heading over to the gym tomorrow morning.

She remembered again about the Nightmare Man and how she was going to call the police so she could tell them about the creep. That would have to wait. She was feeling too wasted to do anything other than crawl into bed.

She fell back onto the couch three times before she got to her feet, and she knew she was staggering like a clichéd drunk in a movie.

Tomorrow morning, she promised herself. *I'll call the police then about creepy, freaky Dale.*

She was snoring loudly seconds after collapsing onto the bed.

Chapter 50

"Thanks to Parker I got red wine all over my favorite blouse!"

Morris arrived home just after midnight and was relieved to see Natalie still awake with his spare thirty-two next to her. She gave Parker an enthusiastic hug before getting off the couch and taking Morris's hands. After they embraced and shared a lingering kiss, she revisited the topic of her stained blouse.

"How did Parker accomplish that?" he asked.

"I was drinking a nice glass of Bordeaux waiting for your TV appearance, and I watched in amazement as Parker plopped on top of Margot Denoir and started treating her like a lollipop. That was it as far as my blouse went."

"Ah jeeze. His hijinks caused you to spit out a mouthful of wine?"

"Worse, I laughed so hard it came out my nose."

Morris grimaced. "Ouch."

"I know it. It stung like you wouldn't believe."

Parker let out several dissatisfied grunts, unhappy that he was being excluded, and he tried to worm his way between them. Morris let go of Natalie so he could thump Parker on his side. That appeased the bull terrier, his tail wagging at a good clip.

"Have you heard from Rachel?" he asked, trying to sound unconcerned.

"I talked with our intrepid daughter a half hour ago. She was safe and sound and busy studying." Natalie opened her eyes wide, her expression showing she had a secret to divulge. "I heard Doug in the background before she shushed him. I didn't mention this to Rachel, since she would've insisted I was hearing things, but Doug must be sleeping over now."

Morris grunted an unintelligible response. Natalie was of course right about how Rachel would've responded to any sort of personal question like that. Their daughter was fiercely protective of her privacy, and had told her parents very little about her boyfriends since she started dating back in high school. Morris wasn't oblivious. His daughter was a beautiful young woman, and she'd been seeing Doug Gilman for over six months. Still, he was as fiercely protective of his daughter as she was of her privacy, and there were certain things he preferred not to think about. But even though he had installed what should be an impenetrable lock on her door, he liked the idea of Rachel not being alone while this Nightmare Man maniac was on the loose. For now he would assume Gilman was only spending the night on Rachel's couch. He decided that would work.

"What?" Natalie asked.

He smiled over being caught during a private thought. "Nothing."

"Hmm." She hooked his arm. "I picked up cheese blintzes at Goldie's Deli just in case you needed a snack when you got home. Do you want me to fry a couple up for you?"

He raised an eyebrow. "Did you get sour cream?"

"What do you think?"

They walked arm and arm to the kitchen with Parker tagging along. While Natalie put two blintzes in a frying pan and watched over them, Morris sat at the table and told her how their investigation seemed to be stalling to a dead end.

"The team's been working overtime, and when I left MBI we'd been able to eliminate every ex-inmate Blount had contact with in Ashfield."

Natalie used a spatula to flip the blintzes. Parker sat like a stone watching her.

"How were you able to do that so quickly?" she asked. "There must've been hundreds of them."

"There weren't as many as you'd think, not when you factored in deaths, hospitalizations, ex-inmates ending up back in jail or prison, etcetera. I don't know, Nat. I was hoping this would lead us to this maniac, but now it's looking like we'll have to get our break another way."

"Any leads from your TV appearance tonight?"

"The hotline got plenty of calls, but nothing useful."

Natalie looked deep in thought, so much so, she almost burnt the blintzes. She got them out of the frying pan and onto a plate in the nick of time but stopped on the way to the refrigerator to retrieve the sour cream. Her eyes had a distant, faraway look, her brow deeply furrowed.

"If this new killer didn't get the Nightmare Man secrets from Blount, who'd he get them from?"

"I don't know," Morris admitted with a pained sigh. "It's possible whoever Blount talked to passed his secrets to someone else. Or someone from the department could've intentionally or otherwise leaked the information. Or a person who saw one of the '84 victims."

"Hmm." Natalie brought her right index finger up to her mouth so that it was touching her lips, and she froze like that long enough for Morris to know she was working out an idea. She said, "You looked at the ex-inmates from Ashfield, but what about prison guards and other prison officials?"

Morris couldn't believe he hadn't thought of that, and he told Natalie he blamed not doing so on lack of sleep. "For now that's the best excuse I can come up with," he admitted. "Give me time and I'll see if I can think of a way to blame Dennis Polk."

Natalie was beaming as she retrieved the sour cream and a container of chopped liver from the fridge while Parker watched intently. She put a dollop of sour cream on the plate with the blintzes for Morris, then scooped out a large tablespoon of chopped liver for Parker.

"I didn't get the chopped liver for Parker, but he made me laugh so hard tonight I figured he earned it," she said, still beaming.

Morris nodded absently as he dug into the blintzes. He was too deep in thought to taste them, which was a shame since Goldie's made the best blintzes around. He badly wanted to call the former Ashfield State Prison warden, Bill Schofield, but he knew he'd be waking him if he did. It would have to wait until morning. He had no doubt that Schofield was an early-to-rise kind of guy.

While Morris might've been too absorbed in his thoughts to enjoy his food, the same wasn't true of Parker, who grunted happily in appreciation of the chopped liver.

Chapter 51

Joplin woke up in the dark feeling awful. Really worse than awful. She was too groggy and her thinking too badly muddled to make much sense of her situation, but several questions seeped through the fog in her brain.

Where's that awful ammonia smell coming from?

Why's my thumb hurting so much?

Where am I?

She remembered getting drunk on vodka and had a vague memory of falling onto her bed. She'd had a few bad hangovers in college, but nothing like this. Well, at least it explained why her mouth felt so fuzzy, like it was filled with cotton. But if she was in her bedroom, why was it so dark? Her bedroom had an alarm clock and a plugged-in carbon monoxide detector that both gave off a soft ambient light, and because of that it never got this dark. And why was her thumb throbbing so much?

She groaned, except the noise that came out didn't sound like a groan, and instead was something badly muffled. As if this was all some kind of bad joke, she said, "Well that didn't sound right," but it came out as the same faraway, unintelligible murmur.

She woke up fully, her heart racing as she realized that the reason her mouth felt so fuzzy and woolly wasn't because of the vodka but because something had been stuffed in her mouth. A rag, maybe? Or even a pair of sweat socks?

She remembered about the creep from yesterday. In her fear, she tried bolting out of bed, but she couldn't move, at least not her hands or feet.

Someone had tied her wrists and ankles together.

An icy fear overwhelmed her as she realized this same person had removed her clothing. She was lying on her back naked and helpless.

Even though she knew at an intellectual level it would be pointless, she tried screaming.

In her extreme terror, she was aware that the ammonia smell had faded. When something metallic clamped onto the nail of the index finger, she understood why her thumb on the same hand was hurting so much.

* * * *

At the beginning there was only suffering and silent pleading and bargaining. Later, there was acceptance and the wish to die and end what seemed like an eternity of pain. Whenever she blacked out there was that awful ammonia smell bringing her back into consciousness, but even during those times when she had lost consciousness, she was still at some level aware of the pain. It just seemed to fill her up, as if it were something unendurable and ever-present.

Near the end, when a hollow metal pipe had been pushed into her throat and the blindfold removed so she'd be forced to see the rat being held in front of her eyes in a gloved hand, she caught a glimpse of her killer's face. Joplin had long since cried herself out, and because of that any further tears wouldn't have been possible. Still, the bitterness she felt seeing her tormentor's face nearly made her forget about the pain.

So unfair, she thought. *Just so damned unfair.*

Chapter 52

Morris patiently waited until seven a.m. to call Bill Schofield. "I hope I didn't wake you," he said.

The former warden sounded surprised by the question. "Heck no. I was up at five thirty so I could take Queenie for her morning constitutional."

Morris chuckled at that. "Parker usually lets me sleep until six thirty before making his demands."

"With Queenie, it's my own fault. For forty years my job required me to wake up at that hour, and I continued the habit after retirement. But as much as I'd enjoy trading bull terrier stories with you, I don't suppose that's why you called. You're looking for those names you asked for yesterday, right?"

"Actually, no. I need a list of all prison officials who had contact with Blount. And I'd appreciate it if you let me know anyone you have in mind who stands out."

Schofield's voice took on a more reserved note as he asked, "*Stands out* as in possibly being this maniac?"

"Yes."

"You're not seriously thinking he could be someone I employed at Ashfield?"

"It's not any of the former prisoners."

"You know that for a fact?"

"I do."

"I see. Let me give the matter some thought. I'll call you if a name comes to me."

Schofield hung up the phone. Morris had picked up something from his voice that told him Schofield already had someone in mind. It wouldn't be an easy thing admitting you had a burgeoning serial killer working for you. He'd give the former warden a few hours to get back to him before pushing him.

Natalie took Fridays off, and she had been sleeping soundly when he rolled out of bed an hour earlier. If she was up, she would've let him know, and he didn't have the heart to wake her, especially since he had kept her up late the last two nights waiting for him. He wrote her a note telling her Parker had already been out and had been given half a bowl of his dried food and that he was leaving the little guy with her to keep her out of mischief. He left the note on the kitchen counter and smiled inwardly thinking of the face she'd make when she read it.

Since eating breakfast, Parker had trudged up the stairs so he could camp outside the bedroom door and wait for Natalie. Morris headed upstairs to say his goodbyes to the bull terrier. Parker was lying on his side, and he consented to lift his head and slowly wag his tail. He looked guilty, and Morris knew why. Parker had already made up his mind he was spending the day with Natalie. He was no fool. He knew Fridays with Natalie meant a trip someplace fun, possibly his favorite place, Runyon Canyon Park.

That was just as well. Morris had a gut feeling Schofield would be giving him the name of the second Nightmare Man, and after that he'd be having a busy day.

"No hard feelings," Morris promised. He scratched Parker a final time behind his ear.

Parker lowered his head back to the floor. He stretched all four legs, then closed his eyes.

* * * *

At a little after nine o'clock, Morris and Charlie Bogle stood in MBI's conference room drinking coffee and staring at the map that showed the locations of the Nightmare Man murders. The 1984 murders were more scattered than the 2001 murders, and took place in Brentwood, Culver City, Inglewood, Marina Del Rey, and downtown Los Angeles. In 2001, the first murder was in Beverly Hills, the next two in the San Fernando Valley, the fourth in Venice, and the final one was again in the valley.

Morris's phone rang. Annie Walsh.

"We've got another murder."

Walsh gave him the victim's name and address. Like all the other victims, she was killed in her bedroom. When Morris got off the phone he stuck another yellow thumbtack in the map—this one also in West Hollywood and only two blocks away from where Lori Fletcher had lived.

"Apartment or private residence?" Bogle asked.

"Apartment," Morris said. "Annie's at the crime scene now. The victim's name is Joplin Cole, age twenty-six, single, not living with anyone. This psycho left her apartment and bedroom doors open. For whatever reason he wanted her body found this morning."

"Was that done with any of the other murders?"

Morris said, "No. According to Annie it's otherwise the same as the last murder. Her lips were sewn shut and the rat was still alive and trying to force its way free from her mouth. But he tortured her the same way as the other victims and left the same message at the foot of her bed."

He had been planning to give Schofield another hour to get back to him on his own, but not after this. When he called Schofield, the former prison warden sounded surprised to hear from him.

"We had another murder," Morris told him. He thought *no more pussyfooting around*, but he didn't say it. He knew that wouldn't go over well with a man like Schofield. "If you have a name, I need it now."

"When did this happen?"

"Medical examiner hasn't shown up yet, but it looks like late last night."

"Not this morning?"

Schofield was really asking whether the murder could've happened because he'd been delaying giving Morris the name of a former employee who he thought could be a psychopath.

"No, not this morning," Morris said.

In his mind's eye, he imagined Schofield saying a silent prayer and crossing himself.

"I have a name for you," Schofield said. "There were stories. Nothing substantiated, mind you."

"What kind of stories?"

"That he got rougher with inmates than he should've." Schofield made a noise as if he were clearing his throat, and added, "That maybe he enjoyed it. But this was a long time ago, and I could be wrong about this."

"How long ago?"

"Over twenty years. Could be over twenty-five. He left sometime in the nineties."

"On his own accord?"

"As far as I know. I didn't fire him."

"His name?"

There was a bit of hemming and hawing from Schofield, then, "I hate the idea of maligning a man who could be innocent."

"Bill, that's not what you'd be doing."

"I guess not." He gave up the fight. "He was a prison guard by the name of Travis Smalley."

"Any idea what happened to him?"

"None. I never heard from him or about him since he left Ashfield. He could be dead for all I know."

Morris hoped not, at least if Smalley turned out to be the one responsible for the 2001 murders. Because if that was the case and Smalley was now dead, they'd have to start looking for a third Nightmare Man killer.

Chapter 53

The human jackals inside Ashfield recognized from the start that they needed to be cautious around Ed Blount, and it was only after cancer had eaten away most of his insides and his weight dropped from 212 to 132 pounds that they started looking at him differently, like he might be vulnerable.

The thought of that made Blount laugh, which quickly turned into a hacking cough that racked his increasingly frail body. He had been lying on his back, but he maneuvered his feet onto the concrete floor and forced himself into a sitting position. Once the coughing fit subsided, he spat out a viscous mix of blood and mucus and wiped a withered hand across his mouth. Every muscle and bone ached. His blood also, as if it had become something toxic. Even so, he still had enough to take out any of these jackals who tried making a play on him. There probably wouldn't be anything left of him afterward, but that would be okay as far as he was concerned.

The horn had blasted minutes ago, warning the prisoners in Blount's cellblock to leave their cells. Blount had heard the other inmates shuffling out, but he had stayed on his cot. If he needed to, he could've gotten onto his feet and made his way to the mess hall, for all the good it would do him. Any food he ate wouldn't be staying down for long. He doubted at this point he had much of his stomach left. But the fact that eating any of the swill they served in the mess hall would be a pointless activity wasn't why he stayed on his cot. He knew Travis Smalley was on duty this morning, and sooner or later he'd be checking up on him, and Blount wanted a chance to talk to Smalley privately.

Smalley had been a guard in Blount's cellblock for the last five years. He could've been assigned to a different cellblock before that, but Blount didn't think it likely. Smalley looked too young for that to be the case. No older than early twenties, and it was a good bet this was his first job after high school. Even if Blount was wrong about Smalley's age, word of him would've gotten around if he'd been working elsewhere within Ashfield.

At first glance, Smalley appeared to be an apple-cheeked all-American type. But Blount was never fooled. He knew right away what Smalley was, even before the first time he caught the malicious glee in Smalley's eyes when the guard rabbit-punched an unsuspecting inmate in the kidneys. Since then he'd seen Smalley dozens of times punch inmates in sensitive areas, trip others and stomp on their fingers as if it were an accident, and inflict other small cruelties whenever the opportunity arose. Smalley had always steered clear of Blount, though, the two of them never exchanging a word. That was going to change today. Blount had a proposal for him.

His mind drifted, and he couldn't say how much longer he had to wait before Smalley entered his cell, a curious smile on the guard's lips. Like the other jackals within Ashfield, Smalley had been careful around Blount, although Blount could see in the prison guard's eyes that he was trying to decide how careful he still needed to be. Him lumping Smalley with the other jackals wasn't really right. He was so much more than that.

Smalley stopped several feet from Blount's cot. He was gripping a baton in his hand, and Blount could see in Smalley's pale blue eyes that he was making up his mind whether Blount was now weak enough.

"Are you too sick for breakfast?" Smalley asked pleasantly. "Is that why you're openly disobeying prison rules?"

"I've got something to offer you," Blount said, his voice a hollow imitation of what it had once been. "I didn't want any prying ears listening in."

The prison guard was amused by that. "What could you possibly offer me?"

"You mean other than the pleasure you'd get from beating me with your baton?"

"Precisely."

"That was a joke," Blount said with a grin that left the little skin remaining on his face stretched tight. "You wouldn't get far if you tried. My bones are brittle enough now I'm sure you'd break some, but I'd still snap your neck before you broke too many."

Smalley's knuckles on the hand holding the baton whitened. "Is that a threat?"

"Just having some fun." Blount was still grinning, but his eyes had deadened, looking as lifeless as sand. "What I want to do is offer you what you want most in life."

Smalley laughed. "You got a million dollars to give me?"

"Money isn't what you want most."

Smalley took a step closer. He licked his lips, his eyes glancing to the right and left of Blount before settling back on him. This was a subconscious habit of his, like a poker tell: looking to see whether there was anyone around to witness his violence. So he must've decided Blount was weak enough now to garner special attention. Also that Blount was off his rocker.

"Get off the cot now," he ordered.

He lifted his baton so that he held it at shoulder level, and at the same time left his groin exposed. Blount was tempted to teach him a lesson by punching him in the balls, then grabbing the baton while the prison guard lay in a fetal position on the cement floor, but whatever satisfaction he would get from that wouldn't be worth the cost.

"Settle down," Blount said. "What I can give you is being able to kill women in the cruelest, most sadistic way imaginable without you ever being suspected. We both know that's what you really want. That your extracurricular activities here aren't giving you enough satisfaction."

"You're crazy," Smalley said a little too quickly. "Whatever has made you sick must've turned your brain into mush."

A weak, rattling noise escaped from deep within Blount's throat. It sounded like a pebble bouncing inside an empty soda can. He was laughing despite himself. He couldn't help it seeing the piggish look of anticipation on the guard's face. Smalley's apple cheeks blushed a deeper red. Blount had been listening to make sure no one else was nearby. He didn't have to worry about lowering his voice. It was already too weak to carry far.

"Do you remember the Nightmare Man murders from '84?" He waited until Smalley said he did before continuing. "The cops never gave out any of the details. I could tell you them and you could take over the killings. You're more than sneaky enough to pull it off, and as long as you use a few brains, the cops will never suspect you."

The hand holding the baton dropped to Smalley's side. He used his free hand to tug on his lower lip.

"You're confessing to me that you were the Nightmare Man?" he asked as if this was a joke.

"I'm not saying one way or the other. But what I can tell you is the genuine article."

"You're serious?"

Blount didn't answer him.

They engaged in a silent staring contest for a good minute, Smalley looking as if he were trying to make up his mind. He must've finally come to a decision, because he shook his head, astonished.

"I could drag you to the warden's office and I'd be a hero," he said.

"You could, but we both know being a hero isn't what you really want, so why kid yourself about it? Besides, all the added attention you'd get would prevent you from ever living up to your true potential."

Smalley's eyes grew distant as if he were searching somewhere deep inside himself. When he looked back at Blount, there was an unmistakable hunger in them.

"Why do you think that about me?" he asked.

He wasn't challenging Blount; he was simply curious.

"Let's say because of my job I needed to be a student of human nature. I see things most others don't."

"You were a hitman?"

"That's right."

"But I thought you insisted you were innocent?"

Blount was surprised Smalley had heard that. He hadn't mentioned anything about his arrest and trial since the first month he'd been in Ashfield. Maybe there was something about it in his prison record. Smalley must've been curious enough about him to at some point read his record. Live and learn.

"What sent me here was a frame, and a damned good one. Not even Houdini could've slipped free of it." He could tell from Smalley's blank expression that he had no clue who Houdini was. "But just because I'm innocent of the one that sent me over doesn't mean I'm innocent. I did more jobs than I can remember."

Smalley sat down on the cot next to Blount, his face taking on a more piggish look. He edged closer, his breath warm and smelling like cheap cat food. In a soft whisper, he asked, "Did you enjoy killing people?"

"I took satisfaction in doing a job well done. That's all."

"The Nightmare Man killings were part of a job?"

Blount didn't answer him.

"You said something before about being able to kill women in the cruelest way. Does that mean you tortured the women before killing them?"

Again, Blount didn't answer.

Smalley correctly interpreted Blount's silence. He had already made his decision and was just being cautious when he asked Blount to explain why the police would never suspect him if he were to continue the Nightmare Man murders.

"How old were you in October '84?"

"Sixteen."

"Where were you living?"

"Bakersfield."

"That should be reason enough. Cops wouldn't believe it possible for a sixteen-year-old kid living in Bakersfield to have done those murders. But that doesn't even matter. They got their sketch from a witness, and the sketch is for a guy in his forties who doesn't look anything like you. If you start these killings up again, that's who they'll be looking for."

Smalley absorbed this. "I remember that police sketch," he said. "They showed it all the time on the news for like a month. I don't remember it looking like you."

"I wore a mask that night. It was something I did when I went out on jobs where I thought I could be seen."

"A true professional," Smalley said with an ugly grin.

"That's right."

His grin shrunk. There was still something on his mind that was troubling him. "Why are you telling me this?" he asked. "What do you want in return?"

Blount had his reason, and he knew it was a lousy one. The evil Trilling had paid him to create should die with him instead of being handed over to someone like Travis Smalley. But as rotten as his reason was, it was important to him. It was all he had left.

He knew Salvatore Penza was behind the frame that sent him to Ashfield. While he was awaiting trial he heard rumors that the massage parlor owner he was supposed to have killed, Arnie Woods, had a problem with Penza over the weekly amount Penza was squeezing out of him, and the moron had made noises about talking to the cops. Blount's blood chilled once he understood Penza had set him up. Penza would've only done that if he had learned about Blount being behind the Nightmare Man murders, and Blount could make a good guess how Penza had learned about that: the client, Donald Trilling, talked with another freelancer before Blount, and that freelancer must've gone to Penza after Trilling's wife was killed. Blount had no idea how Penza was then able to figure out that he took the job, but somehow he did and decided to apply his own brand of justice. It made sense that was what happened and explained why Trilling included in his note that torture was necessary. He'd already been turned down once, and he wanted to make sure other freelancers knew up front what the job required.

Blount could accept a life sentence for killing Arnie Woods, even though he had nothing to do with the hit. He could also handle Lauren and his boys thinking he was a hitman, even if they learned how extensive his career was. He'd do anything, though, to keep them from ever finding out that he'd been the Nightmare Man. He'd rather cut out his own heart than have them ever discover that, and that was why he had to accept the frame and keep his mouth shut.

He had planned to take his Nightmare Man secret to the grave, but how does that saying go about the best-laid plans of mice and men? How quickly they can go to shit? Lauren visited him during his first four years before sending him divorce papers; his oldest boy, George, visited him a handful of times, his last visit being three years ago; his middle son, Tom, not a single visit, letter, or phone call ever, and it looked like the same was going to be true with his youngest boy, Jack. Then out of the blue Jack came to see him a year ago, but one look and Blount knew it wasn't a social call, that his son had a specific purpose in mind. Jack wanted to know the truth about Blount working as a hitman, and Blount didn't lie to him. When his boy pressed him about whether Woods had been his only hit, Blount admitted that he'd done more jobs over two decades than he could remember. If Jack wanted to tell the cops any of that, Blount wouldn't hold it against his boy. The cancer hadn't ravaged him yet, but he knew it was inside him and that he'd be dead long before the DA would ever be able to put him on death row, if it ever went that far.

It turned out that Jack wanted to ask him about the mask that looked like the police sketch of the Nightmare Man. Blount could've sworn he had gotten rid of the mask the night he cleaned out his workshop, but somehow his boy had gotten his hands on it. While Jack danced around the subject, what he really wanted to know was whether Blount had been the Nightmare Man. He gave Jack some cock-and-bull story about the mask, which Jack acted as if he believed, but Blount knew he really didn't. That Jack might become convinced he was Nightmare Man ate away at him worse than the cancer. Even worse was knowing that Jack might share his suspicions with Lauren and his brothers. The only way Blount could make sure none of that happened was if the Nightmare Man were to kill again. That was why he needed to tell a sicko psychopath like Travis Smalley his secret. Besides, what difference would it make? He was damned either way.

Smalley was waiting patiently for an answer about what Blount wanted in return, and Blount told him that he wanted his masterpiece to live on.

It was a sicko deranged answer, total bull, but he knew it would make perfect sense to someone like Smalley. From the way Smalley smiled, it hit a bull's-eye.

Blount stared down at his heavily veined hands, the cancer leaving them gnarled and desiccated. He knew he deserved the worst hell imaginable for the decision he had made, and he accepted that.

"I also want enough horse so I can check out tonight," Blount said. "This whole suffering with cancer business has gotten old. You think you can arrange for that?"

Smalley's eyes were burning with an eagerness to learn the Nightmare Man's secrets.

"I'll fix you up right," he promised.

Chapter 54

Woodland Hills, 1999

Travis Smalley accepted Joanne Krate's offer for coffee, and while she busied herself, he sat at the kitchen table and munched on an oatmeal cookie she had offered him. She had already mentioned that she was divorced and living in the house with her teenage daughter. Smalley guessed she was in her forties. A plump, moonfaced woman with mousy brown hair who couldn't shut her mouth if her life depended on it. Smalley smiled pleasantly as she rushed around the kitchen to get out her best china and add sugar to a bowl and two percent milk to a creamer, all the while blabbering away about all the hidden benefits of renting her guesthouse.

"It's such a safe neighborhood, Mr. Smalley. Or can I call you Travis?"

His mind had wandered and he'd been imagining himself doing terrible things to this woman. He snapped back to attention. Somehow he played back in his mind what she had just asked.

He gave her a naughty smile and said, "Joanne, I'd be insulted if you called me anything else."

She tittered. No exaggeration. She actually brought her hand to her mouth and tittered.

"Travis, I can't tell you how nice it is to have a clean-cut, respectable man in my kitchen for a change. My ex, well, all I can say is good riddance. And I'm being charitable at that." She laughed, but bitterness soured her expression. "What was I talking about before? Oh yes, I remember. About how convenient we are to almost anywhere. You can get onto the 101 in less than three minutes, and that will take you right to downtown LA. Really, Travis, I can't think of a better value anywhere in the valley."

She poured them both coffee and joined him at the table. She stopped talking long enough to take a bird-like sip, and then she was back at it, giving him the hard sell, breathlessly telling him how easily he'd be able to drive anywhere from the house. Goddamn, he'd enjoy shutting her up for good; well, after first having her scream for her life. But he had come here to rent a guesthouse that would give him the privacy he needed, and the pickings in his price range were slim. This one would do nicely. The cul-de-sac the house was situated on had little traffic, and the guesthouse provided a secluded entrance in the back—if you had the audacity to call the four-hundred-and-fifty-square-foot apartment added to the small ranch-style home a guesthouse. So as tempted as he might have been to unleash his hidden demon on this blathering woman, he had already decided he wouldn't be killing anyone until the seventeen-year anniversary of when the Nightmare Man took his first victim. That was his own idea, not Blount's. The symmetry seemed too perfect to do anything other than that. Besides, he had already waited this long, what was two more years? He accepted that for now he'd have to keep his desires tamped down, just as he'd been doing ever since Blount handed him this gift, and keep reminding himself that the anticipation would make the killings that much more delicious. The next two years were for planning only, even when he met someone like Joanne Krate who so badly needed to be tortured and killed.

She was still going on about what a great deal the guesthouse would be for someone like himself when she was interrupted by the kitchen door swinging open. An awkward-looking teenage girl walked in. This had to be Joanne Krate's daughter. Smalley guessed she was thirteen. Skinny as a stick in her jeans and T-shirt, but she had her mom's round, puffy face that was made even puffier thanks to a mouthful of braces. Also like her mom, she had a slightly upturned nose and mousy brown hair, except hers was pulled into pigtails. She stopped when she spotted Smalley and looked timid as opposed to shy as she glanced down at her feet as if she'd die of embarrassment if she didn't. Smalley smiled seeing how self-consciously she pulled at her fingers, as if she had no idea what to do with her hands.

"Rosalyn, honey," Mrs. Krate said. "This is Mr. Smalley. He's thinking about renting our guesthouse. Wouldn't that be swell?"

Smalley got up from the chair and extended a hand. "Pleased to meet you, Rosalyn," he said, grinning like the cat who'd swallowed the canary.

Her blush deepened. When she took his hand, Smalley noticed that she had especially slender and delicate fingers. His smile broadened as he imagined using needle-nose pliers to rip out her nails. He could only imagine how small her toes would be. But this was only a nice fantasy. If he rented the guesthouse he wouldn't be able to make her one of his victims, at least not in 2001. He could perhaps keep track of her and choose her when the Nightmare Man struck again in 2018. The anticipation of that would be quite something.

"I hope you rent our guesthouse, Mr. Smalley," Rosalyn said softly. She peeked up at him, and he realized she wasn't as timid as he had first thought.

"Please call me Travis." He laughed. "All my friends do."

This time when she peeked at him her lips were twisted into a secretive little smile. *Yes, not so timid at all, are we?*

"Okay, Travis," she said.

"Travis is a security expert," Mrs. Krate said, beaming.

"I don't know if expert is the right word," Smalley said with a modest, aw-shucks grin. "But I will be managing security for five apartment buildings here in the valley."

"He used to be a prison guard!" Mrs. Krate said. "Imagine the stories Travis could tell us!"

Smalley said, "They'd curl your toes."

Both mother and daughter gasped at that. He was exaggerating. He had stories of his own little cruelties that would sicken them, but he only had one story that would curl their toes, or at least curdle their blood, and he was keeping that one to himself.

Mrs. Krate put down her coffee cup. It was time to get serious, and so she put on her serious face. "Travis, dear, I'd feel so much safer having a man of your character and expertise staying here, enough so that I'm willing to drop the monthly rent to four hundred and twenty-five a month if that will help you make up your mind."

"I'm sold," Smalley said. He got careless and let his smile become something wolfish. He quickly corrected it. Mrs. Krate didn't notice, and if Rosalyn did, she kept it to herself. He added, "How could I pass up the opportunity of living in the vicinity of two such lovely ladies?"

Mrs. Krate tittered again. Rosalyn smiled in a way that showed he had completely misjudged her earlier. She wasn't timid at all. He also realized he had to be careful with her.

He decided then he would someday kill her. He would let the anticipation build into something nearly unbearable, but when the day finally came, it would be pure, unadulterated bliss.

Chapter 55

Los Angeles, October 8, 2001

Detective Martin Hadley took the call, and when he got off the phone he growled at Morris to get his ass in gear—they had the murder of a housewife in Beverly Hills to investigate. Morris held his tongue. When Hadley peered across Morris's desk at a recent photo of Natalie and Morris's seven-year-old daughter Rachel and wisecracked that he couldn't see why a pretty gal like Natalie would have anything to do with any ugly squirt like him, Morris shrugged it off and admitted it was a mystery.

Morris had earned his detective's shield and joined LAPD's Homicide and Robbery division almost a month ago and, as he was learning, it wasn't all milk and honey. He'd been assigned to work with Hadley, or more specifically, Hadley had arranged for him to be his partner so he could ride him and break his chops whenever possible. Morris hadn't known the man before joining the force and had had nothing to do with him when he was a patrolman other than catching Hadley's dirty looks. Because of that, it didn't take a genius to know that whatever Hadley had against him was really directed against his dad, Sam Brick, who had retired six years earlier. When he asked his dad about it, the senior Brick told him he'd just have to grin and bear it for the time being.

"Sins of the father, I guess," Sam Brick had said with a hard smile. "I chewed him out once in front of the precinct for sloppy police work that forced us to cut a suspect loose. A man like Martin Hadley doesn't forget something like that. But I don't suspect he'll be your partner for long. He's a political animal if there ever was one. Even six years ago I could see him laying the foundation and working angles to finagle his way into a command position, and it's only a matter of time before he succeeds. Son, in this job you'll be learning it's not only cream that rises to the top."

"He doesn't let me do detective work," Morris complained.

"Give it a full month," Sam Brick said. "That's enough time for the other detectives to get used to you and think of you as one of their own. Then stand up to the blowhard. Punch him in the jaw if needed. Hadley's all bluster and noise, but he doesn't have the stones to go toe-to-toe with you if he knows you mean business."

* * * *

When Morris and Hadley arrived at the Beverly Hills home, another detective, George Landrigan, was waiting for them outside and filled them in. The husband, Michael Buchalla, age forty-two, had come home that morning after a week of traveling to find his wife, Silvia Buchalla, age thirty-six, brutally murdered.

"The wife was found in the bedroom. Sicko stuff like you wouldn't believe." Landrigan's hard exterior softened if he were reliving the murder scene. "I just might've become a vegetarian today."

Hadley asked in his gruff, raspy voice, "Where's the husband?"

Landrigan checked his watch. "As of three minutes ago, he was in the kitchen sobbing his guts out, or at least putting on a good act. Hutchings is talking to him. I came out here for some fresh air and to wait for you." He leaned closer to Hadley and Morris and lowered his voice. "Here's the kicker: According to the ME, the wife could've been dead for as long as a week. He won't be able to give us anything more definitive until he does an autopsy. This Buchalla is gone a week and doesn't once call his wife."

Hadley asked, "He have a reason?"

"He claimed he and his wife would go on separate vacations, and when they did, no phone calls. Something about absence making the heart grow fonder. Christ on a stick. No way my wife would ever let me get away with that."

Hadley laughed. "My ball and chain would skin me alive if I even hinted at it." His thick, rubbery lips twisted into an ugly smirk and he waved a fat thumb toward Morris. "I wouldn't bet against Brick's hot little number paying him to disappear for a week, ain't that so, Brick?"

Landrigan joined in, chuckling at Hadley's jibe. Morris smiled good-naturedly.

"You're a funny man, Martin," Morris said. He asked Landrigan whether there was any other indication the husband might be involved.

Both Hadley and the detective looked taken aback, as if neither of them expected any questions from a freshly minted detective. After all, he was just supposed to keep his mouth shut and stay out of the way of the real detectives on the job. Hadley recovered enough to glower at Morris and his jowl began quivering, but before he could work up enough steam to shut down Morris's question, Landrigan consented to answer him.

"No visible signs of a break-in," Landrigan said. "Buchalla not calling his wife for a week sounds fishy, and what was done to her was so demented it makes me wonder whether it was staged to look like a sicko serial killer. His sobbing act appeared genuine, but a psychopath can fake that, and someone would have to be a flat-out psychopath to think of the things that were done to the victim."

Hadley made a harrumphing noise as if Landrigan's answer put Morris in his place. "Who do we got in there?" he asked Landrigan.

The detective counted with his fingers that inside the house were Hutchings, the ME, the two uniformed officers who took the call, and five members of the crime scene team.

"You heard him," Hadley snapped at Morris. "Go out and get eleven coffees." He magnanimously suggested Morris make it a dozen if he wanted one himself. "And two dozen donuts. Make sure to get a couple lemon crème."

"I better check inside so I get the orders straight," Brick said. He winked at Hadley. "You never know, someone might prefer tea."

Hadley hadn't expected this insubordination and was too slow on the uptake to stop Morris from steamrolling past him and leading the way into the house.

The interior was expansive. Rich cream-colored wall-to-wall carpeting, large rooms, fifteen-foot-high ceilings, expensive furnishings. From the back of the house Morris heard the faint sounds of what must've been the husband sobbing. From behind, he heard Hadley barking out an order for him to do as he was told. He pretended not to hear him, nodded at a crime scene specialist collecting dander and hairs from the carpet, and continued to the staircase to the second floor. He wanted to get a look at the husband in the kitchen, but that would give Hadley a chance to catch up to him.

He smiled as he imagined Hadley red-faced and breathing hard chasing after him. He heard noises coming from the first room on the left, and when he entered it he saw the murder scene. The grisly "17" left in front of the bed stopped him for a heartbeat. As he continued toward the dead woman lying on the bed, he blanched seeing the damage that had been done to her. His movement became almost dreamlike, and he wondered if that was really a rat's tail hanging out of the victim's mouth. Hadley was making noise behind him, but he stopped when he stepped into the room and saw the carnage.

Morris had seen his share of dead bodies during his eight years as a patrolman. Shooting and stabbing victims. Bodies pulled from auto wrecks. Motorcyclists smeared across roads after wiping out. Pedestrians struck by speeding vehicles and split open like cantaloupes. Shut-ins found weeks after death, their bodies streaming with maggots. But this was different. This was depraved, and the thought of what the woman must've gone through during her last hours of life sickened him.

"Is that a rat?" he asked the ME, Dr. Joel Katzenberg.

Katzenberg turned to offer him a grim look. "Yes," he said. "The animal was pushed deep into her trachea."

"Is it alive?"

"Not now. But it was when it was forced into her. I've found a number of bite marks."

Hadley had caught up to Morris and stood beside him. His bulldog-like face had turned chalky white.

"Jesus," he murmured, his small, pale blue eyes bulging.

Katzenberg said, "I assure you Jesus had nothing to do with this."

Hadley was too stunned to notice the ME's crack. Morris recovered enough from his own shock to tell the ME that he was making a coffee run, and asked whether the ME had a special request.

"The largest size of high-octane they offer," he said without much enthusiasm. "This is going to be a long day."

Morris's stare fixed on the woman's death mask. The killer had been more than cruel. He not only used a sharp blade to sever flesh from her torso, but he cut off most of her nose and gouged out a large chunk of flesh from her cheek, and from what he could tell, the killer used something red-hot to brand both wounds. There was either a tremendous amount of hatred at work, or a sadism that knew no bounds.

Morris asked, "The victim's been dead a week?"

"Could be five days, could be as much as a week," Katzenberg said. "I won't know until I do some tests."

Morris turned to head out for a coffee run, and Hadley was hot on his heels, mumbling to no one in particular that he wanted to talk to the officers who took the call.

Once Morris was outside, he used his cell phone to call his dad. Before he could say more than "hi," the senior Brick asked whether Hadley was still pushing him around.

"He is, but that's not why I'm calling. We picked up a murder where it's either a husband trying to fool us into thinking it's a serial killer at work, or it's the real thing."

When Morris had gotten his dad on the phone, the senior Brick sounded like he was spoiling for a fight, like he wanted an excuse to seek out Hadley and kick the man's ass. This changed immediately, and his voice sounded tired as he asked whether a message had been left.

"Yeah, I'd say so."

"The number seventeen made up of severed flesh and nails? A rat found stuck in the victim's throat?"

An iciness crept down Morris's spine. "You've seen this before?" he asked.

"I did. Seventeen years ago. Do you remember the Nightmare Man murders?"

Morris remembered them. He had been a kid at the time, only fourteen. He remembered how worn out his dad had looked during the months when he investigated the murders, and that his dad never spoke a word about them to the family.

"We need to talk face-to-face," Sam Brick said. "The sooner the better."

Chapter 56

Los Angeles, October 8, 2001

Hadley sputtered with outrage when he saw Morris had returned empty-handed. "You've been gone almost an hour!" he barked. "Where's my coffee and lemon crèmes? Can't you do anything right?"

If Hadley's outburst bothered Morris, he didn't show it. "I consulted with my dad instead," he said.

Hadley was too livid at first to talk, his mouth pushing in and out as if he were adjusting dentures. Finally he spat out, "What was that?"

"My dad has seen murders like this one before."

"You discussed an ongoing investigation with a civilian?" he asked, indignant.

Morris was still three days shy of his one-month anniversary, but he decided he was close enough to take his dad's advice. Besides, he was sick of Hadley's antics, and he found it infuriating that Hadley was so caught up in his little power trip that he would dismiss what he'd just been told.

"Martin, don't get your boxers in a twist. I discussed the situation with a retired LAPD homicide detective who had thirty years on the job. This murder matches unsolved homicides from 1984 attributed to the Nightmare Man."

Hadley was flabbergasted. He opened his mouth and closed it. Like a fish gulping. "Disobeying orders from a higher-ranking detective," he croaked in a raspier than normal voice. A stubby index finger was raised. "Violating departmental rules." A second finger joined the first to form a backward peace sign. "That's it, sonny boy, I'm going to see you busted back down to patrolman, if you're lucky."

Morris said, "You can try. But how about for now we get the FBI involved?"

Hadley was angry enough that Morris could imagine steam rising from his fat head. Before Hadley could utter a word, his phone rang. He barked out at it, demanding, "What do you want!" and then his face deflated as he listened to what the caller had to say. Morris stood close enough to listen in. A woman had been murdered last night in her San Fernando Valley apartment, and a grisly "17" was left behind.

* * * *

Aside from the gray hair and deeper lines in his face, Captain Jim Marshall looked pretty much the way he had back in 1984. He still had the same office and command position, but he was now addressing a different Detective Brick, and after clearing his throat, he informed Morris that Hadley wanted him drummed out of the LAPD.

Morris said, "I was only doing my job."

Marshall sat erect in his chair, his clasped hands resting lightly on his desk. He forced a patient smile.

"You've still got training wheels on, son," he said.

"Don't you think it's about time they came off?" Morris didn't give Marshall a chance to contemplate an answer. He shifted forward onto the edge of the seat and quickly went into the speech he'd been practicing in his head. "My dad's ideas on this murder make a lot of sense," he said. "If my dad was right and Donald Trilling hired a hitman in 1984 to kill his wife, then this same hitman could've been laying low or been in prison until recently, and he could've brought back the Nightmare Man to hide another contract killing. We need to work with the OC task force and put pressure on these mob guys to give up this hitman. We also need to look hard at Buchalla's finances. His home has got to be worth at least five million, and he'd be a perfect candidate to be hiring a hitman."

Captain Marshall stared blankly at Morris.

"You've been a detective a week now and you're already giving orders?"

Morris said, "Almost a month."

"Almost a month. Imagine that. And you're already turning out to be the same pain in the ass as Sam." His tone softened. "But your old man was a good detective, and maybe someday you'll be the same, so I'll tell you how this is going to work. We're going to follow the book on this, and you're only doing what the ranking detective on the case tells you to do. Within reason. If I hear anything about you bothering Mr. Buchalla, or about you freelancing and interfering with organized crime investigations, or wasting even a minute of their valuable time, you'll be looking for another job. Have I made myself clear?"

Morris sat grinding his teeth, not wanting to give in. "Sir, with all due respect, I think we'll be ignoring an important avenue of investigation."

"That will be Martin Hadley's call, not yours, since he's the ranking detective on this, not you." Captain Marshall's expression weakened, and in a confidential tone he added, "These murders tormented me seventeen years ago. Back then I gave your old man months of leeway to explore this same hitman theory, and he got nowhere. We're not going on any more wild-goose chases. This time around, we're following procedure straight down the line."

He checked his watch and told Morris he believed they were done. Morris got up and closed the door behind him on his way out. Hadley was waiting for him at his desk, his pale blue eyes watching Morris carefully.

Hadley asked, "You still employed by the LAPD?"

"As far as I know."

"So I'm still stuck with you, huh? That's a shame."

Morris swallowed back what he wanted to say and sat down behind his desk, ignoring Hadley as he leaned against it.

"I thought about your dumbass idea about this being a hitman," Hadley said. "We're not wasting any time on that. *Capisce?*"

Morris said, "You're the ranking detective on the case."

"You're damn straight I am. And don't you forget you're a know-nothing waste of space. There's a chance, mind you, a small one at best, that if you keep your eyes open and mouth shut you just might learn enough from me so you're not totally useless."

If Hadley expected a thank-you from Morris, he didn't get one. After a minute of waiting, he lost patience.

"I take that back," Hadley said. His gaze had shifted to the framed picture of Natalie and a seven-year-old Rachel, and he was staring at it in an almost obscene way. "As long as you've got that photo on your desk you're not completely useless. But how about doing all of us here in Homicide a favor and getting one with the wife in a skimpy bikini?"

He let out a guffaw.

Morris pushed himself to his feet, and he used his right hand to grip Hadley by the shoulder. It was a gesture that could've looked friendly, but from the way Morris squeezed the shoulder, it was anything but. He had gone to UCLA on a full baseball scholarship, a starter at third base all four years. He was good enough that he disappointed Major League scouts when he told them he had no interest in playing professional baseball and planned to go into law enforcement instead. Third basemen and bricklayers tended to have powerful hands, and Morris's hands were as strong as any. He soon had Hadley squirming under his grip.

"If you ever say another word disrespecting my wife, I will tear you apart," Morris said softly into Hadley's ear. "*Capisce?*"

Hadley was struggling to break free but had no chance. "Okay, okay," he forced out, wincing from the pain.

Morris let go of Hadley's shoulder. They exchanged a look then, and it told Morris that Hadley was afraid of him just enough to stop his nonsense. His dad had been right. When it came down to it, Hadley didn't have the stones to stand up to him. But he also knew Hadley wasn't going to change his mind about talking with organized crime. The fact that the idea came from Morris's dad sealed that.

Hadley said, "I want you back at Leary's apartment building at five this evening, and I don't want you leaving there until you've talked with every single tenant. You got that?"

Cynthia Leary was the name of the twenty-seven-year-old woman murdered last night in the valley. Earlier that afternoon while Morris was given busywork, Hadley and two other detectives canvassed the apartments, but only a handful of tenants were home. So Hadley was now consenting to give him real detective work. At least that was something. Still, in Morris's gut he didn't believe following standard procedure would lead them to the Nightmare Man. Talking to organized crime was out—he knew Captain Marshall meant business—but he still planned to go through the mugshot books and look at every prisoner photo. If the Nightmare Man was a hitman who had gotten out of prison, Morris still had a chance of finding him. At least if the police sketch from 1984 was a close enough match to the real killer.

"Yes, sir," Morris said.

That seemed to mollify Hadley. The older detective nodded in a way to show they had a truce, and that as far as Hadley was concerned, Morris had earned his respect. Or at least his fear.

Morris checked his watch. Four thirty-five. If he was going to get to the San Fernando Valley apartment building by five, he should've left ten minutes ago. He waited until he was in the car and started driving before calling Natalie.

"It's going to be a late one," he said. "I might be out until midnight. My folks would like to come over and keep you company until I get home. Is that okay?"

"Of course, Rachel will be thrilled to see Grandma Ruthie and Pops." Natalie lowered her voice. "They've been reporting about the Nightmare Man on the news. Is that what you're investigating?"

In his mind's eye, he could see Natalie's brow furrowed deeply as she tried hard to sound unconcerned and cheery. Rachel had to be in the room with her.

"It is," he admitted. "How many murders have they been reporting?"

"One." He caught the hitch in her voice as she asked if there had been more than that.

"There have been two. I'll be spending part of the night canvassing the apartment building where one of the murders took place, part of it searching through mugshot books."

"There's a witness?"

"From 1984. We've got a police sketch from back then. It's being updated now to age the suspect seventeen years."

"Oh."

"You know why I want my parents with you until I come home?"

Her voice dropped to a whisper, "I know." Then sounding especially cheery again, "I've got a mischievous little girl who's eager to talk to you."

Morris heard Rachel giggling in the background. "Has she been causing trouble?" he asked.

"I'll let her tell you."

The giggling got out of control as the phone was handed to Rachel.

"I didn't do anything, Daddy," Rachel insisted earnestly. "Simba jumped up on the counter and knocked over the flour canister and got flour everywhere. It was so funny!"

She broke out into a giggling fit. Simba was the family cat. Morris had no idea what type he was, only that he was black and white, and that he liked to dig his claws into Morris's stomach whenever he settled down on him. When Rachel was four, she had won the cat at a Purim party. A dirty trick, giving away kittens that way. Morris and Natalie had been talking about getting a dog when their daughter was older, but what were they going to say to their four-year-old little girl when she came running to them with the kitten she'd just "won"? And so they were stuck with a cat who liked to jump on kitchen counters and leave Morris dead little gifts in his shoes.

Rachel's giggle wound down, and she proceeded to tell Morris all about the trouble Simba had caused and how funny it was.

Morris asked, "Who's cleaning up the mess?"

"Mommy did, but I helped."

"Don't you think Simba should've cleaned up his own mess?"

"That's silly, Daddy," she said in a patronizing voice. "Cats don't clean up their own messes. That's why they have us."

Morris couldn't argue with that logic.

Chapter 57

Los Angeles, October 27, 2001

Travis Smalley found the next woman he was going to kill in a downtown nightclub. The instant he saw her, he knew she was the one. Mid-twenties, long mousy brown hair hanging well past her shoulders, and a cute face bordering on pretty, even with her slightly upturned nose. What made her so perfect was (a) this could be Rosalyn in ten years and (b) she was skinny.

The fact that she strongly resembled an older version of Rosalyn Krate was what first drew his attention, but he had learned during the last three weeks that the pain he administered was so much more excruciating when he was carving the flesh off of women who didn't have much to spare.

The last three nights he'd been to two dozen bars and almost a dozen nightclubs hunting for his next victim, and he'd spent a good chunk of money on cover charges and buying drinks he barely sipped. That was all part of the process and to be expected, and to be fair, he saw other women he almost chose instead. He even had several drunken or stoned women approaching him, and any one of them would've been easy to take. Somehow, though, they weren't quite what he was looking for. Once he saw this woman, he understood the reason for that.

He first spotted her on the dance floor where jammed bodies gyrated to ear-splitting, head-banging heavy metal music. It was a miracle he saw her at all. When the people blocking her parted long enough for him to see her, he took it as a sign that this was meant to be. She wore a T-shirt that looked painted on and fit so tightly he could make out her ribs, and a black leather mini-skirt barely covering four inches of her skinny thighs. Completing the outfit were black ankle boots. Before she was swallowed up again by the crowd, he watched her raise both skinny arms high above her head, the movement pulling up her shirt and revealing an emaciated stomach and a pierced belly button. Since then he'd been spying on her from a distance, following her around the club while he carried an untouched rum and coke. She was with a ratty-looking dude her age, also skinny, and with tattoos covering both arms from his shoulders to his wrists. As far as Smalley was concerned, this was a plus. He liked the idea of butchering his next victim while her boyfriend was tied up and forced to watch. More than that, he was anxious to venture into new territory.

Blount had been right. Smalley followed Blount's playbook to the letter, not deviating once from the formula he was given, and because of that he'd been able to kill five women without the police ever suspecting him. Even better, he had them chasing after a phantom. He got a charge every time he turned on the TV and saw their updated sketch of the Nightmare Man: A sixty-year-old geezer who never existed.

Blount had also been right about how this was his destiny. Travis Smalley had found that it was pure ecstasy torturing and snuffing out his victims, his senses heightened to a level he never would've imagined possible. He didn't just watch as they squirmed in their final agonies; instead it was as if he could smell and taste their suffering, as if he could feel vibrations of it on his skin. The experiences left him hungering for more.

At first, he tried to ignore this hunger. There was a simple symmetry with the number seventeen. He'd done as Blount suggested, killing five women in seventeen days, and his original plan was to wait seventeen years and then do it all over again. Easy peasy. He was thirty-three, and he could remember back to when he was eleven and first felt the urge to kill. The little girl he first wanted to torture and snuff out was five-year-old Betsy Jackson who lived three doors away, but he fought against the urge then. He even let her tag along after him, and he would listen patiently as she droned on about her favorite dollies, all the while daydreaming about what he'd like to do to her. If he could tamp down those urges for twenty-two years, he should be able to ignore them for another seventeen years. Except easier said than done.

The genie was out of the bottle.

Four days ago he had woken up with a throbbing head and his mouth so dry he would've sworn he had swallowed a handful of sawdust. It didn't matter how much he drank or how many aspirins he took; he couldn't get rid of the dryness or stop that unrelenting drumbeat deep in his head. He also couldn't stop thinking about killing more women. He knew the reason. He was an addict. When he had his way with his victims a flood of endorphins was released, so he experienced the mother of all highs.

He couldn't go cold turkey, even if he wanted to, and he was just like any other junkie badly needing a fix. Barely sleeping, jittery every waking second, brain throbbing, an endless cold sweat. He was still living in the Krates' guesthouse and he almost gave in to his impulse to slaughter Rosalyn, her freakin' annoying mother, and the equally annoying fat slob who had moved in with them six months ago, but as satisfying as that might've been, the police would be chasing after him if he did that. And then he realized he didn't have to give up the Nightmare Man. Just because Blount only took five victims didn't mean his own hands were tied. He could still make the police think the number seventeen was special if he took seventeen victims, spreading out the killings so that each were further away from the last. This way he could wean himself off this oh-so-powerful drug. But that would be for later. For now, all he could think about was his next fix, and just the sight of the skinny woman who looked so much like an older Rosalyn made his mouth drier and the drumbeat in his brain louder.

The woman's punk boyfriend had disappeared—either a trip to the men's room or the bar for drinks—and Smalley watched as she moved rhythmically to the music. As her body swayed, he imagined all the places he'd be cutting off her flesh. She surprised him by turning his way, and before he could move her eyes caught his. She maintained eye contact, challenging him. He didn't look away either. Of course, she mistook his interest in her, thinking it was sexual.

He considered approaching her, but tonight was only for hunting his prey. Tomorrow night would be for killing. When he spotted her boyfriend making his way toward her, he slipped back into the crowd.

He was more careful after that, staying in the background and keeping them in his peripheral vision. When he saw they were getting ready to leave, he made a quick beeline for the back door, which led to an alley. The next step would be tricky, as he needed to follow them home so he could surprise them tomorrow night. He'd been choosing neighborhood clubs and bars for his hunting grounds, hoping to be able to follow his prey on foot, but if these two hailed a cab or got into a car, he planned to sprint to his car a block away and tail them.

He watched them leave the nightclub and walk past the alley. They didn't hail a cab or walk to a car. Good. It would be easier following them on foot. He guessed that they lived together in an apartment. Most apartment buildings had standard locks that were easy for someone like Smalley to pick, but it didn't matter where they lived—he would find a way in tomorrow night.

He followed them for three blocks, staying in the shadows. When they stopped in the middle of a block to kiss, he slipped into an alley. Maybe he was wrong about them living together, and they could be saying their goodbyes before separating for the night. He'd give it a minute before checking on them. He didn't want either of them seeing him.

He was counting down the minute when the boyfriend walked into the alley.

"You're the perv who's been eye-raping my lady all night," the boyfriend accused. "What the fuck, man? You following us?"

Smalley was rattled. He knew she had caught him looking her way once, but there must've been other times he wasn't aware of. And how'd they know he'd been following them?

"I don't know what you're talking about," he insisted.

"You don't, huh? That's why you're hiding in an alley?"

Smalley recovered enough of his wits to realize he didn't have to wait until tomorrow night. It was almost three in the morning, and he hadn't seen anyone out in the streets other than these two, and they were the only ones who could've seen him. This skinny-assed punk was maybe a hundred and fifty pounds soaking wet, while Smalley was a strapping two hundred. He'd broken hardened men at Ashfield twice the size of this scrawny Tom Petty look-alike. He could beat him to death right here in this alley, and when the girlfriend came to investigate, he'd bash her head into pulpy gore. It wouldn't be as satisfying as being the Nightmare Man, and he'd have to be careful about leaving any DNA behind, but it would take the pressure off and maybe stop the drumbeat pounding in his brain.

Smalley made up his mind. He could get away with it, and just as importantly, he'd enjoy it. He jutted out his chin and took a step toward the boyfriend.

"I'm just minding my own business," he said.

"Hey, my bad, then. If you're just minding your own business, that's cool with me."

The boyfriend extended his hand as if they'd shake and everything would be cool, and Smalley smiled thinking how easy he was making it for him to drag the man deeper into the alley so he could have his fun. He took the offered hand. The boyfriend had the same idea, and he was faster than Smalley. He might've been skinny, but he had a wiry strength, and he jerked Smalley toward him, catching him off-balance. Smalley caught the glint of the knife's blade as it swung open, but it was too late for him to stop the blade from being pushed into his stomach. The boyfriend not only had a wiry strength but was as quick as a weasel, and he stabbed

Smalley three more times in rapid succession before Smalley fell to his knees. A kick in the face sent him onto his back, and then the man was straddling him, stabbing him over and over again.

Smalley couldn't do anything to stop him. He didn't have the strength to lift his hands or make any noise other than a sick, gurgling sound. He was completely, utterly helpless, as much so as the five women he had butchered.

He lost track of how many times the knife's blade penetrated him. At least at the very end the infernal drumbeat in his head went silent the second the blade pierced his heart.

Chapter 58

Samantha Fine knew rolling her eyes was a useless gesture since her mom was calling from Kansas, but she couldn't help herself.

"Mom, I'm not flying home," she said.

"But honey, you have to! There are stories on the news here about a madman killing people," her mom said, as if she were mystified by Samantha's stubbornness on the matter. "It's not safe for you to be in Los Angeles by yourself!"

Another eye roll. "I'll be fine."

"How can you say that? He's already murdered two girls this week—"

"Women," Samantha interrupted.

"What?"

"The victims who were murdered were women, not girls."

"Really? That's what you have to correct me on? All right, women." Susan Fine from Wichita, Kansas, made a harrumphing noise to demonstrate her irritation. "As I was saying before you so skillfully tried distracting me regarding the semantics of whether these poor unfortunate victims were women or girls, they were murdered right in your neighborhood!"

Samantha knew that, but she was surprised her mom did, especially since news about the second murder only came out ten minutes ago. It figured less than five minutes later her mom would call her. "How'd you know that?" she asked.

"You don't think I know how to use Google to get stories from Los Angeles newspapers? Or that they don't provide the addresses of where those women were killed? Or that I wouldn't be able to use Google Earth to see how close their apartment buildings are to yours? Both of them lived only blocks from you!"

"I wouldn't have thought so," Samantha admitted. "You're more tech savvy than I imagined."

"I know a lot more than you give me credit for." Mrs. Fine made another harrumphing noise, this one showing she felt insulted. "For starters, you don't argue with your mother just for the sake of being stubborn when there's a madman breaking into apartments near where you live and killing other young girls who could be you. Excuse me. Young women!"

"Mom, you're acting as if this lunatic is targeting me. Do you have any idea how many thousands of people live in West Hollywood?"

"That's supposed to make me feel better?"

"The police will be catching him," Samantha said.

"They've been trying for thirty-four years, and they haven't yet," Mrs. Fine fretted. "Jeff shouldn't have left you alone."

"Jeff flew to New York on Monday. The first murder was reported on Wednesday."

"He should've gotten on the first flight he could back to Los Angeles then."

"He couldn't. He's contractually obligated for the next three weeks. Besides, filling in on this play could be a big break for him."

"Then you should fly to New York and be with him!"

Samantha couldn't help smiling at that. Her mother the worrywart suggesting that. When she moved to Los Angeles five years ago to pursue an acting career, her mother had conniptions, but at least consoled herself that her daughter wasn't moving to New York where a young woman could be mugged just riding the subway!

"New York's okay with you now?"

"At least there's no one named the Nightmare Man killing people there! Give me one reason why you have to be so stubborn and tempt fate? What would be so wrong about being with your husband for the next three weeks?"

Samantha could've told her the truth, that she had a callback that afternoon for a lead in a new TV series, but she didn't want to jinx it. The only ones outside the show who knew about it were Jeff and her agent, and Jeff was worried also, but he wasn't about to ask her to give up what could be her huge break. She didn't want to think about anything other than the callback. The truth was she was more worried about the Nightmare Man than she was letting on, and her bravado was for her mom's sake. She also knew it was ridiculous to think that this freak would pick her out to be one of his victims, but she'd been having a weird déjà vu feeling, almost as if she'd been having dreams about the Nightmare Man that she couldn't quite remember. Or her mind was playing tricks on her. When minutes ago she saw the news story about the freak killing a second woman, an icy panic gripped her heart, but with deliberate concentration she forced the fear from her mind. And then, of course, her mom called.

Samantha said, "The odds are better I'll be hit by lightning than this lunatic doing anything to me."

Mrs. Fine snorted out angrily. "Miss Know-it-all."

"It's true. And it's Mrs. Know-it-all. As you're well aware, Jeff and I were married four months ago."

Mrs. Fine decided to try a different tactic. "Sam, honey, I'll buy you a plane ticket to either Kansas or New York, your choice. Your father is so worried about you."

Even if Samantha was inclined to take her mom up on her offer, she wasn't going to. Her dad worked as an elementary school teacher, her mom as a librarian. They had already spent more than they should've on her wedding, and they didn't have the money to throw away on a last-minute plane ticket because some crazy lunatic called the Nightmare Man might choose her out of the millions of other women in Los Angeles to kill.

"Mom, I'm going to hang up now," she said. "I promise you I'll be careful, and nobody is going to hurt me, okay? I love you. Dad too."

She disconnected the call before her mom could try another tactic. The phone call had left her uneasy, as if there was actually a chance that lunatic might try to come after her. She checked the time. Ten minutes after twelve. Her callback wasn't until three thirty, which left her time to head over to the gym and work off her nervous energy.

She forced a determined look. Screw the Nightmare Man.

Chapter 59

Morris was disappointed to see that the woman answering the door was in her early thirties and had a three-year-old munchkin wrapped around her leg and an infant in her arms. Unless she had grown up in this ranch-style house and gotten it from her parents, she wouldn't have lived here when Travis Smalley had rented the guesthouse in 2001. He introduced himself and Charlie Bogle, explained why they were there, and asked a question for which he already knew the answer.

"Me and my husband have only been here four years," she said. "We're renting the main part of the house. A very nice young woman who's going to medical school is renting the apartment."

The tiny munchkin hiding behind her leg peeked out at Bogle and made a "nyah-nyah" gesture with thumbs to his ears and tiny fingers wriggling. Bogle stuck his tongue out at him, and the boy disappeared again behind his mother's leg. The woman caught Bogle doing this and gave him a cross look. Morris brought her attention back to him by asking whether she could give him the landlord's name.

"If you wait here I'll get you the address and phone number for the management company," she said curtly. She shot Bogle another cold look before disappearing into the house.

"You're worse than Polk," Morris told Bogle once the door had closed on them. "If you had behaved yourself, she would've invited us in, maybe offered us some coffee."

"We're all Polk at one time or another," Bogle offered philosophically. "Besides, the kid started it."

Neither of them were in good moods. They had visited Joplin Cole's apartment and saw what had been done to her, and that by itself would've been enough to dampen anyone's spirits. They'd also learned that Travis Smalley had been stabbed to death sometime during the night of October 27, 2001, his body discovered in a downtown alley with fourteen knife wounds to the stomach and chest. The timing of his death was suspicious, occurring a week after the Nightmare Man finished killing his fifth and final victim that year, but it didn't prove that Smalley had taken over for Ed Blount. They were looking at him for the 2001 murders because they had no other likely suspects to look at. If he turned out to be the second Nightmare Man, that meant he had passed the baton to someone else before he died, and they'd have to be hunting for a third Nightmare Man.

The front door opened and the woman fixed another cold stare Charlie Bogle's way before handing Morris a note with the management company's contact information. She had put the infant down before returning, but the three-year-old was once again hiding behind her leg, and this time he peeked out long enough to stick his tongue out at Bogle. The woman closed the door on them before Bogle could retaliate.

Morris said, "You certainly made an impression on them."

Bogle said, "One of those days."

Morris sent Adam Felger a text message, then suggested they find a place for lunch. Bogle shrugged. They might as well, since they couldn't move forward until Felger identified who owned the Woodland Hills house back in 2001 when Travis Smalley had rented the back apartment.

They found a diner two miles away. Morris was munching on a turkey club and Bogle the meatloaf dinner when Polk called. He had gone to the apartment management company in Van Nuys where Travis Smalley had worked in security before his death.

"Krenshaw Properties managed the apartment building where Cynthia Leary lived," Polk told Morris. "Up until December 2000, they also managed the building where Tina Ellison lived. In Travis Smalley's position as head of security, he would've had access to keys for both units and would've had no problem making copies of them."

Cynthia Leary was the second woman killed by the Nightmare Man in 2001, Tina Ellison the fifth. Both had lived in Van Nuys. Morris asked about Fiona Connolly, the third victim from 2001, who had also lived in the San Fernando Valley.

Polk complained, "You're never satisfied."

"That's not necessarily true. I remember a time back in 2009—"

"Yeah, well, save it. I'm heading over now to the Lasher Management Group in Sherman Oaks and see if I can find a connection between them and Smalley. But as that old '70s song said so eloquently: two out of three ain't bad."

"Three out of three would be better."

"No kidding. I'll let you know what I find out. Am I mistaken, or are you eating something?"

"You've got a good ear. I didn't realize I was chewing that loudly. A turkey club. Charlie and I found a diner in Woodland Hills."

"Yeah? Any good?"

"Very tasty," Morris said. "They use real roast turkey, not the processed stuff." He looked up at Bogle and asked about the meatloaf plate. Bogle had a mouthful of meatloaf and mashed potatoes, and he gave a thumbs-up sign. Morris told Polk, "Charlie approves of the meatloaf."

"Meatloaf, huh?" Polk said. "That's the name of that chunky, sweaty rock singer who did the song I mentioned. Serendipity, if you ask me. I haven't had lunch yet, but Woodland Hills has got to be at least fifteen miles away."

"At least twenty," Morris said.

"I guess you two would be done by the time I got there," Polk inquired.

"No doubt."

"All right, all right, you don't have to hit me over the head for me to take a hint." Polk had taken on an injured tone. "I'll call you after I dig around at Lasher Management Group." He sniffed and added, "I'm sure they've got good diners in Sherman Oaks."

"I'm sure they do."

Polk hung up.

After Morris put his phone away, Bogle commented that it sounded like Morris had been giving Polk a hard time.

Morris stared back blankly as if he had no idea what his friend was talking about.

Bogle studied him carefully. "What gives?"

Morris gave up the poker face and told Bogle about what Polk had discovered.

"What do you know?" Bogle said. "We can now tie Smalley to two of the 2001 victims. So we've actually got a legitimate reason to look at him as the second Nightmare Man."

"That and the fact that we eliminated everyone else from Ashfield State Prison."

"You could've been nice and invited Polk to join us," Bogle said.

"I'd rather have him spending his time looking for a connection between Smalley and the third 2001 victim. You also must've forgotten what it's like to watch Polk eat."

Bogle shuddered. "A memory I've been trying hard to repress." His eyes took on a thousand-yard stare as he chewed on another mouthful of food, then washed it down with coffee. His gaze shifted back to Morris. "Let's say Smalley killed these women in 2001. Why was he killed in that downtown alley?"

"Maybe he was trying to procure a sixth victim and someone stopped him. Ed Blount killed those five women in 1984 for money, not because he enjoyed it. Smalley would've been a totally different kind of animal. He might not have wanted to stop after five."

Bogle chewed more of his food. "Why didn't the Nightmare Man secrets die with him?" he asked. "Is it possible he had a partner?"

Morris held his hands palms up in a hell-if-I-know gesture. This was now the million-dollar question. Travis Smalley was killed suddenly and violently and wouldn't have had time to pass along his secrets while he was being stabbed repeatedly in a downtown alley. If he had really been the Nightmare Man in 2001, it made sense that he had had help with the murders and had a chance to train his replacement if someone else was now taking over for him. While serial killers rarely had partners, there had been cases of it. They now had enough to justify digging more into Smalley's background and finding out who his friends were. Going back seventeen years wasn't going to be easy.

Bogle said, "If this Smalley character turns out to be the second Nightmare Man, that would mean we had to go back thirty-four years to solve murders that took place seventeen years ago. And then had to go back seventeen years to solve murders happening today. When I think about it, it gives me a headache."

They ate in silence after that, and when they finished lunch, Morris called his computer specialist, Adam Felger, to see if he had found the owner of the Woodland Hills home in 2001. Felger had a name: Joanne Krate. She had sold the house in 2007, and he was trying to find out where she lived now. Felger told Morris he hoped to have that information soon—that Gloria Finston had a call in with the FBI.

They had more time to kill. Morris asked Bogle if he wanted some pie, and Bogle shrugged why not. Morris waved over the waitress, a wrinkled grandmotherly type who walked as if she had pebbles in her corrective shoes.

"What's your best pie?" he asked.

"That would be our peach, hon."

Morris looked at Bogle, who signaled he wanted pie also. "Slices for both of us, please," Morris said. "A scoop of vanilla ice cream on one."

"Make it two," Bogle said.

The waitress gave Bogle a confused look. "Hon, are you asking for one or two scoops?"

"One would be plenty."

The waitress had a pot of coffee with her and refilled their cups before hobbling away, muttering under her breath that people needed to be clearer when asking for things, that she wasn't a mind reader.

While they were finishing up their pie, Felger called back. The FBI had tracked Joanne Krate to Las Vegas from her last tax return. He gave Morris her home address and the name of the casino where she worked as a blackjack dealer. "I'm still trying to find a cell phone number," Felger said. "I warned Greta, and she's looking into travel options. Do you want me to transfer you?"

Morris told him he did, and Greta was soon on the line. The earliest flight she could get him on was a five ten that would be arriving at six twenty-five, and if everything went smoothly they'd have a rental car by seven. Las Vegas was a four-hour drive, and if he and Bogle left now, they'd get there by five, and possibly as early as four thirty depending on how heavy a foot they used on the gas. It made the decision easy.

Morris dropped enough cash on the table to leave the waitress a nice tip, and he and Bogle sucked in their bellies and squeezed their way out of the booth.

Chapter 60

The freak was pacing in his apartment. He knew he had acted stupidly the other day. Not just stupidly, but impulsively. Recklessly, to be completely honest about it. Yes, it was a thrill stalking Joplin Cole and following her to the fitness club, and it would've been okay if he'd just left it at that. It also would've been fine if he had limited himself to simply getting on the machine next to hers. But he shouldn't have spoken to her, and he most definitely shouldn't have followed her to the restaurant.

Dumb. Dumb. Dumb.

But to be fair, what did he say to her at the fitness club that was so egregious? She should've just taken his comments as friendly small talk. For cripes' sake, it wasn't as if he had told her that the Nightmare Man would be having his way with her later that night! It had actually shocked him the way she reacted when he introduced himself as Dale. What would've been so difficult about being nice and simply shaking his hand instead of looking at him as if he were a giant turd and jumping off her machine as if she couldn't get away from him fast enough? Not that it would've mattered how she had acted. She had been chosen to be the Nightmare Man's second victim for this cycle, and nothing would've changed the fact that she was going to die last night.

Still, though, what a bitch!

At least he wasn't stupid enough to tell her his real name. But the incident at the restaurant was bad enough. The freak's lips pressed into a harsh slash when he thought about what had happened. No matter how you look at it, it was really her friend's fault. He had carefully kept his distance when he followed them from the office building to the restaurant and used field glasses to watch for a table to open up so he could spy on her. But her blond bimbo friend must've caught him looking and warned her. If the bistro had security cameras, the police might now have photos of him. Even if they didn't, her friend had gotten a good enough look at him to help with a sketch, and it was too late for him to do anything about it. If he was going to kill Joplin Cole's friend, he would've had to do it last night, and that just wasn't possible—he had been too busy setting up an alibi.

He stopped in front of the TV, picked up the remote control, and tried to work up the courage to turn it on. He couldn't do it. He just wasn't up to seeing whether they were showing a surveillance photo or sketch yet.

He took a deep breath and focused on calming his nerves. He was making too much of this. People had incidents all the time in LA, and besides, she was the one who had accosted him, not the other way around. And just because she was butchered later that night didn't prove anything. Even if they were right now plastering a sketch or surveillance photo of him everywhere on TV and the internet, that didn't necessarily mean the police would find him. There were probably thousands of guys here in LA who had his same blond, clean-cut good looks. And just because Joplin Cole recognized him as a freak didn't mean her friend did also. Not everyone was as perceptive as Cole proved to be, and in the freak's experience, most people never spotted him for what he was. Besides, even if Cole's friend also saw him as a freak, that wouldn't translate well to a police sketch.

Another long, deep breath. He needed to think this through. Let's say the police tracked him down to Cole's fitness club. How would that help them? He had bought a one-month pass using cash, and when he filled out the paperwork he used his *Dale Cooper* alias along with a fake address. He chuckled thinking of his chosen alias and its appropriateness. When the 1990s cult TV show *Twin Peaks* ended after its second season, Dale Cooper, the FBI agent, was left imprisoned within the mysterious black lodge while his evil doppelganger was free to create mischief and mayhem.

The freak's mind wandered back to the problem at hand, and he started panicking again. Another long, deep breath. So what would happen if the police found him? If they searched his apartment, they wouldn't uncover a single trace of the Nightmare Man. He also made sure to have rock-solid alibis for Tuesday night when Lori Fletcher was murdered and last night. So what would happen next? They'd have to look at the restaurant incident as just being one of those things. A coincidence, and nothing more. A hysterical woman making a scene and attacking an innocent guy sitting quietly minding his own business. They might look at him as a person of interest, but that would be it…unless they found out what he had whispered to Joplin Cole before he fled the restaurant.

The freak sat down heavily on the couch, his right leg bouncing like a jackhammer.

Oh shit.

If Cole had repeated to her blond friend what the freak had told her, the police must know it now. And that meant if they ever found him, they'd do whatever they had to do to crack his alibi.

Oh shit.

The freak had earlier considered going to the police and telling them he had learned about Cole's murder from TV, recognized her from their bizarre and unfortunate misunderstanding, and wanted to clear the air. But he couldn't do that, not if they knew what he had whispered to her.

She had gotten his goat by yelling at him in front of everyone in the restaurant. The last thing a freak wanted was to be made the center of attention, especially of an unpleasant incident. But still, it had been so stupid of him, saying what he did. He had put everything at risk.

Stupid, stupid, stupid!

But there was a good chance the police wouldn't find him. He also realized he had been wrong before—it still made sense to find and kill Cole's friend, because even if they had a sketch of him, the sketch would be useless if she wasn't around to identify him. There was the waitress also, but she hadn't seemed to pay much attention to the freak when she took his order. Others in the bistro must have turned his way once that bitch yelled at him, calling him a creep, but he left quickly after that, and besides, the situation was too embarrassing and uncomfortable for them to pay close enough attention to later pick him out of a lineup. The freak had read articles about how witnesses weren't reliable when identifying a person they'd only seen for a second or two.

No, Cole's friend was the only one he had to worry about.

The freak would find her soon. He'd also stop stalking the other women chosen to be slaughtered this year, no matter how much he enjoyed doing it. Even moonfaced Rosalyn.

He felt better after sorting it out.

* * * *

Morris and Bogle were driving in the middle of the desert when Fred Lemmon called. Morris put the phone on speaker, amazed he could pick up a signal.

"We've got something interesting," Lemmon said. "This Nightmare Man maniac might've been stalking Joplin Cole yesterday."

"Wait a minute," Morris asked. He pulled over on I-15. He didn't want to risk losing the signal. An eighteen-wheeler roared past, shaking the car. He looked in the rear-view. There didn't appear to be any other vehicles behind him on this dusty stretch of highway. "Okay, go ahead," he said.

"The victim had lunch yesterday at a downtown restaurant called the Petit Bistro with a work friend named Jamie Siegel. Halfway through lunch Siegel noticed a guy eyeballing Cole from behind. When she told her friend she had an admirer, Cole turned around, and when she saw who it was she left her chair, approached him, and made a scene, calling the guy a creep and yelling at him to leave her alone."

"By any chance, does the Petit Bistro have surveillance cameras?"

"I already called them. They don't. I'm heading over there now to see if there are any cameras between the office building where Cole and Siegel worked and the restaurant."

"Because you think this guy followed them from work to this restaurant," Bogle said.

"Is that you, Charlie?" Lemmon asked. "You're still playing hooky from your babysitting job to slum as a real detective?"

"Nah, just wanted a ride to Vegas so I can catch the floor show at the Sahara and heard Morris was heading over there."

Lemmon laughed at that. "To answer your question, I'm hoping that's the case and we've got this guy on surveillance video. From the way Siegel described him, he's kind of a bland Ken doll in his thirties. There are probably thousands of surfer dudes and preppies in LA who'd fit his description. Annie is taking Siegel to the Wilcox Avenue station for a statement and to see if we can get a police sketch out of her."

"Did he have a man bun?" Bogle asked. "I hear they make Ken dolls like that now."

"Nah. He sounded like one of the old-fashioned types. Blond, Dockers, polo shirt, tennis shoes. Nothing distinguishing. No tattoos or scars. I'll be interviewing the staff at the bistro to see if anyone remembers anything else."

Morris asked, "What happened after the confrontation?"

"Ken Doll whispered something to Cole, then got out of there fast. Siegel doesn't know what was whispered."

"It would be good to find that out," Morris said.

"Yeah, I know. No one else in her office heard anything about it. Once we get her cell phone unlocked, Annie and I will be going through her call log to see who she might've spoken with afterward. But if she didn't tell Siegel there's a good chance she didn't tell anyone."

Morris sat rubbing his jaw, deep in thought. "She met him somewhere before the bistro," he said.

"We'll be trying to find that out, boss. One step at a time."

Bogle said, "It's possible he's an old boyfriend, or even just a jerk who struck out with her at a bar. This might not be related to the Nightmare Man murders."

Morris made a face. That wasn't likely.

"Coincidences happen," Bogle argued.

"Not as often as you'd think."

Lemmon interrupted them, asking Morris what they should do with the police sketch. "Advertise it or keep it among ourselves?" he asked.

That was a tough question. If they advertised it, they might get a legitimate lead or send the suspect underground. In this case, there were other considerations. If the suspect was as generic looking as Lemmon described, publicizing the sketch could cause thousands of innocent men to be looked at potentially as the Nightmare Man, leading to lost jobs and relationships. But if they could stop this maniac before he killed again, they had to do it.

"We get the sketch out there, but we make it a soft sell. The police believe this individual seen yesterday at the Petit Bistro has important information in the Nightmare Man investigation, and we're asking for him to come forward."

Lemmon made a snorting noise at his end. "If he's the Nightmare Man, he won't be voluntarily walking into any police stations."

"You never know," Morris said. "He could come in thinking he could outsmart us. But it doesn't matter. It gets his face out there. If people know him, they'll call the hotline. And if he doesn't come in on his own, we know he's the one we want."

"We already know he won't be coming in," Lemmon said. "I'd suggest we make it more of a hard sell. We could call him a person of interest. Let's see if we can put maximum pressure on this bastard."

"Let's try it the other way for now."

"All right, if that's how you want to play it. After I finish up downtown, I'll be meeting up with Annie again, and we'll work to trace back Cole's movements and see if we can figure out where she met the Ken doll. I'll text you the sketch when we've got it."

Lemmon got off the call. Morris turned to Bogle and asked if they should turn back.

Bogle said, "We're already more than halfway there."

"By maybe a mile."

"What are we going to do if we go back?" Bogle asked. "Fred and Annie have the Ken doll search covered. If you think you need more bodies on it, put Polk on it. Or one of the LAPD detectives. My gut's telling me we're going to find this psycho by following our Travis Smalley thread."

"You just want to see Wayne Newton at the Sahara."

A thin smile crept onto Bogle's lips. "I don't think he's playing at the Sahara."

Morris put the car back in drive, got back on the highway, and continued toward Las Vegas.

Chapter 61

Samantha Fine was sure she killed it. She stood breathless watching the faces of the showrunner and producers, the look in their eyes seemingly confirming that she killed it. None of them looked bored or uninterested, and the showrunner gave Samantha a hint of a smile and an encouraging nod. They were sitting behind a table, and they huddled together to confer among themselves, talking in hushed whispers. Samantha wished she could read lips. Their conference didn't last long, and the head producer got up and headed toward Samantha, a broad smile breaking out over her lips.

"A beauty who can act," she said.

Samantha could barely believe this was happening. She'd been working toward this moment since she was seventeen. She'd acted in commercials, several small parts on soap operas, and a fifteen-second, one-line appearance in a movie that was still searching for a distributor (and for all she knew, they'd already cut her out of it), but this would be a starring role on a new TV series. And the script was smart and funny. The show had a chance of being something big, especially with the pedigree behind it.

She asked whether she had gotten the part, the words tumbling out.

The producer grinned at her. "We can't make it official until Monday," she said. "We'll want you to come back then, and we'll be having a press conference and announcing it then." The producer looked taken aback. "Why so glum? I thought you'd be doing backflips."

"No, it's not that," Samantha said. She forced a smile. "I really am thrilled. It's just that hubby is in New York, and I was planning to take the red-eye tonight to see him. But that will have to wait. I'll be here whatever time you want Monday."

"Good." The producer's broad smile came back. "We'll see you here at noon sharp on Monday."

The two women hugged. The producer said softly to Samantha, "Sweetie, you're shivering."

"I'm just so happy."

She had lied about why she had shivered. Of course she was happy about getting the part. Ecstatic, really. But now that she wouldn't be flying out of Los Angeles as she had planned, she realized just how frightened she was of the Nightmare Man. The idea of it was ridiculous. Insane, really. She had let her mother's earlier phone call inflame her fears. But there was something more than that. There were those whispers in the back of her mind that she couldn't quite get a handle on, the ones she was sure were warning her about the killer. God, what was wrong with her? The biggest break of her life, and she was going to worry about some crazy lunatic on the loose?

The head producer brought Samantha to the showrunner and her two associates, and they chatted. The showrunner, Mitzi Helgund, was the creative force behind the wildly successful *Purple Is the New Sad*, and she told Samantha that the callback had been only a formality. "I knew the second I saw you that you were our Jane," she said. "Sassy, tough, and vulnerable. And of course, cute as hell. You also have *it*."

Samantha was flustered, embarrassed, and giddy at this point, and said, "I hope *it*, whatever *it* is, isn't contagious!"

Mitzi laughed. "If *it* were, we'd be lucky to catch *it*."

Later, as she was leaving the building, she started to call Jeff but remembered the time difference and knew he'd be preparing himself to go onstage in an hour. His play was a heavy drama, and his character was especially morose throughout it, so it would be better if she called him later, or he might accuse her of causing him to break out grinning during his performance. Instead she called her best friend Toni and told her the news.

"How fast can you get over to Divine's?" Toni asked.

Divine's on Vine was a popular Hollywood bar. "I could be there in twenty minutes," Samantha said.

"That's good, 'cause girl, we need to do some celebrating!"

Chapter 62

Las Vegas, the present

Morris and Bogle found Joanne Krate dealing blackjack at a five-dollar-minimum-bet table. The table had four open seats, and they took two of them. While they played hands, Morris explained to Krate that they had driven up from Los Angeles to ask her about a former tenant, Travis Smalley. She seemed surprised to hear that and told Morris that she needed to concentrate on her dealing but would be happy to talk to him during her next break. Over the next twenty-five minutes, Morris lost sixty dollars while Bogle won three hundred twenty. After Krate's replacement arrived, Morris and Bogle left the table and quickly caught up to her.

"Dealers aren't supposed to fraternize with the clientele," she told them. She shot Bogle a dirty look and added, "Especially not clientele who win money at the dealer's table. I need to clear this first with my floor manager."

Krate was a plump woman in her sixties who dyed her thinning hair a mousy brown. After fussing with her standard-issue purple and dark green uniform and making sure her bowtie was straight, she scanned the casino floor until she spotted a man in his late thirties with a heavy five o'clock shadow who was carefully watching one of the tables. Unlike the dealers, he wore a black tuxedo. Krate made a beeline for him while Morris and Bogle followed her. She told him about Morris's request and how the two had done at her table. He shifted his gaze from the blackjack table he was studying to Morris and Bogle for all of two seconds before fixing his stare back onto the goings-on at the table he'd been observing.

"Have you two ever met Joanne before?" he asked.

"No," Morris said.

"Do you plan on ever sitting at her table again?"

"As pleasant as I found Ms. Krate, I'm not much of a gambler and rarely go to Vegas," Morris said. "I can promise I will not do anything to get Ms. Krate in trouble."

"Ditto," Bogle said.

"How serious is this business you want to talk to her about?"

"Serious," Morris said. "But nothing she was involved in."

"Okay, go have your talk. Just be discreet. Joanne, how about you take your dinner break now."

The floor manager seemed satisfied with the table he'd been watching and moved on so he could observe another one.

Joanne Krate's face brightened. "I know a place nearby that has the best open-faced roast beef sandwiches. They're to die for. How about you two buy me dinner and we'll talk there?"

Morris said, "Sure thing."

Joanne Krate seemed especially happy over the prospect of being treated for dinner. Her smile weakened. Guilt.

"I should warn you that you're wasting your time," she said. "Whatever you suspect Travis of having done, you're wrong. He was a gentleman, through and through, and his death was just too tragic for words. But I'll tell you whatever I can."

"That's all I can ask," Morris said.

He let Krate lead them off the casino floor.

* * * *

Morris and Krate ordered the open-faced roast beef sandwiches while Bogle had the French toast and sausage patties. After one bite of the sandwich, Morris agreed it was very tasty, and Krate seemed tickled to hear that.

"I tried calling your cell phone during the drive and didn't get an answer," Morris said. "I couldn't tell from the automated voicemail greeting whether I had the right number." He repeated to her the number Felger had given him.

"That's the right one." She sighed and showed a pout before adding, "But we're not allowed to have our cell phones on while we're working. God forbid someone needed to call us about an emergency."

Morris didn't want to send her off on a tangent about the casino's employee policies; he just wanted to make sure he had the right number. He had learned during the car ride to the diner that Joanne Krate could talk up a storm if given the chance.

He asked, "Mr. Smalley was renting your guesthouse at the time of his death?"

"That's right," she said, nodding fervently. "The dear man had been with us for two years, and I couldn't have asked for a better tenant. He was just so polite and helpful. And quiet! I never heard a peep from his apartment. And handsome! Like a young Rock Hudson." She blushed a light pink. "Craig was so jealous of him. But he had no reason to be. Travis was just a perfect gentleman."

"Who's Craig?"

"He was my second husband." Bitterness wrecked her mouth. She cut off a piece of the sandwich and chewed until the bitterness passed. "Craig Farrow. When I rented the guesthouse to Travis it was just me and Rosalyn. I met Craig later, and he was always harping on me to kick Travis out. He had no good reason; he just kept claiming he didn't like Travis's looks." More bitterness whitened her face, and her lips pressed tightly, pruning the skin near her mouth. "It was Craig's idea that I sell the house and we move to Las Vegas."

"How can I get ahold of him?"

"You can't. At least not in this lifetime. He died of a heart attack three years ago, but not after first gambling away all my money. This was supposed to be my retirement—"

"Is Rosalyn your daughter?" Bogle asked to distract her and keep her from tumbling into full-blown resentment.

She stared at Bogle as if she'd forgotten he was there. "Yes," she said. "Rosalyn had such a crush on Travis, always mooning over him. The poor thing was devastated when he died. To be honest, I cried like a baby myself."

Morris asked, "Did he ever keep caged rats in his apartment?"

She blinked several times at Morris and made a face as if she didn't understand what he was asking her. "That's such an odd question," she said.

"I agree," he acknowledged. "But it's an important one."

"Why in the world would Travis have kept rats?" she asked, frowning.

"How about metal cage traps?"

Her frown deepened. "I couldn't tell you what he kept in his apartment," she said. "I don't believe I ever stepped foot in it while he was renting. Travis was a very private person, and I respected his privacy."

Bogle asked, "What about your daughter?"

Confusion marred her soft, round face. "What about Rosalyn?"

"Was she ever in Smalley's apartment?"

"Of course not. She was only thirteen when Travis moved in. He wouldn't have had her alone in the guesthouse!"

"Can you tell me about his friends?"

Her face went blank. "I can't remember Travis bringing friends around," she said. "That didn't mean he didn't. The guesthouse has a private entrance. But I don't remember ever seeing anyone."

"So no girlfriends?" Bogle asked.

Joanne Krate looked astonished by the fact, as if she'd never thought of it before. "Of course, Travis knew I had a young, impressionable daughter, so that could be why he never brought anyone over."

Morris asked, "How about his hours?"

"He had a very demanding job and would often come home late from work. There were times I'd hear his car at two in the morning, or even later. But it wasn't as if he made a racket. He was very conscientious. I'm just a light sleeper."

She closed her mouth, and her head cocked to one side as if she were listening to whispers from far away. "I'd forgotten about this, but Rosalyn was in Travis's apartment once," she said. "This was after Travis died and we needed to clean out the guesthouse. Rosalyn volunteered to do it." She sat quietly kneading her fingers. "I shouldn't have let her," she said. "My daughter was only fifteen at the time, and I should've put my foot down, but Rosalyn was so insistent and Craig didn't want me spending any money hiring someone, so I gave in. But I'm sure if Rosalyn had seen rats or cage traps or anything odd like that she would've told me."

Morris asked for Rosalyn's contact information, and Joanne Krate's eyes filled with tears. She used a napkin to wipe away some of the wetness and told Morris that she had had a falling-out with her daughter over Craig.

"Rosalyn didn't like him and threatened to have nothing to do with me if I married him. I should've listened to her. She knew." She sniffed several times and bit her bottom lip as she struggled to keep from sobbing. She showed Morris a sad clown smile and told him she hadn't talked with her daughter since she had sold the house. "I don't know where she's living," she said. "If you find her, could you please give her my phone number and ask her to call me?"

"I will," Morris promised.

Joanne thanked him. She cut off another piece of roast beef, and after putting it in her mouth, her face crumbled.

"It's gotten cold," she said.

She started sobbing quietly. It had been too much disappointment for one night. Morris told her he'd order her another one, then bolted from the table to look for the waitress.

If looks could kill, the one Bogle gave him right then for leaving him alone with the distraught woman would've put Morris six feet under. Later, when they were driving back to Los Angeles, Bogle admitted he was angrier at himself for not thinking of the trick first.

"We know Smalley was a sadist, a loner without any friends, that he could nearly charm the pants off a middle-aged woman like Joanne Krate, and kept odd hours. Sounds to me like a prime candidate to be a serial killer."

They knew more than that. They could connect him to Ed Blount and two of the 2001 victims. Polk didn't have any luck connecting him to the victim who had lived in Sherman Oaks, but the apartment building had had a rash of break-ins in 1996, and they had replaced all the locks then. The management company had hired a subcontractor for that work who was no longer in business, so Polk had hit a dead end. Smalley could've been involved.

"If we can find the daughter, she might be able to enlighten us whether Smalley had any friends," Morris said, one hand loosely on the wheel as he navigated through the slow-moving Las Vegas Strip traffic. "She should also be able to tell us if he kept caged rats in the apartment."

Bogle dozed off once they drove outside the Las Vegas city limits and were in the desert. They had planned to switch places after two hours, but Morris let his friend sleep.

Before they had tracked down Joanne Krate, Fred texted him the police sketch of the man who had upset Joplin Cole at Petit Bistro, and Morris was disappointed with what he saw. Fred had been right earlier; the guy looked like thousands of other blond thirty-something guys floating around Los Angeles, or at least his sketch did. Fred also didn't have any luck finding surveillance video. Maybe they'd get the guy from someone calling the hotline number or by tracing back Joplin Cole's movements and discovering where she met him, or maybe Bogle had been right earlier, that if they kept pulling on this Travis Smalley thread it would somehow lead them to this guy. Morris was all but convinced Smalley had been the second Nightmare Man, which meant there had to be a connection between him and his replacement.

Morris felt there was something he was missing, maybe a link between Lori Fletcher and Joplin Cole that he should be seeing but wasn't. Whatever it was, he couldn't figure it out. When he was an hour from LA, Felger called. He had Rosalyn Krate's address but couldn't find a phone number. Like Fletcher and Cole, she lived in West Hollywood.

Bogle woke up as Morris pulled into MBI's parking lot, his face craggy from sleep.

"Same time tomorrow?" he asked.

"Same time, same bat channel." Morris pulled up next to Bogle's car. Bogle gave him a wave before getting into his car and driving off. Morris parked and headed up to the office. Once inside the conference room, he located Rosalyn Krate's address on the map he had taped to the wall. She lived two blocks away from Lori Fletcher and three blocks from Joplin Cole's apartment building. A chill ran through him. He couldn't explain the reason for it. Did he really think she was going to be targeted as one of the Nightmare Man victims? For what reason? Because she had a connection with Travis Smalley seventeen years ago?

He checked the time. Eleven twenty-five. All the driving had made it seem like a much longer day. He left the office and got back in his car, but instead of heading home he drove to Rosalyn Krate's apartment building. He frowned at the setup: There was no doorman, no buzzer, no security of any kind. Anyone could just walk in. Rosalyn lived on the fourth floor. No elevator either. He climbed the stairs, listened for a minute to dead quiet coming from inside her apartment, and resisted the urge to pound on the door to see that she was okay. It would've been crazy to wake her up based on a hunch he couldn't explain. He'd talk to her tomorrow.

He wrote a note on a business card asking her to call him and slipped it under the door.

Chapter 63

The killer used a key to enter Samantha Fine's apartment. A large gym bag slung over one shoulder held an angry caged rat and all the materials and tools needed for the Nightmare Man killings.

The killer set the bag down next to the dining room table and proceeded to empty it, placing each item on the table and being careful not to make a sound. The rat had become exceedingly agitated and began scratching furiously against its metal mesh enclosure, but this made less noise than the refrigerator in the adjoining kitchen. It certainly wouldn't wake Samantha, especially since the bedroom door was closed.

It was a little after three a.m., and there was enough ambient light from outside streetlamps that the killer didn't need to use a penlight. This was the fifth time the killer had been in Samantha's apartment. During the earlier visits the killer had crept quietly into the bedroom and whispered to Samantha while she slept, just like with Lori Fletcher and Joplin Cole. Samantha never woke during these times, although her husband had once, but he had fallen quickly back to sleep without realizing they had an intruder. While Samantha might have slept through these whispers, they still affected her, causing her to frown and her brow to become deeply furrowed. A few times she even whimpered.

The killer last visited a week ago. At that time the killer not only whispered terrible things to Samantha Fine but had also gone through papers that were left stacked on the kitchen counter and discovered that the husband planned to fly to New York on Monday, which meant his gorgeous wife would be all alone tonight. Of course, calling Samantha gorgeous was an understatement. Lori Fletcher and Joplin Cole were both very pretty, but Samantha was something else entirely. Vivacious.

Stunning. Jaw-droppingly beautiful. A star in the making. That was why she was chosen. When people saw her picture and learned what had been done to her, it would cause outrage and immense sadness that would dwarf that of any of the other victims. Their deaths would be considered tragic, of course, and people would mourn them, but with Samantha the focus would be on the potential that had been stolen from the world. More than the other victims, she would be inextricably linked to the Nightmare Man, and that would only heighten the mystique.

The killer took off leather gloves and replaced them with a pair of protective rubber gloves. The killer then brought a rag and a bottle of chloroform to the kitchen sink and proceeded to saturate the rag. Later, the sink would be cleaned, but for now Samantha needed to be anesthetized. Once she was helpless, the killer would cut off her pajamas (such a disappointment to discover during previous visits that she wore pajamas to bed instead of sleeping nude), gag her, and bind her wrists and ankles. After that the killer would use needle-nose pliers to pull off one of her thumbnails. If that didn't wake her, smelling salts would be used.

The killer was careful not to drip chloroform on the floor, not that it mattered. The medical examiner must know by now that chloroform was used, just as in 1984 and 2001. Still, why leave any traces that didn't need to be left?

A slight click could be heard when the bedroom door was opened. The shades were down, making the room darker than the rest of the apartment. The carpeting deadened any sound the killer's rubber-soled shoes might've made, but the killer still moved cautiously to where Samantha slept so as not to bump the bed.

The killer reached down to where Samantha's head should've been resting on the pillow, except there was nothing. Well, that wasn't right. A penlight showed the bed was empty. The killer found the light switch. Not only was the room empty, but the bed was made. The killer had already checked the apartment's lone bathroom. Samantha wasn't home.

There was nothing else to do but bring the chloroform-soaked rag back to the kitchen so that it could be cleaned in the sink. The killer spent minutes soaking the rag with water and rinsing it out, all the while thinking things through. Once the sweet chemical smell from the chloroform had dissipated, the rubber gloves were stripped off.

Samantha Fine was supposed to die tonight at the hands of the Nightmare Man, but that no longer seemed possible, which was more than upsetting. Plans had been so carefully drawn out, and not just for Samantha but for the other victims as well. After all, Samantha Fine was only going to be victim three, and five lives were going to be taken before the Nightmare Man disappeared for another seventeen years. But sometimes you had to roll with the punches. Accept life's disappointments and move on. There was always tomorrow night for Samantha to die.

The killer packed up and left quietly, making sure no trace of this nocturnal visit was left behind.

Chapter 64

Saturday morning at ten minutes past seven, Morris was taking Parker for a walk in the neighborhood when his phone rang. He frowned when he saw there was no caller ID information. He answered anyway.

A woman's voice cooed, "I know who you are from TV. I saw you on *The Hollywood Peeper*."

"Okay," Morris said. "And whom am I talking to?"

The woman sounded confused. "Rosalyn Krate. You left a business card under my door. Or somebody did who was pretending to be you."

"I left the card late last night."

"Well, it scared the heck out of me! I know from TV you're working with the police to arrest the Nightmare Man. Does this mean I'm in danger?"

"I'm sorry if I scared you. We need to talk face-to-face. As soon as possible."

"What about?"

"I'm hoping you have information that can help us."

"What could I possibly know that could help?"

"We'll talk about that when we meet. How soon can that be?"

"Can you buy me breakfast?" She got coy, adding, "I think that's the least you can do for getting me so worried."

"Sure, I can do that. Give me a place and time."

"Do you know Stephanie's in West Hollywood? On Santa Monica Boulevard? Eight o'clock?"

"I'll be there."

* * * *

When Morris and Parker arrived at the restaurant, Rosalyn Krate was already seated at a table, or at least Morris assumed the thin and pretty woman was Rosalyn. Early thirties, light brown hair, and a clear resemblance around the eyes and nose to Joanne Krate, as well as a similar moon-shaped face. She faced the door, and her expression when he walked in was a dead giveaway that she knew who he was and that she'd been waiting for him. When Morris got within ten feet of her, Parker began misbehaving, growling and trying to bull his way forward. That was unusual for him. Morris saw the frightened look on Rosalyn's face, and he shortened his hold on the leash and scolded Parker. The dog mixed in a few angry pig grunts with his growling, but after more scolding he complied.

Morris continued on to the table, making sure Parker stayed close to his side. He asked the woman if she was Rosalyn Krate. She nodded, her eyes large as she watched Parker.

"He's not going to bite me?" she asked.

"No, he won't. I don't know what got into him, but he'll be good."

Morris took the seat across from Rosalyn and had Parker lie down by his feet. A low rumble came from the dog as he started growling again, but another stern warning stopped him.

"I've always been afraid of dogs," Rosalyn said. She chewed her bottom lip and added, "I think they can sense when you're afraid."

"That must be it. I apologize. He usually doesn't act like this."

An unhappy moan eased out of Parker, his eyes fixed on Rosalyn as he lay on his stomach, his snout resting on his paws. At least he wasn't growling.

More lip chewing, then, "I knew you had a dog. I saw him when you were on *The Hollywood Peeper*. It just didn't occur to me you'd bring him here."

Her complexion had paled a shade since Morris first spotted her, and this helped him notice the dark circles under her eyes.

"You haven't been sleeping well," he said.

"It's not just dogs I'm afraid of these days." She leaned forward so she could confide in Morris, and in a softer voice said, "This is going to sound silly, but I've been afraid of the Nightmare Man. It's almost as if I've been having premonitions that he's going to hurt me. Crazy, huh?"

A waitress came over with menus. Morris had suspected when he walked into the restaurant and saw the food on one of the tables that it was a crunchy-granola vegan place, and sure enough the menu only had items like chia pudding, tofu omelets, and beet burgers. He smiled inwardly thinking this was why Parker had gotten so upset—she had dragged them to a place that served tempeh bacon!

Rosalyn informed the waitress that she already knew what she wanted and ordered a banana, apricot, and hemp milk smoothie and a tofu scramble with quinoa, spinach, black beans, and a cheese made out of something called cassava and arrowroot. Morris stuck with coffee. He waited until the waitress had walked out of earshot before telling Rosalyn that it wasn't crazy for her to be worried about the Nightmare Man.

"It could be something your subconscious picked up on from when you were a teenager and is now sounding an alarm," he said. "I'd like to ask you what you remember about Travis Smalley."

She blinked several times as if she weren't sure she had heard that right. "Travis rented my mom's guesthouse," she said. "But he died when I was fifteen. What could he have to do with the Nightmare Man?"

"That's what I'm trying to figure out. Your mom told me you cleaned out the guesthouse after he died."

"You talked with my mom?"

"Yesterday." Morris dug out of his pocket a piece of paper that had Joanne Krate's phone number and he handed it to Rosalyn. "She'd like you to call her."

She looked blankly at the paper, then crumpled it and dropped it on the floor. Pink peppered her cheeks.

"That's not going to happen," she said in a hurt voice.

"If you change your mind, you can call me and I'll give you her number again. Her second husband is out of the picture for good, if that helps at all."

"If you don't mind, I'd rather not talk about her." She closed her eyes as if she were trying to wipe the memory of her mother from her mind. When she opened them again, a peacefulness had settled over her face. A tranquil moon once again. "Yes, I was the one who cleaned out the guesthouse after what happened to Travis."

"Was that the first time you were in there after he moved in?"

She nodded.

"Did you notice anything unusual?"

"Like what?"

"Cage traps."

"What do you mean? Like for rabbits?"

"Sure."

"I remember those," she said. "He had a bunch of them stacked up inside his apartment. But he was head of security for a bunch of apartment buildings, and I thought he must've needed the traps for his job. Like what if any of these buildings had flower gardens and he needed to catch rabbits infesting them? But I did find it odd."

"How about a hunting knife?"

She squinted and scrunched up her slightly upturned nose as if she were digging deep into her mind. "I don't remember weapons of any kind," she said. "He had a tool chest. I remember that. But I didn't open it. I didn't want Craig to take it—he was the awful man my mom hooked up with and married—so I packed it up to be stored, but all of Travis's belongings ended up being thrown out. You're acting as if you think Travis might've been the Nightmare Man?"

"There's a chance of it," Morris admitted.

"But how would that be possible? He's been dead for years." Her eyes opened as wide as half dollars and her mouth formed a small perfect circle. "Oh my God," she whispered. "What if he really didn't die? What if Travis is still alive?"

Morris felt his heart beat a tick faster. Was it possible that wasn't Smalley's corpse found in a downtown alley back in 2001? Smalley could've found someone who looked like him and planted his wallet on the body so it would be mistaken for him. But why would he do that? No obvious answer came to mind, but it explained one of the riddles that needed solving—how the Nightmare Man's secrets were able to live on after Smalley was killed so suddenly and before he would've had a chance to train his replacement.

"I'll find out today if it really was Travis Smalley killed in that alley," Morris promised. "Do you know if he had a girlfriend?"

"I was just thirteen when he moved into the guesthouse, but I had a hopeless crush on him and he knew it." She smiled tragically. "He used to tease me about it all the time. Telling me that when I got older, he'd make sure to find me and that we were destined to someday be together. But he was just joking and seeing how much he could make me blush. He wouldn't have told me about a girlfriend if he had one. He knew it would've absolutely destroyed me."

Morris decided he'd have Polk watch Rosalyn, at least until he knew for sure whether Smalley was really dead. Which also meant he needed the body exhumed and dental records checked, assuming the body had been buried and not cremated. He dug into the briefcase he had brought along and pulled out the police sketch of the blond thirty-something man who had bothered Joplin Cole. He showed the sketch to Rosalyn and asked if she had seen him.

"I probably see dozens of guys each week who look like that," she said. "I couldn't tell you who this is. But how is he connected to Travis?"

"I don't know," Morris admitted. "Did you know any of Travis's friends?"

"I never met any of them," she said. "I can't remember him ever talking about any."

"Anything you can think of about him that you found peculiar?"

"You mean something that makes me think he was the Nightmare Man when I was fifteen?"

"Yes."

She gave it a try but shook her head. "Nada. Sorry."

"If something comes to mind, call me?"

The waitress came with their food. Rosalyn might've been showing a tragic smile, but it didn't adversely affect her appetite, and she attacked her tofu scramble with vigor. Morris took a sip of coffee. It tasted like the real thing. At least they didn't make it out of soybeans. He put his mug down and took a couple of photos from the briefcase. He first showed Rosalyn a photo of Lori Fletcher and asked if she had ever met her.

"I recognize her from TV," Rosalyn said after swallowing a mouthful of tofu scramble. "She was one of the victims. But no, I never met her."

Morris next showed her a photo of Joplin Cole, and Rosalyn told him she hadn't met her either.

"Okay, I'll take care of the bill. Thanks for your help." Morris pushed his chair away from the table and stood. He gave Rosalyn a long look. "You still have my business card?" he asked.

"Yes, of course."

"If anything weird happens, call me immediately. Anytime."

She smiled at that. "And you'll come running. Because I've got a friend?"

Morris smiled over the Carole King reference. "Exactly."

He had to tug on Parker's leash to get the bull terrier up on his feet. The dog let out a bunch of grumpy, unhappy grunts as he plodded along behind Morris. He found the waitress and handed her enough money to cover the bill and a nice tip, and once he was outside, he called Polk.

Morris asked, "I didn't wake you?"

"Uh uh. I'm here at MBI drinking coffee, reading everybody's notes, and trying to piece together in my mind what we know about this investigation. You know what conclusion I've come up with?"

"Enlighten me."

"It's a mess."

"I can't argue with you there." He gave Polk the address for Stephanie's. "There's a woman here I'd like you to tail and make sure she stays safe. How fast can you be here?"

"Ten minutes?"

"Good enough. I'll stick around so I can point her out to you."

"Are you expecting this Nightmare Man psycho to target her?"

"To be honest, I'm not sure what I'm thinking right now."

After he got off the phone with Polk, he called Roger Smichen and told him what he needed. Smichen sounded grumpy over the idea of searching for a seventeen-year-old record from the coroner's office but told Morris he'd handle it personally. He also warned that Morris would need to work the proper channels for an exhumation, assuming the body still existed. Polk had also sounded grumpier than usual, and Morris wondered whether Parker's grumpiness was contagious.

There was a fast food joint on the same block that sold breakfast sandwiches, and Morris bought egg and bacon sandwiches for himself and Parker. He didn't want to reward Parker's earlier aggressive behavior, but he knew bad moods could be contagious also, and it was time to turn things around.

Chapter 65

Woodland Hills, October 29, 2001

Rosalyn couldn't stop weeping. When she came home from school and her mother told her Travis was dead, she refused at first to believe it.

"You're making that up," she insisted.

"Now honey, why would I do that?"

"I don't know. But it must've been Craig's idea!"

"You're always thinking the worst of Craig." Mrs. Krate sighed. "I don't know why you do that. But honey, the police came today and they showed me Travis's driver's license. They also brought back his house key."

"Prove it!"

Mrs. Krate searched through her pocketbook and found a key, which she held out to her daughter. Rosalyn started trembling. If she took the key and used it to open the door to the guesthouse, that meant Travis was really dead.

"You poor thing."

Mrs. Krate made a clucking sound and took a step toward Rosalyn with the intention of hugging her. Rosalyn would've let her if it wasn't for Craig. She remembered every nasty comment and innuendo he had made about Travis when Travis wasn't around to defend himself. Rosalyn despised her mother's live-in boyfriend, and because of that she ran from her mother and fled to her bedroom, slamming the door behind her and flinging herself onto the bed. For several minutes she felt too numb to even think. Then it hit her that her mother was telling the truth and this wasn't a nasty joke Craig thought up. The realization that Travis was really dead left her feeling like she could be crumpled up like a piece of tinfoil.

Rosalyn wasn't a foolish, empty-headed girl, even though Craig routinely called her that. She had been well aware that Travis was twenty years older than her, but she also knew in ten years their ages wouldn't be all that insurmountable. She also understood he was joking when he talked about how they were destined to be together someday, but she wasn't just a silly child either. She'd see the flashes of hunger in his eyes, and in her heart she knew they truly were each other's destinies. But if he was really dead, that meant she was rudderless and utterly alone. And so she wept.

At five thirty her mother knocked on the door and told her dinner was ready. Rosalyn got up, wiped her eyes and nose, made a stop in the bathroom to wash her face, then headed to the dinner table. She felt completely dead inside and had no intention of eating even a morsel of food, but she wanted to be at the table in case Craig said anything mean about Travis. If he did, she was going to stab him in his fat face with a fork!

Her mother had made Rosalyn's favorite—vegetable lasagna. Craig, of course, had to complain about it. "You couldn't add any sausages?" he grumbled.

"Hush! It's good the way it is. And Rosalyn needed something special tonight."

"She's not even eating it," he said, his face folded into a surly frown.

Mrs. Krate looked with alarm at Rosalyn. "Honey, I know how fond you were of Travis, but starving yourself isn't going to do you any good. And I did make tonight's dinner specially for you." She put her fork and knife down and fretted with her hands. "Please, Rosalyn. I even added roasted eggplant. Just try taking a bite."

Rosalyn conceded to cutting off a piece of the lasagna and pushing it around her plate with her fork. She had no appetite for food. That wasn't why she had joined them at the table. She wanted an excuse to stab Craig in the eye! He must've sensed this, because he behaved himself and only made disgusting eating noises as he shoveled food into his mouth. Sausage or no sausage, he cleaned his plate and waited until then to comment that they needed to box up Travis's belongings.

"There's no reason you should miss out on any rent," he told Mrs. Krate, one eye carefully watching Rosalyn.

Rosalyn was furious that he'd suggest that, even though logically she knew there was nothing unreasonable about it. But Craig was a freeloader, and that he believed he had the right to tell them how to handle their affairs left her fuming.

"We can wait a few days on that," Mrs. Krate said.

"Why throw money away?"

Rosalyn's hands tightened on her fork.

"I'll hire someone to box up the guesthouse," Mrs. Krate said.

He made a snorting noise. "Why do that? Why not have Rosalyn earn her keep for a change?"

Rosalyn was ready to leap across the table and unleash all of her grief on this fat, hideous man by plucking out one of his eyes with the fork, but then she realized how much she wanted to do what he was suggesting. The idea of spending time in Travis's room and being the one to fold up his clothing and other belongings was all she wanted right then.

"That wouldn't be right," Mrs. Krate insisted. "I'll hire someone first thing tomorrow."

Craig started grumbling some more and was going to argue about the matter, but Rosalyn cut him off. "I'll do it tomorrow when I get home from school," she said.

"You bet you will," Craig muttered under his breath.

Mrs. Krate ignored him. Concern weighed heavily on her face as she studied Rosalyn.

"You'll need your strength, then," she said.

Rosalyn accepted that they had a deal. She halfheartedly began eating the lasagna on her plate.

* * * *

When Rosalyn returned home from school she found the boxes and packing material her mother had delivered beside the door to the guesthouse. The plan was for Rosalyn to box up Travis's belongings, and they'd store everything in the basement until they found a relative to claim them. She wasn't sure they'd find anyone. Travis had once told her that both his parents were dead and, like her, he was an only child.

The key for the guesthouse had been left next to the phone in the kitchen, and Rosalyn felt lightheaded as she walked around the outside of the house so she could enter the apartment where Travis had lived for two years. She'd had many sleepless nights lying in bed wondering what it would be like to sneak into the guesthouse and cuddle up next to Travis. She had dropped hints that she wanted him to invite her into his apartment, but he either acted obtuse or made it into a joke. "God only knows what I'd do to you if we were ever alone together," he said with a wink that made Rosalyn blush down to her toes.

She felt as if she could start weeping at any moment, but she steeled herself and unlocked the door, then entered the apartment. He appeared to have lived a simple, austere life. There were no photographs or paintings on the walls, no little knickknacks or souvenirs, no expensive Sony PlayStations or stereo systems. Nothing to give his life any special meaning. Aside from his clothing there was only a small TV, a clock radio next to the bed, and a few dozen books that had been carefully arranged on a bookshelf. Most of the books were about criminal investigations or deviant psychology, although there were a few others mixed in—*Silence of the Lambs*, *Helter Skelter*, and something called *The Killer Inside Me*. Tears began streaming down her cheeks as she walked around the apartment and saw how Travis's life had been reduced to so little. It was just so unbearably sad.

When she opened the closet, she saw the metal cage traps stacked up inside as well as a toolbox. The cage traps were an odd thing to find, but she assumed he needed them for his job. She carefully, reverentially, folded the clothing hanging in the closet and placed it in the boxes. Then she moved to the three-drawer dresser so she could do the same. This dresser used to be hers, but four years ago her mother had bought her new furniture and she and her mother had moved her old dresser to the guesthouse. It broke her heart all over again knowing that she and Travis had shared this piece of furniture. Of course, he had changed the lining paper inside the drawers. Hers had rainbows and unicorns, and the paper being used now was a solid dark gray. This made Rosalyn smile. Of course he'd pick paper like that. Solid, dependable. And of course he had his clothing neatly stored away, all his shirts and pants folded precisely. Still, after she took them out of the drawers, she refolded everything before packing it. After all, this was the last possible thing she could do for Travis.

Rosalyn worked quickly, efficiently, and soon had the dresser emptied, but she found herself staring with befuddlement at the bottom drawer. It wasn't as deep as she remembered it. Curious, she felt around inside. The dark gray lining paper did a good job camouflaging the small finger hold that allowed her to lift up the false bottom revealing Travis's secret cache: a handwritten journal, camera, stack of photos, large envelope, pair of panties, stockings, lipstick canister, women's sunglasses, and a cheap pair of earrings.

Rosalyn first looked at the photos. They were taken in the dark with a flash, and each one showed a different woman lying naked on a bed. The women were all gagged, and their wrists and ankles were bound. She next looked at what was inside the large envelope and found clipped newspaper articles about the Nightmare Man murders. She read a few of these before storing the articles back in the envelope. The articles she read had shown photographs of the victims when they were alive, and she recognized these women from the other photographs. A coolness filled her head as she took the handwritten journal and brought it to the beat-up La-Z-Boy recliner that her mother had put in the guesthouse years ago.

There was no doubt Travis had written the journal, and it talked about how a dying inmate at Ashfield State Prison had been the Nightmare Man back in 1984. The journal further revealed all of the Nightmare Man's secrets, and how Travis hunted and chose the women to kill in 2001. He wrote in detail about each of his victims and how euphoric he found the killings. Rosalyn soon understood that the lipstick and other items were trophies Travis had taken from his victims. When she read about his plans for her, she also understood her true destiny.

Chapter 66

Los Angeles, the present

Samantha woke up with the mother of all headaches and her mouth tasting like she'd been gagged with a pair of wool socks. She slowly remembered drinking heavily last night with Toni, then returning to Toni's apartment to smoke weed and eat pizza. She was so wasted that Toni insisted she sleep on the couch.

"Gah!"

Samantha bolted up, contorting her mouth as she tried to get rid of that awful taste. She noticed she was wearing a pair of Toni's pajamas, which was a good thing since Toni's boyfriend Ben was sitting at the dining room table drinking coffee and reading the paper.

"Coffee, please," she begged.

He looked up from the paper and grinned. "Ah, you're up. Toni's still sleeping it off. You two were so wasted last night."

"Ben, I'm begging you. I might die without coffee."

He bowed. "Right away." He walked into the kitchen and began listing different flavors of coffee, and she chose the first one mentioned. Seconds later she sighed with relief hearing the whirring from the single-cup coffee maker. Ben called out again, asking about milk and sugar.

"Plenty of both, please."

He brought her a mug, and her hands shook as she took it from him and sipped the coffee as if her life depended on it.

"You're a lifesaver," she said.

"I do my best. Congratulations are in order. Before Toni started snoring like a lumberjack, she told me you got the big part. Jeff must be thrilled."

She remembered then about getting the part. She also realized she had never called Jeff last night. She told Ben that.

"You better call him, then."

She found her pocketbook next to the couch and fumbled for her phone. Once it was powered on, she saw a screen full of text messages from Jeff. He wanted to know that she was okay, and without spelling it out, he was worried about the Nightmare Man. Her eyes misted up with tears seeing that. He had also left voice messages, and it was obvious that he was trying hard not to sound worried.

It was nine fifty, which meant it was twelve fifty in New York. Jeff's play had a one o'clock matinee show on Saturdays. She hated the thought that she might screw up his performance, but she wasn't going to wait another second to call him. He answered on the first ring, and Samantha began apologizing profusely. She told him about getting the part, that she and Toni had gone out celebrating afterward, and that she had crashed last night at Toni's apartment.

"Later I'll be excited for you for winning that part, but right now I'm just relieved you're okay." He laughed and added, "I let some really crazy thoughts get into my head."

"About the Nightmare Man."

Samantha didn't say that as a question. More as a statement of fact.

"That's true," he admitted. "How about taking the first plane you can to New York?"

"Monday after my meeting. I promise."

"I'll hold you to that." He laughed again. "It's crazy I let myself get as worked up as I did. With all the millions of people in Los Angeles, I had to drive myself nearly insane thinking absolutely crazy thoughts. As if that nuttiness was actually a possibility."

She wanted to laugh and cry at the same time. She bit her tongue to keep from doing either and wiped the back of her hand across her eyes. "As if," she said.

* * * *

The freak discovered that Joplin Cole's friend was named Jamie Siegel by perusing Joplin's Facebook page. There were nine Jamie Siegels living in Los Angeles, and he had already visited four of them, knocking on their doors and seeing that none of them were the Jamie Siegel he wanted. If any of them were that Jamie Siegel he would've used the knife he had brought to cut the woman's throat, but instead he simply asked if he could interest them in a magazine subscription, and all of them closed the door quickly on him after that.

He was approaching the apartment building for the fifth Jamie Siegel when he saw a sedan pull up in front of the entrance and two men get out, both of them looking like plainclothes detectives. The freak was wearing dark sunglasses and a baseball cap pulled down almost to his eyes to hide his hair. The odds were good no one would recognize him from the police sketch they'd been showing, but he stepped back anyway and hid behind a tree. His Spidey sense was telling him this meant trouble, and sure enough, a few minutes later the two men escorted the fifth Jamie Siegel into their car. They must've been bringing her to the police station for more questioning. That was a shame, but it didn't matter. He'd just have to come back later.

Chapter 67

Morris and the rest of the team had a busy morning. The police sketch brought in ninety-seven calls from concerned citizens who thought they recognized the human Ken doll, and caused eighteen blond thirty-something guys to voluntarily show up at the Wilcox Avenue precinct to claim they weren't the person in the sketch. Jamie Siegel agreed to come in, and Franklin Strong and Ray Vestra picked her up and brought her to the precinct so she could look at potential suspects through a one-way glass. While this was happening Morris and the rest of the team tracked down potential suspects from the hotline calls. Some could prove they weren't at Petit Bistro, others had their pictures taken or, if they acted suspiciously, were brought to the precinct. By three o'clock the team had eliminated these potential suspects, and Morris, Bogle, and a still grumpy Parker were in MBI's conference room eating lunch.

Morris asked Bogle, "You know what I'm thinking?"

"That you should've gotten yourself prosciutto and mozzarella instead of tuna fish?"

"That too," Morris agreed. "But I keep thinking that there's a connection between the two victims and if we dig deep enough we'll find it."

"Like what?"

"I'm not sure exactly." Morris took another bite of sandwich. "Maybe they frequented the same bar or restaurant or spa or whatever, and that's where this guy found them."

Parker had gotten under the conference table and made a demanding grunt. Morris ordered the bull terrier to get out from under there. Parker made several more unhappy grunts before complying.

"He's been in a pissy mood all day," Bogle remarked. "What's gotten into him?"

"I couldn't tell you."

Lemmon and Walsh joined them. They had done what they could to trace back Joplin Cole's movements and had gotten nowhere. Morris told them his thoughts about trying to find a link between Fletcher and Cole. He added, "It would help if we had their credit card statements."

Walsh showed a helpless gesture. "The request has been put in," she said. "I'm still waiting, just like I'm still waiting for the FBI to unlock Cole's phone. What's up with your dog? Every time I've seen him today he's been moping around."

"It's a mystery."

They decided to split up the calls. Lemmon and Walsh would focus on bars and restaurants, and Morris and Bogle would cover everything else. Twenty minutes later while Morris was on hold with a nail salon, his cell phone rang. Roger Smichen.

"I've got good news and good news," Smichen said. "Which do you want to hear first."

"You sound as punch drunk as I feel," Morris said.

"No doubt. It's what can happen when you spend a day chasing after a seventeen-year-old coroner's report. So I'll give you the good news first. You can't do an exhumation. Smalley's remains were cremated."

"How is that good news?"

"Because an exhumation isn't needed. The coroner, bless him, was exceedingly thorough and took dental X-rays and included Smalley's dental records in the report. The X-rays match up. Travis Smalley was killed in that alley. No other possibility."

"Okay. Thanks, Roger, and sorry for having you spend your Saturday on that goose chase."

"It happens."

Morris was still on hold with the nail salon. He called Polk to tell him he could drop the tail.

"Thank God," Polk said in a hushed voice. "I followed her into a movie theater where she's watching the sappiest chick flick imaginable. Another minute of this and I might've gone blind."

"If you want to wait until the movie's over before heading back, feel free."

Polk chuckled at that. "I don't think so. Assuming traffic's not a bear, I'll be there in ten."

The owner of the nail salon finally came on, and like the other calls Morris had made, it was a dead end. Two hours later he had finished calling all of the West Hollywood nail and hair salons and was feeling as grumpy as Parker was acting when Bogle entered the office with a hard grin etched on his face. "Bingo," he said.

"Sure, go ahead. Keep me in suspense."

"They were both members of the same West Hollywood gym. A place called Muscles Incorporated."

Morris frowned hearing that. Neither woman had gym membership cards in their pocketbooks. The killer must've taken them.

"Do you know by any chance whether they give you keys for a locker or if you need to supply your own lock?"

"I asked that exact question," Bogle said, his grin hardening. "They give you a key to a locker. And yes, they have duplicates for every locker in case a key is lost. Or in case a psycho serial killer working there needs access to a locker so he can make a silicone putty impression of a person's apartment key."

A grimness tightened Morris's features. Lori Fletcher and Joplin Cole never had a chance.

"Let's get the hell over there," he said.

Chapter 68

Morris caught the way Bogle eyed the stunningly gorgeous redhead who walked into the gym ahead of them.

"So all that talk about you changing your ways and only wanting to get back together with Jenny was lip service," he said.

Bogle gave him a look as if he were nuts. "You're acting as pissy as your dog," he said. "Even if I were twenty years younger I wouldn't have a shot with a babe like that. I was only practicing my deductive powers. For example, from her lithe body and the way she carried herself, she's trained as a dancer and is most likely an actress."

"Lithe, huh?"

Bogle grinned. "A word I picked up working at Starlight Pictures. After spending two months working with a more erudite crowd, I might even now be able to fill in a word or two in a crossword puzzle."

"Erudite, huh?"

"Keep hanging around me now, and you'll have to get a dictionary. Another deduction I made regarding that lovely lass is from her slightly blotchy skin and less than clear eyes, she got blotto last night. But it takes a special kind of woman to work out while hungover."

"Charlie, I hardly know you right now."

Bogle's grin soured. "I'm just punchy from this case. Or maybe I caught whatever your dog has."

Almost on cue, Parker let out an irritable grunt. Morris gave the bull terrier a hard look. He had never seen the dog in such a bad mood, and he considered calling Natalie to take Parker off his hands. First, though, he wanted to see if Muscles Incorporated could help them identify the guy in the sketch.

The woman working at the front desk was expecting them, and her face flushed with excitement as she pointed out where the manager could be found. The manager, an attractive woman in her thirties who Morris guessed was also quite lithe, was waiting for them. But in her case she was nervous rather than excited. He could appreciate why. Not only did this involve the Nightmare Man, but she understood that two of her gym members might've met the killer here.

"Anything I can do to help," she said.

Morris showed her the police sketch. "Do your gym ID cards have photos?" he asked.

"Annual membership cards do," she said. "But we also sell daily, weekly, and monthly passes, and those only have barcodes so we can track their use. Let's see if he's in our database."

Morris and Bogle stood behind her as she brought up each photo that was on record, but none of them was the guy they were looking for.

"I'm sorry," she said, but she also sounded relieved that the Nightmare Man wasn't a member of her gym, or at least not an annual member.

Morris asked, "Your software records each member's visits?"

"Yes."

"Can you tell me the last time Joplin Cole was here?"

She typed in Joplin's name and hit a button with the mouse, and that brought up a screen showing dates and times. She squinted as she read the last entry on the screen.

"That would've been last Thursday," she said. "She was here at five minutes to seven and returned her locker key at eight twenty-seven."

"Were any of your daily, weekly, or monthly pass members here then?"

This took more typing and mouse-clicking, but she brought up a screen with a single name.

"Someone who had bought a monthly pass. His name is Dale Cooper."

Bogle remarked dryly that that was the name of the FBI agent from *Twin Peaks*.

"Did he use a credit card when he bought his pass?"

Another mouse click. The manager told Morris that Dale Cooper paid with cash. "I can print out his phone number and address if you want."

Morris expected it to be fake, but he told her that would be helpful. Odds were this fake "Dale Cooper" had bothered Joplin that morning and stalked her to Petit Bistro, which meant he needed to talk to whoever had been working at the front desk that morning, and he asked the manager for the information. Her brow furrowed with concentration as she clicked on more buttons.

"Rosalyn Krate was working that morning."

Morris felt as if he'd been slapped in the face. "What was that?" he asked. She looked at him with alarm. "Rosalyn Krate," she said. "Do you know her?"

"We've been introduced. Would you have expected her to recognize Joplin Cole and Lori Fletcher as members here if she were shown their pictures?"

"Rosalyn has been working here for quite some time," she said. There was a flurry of mouse clicks, and her eyes narrowed as she scanned through several screens of information. "The times when Ms. Cole and Ms. Fletcher came here coincided enough with Rosalyn's work schedule that I would expect her to know them both by sight. Would you like me to print out Rosalyn's address and phone number?"

"Not necessary. Thanks. You've been very helpful."

After leaving the gym, Bogle asked Morris whether Rosalyn was in cahoots with the blond guy from the sketch. "Could Smalley have told her his Nightmare Man secrets?"

Morris said, "All I know right now is I want to talk to her again."

They drove in silence to Rosalyn's address, and Morris had to restrain himself from racing up the four flights of stairs. When they got within five feet of her apartment, Parker started growling again and bulling his way to the door.

Bogle asked, "What gives with him?"

Morris held a finger to his mouth. He knocked on the door, and when no one answered, he told Bogle, "Terriers are natural ratters. Ten to one odds there are rats in there."

Morris got down on one knee and rubbed Parker vigorously behind the ears and on the snout. "You smelled rat hair on her earlier, didn't you?" he said. "You were telling me she's our killer, and I was too stupid to listen to you. No wonder you were in such a rotten mood."

Parker stopped his growling to let out several appeased grunts, his tail wagging. Just like that, his bad mood was gone. All was forgiven.

"Sonofabitch," Bogle whispered under his breath, because it all made sense. "What about the blond guy?"

"She must be working with him. Maybe he's the one who's doing the killing, but she's the one picking out the victims, sneaking into their gym lockers to make copies of their keys, and trapping and keeping the rats." Morris let out a bitter laugh. "She even tried to convince me today that Travis Smalley is still alive."

Bogle said, "Maybe not just you."

Morris agreed that made sense, and he called Felger to ask him to see if anyone was trying to make it look like Travis Smalley could still be alive. "Check social media or anywhere else where he might have a presence." After he got off the phone with Felger, he called Annie Walsh and told her they needed a search warrant. She didn't like the thinness of what he had. "You don't even know if Smalley committed the 2001 murders, which makes her connection with him irrelevant. Can you give me one solid piece of evidence?"

"She lied to me, Annie, and tried to mislead me."

"Speculation."

"Come on, you've gotten warrants on less than that."

"I'm just telling you what a judge will say."

"How about this, a trained ratter is indicating that rats are being kept in her apartment."

She sighed. "I'll see if I can pull off a miracle. I'll call you."

After Morris got off the phone, Bogle gave him an unhappy look. "So we wait?" he asked. Morris shrugged. He had his lockpicks with him, but he couldn't afford to break in and let Rosalyn skate on a technicality.

Bogle said, "I know the name is spelled differently, but a krait is one of the deadliest snakes in the world."

Morris hadn't ever heard of that before. "It figures," he said.

Chapter 69

Annie Walsh called Morris to tell him that Judge John Kelley had some questions for him. She lowered her voice to a whisper and added, "Morris, he's the fourth judge I've been able to track down, and I'm running out of ideas of whom to try next. Just saying."

"Understood."

The phone must've been handed to the judge, because Morris heard a man making a show of clearing his throat, and then a gruff voice asked, "Mr. Brick, are you the one who's determined to ruin my Saturday night?"

"Judge, if I don't get that search warrant, someone else's night might be ruined far worse."

That seemed to have an effect. The judge's voice sounded more restrained as he asked about Morris's dog's professional training as a ratter.

"He doesn't have professional training per se, but his father was a champion, so it's in his bloodline."

"I see. You've witnessed this behavior before?"

"Many times."

This was partially true if you looked at it sideways and squinted enough. Parker liked to chase squirrels, but Morris couldn't remember him ever encountering a rat before.

There was more throat clearing from the judge, then, "Tell me what evidence you have that Ms. Rosalyn Krate purposely deceived you earlier today."

"It's my professional judgment that she did."

"I see. In other words, you have no evidence."

"Only if you want to discount my many years as a decorated and accomplished police detective."

"You're making this hard for me, Mr. Brick."

"Judge, if I don't get the warrant there's a chance somebody will be dying tonight."

"There's a chance every night that somebody will be dying. In fact, it's a near certainty."

"But not in the way the Nightmare Man forces his victims to die."

"I see. You understand that if I give you this warrant and you don't find rats being kept in the apartment, it will all but ruin any case the district attorney might want to bring against Ms. Krate, assuming she's involved."

Morris thumped Parker on the side. "I trust my dog."

The phone was handed back to Walsh, and two minutes later she told Morris she had a signed warrant. Twenty-five minutes later she arrived with the warrant in hand. Morris had already arranged with the landlord to unlock Krate's apartment door once the warrant arrived, and a representative from the management company gave the paper a quick look, and then did just that. Once the door was opened, Parker bulled his way into a small living room and strained on his leash, pulling Morris to the back of the room. The bull terrier then stood grunting and growling and pawing at the wall. Morris took down a ceiling-to-floor wallcovering that exposed a seam for a hidden door. Bogle moved a chair and end table, and this revealed a keyhole. There was no knob for the door, just the keyhole.

"The tenant must've had part of the room partitioned to whatever this is," the management company representative said. "I guarantee you none of the other units have this."

Morris used a lockpick, and after he felt the lock release he pushed the door inward. A flashlight revealed four rat cages on the floor, two of which were occupied. He found a light switch, which turned on a sixty-watt bulb. Hung on the wall were photos of women he recognized as the 2001 Nightmare Man victims. There seemed to be a flimsy homemade altar. He walked over and shined the flashlight on it. He guessed the lipstick canister and other items were trophies Travis Smalley had collected from his victims. Added to the altar were the gym membership cards taken from Lori Fletcher and Joplin Cole.

Bogle called him and Walsh over to look at photos he had found. They were all taken in darkened rooms, but Morris was able to recognize Lori Fletcher in the first four pictures. In all of them, Fletcher appeared to be sleeping. The next ones were of Joplin Cole, also taken while she slept. The next subject was a familiar-looking woman who also appeared to be sleeping.

Bogle said to Morris, "This is the redhead we saw at the gym tonight."

Morris recognized her, and Bogle showed them another photo, this one a brunette in her twenties.

Bogle said, "We don't know who she is either."

Walsh asked, "How about the fifth woman?"

"There are only four."

"I thought the Nightmare Man kills five women before disappearing?"

Bogle said, "I don't know what to tell you. But here's something else. I found three door keys. I'm guessing two of them are for the victims he already killed. Or I guess I should be saying she, but for now let's assume the blond dude is doing the killing and Krate the planning."

"So a key's missing," Morris said.

"That's right."

"Shit," Walsh said.

"We need to identify these two women," Morris said, referring to the redhead and brunette. "Pronto."

Morris grabbed a pair of handwritten journals that he spotted, and they left the Nightmare Man room or temple or whatever it was supposed to be. Once they were back in the living room where there was more light, he took pictures of the photos of the two unknown women, texted them to the gym manager, and asked for her help in identifying them. Walsh took the photos. She told Morris she planned to head over to the gym and make sure the manager made it a priority. "I'll also have someone check these against the DMV database. I hope the brunette's a member of that gym also. It could take hours to identify her through license photos."

Once Walsh left, Morris tossed Bogle one of the journals, and the two of them settled in for some reading.

Chapter 70

Samantha found a policeman waiting at her door. When he saw her approaching, he asked whether she was Samantha Fine. She nodded, too flustered to say anything.

He asked, "Have you been at home yet this evening?"

"Not yet." She held up her gym bag. "I was at the gym earlier, then dinner and a movie. What's this about, Officer?"

He gave her what looked like an attempt at a reassuring smile. "I need to check your apartment to make sure it's safe. This is only a precaution and nothing to be upset about. A detective will be here soon to explain what's going on."

Samantha's hands shook slightly as she unlocked the door. Even though the officer didn't say this was about the Nightmare Man, she knew it had to be about that.

"Should I come in with you or stay out in the hallway?" she asked.

"How about you stay out here until I tell you it's safe."

She watched as he removed his service revolver and entered the apartment. It was a small one-bedroom, and she heard him moving through it. Less than a minute later, he yelled out that the coast was clear. She walked in and found him grinning at her, relief washing over his face, his gun back in its holster.

"As I said, nothing to worry about," he said. "Do you want me to wait with you until the detective shows up? He should be here in less than fifteen minutes."

"That won't be necessary, Officer."

He took a step toward the door but frowned as he glanced in the direction of a hallway coat closet. "I missed that earlier," he said. He grinned again at Samantha. "Better safe than sorry."

The officer walked to the closet and opened the door. He froze before reaching for his service revolver. A gunshot rang out. Blood exploded from the officer's chest, and he collapsed onto his back. Samantha's natural instinct was to go to the fallen officer's aid as opposed to fleeing, and she rushed toward him. A vaguely familiar-looking woman came out of the closet and pointed a gun at her.

Samantha was terror-stricken. Her voice came out as a whisper as she told this woman that the officer was still breathing. "I need to apply pressure to his wound. He doesn't need to die."

"I'm afraid he does. And I'll be shooting you in the face if you touch him." The woman was carrying a large gym bag, which she tossed to Samantha. Samantha thought she heard a squeal come from inside.

"You're going to carry this," the woman said. "And you're going to do exactly what I tell you to do, or I'm going to shoot you. Now turn around."

Samantha had never stared down the barrel of a gun before, and it was frightening now doing so. She turned around and felt the barrel push into her spine.

"We're going to walk to the stairs and exit the building from the back fire door. If you scream or try to run away from me, I will shoot you and leave you paralyzed. Do you understand me?"

Samantha bit her lip to keep from crying.

The woman must've taken out a cell phone, because Samantha could hear a phone dialing, then the woman arguing with someone before ordering the person to meet her at an alley behind the building. When the call ended, the woman ordered Samantha to start moving.

"You ask anyone for help, and I'll shoot both of you," the woman threatened.

She marched Samantha out of the apartment and into an empty hallway. None of her neighbors had bothered investigating the gunshot. Maybe they thought it was only the TV.

A promise that Samantha had made to her mom when she moved to LA was that she would take self-defense classes, but they never taught her what to do when someone was pushing a gun into her back. As she made her way down the back stairs, she tried desperately to remember something from her class she could use, but her mind was blank. She was just too frightened. After they left the building and were walking across the parking lot to the connecting alley, she remembered something. Would it work? She didn't know, but it was all she could think of. Soon she was being marched down the darkened alley, and she steeled herself, playing out in her mind what she planned to do.

They made their way out of the alley, and a car tapped its horn. Samantha could almost feel the woman look toward the noise, and she acted then, throwing the gym bag into the air, then sweeping her left foot toward her right and then outward and back so that her leg was now behind the woman and she could feel the woman's thigh against her thigh. An elbow in the face sent the woman toppling backward, and Samantha started running.

* * * *

Rosalyn Krate picked herself up off the sidewalk. Samantha was gone, and the blond freak had left the car and was giving her a dumbfounded look.

"You couldn't stop her?" she hissed.

His head jerked back as if he'd been slapped. "It happened too fast."

Useless. Absolutely useless. She heard police sirens in the distance. The gym bag had landed a few feet from her. She picked it up and heard the rat inside squealing. She got into the car's passenger seat and ordered the freak to get back behind the wheel.

"What happened?" he asked.

"A change of plans," she said. "Start driving."

"Where to?"

"You know where."

The freak drove five blocks before pulling into the back of a building and parking in an assigned spot. Without saying a word, they walked to the back door, then up three flights of stairs before using a key to open an apartment door. The apartment was a studio, and the only piece of furniture was a small bed. Once the door closed, the freak asked Rosalyn again what had happened, and she slapped him in the face.

Tears welled up in his eyes. "Why'd you do that?"

"You really have to ask me? You pull a dumb stunt like stalking Joplin, and you're going to ask me that? You put everything at risk!"

He touched his cheek. "I'm sorry," he said. "I made one mistake—"

She kneed him in the groin, and he fell to the floor, tears now streaming down his cheeks. She grabbed his earlobe and twisted it.

"One mistake? I caught you stalking me also. You really didn't think I'd see that? How many of the others did you stalk? Samantha too?"

"I swear I didn't stalk her! Only you and Joplin! I swear!"

She let go of his ear. She didn't believe him. The police had visited Samantha's apartment for a reason, and the only thing that made sense was that the freak had been seen stalking her. But it wouldn't do her any good beating up this pathetic excuse for a freak. The Nightmare Man was too important. She could still salvage this.

She said, "You need to kill me now."

His mouth dropped open as he stared at her. "I wasn't supposed to kill you until the nineteenth," he sputtered.

"It can't be helped."

"But what about the other two victims? There has to be five of them, right?"

"You'll have to find two more on your own and complete the cycle on the nineteenth. You can do it, Duane. I made you a part of this for a reason. I can see greatness in you."

He looked like he was fighting to keep from bursting out crying. He'd been planning to kill Jamie Siegel later that night, but he was still a virgin having not yet taken a life. Never really even hurt anyone badly. He told Rosalyn this.

"I thought I'd have more time to prepare myself," he moaned.

"Tonight's as good a night as any to pop your cherry. And you know you want to do it. You know you've been aching to do it."

"I guess," he said.

She laughed. "Duane, come on, show some enthusiasm. You're going to be part of something great. Something Los Angeles will never forget. The Nightmare Man will live on forever because of you."

A determination now showed in his face.

"After you kill me, you'll need to go to my apartment and clean out the sacred room. We can't allow the police to find it. But you'll be safe doing this. The police won't be discovering my body for days. If you want, you can punch me in the face and knock me out before tying me up and cutting off my clothing. Would you like to do that?"

His jaw was clenched, and his eyes now shone with a dark cruelty.

"Just make sure to use smelling salts on me every time I pass out. And follow the formula precisely—"

"How about you shut up already!"

The freak jumped to his feet and slammed a fist into Rosalyn's jaw. He then carried her unconscious body to the bed.

Chapter 71

Morris's cell phone rang. Felger.

"I found something about Travis Smalley," he said. "Bottom line, it appears as if a month ago he rented an apartment in West Hollywood." Felger gave Morris an address.

Morris told Bogle the news. "That's less than a block from here."

A crime scene team had arrived, and Morris asked one of the team members if he could keep an eye on Parker; then he and Bogle moved in a half run toward the address Felger had given him. On the way, he called Walsh and asked her to send a unit to the address.

As with Rosalyn's building, this one also had no elevator, and Morris was breathing hard by the time they got to the apartment. Bogle appeared to be in better shape and barely showed any effect. They drew their guns and tried the door. It was locked. When they heard a whimpering noise inside, Bogle kicked it open. Their blond suspect was in the process of carving out a large chunk of flesh from a naked woman's face. A grisly "17" had already been arranged on the floor, so he must've been nearly done with the carving phase of the murder. He turned toward Morris and Bogle, surprise flooding his eyes.

Morris was still breathing too hard to yell out a command, so Bogle ordered the man to put down the knife. The man looked from them to his victim and then back at them, his face frozen in a funny expression, as if he wanted to explain something to them. He didn't drop the knife, though. Instead he came running at them.

Morris wasn't sure whether the man's intention was to attack them or to try fleeing the apartment, but Bogle fired three shots into the man's chest, dropping him. Bogle knelt by the body while Morris checked on the woman lying on the bed.

"Perp's dead," Bogle yelled out.

Morris knew from reading Rosalyn's journal that the woman on the bed had to be Rosalyn, but it was hard to recognize her with her nose cut off and through all the damage and gore. She was conscious, but the only thing he could make out in her eyes was supreme disappointment. If she hadn't been gagged, he knew she would have been begging him to finish the job.

He took out his phone and called for an ambulance.

Chapter 72

Morris entered the hospital room and found a heavily bandaged Rosalyn Krate with her wrists and ankles chained to the bed. Her jaundiced eyes caught his. "I didn't think you'd come," she said.

Maybe it was because she didn't have a nose anymore, or it could've been because Morris now knew what she really was, but her voice sounded very different to him. More like a snake's hiss. He guessed she had tried smiling through her bandages.

She said, "But you came running. Because I've got a friend."

Morris said, "We're not friends."

"It doesn't matter," she said. "I wanted to tell you that what you did won't change anything. I'll find someone else to be the Nightmare Man."

Morris had read her journal and understood that while she had a number of bullshit reasons to explain why the Nightmare Man had become a part of the fabric of LA's history and his legend needed to continue, what really drove her was a twisted psychosexual fantasy involving Travis Smalley coming back from the dead to claim her. The newspapers and TV would soon be running stories about the four people who had acted as the Nightmare Man over the years, and they'd be showing Ed Blount as a ruthless hitman, Smalley as a small-minded sadist, Rosalyn as a lonely and psychologically damaged woman, and Duane Hopper (the blond man whom Charlie Bogle had shot dead) as a pathetic freak. Once the harsh light of truth was shone on the Nightmare Man, the mythology would wither and die. The Nightmare Man was done and dead, and there was nothing Rosalyn could do to resuscitate him. But explaining that to Rosalyn would be like pulling wings off a fly. Still, Morris felt impelled to reach something human within her.

He said, "You didn't ask about Sean Maguire."

She gave him a puzzled look.

"He's the officer you shot in the chest. Sean has a wife and four kids, and it was touch and go for a while, but he survived a seven-hour surgery and is expected to make a full recovery."

"It doesn't matter," she said. "Whether he lived or died wouldn't matter to the Nightmare Man."

"I went to both their funerals," Morris said. "Lori Fletcher's and Joplin Cole's. They both had parents who had to bury their daughters. They both had families and friends who are now devastated."

"They had to die," she insisted. "The Nightmare Man needed their deaths."

Morris accepted that he couldn't argue with insanity. He got up and left.

Epilogue

Parker rose to his feet and trotted out of Morris's office. Seconds later Morris heard the commotion coming from the reception area and got up from his desk to see Charlie Bogle joking and shaking hands with Fred, Polk, and Greta, while Parker wagged his tail and wormed his way through the crowd so he could force Bogle to rub his snout. Even Adam Felger had ventured out of his office to join them. Morris walked over to them. It had been three months since the Nightmare Man business was finished.

Morris didn't shake Bogle's hand but instead gave him a hug, which he knew embarrassed Bogle since Bogle wasn't a hugging type of guy. Truth be told, neither was Morris.

"Good to see you, Charlie," Morris said.

A sheepish grin forced its way onto Bogle's face. "Same here. Can we talk?"

"Anytime."

Morris led the way back to his office, with Parker joining them. Bogle closed the door and took the chair across from Morris's desk. He put his feet up like he owned the place.

"I was surprised to see a full contingent on hand," Bogle said. "I would've expected people out in the field working."

"Looks can be deceiving. We're busy like you wouldn't believe." Morris checked his watch. "We have a staff meeting in ten minutes. How's life in the movie business?"

"I gave my two weeks' notice today." Bogle's grin grew wistful. "I don't know. Spending my days fixing problems for these actors didn't seem quite so rewarding after what we did three months ago. Anyway, I'm going to be looking for a new job."

"I told you when you left I'd keep your position open for a year before I looked to fill it."

Bogle showed his best poker face. "I'll need a pay bump, of course. After all, I was the one to shoot the fourth and final Nightmare Man."

"I don't know if you can call him the fourth Nightmare Man. It wasn't as if he finished the job."

"The papers are calling him that."

Morris waved away the issue with his hand. "Let's not split hairs. What type of bump are you looking for?"

"A hundred a week."

"Jenny's okay with you doing this kind of work again?"

Morris knew Bogle had moved back in with his wife two months ago. In fact, he, Natalie, Rachel, and Parker had joined them for a celebratory dinner.

"We discussed it. She's not thrilled by the idea, but she understands why I need to do this."

"In that case, deal."

Morris got up from his chair, and this time they shook hands.

Don't miss the next spine-chilling thriller starring
Morris Brick....

UNLEASHED

Coming soon from Lyrical Underground, an
imprint of Kensington Publishing Corp.

Keep reading to enjoy a sample excerpt....

UNLEASHED
Jacob Stone

Duncan Moss bought coffee at the counter and took it outside so he could sit at one of the patio tables. This was a nice, upscale downtown LA neighborhood, and the people walking by all looked nice and upscale. Or at least clean, fit, and well-off. Quite a contrast from the boardinghouse where he was staying half a mile away. That area could best be described as dingy and downbeat. More than that, a heavy oppressiveness seemed to hang in the air like a bad stench that just wouldn't go away, and the people living there carried an unmistakable hopelessness. Duncan much preferred that neighborhood. He could barely stand to see all these happy, privileged people who thought nothing bad could ever happen to them. They were so wrong. *So very wrong.*

On the same block as the coffee shop there was also a bakery, a café advertising Los Angeles's best breakfast, and a diner, and across the street was a small park with neatly arranged flower beds and benches, and while it wasn't quite nine thirty yet, it was one of those near-perfect early spring days, and all of that was enough to bring out a small parade of people. Duncan sipped his coffee and watched as fellow millennials walked past him. Older people were also in the mix, but it was the millennials that he focused on. They were the ones who stirred up a toxic and near-suffocating mix of rage, jealousy, and psychotic need to cause pain. All of them trying so hard to look hip and cool with their tattoos and piercings, the dudes with goatees, soul patches, and man buns, the women with brightly colored dye jobs. There was barely a pound of body fat among them. They kept themselves in shape by dieting and CrossFit-type training classes. Duncan was also as lean as a rail, but he accomplished this the old-fashioned way. Survival. And while he had never in his life stepped into a gym or taken an exercise class, he had a wiry strength that few of them would've been able to match.

Of course, most of them had their noses stuck in their cell phones. Some sort of strange sixth sense kept them from colliding with each other as they crisscrossed on the sidewalk. Jesus, what a bunch! Most of them were so oblivious to the world around them that Duncan could've gotten up and punched them in their smug faces without any of them having a clue what was happening until they hit the pavement. As tempting as it was, he stayed seated. He had a plan, after all. He'd later be unleashing his rage in a very specific, controlled way. Besides, none of them were what he really needed.

While he remained invisible to most of them, one of them noticed him. A blond woman walking a little four-legged fuzz ball that was supposedly a dog. She was in her early thirties, maybe five years older than him. Slender, yellowish hair that fell past her shoulder, cute heart-shaped face, a short dress showing off long, thin legs. She smiled at him. An invitation of sorts. Why wouldn't she? He was a good-looking guy with dark features and was impeccably groomed and dressed smartly in slacks, sports jacket, and boat shoes. He was also making a concentrated effort to show only a carefree, pleasant expression.

If this had been three months ago, she certainly wouldn't have smiled at him, and not just because he had lived three thousand miles away in the Jamaica Plain neighborhood of Boston. If she had caught sight of him then, she would've fled to the other side of the street. Back then he was a mess. He had gone over a month without showering or shaving or changing his clothes and almost six months without getting a haircut or even combing his hair, but more than his ragged, disheveled appearance, it would've been the craziness shining in his eyes that would've frightened her. He had reached rock bottom and was consumed with dark, suicidal thoughts.

He no doubt would've ended his life if he hadn't received the postcard when he did. It had been mailed from Los Angeles, and at first it nearly sent him out of his mind with rage and homicidal fury, but later that postcard allowed him to see as clear as day what he needed to do. After that he came up with his plan.

Once he had the plan, everything was okay, at least as okay as it could be. He cleaned up his act—first clipping off his beard and cutting his hair short, then making sure to shower and shave each day, and taking care of other personal hygiene issues. He also made it a point not to glare with homicidal rage at the lucky, happy people he would see and instead hide his true self behind a pleasant facade. It took effort and concentration, but it became easier once he had his plan. And while the sight of the happy, lucky people made him feel like a heavy stone was crushing his chest, at least he no longer felt like he was on the verge of suffocating. Because he had a plan....

He couldn't come out to LA right away. He was broke and he needed to raise enough cash to bankroll his plan. It had been almost five years since he had burglarized any homes or rolled drunks or robbed anyone at gunpoint, but certain skills come back quickly, and these were skills he had always excelled at. It didn't take him long to raise the money he needed.

After that, he bought a 2002 Cadillac Eldorado for five hundred dollars at a police auction, and a week ago hit the road. He drove almost nonstop for two days, drinking enough coffee to keep him awake, and arrived five days ago in LA. Since then he'd been getting a lay of the land and making plans for where to go hunting. He also bought himself an appropriate wardrobe so he could fit in with the happy, privileged people. Money wasn't an issue. He had the necessary skills to always get more.

The blonde walking the fuzz-ball dog slowed down a step, her smile turning more hopeful. Duncan smiled back, but in a noncommittal way. He had no intention of inviting her to join him. She wasn't what he needed. She tried to maintain her smile as she walked past him, but it cracked, the hurt weakening her mouth betraying her.

He looked past her toward a couple holding hands half a block away. So happy, so much in love. But they weren't what he needed either. While they were privileged and charter members of the Beautiful People's Club, they were in their fifties, and Duncan needed them to be younger. He needed them to have their whole lives ahead of them so that the loss and pain would be all that much more profound.

He tilted back the cardboard cup and finished off the last few sips of coffee, then got up, crushed the cup into a ball, and tossed it into a trashcan. He hadn't come here to hunt, at least not exactly. If he had seen exactly what he was looking for, he would've gotten on their trail. But today was Saturday, and if you wanted to find a young, well-off couple who are oh-so-in-love, why not go directly to the source and crash a wedding?

Acknowledgments

I would like to thank my editor, Michaela Hamilton, as this book, as well as my Morris Brick thriller series, wouldn't exist without her.

In advance I'd like to thank the Kensington team who'll be supporting this book and doing their magic to make it shine: Lauren Jernigan, Michelle Addo, Vida Engstrand, Claire Hill, and Alexandra Nicolajsen.

A big thanks also to my college buddy Alan Luedeking who, as with all my books, muddled through my initial draft and helped smooth out the language. Also my longtime friend (since second grade) Jeff Michaels for also providing feedback.

As always, I'd like to thank Judy, my wife and best friend, for her encouragement and support, and for also helping to make my manuscript more readable.

About the Author

Photo by Judy Zeltserman

Jacob Stone is the pseudonym chosen by Dave Zeltserman, an award-winning author of crime, mystery, and horror fiction, for his Morris Brick thriller series. His crime novels *Small Crimes* and *Pariah* were both named by the *Washington Post* as best books of the year, with *Small Crimes* also topping National Public Radio's list of best crime and mystery novels of 2008.

His horror novel, *The Caretaker of the Lorne Field*, was shortlisted by the American Library Association for best horror novel of 2010, a Black Quill nominee for best dark genre book, and a *Library Journal* horror gem.

His Frankenstein retelling *Monster* was named by *Booklist* as one of the 10 best horror novels of the year, and by WBUR as one of the best novels of the year.

His mystery fiction is regularly published by *Ellery Queen Mystery Magazine*, has won Shamus and Derringer Awards, and twice has won the *Ellery Queen's* Readers Choice Award.

Dave's novels have been translated to German, French, Italian, Dutch, Lithuanian, and Thai. His novel *Small Crimes* has been made into a film starring Nikolaj Coster-Waldau, Molly Parker, Gary Cole, Robert Forster, and Jacki Weaver, and can be seen on Netflix. His novels *Outsourced* and *The Caretaker of Lorne Field* are currently in development.

JACOB STONE

DERANGED

A MORRIS BRICK THRILLER

JACOB STONE

CRAZED

A MORRIS BRICK THRILLER

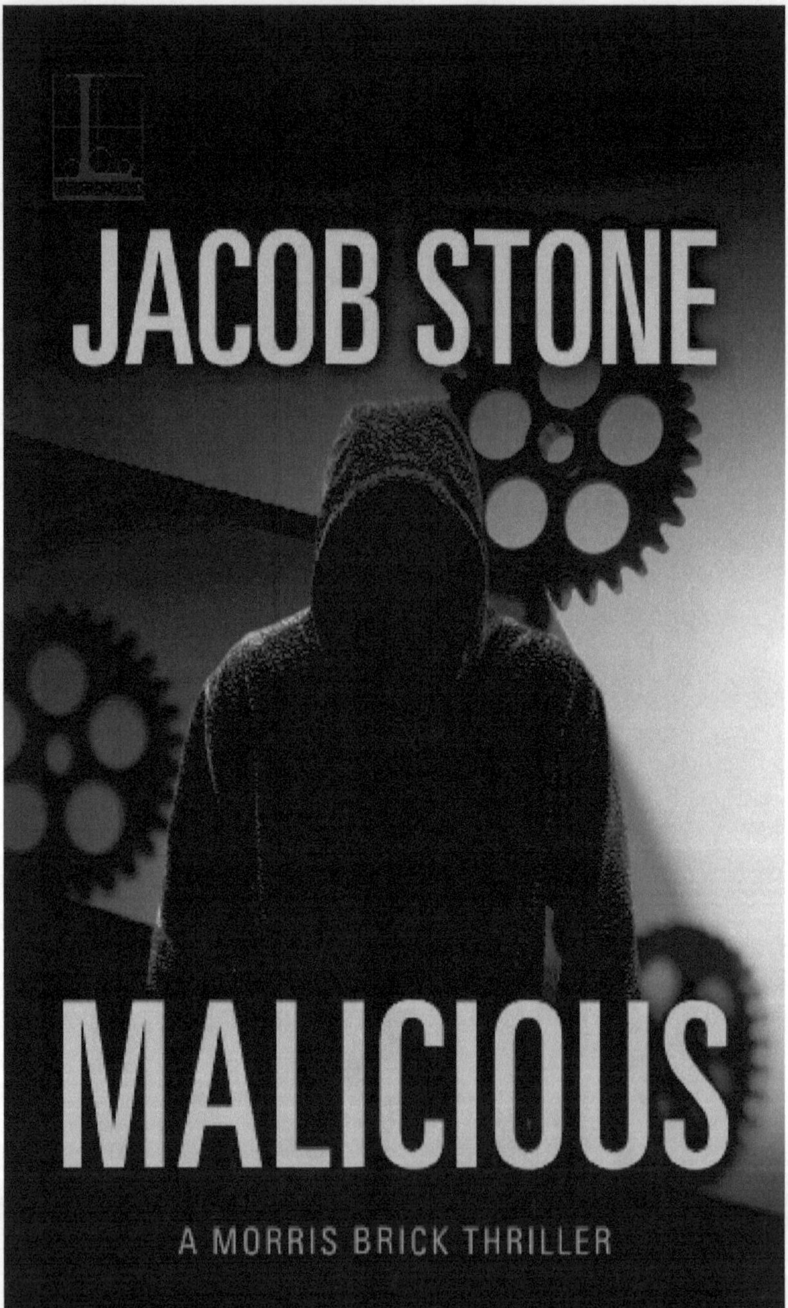
JACOB STONE
MALICIOUS
A MORRIS BRICK THRILLER

JACOB STONE

CRUEL

A MORRIS BRICK THRILLER